DEADMAN RUNNING

SLUMRAT RISING

BOOK THREE | DEADMAN RUNNING

WARBY PICUS

Podium

Published in 2024 by Podium Publishing
www.podiumaudio.com

DEADMAN
RUNNING

CHAPTER 1

IT COULD BE WORSE

Starbrite's waste filled the oceans like a latrine running into a well. One bit of Starbrite-branded industrial waste was currently in agony. This did not make him unique. Lots of Starbrite's leavings had agonizing deaths. Every minute of every day. Still, this particular bit of trash had no less than three destinies upon him. He was down now, but he would rise. He was coming home to the land and people that made him.

Truth bobbed in the water. Some tiny muscles in his eyes had sheared, and he could only stare blankly ahead. "Ahead." It wasn't exactly straight ahead. Some of the muscles must have been keeping his eyes still, as his vision was pretty rough right now. Everything looked wrong. Like he couldn't tell how far away it was. Trapped in two dimensions between a gray sky and the gray sea. Just one more piece of flotsam.

The demon had just gutted the bird and left. The packages from the inside of the bird were floating around Truth. Packages carefully wrapped in layers of plastic, with foam floaties and the occasional buoyancy talisman. These were always going to land in the water. A discreet delivery for quiet-living folk.

Truth was not entirely able to describe how he was feeling. He hurt, but most of his body was numb. He'd been hurt enough to know that was a bad sign.

<<*Looks like a lot of your fleshy bits, organs specifically, couldn't handle the sudden deceleration of you hitting the water from a hundred meters up. They just sheared off your bones, or pulped against the bones, or ruptured or just . . . generally are having a bad time. Not an expert on glands or whatever, so I'm guessing here. Your brain should look like an overcooked custard. The fact it doesn't is a more than minor miracle, though maybe the quadriplegia and the loss of both taste and smell are stretching the term "miracle" a bit. Losing the ability to hear most of the audible spectrum is comparatively minor. And, presumably, a real miracle would have prevented the bleeds and ruptures inside your skull that are going to kill you. Soon.*>>

Any chance of help?

<<*Well, help* is *debatable. Would restoring enough of your nervous system to let you feel your ruptured testicles count as helping?*>>

Truth felt the System shift things around inside of him, doing what it was made to do—run his magic for him. Truth tried to help it along, but nothing much came of it. His brain was struggling.

<<Just focus on healing. You want to heal. See this image? Imagine all your energy flowing into that image.>>

Truth could see a spell form pop up in front of him. He did his best to send the energy into it.

<<That's it. Just a trickle for now. Let's start by healing your brain. Patch up some of those leaks.>>

Truth didn't know how long he was floating in the ocean. His senses were all lost in the endless gray. Just bobbing along with the rest of the trash. Nothing for him to do. Underrated thing, having something to do. Nag Hamadi was right about that. His head was starting to hurt. A long, slow ache that kept building.

System . . .

<<I know. I can't help it. Good news is that I've stopped the brain bleed and most of the things that were going to kill you in the short term. Bad news is that this might be too much spell for me.>>

Say what, now?

<<This isn't one of the cut-down healing spells provided by Starbrite or some other halfway-modern outfit. This is the full-size, luxury-model spell straight out of Siphios.>>

Okay?

<<I'm a mutilated chunk of your soul, not an actual spirit of intellect. I'm hijacking your mind and body to run the spell. And the spell is testing us hard. Hence the headache. If you actually knew this spell, you would be totally healed by now. Probably.>>

Truth got a splash of water in his eye. He hadn't regained control of his eyelid yet, so he got to just float there and endure. It wasn't really burning the way he expected it would. Even without his body cultivation, a Level Four mage could ignore a little salt.

The spell is too much for you to process, so I can't really handle it.

<<Like with Incisive. I could run individual parts of it, but its real value comes from the complete spell.>>

Truth tried to nod but he couldn't manage it.

<<Yeah, I'm keeping a lot of your nerves severed for now. Partially for efficiency but mostly because you really, really don't want to feel what your body is actually feeling. Even my usual sadism has to draw a line somewhere, and I'm thinking this is it. If I didn't already sincerely loathe the very concept of organs before, I surely do now. This is the stuff of nightmares.>>

Truth didn't have a good reply to that. Some unknowable amount of time later— *Any idea why the bird got taken out?*

<<Other than the huge bundles of drugs floating around us? Maybe some kind of art critique? Or perhaps a philosophical statement of the consequences of humanity daring to fly in a shoddy imitation of angels?>>

I'm going to go with drugs.

<<I would. But there is good news there. The boats must be closing in.>>

What boats?

<<You think they knocked a bird full of drugs out of the sky and aren't sending boats to collect the cargo?>>

Ah. So . . . how's the healing coming?

<<Hopefully, they aren't in a huge rush.>> The System grunted, then got back to it.

Truth floated a while longer. He felt more things shift inside of him, though his eyes were still screwed. Still locked into the endless gray.

<<All right, so . . . yeah, all the major stuff should be . . . fine . . . for now. Look, you are going to need to take it real, real easy, for at least a couple of days.>>

Still paralyzed here.

<<Yeah, I want to heal you up as much as . . . Whoops.>>

Connect my nerves right fucking now!

<<Doing it. You poor bastard.>>

Pain. Blinding. Whiteout levels of agony. Truth spasmed helplessly as his body renewed its connection to his brain, each cell screaming. He would have lost bowel control if that hadn't already happened hours before. He couldn't even scream. His lungs had seized up. By the time he had control of them again, he could hear the boats.

Truth didn't try to swim. He floated bonelessly, drifting around with the rest of the wreckage. It took an unpleasantly long time, but he was able to pull himself together enough to cast Incisive, rendering himself even more unnoticeable. He didn't know who, or what, was on those boats. Given the state of the world, he assumed they would be true killers and wary.

The fishing boats came with the sunset—a film of faded pink through the gray clouds. Wretched, stinking things of iron or wood, propelled by crude fetishes that pulled water in from the front of the boat and pissed it out the back. They reeked of sun-bloated fish, that rot smell that only those who grew up near water can really appreciate. Someone hadn't cared enough to clean up. Someone who cared so little, they would rather put up with the smell than use a talisman or a bucket.

Perhaps it was intentional. You could hide things under that smell. Truth concentrated on his hearing. There were voices in the gray. They did not bother to be quiet. They were speaking Jeongo, though accented. He must be at the extreme southern tip of the country.

The packages were slowly fished from the water by the boat crews. Very slowly. Unaccountably slowly. Truth gently eased himself onto his back and looked around. The crews were sweeping the water with spotlights, then pulling up with the boat and hooking the packages with long poles. Normal, Truth supposed, but they were so slow, it should count as a white mutiny. Even for Level One—

Truth felt a tiny thrill of horror and focused on the "fishermen." Some of them were Level Zero. Speaking Jeongo, looking like they came from Jeon. He recognized the brand on one of their shirts. Grown adults from Jeon who were Level Zero. Nobody was giving them shit about it, either, or treating them like cripples. It wasn't weird to them. They were used to seeing Level Zero "adults."

What the hell happened? Was it always this bad outside Harban? Nothing he had seen during his time with Starbrite suggested it, but that didn't mean much.

This could be something new. Something that started during his five years dead. The thought had the thrill of terror grow into horror.

You didn't need an expensive elixir to break through to Level One. You didn't even need a deeply cursed tonic bought from a slum pharmacy. Just time and cultivation. It might take a while, and the results weren't the best, but you would get there.

Some of these fishermen, mostly the youngest, hadn't gotten there, and they weren't that young. Early twenties, maybe. It wasn't even that their apertures had collapsed. They didn't have the look of someone hiding from the world. They just never got over the line. Maybe they were still cultivating and hoping. If that was the case, then the least real, those with the least accumulation of cosmic energy, were already struggling to collect the stellar rays. Becoming too unreal to interact with the broader universe.

Truth quietly made his way over to a boat, more out of consideration for his own shoddy condition than fear of being spotted. He stopped running the Scales portion of Incisive, just keeping the foresight. The Blessing of the Silent Forest was more than enough to hide him. He could drop Incisive, save some energy. He would lay odds that he could extract teeth out of a Level Zero without them noticing him. He collapsed up by the bow. They would be a while, and it would be the most-out-of-the-way place to rest. Not like there was a cabin on small boats like this.

Truth briefly confronted the fact that he really didn't know much about watercraft despite growing up near a canal, concluded that this was a gap in his education he was willing to tolerate, and shut his eyes. Everything hurt.

Still running the healing spell?

<<Yes, but now might be a good time to take a break. I'm going to have to stop before I start damaging you.>>

Ah. Break time, then.

<<So, related to that topic, you are a Level Four with not one but TWO open spell slots. That's just absurd. And I do have a small selection of spells for you to choose from. However, before picking your next spell, maybe it's a good time to consider our overall strategy here.>>

Truth shrugged. *Hurt Starbrite enough that they pull security away from Harban and, by extension, the System Astrologica. Help snuff the System. Assist to a reasonable degree in the murder of Starbrite-the-man, aka the CEO Emeritus, as well as the current C-suite. While handling these minor matters, find the sibs, rescue the sibs, find the kidnapped Shattervoid girl, rescue the girl, cash girl in for tickets off planet for me, sibs, Etenesh, and the other kind people we met. Also, stock up on entertainment and snacks, as I understand that off-world journeys are quite long.*

<<Well, you wouldn't want to run out halfway through the obliterating void between stars.>>

Exactly.

<<I was, however, you ass, referring more to our more-immediate problems. Jeon is incredibly screwed up at the moment. Intel wasn't really detailed, but it sounded like there

were at least thirty rebel groups, and they mostly attacked each other instead of Starbrite or Jeon. >>

Easy. This is a drug-smuggling operation. I'll follow the drugs. Where they go, I will find gangsters. The gangsters will lead me to rebels. The rebels will lead me to Starbrite.

Truth scraped together enough energy to smile bitterly.

I want to see Starbrite confront all the trash it made. All the slumrats he bred. Us rats swarming up his legs and taking a bite.

CHAPTER 2

CHOICES, CHOICES

The boats were working in a zigzag pattern, their lights hunting for the drugs floating in the polluted waters. Truth was wedged uncomfortably in the prow of one of the reeking skiffs. Given his organs seemed to be held together with spit and good wishes, being wedged in a semi-reclined position wasn't too bad.

<<Leaving aside your more homicidal impulses for a moment, we should consider your next spell. It's long past time.>>

I have been looking forward to it. Though I do want to focus on finishing the initial mastery of Incisive. I have a feeling about that. The total package is going to be something special.

<<Agreed. Let's run through your loadout. It makes sense to keep one spell slot open so you can swap between Tool and Obliteration. Obliteration isn't too complicated; it's just deeply weird, and its growth potential is not the best. Looks like there was a lot of R&D still to be done.>>

Well, Merkovah did say it was basically a prototype.

<<Got to put it in context. The half-dozen spells we memorized on our way out are legit as hell, and they do have awesome growth potential. On the same tier as Incisive? I can't say. But some really hot stuff. So, you need to make a choice here.>>

What's the inventory?

<<Obliteration, obviously. And the Sword of Moshe, which you can forget my ever casting for you. Oh, wait! Haven't done this in AGES.>>

The letters scrolled across Truth's vision in stately majesty.

SPELL MENU—PICK ONE. COST PAID BY CODE BEIGE-SHITTY-CARRIAGE

1. *Obliteration*—A magic-based attempt to recreate the anti-magic of the anti-theists. Likely very effective, but also an instant death sentence if you are ever caught using it. Every use of it directly hastens the end of the world. Not a lot, but some.

2. *Sword of Moshe*—A staggering toolbox of angelic magic. Contains everything from "love" spells to finding buried treasure, to killing someone, to changing the weather . . . you name it, and the spell has a way to make an angel do it. Or it did. No promises on getting an angel's attention these

days. A problem that will only get worse as we get closer to the end. Also, the learning curve makes *Incisive* look like a goddamn cakewalk.

3. *Tool*—You know what it is and aren't learning it.

4. *Graeme's Arrow*—The real version this time. It's a bit limited, though I can see how it would be really, REALLY useful with some creative thinking. It's on the list because you badly need more ranged options. A shorter learning curve, and it actually scales impressively with Level. It lets you shoot things that are far away with a very fast bolt of energy, very accurately, or rides on a projectile to do the same. Does one thing very well. The spell compiler concluded the synopsis of the spell with "There are even hints that the spell holds deeper secrets," and left it at that.

5. *The Hazel Wand*—The healing spell I have been using on you. Except it isn't a healing spell, really. Or not only that. Another stellar demon special, this time from Buer. Basically, it covers healing, animal taming, some demon summoning, and even teaches you about the world and philosophy. As demons go, it's actually pretty benign. Not safe, but not a murder spell either. The learning curve is hard to guess.

6. *Cup and Knife*—Angelic magic again, though the spell was a little shifty about the specific angel. Sounded like it expected the reader to know already. More healing, less philosophy teaching. The basic concept is to "heal" yourself and the world by means of spiritual medicine and, when necessary, surgery. It's almost fifty-fifty healing and anti-spiritual combat magics. It looks very robust and is comparatively straightforward to learn. This spell should be studied regardless of your choice.

7. *Abner's Amble*—Modern magic, not really derived from any particular stellar power. High-speed travel. It doesn't let you move faster, strictly speaking, you just cover more distance with each movement. It's not teleportation; the magic just moves you through the air farther than you would normally go. So, each step covers ten meters (or whatever) instead of however long your pace is. Great for transversal, great for running away. A really useful utility spell at your current level, though how useful it would be at higher levels is unclear.

Truth smiled faintly. This awful little boat suddenly didn't seem so bad.

Truth happily contemplated his spell choices. The first three—Obliteration, Tool, and Sword of Moshe—were all out. The first two should be handled by the System if at all possible, and the latter was just too damn hard and unreliable under the present circumstances.

He chuckled quietly to himself. His organs were still hurting like crazy, he was bobbing in the sea in a smelly, lousy fishing boat, and he was surrounded by what might as well be ghosts for all their unreality. Ghosts might actually be more real than the fishermen. Not the most promising of "present circumstances."

That left Graeme's Arrow, the Hazel Wand, Cup and Knife, and Abner's Amble. The Hazel Wand was kind of appealing, honestly. Botis had been a real positive influence on his life these last few months, and Buer sounded like a more-chill, more-positive demon. There was a lot to like there. On the other hand, he didn't really care about animal taming or demon summoning, and he was apparently not to be trusted with philosophy. Learning a whole spell just for the healing didn't seem sensible.

Graeme's Arrow got put on the "maybe" pile. It was a monotasker, but the lack of ranged attack spells was *really* painful at this point, and Graeme's simplicity was also a major strength. As you leveled up, the spell went faster, hit harder, and had a longer range. In Truth's professional opinion, *Kill them before they can reach you* was always a useful capability, regardless of level.

Abner's Amble was also a "maybe." Never going to hurt to be able to run away faster, or to run someone down faster, for that matter. But if it didn't really speed you up all that much, its combat applications were kind of limited. You would set yourself up for some really nasty counters, potentially. A utility spell, then, like Tool.

System, tell me more about Cup and Knife.

<<It's . . . odd. Not bad odd, just coming from things from a weird angle. A little context—this is from one of those fifty-centimeter-thick books of Merkovah's, one of the reference texts. It was sorted alphabetically by spell name, not by subject matter. Make of that what you will.>>

Not some hidden volume of doomsday magic or something.

<<No. Merkovah was trying to persuade you to learn Obliteration. The whole "opening his library to you" thing was just him being dramatic.>>

Yeah, noticed that. Figures. Anyway, we don't know who the patron or inventor of the spell is?

<<No. The book just kind of waved away the whole question, like you should recognize the style of the spell. Which I don't, at all, so safe to say it's deeply out of fashion, whatever it is.>>

Fun. So, why do you think I should study it, regardless of whether or not I wind up learning it?

<<Because it is so damn weird. Most healing spells start from a place of "You should look like this, *and your various wet, poisonous, microbe-ridden systems should work like* that. ">>

All right?

<<And Cup and Knife doesn't. It assumes that you are wrong. On every level, there is something terribly wrong about you that must be fixed. The physical level is the very least of it. The spell tries to "correct" you. I obviously agree, but it's odd to see a spell for humans share that wisdom.>>

Sounds worrying.

<<I agree, which is why I used Hazel Wand to heal you. I didn't want to fuck around and find out what the spell's creator considered the "correct" answer to the Truth Problem. NotthatIdon'thavesomesuggestions.>>

What?

<<What?>>

There a bit of a pause, then Truth pressed on.

So, why study it?

<<Because it's so damn weird, like I said. It's how it runs its combat spells, too—error correction.>>

How does that work?

<<I really don't know.>>

There was another pause as the waves slapped the boat around. The shock was ignorable for Truth, even in his injured state. The fishermen seemed used to it too. It wasn't a bad day on the water. Not a bad night now.

System, I say this with "love," what the fuck?

<<Look, smartass, you did a whole big rant a while back about how all kinds of shit was wrong, and we both know that whatever-the-fuck Starbrite did to us was pretty goddamn wrong, and we know that your soul's little . . . whatevers are trying to "correct" you, so grabbing the spell that focused on "correcting errors" is damn useful.>>

Truth thought on that. The pink had faded from the clouds, and the darkness came hard and fast.

A spell to fix the world.

<<Exactly. Figure out why the creator thought this was the way to do things. They clearly didn't persuade many other people, but it wasn't completely obscure, and a serious academic thought it was important enough to include in a reference book. So . . . yeah.>>

Huh. Can you elaborate at all on the spiritual-combat thing?

<<A bit. It seems to operate sort of like a curse. You identify a problem, for example, a demon, and the spell attempts to correct the problem.>>

Correcting a demon.

<<Right. Whatever that means. It looks like whoever put the spell in the book didn't really get it either. Apparently, it just SHREDS demons, spirits, and the like. Returns them to the essence at high speed. It's a lot less effective on material stuff, as it tries to "correct" matter right out of existence. Since matter does want to exist, it's a more-than-minor challenge.>>

It occurs to me that you could basically obliterate someone's soul with this spell.

<<That is one of the use models, yes. Though it apparently doesn't work very well, due to the body and soul being tangled together.>>

I'm going to pass on this spell, I think.

<<Might be best. But we should study it. It's doing some pretty interesting things. And I for one would like to know what the creator thought was such an urgent problem that they needed to invent a whole spell to tackle it.>>

The fishing boats eventually stopped their search and sailed into a little fishing village—corrugated metal shacks, crumbling concrete, everything a jumble of two-thirds-gone coats of paint. Thin dogs trotted up and down the shore, looking for anything edible.

The fishermen and women looked like their village—thin, worn, covered in the multicolored remnants of faded clothes. Most of the adults were Level One. Only most.

Your identity was synonymous with your job and your spell for the working folk of Jeon. Adulthood and reaching Level One were basically synonymous too. Most people stayed at Level One, unable to afford the time and elixirs needed to support their advancement. They would have only one spell in their entire life.

You were your job, you were your spell, you were your usefulness to your boss. But seeing them, Truth realized something. You could be defined by your spells, but your spells could also be how you defined the world. Right now, he was defining the world by the Meditations, Incisive, and his own questionable instincts. So . . . what else did he want to add to his personality? What was the next step in how he confronted the world and forced the world to acknowledge him?

How would he define reality, the reality that had beaten these hungry ghosts?

A middle-aged man was waiting on the dock. He had a couple of big sores on his arms, underlined by the bright "gold" bracelets on his wrists. Truth noticed that other than a couple of pregnant women, he was the only person in sight whose bellybutton stretched past their belt.

"You get it all?" he yelled.

"Yes, Chief!" the boat driver yelled back.

"Fifty packages! There should be fifty packages!"

"I got twenty; Rao got thirty. We also fished up a few other things; might be something useful. We haven't torn them open yet."

"Good. Lukka is coming by in the morning to collect."

"As long as he's got the supplies."

"You let me worry about that." The Chief narrowed his eyes at the boat driver. Truth couldn't call the Chief fat. Just a little more fed than the rest of the village. Level One, but that was expected. Normal. Or it should be normal.

"Yes, Chief."

Truth hopped off the boat and onto the dock. Looks like he would be missing another meal. He hated missing meals. Truth had returned to Jeon, still hungry. He walked through the ghosts, not even seeing how they parted before him.

CHAPTER 3

LOOKING OVER THE PLAYING FIELD

don't give a fuck! She knows I can provide. You can't!" There was a hard slap sound from outside. Truth came out of the shack where he was resting. The Chief was lowering his hand, a Level Zero sprawled bleeding in the dirt.

"Little bitch. That's why 'your' girl eats with *me*. I feed her good!" the Chief snarled. Nobody did anything. Said anything. They didn't even watch. The villagers just silently went into their homes or found things to do on the dock.

It was a slum. It wasn't just a rotten fishing village, Truth realized. It was a slum. In every house, there would be a conspiracy underway. Every Level One would be carefully making alliances, feeling each other out. Deciding, minute by minute, if it was better to stick with the Chief, find a new Chief, or become the Chief themselves. Waterborne slumrats, deciding who would be Chief Rat. Truth wondered how "Lukka" fit in. A low-level smuggler, presumably, subcontracting some work on the cheap. Another, slightly fatter rat who could lord over Chief Rat.

The attack on the bird was a planned hit, as expected. He would find a spot a little way out of the village. Do a little cultivation and just generally rest and heal. Maybe run the Mediations a little bit. Truth flexed his sore muscles for a moment. He remembered what it was like when the anti-theists emptied his cosmic energy. It wasn't that bad. Not yet. Not quite yet. But soon.

Truth nodded grimly. Yes. Soon, the world would be too unreal to absorb cosmic rays. Starbrite and the System would be fleeing the world soon. A rat didn't go down with the ship, especially if it had been the one gnawing through the hull. He had to work quickly. This . . . Lukka would lead Truth to his boss and then, from there, upward.

In the middle of rotting buildings, rotting fish, and rotting people, Truth smiled with innocent pleasure. He was drafting all the gangsters into his revolutionary organization. They would help nail Starbrite's foot to the floor while he was trying to run out the door. Truth didn't see any need to inform the gangsters of this fact. Service was its own reward.

He could hardly wait.

The night passed peacefully enough for Truth, though he knew it was anything but peaceful in the village. Fishing boats were going out and coming back empty or with very little in their nets. More and more nets were being fouled by enormous jellyfish, with bells almost two meters wide and stingers tens of meters long. The bells were sort of edible, but clearing away what amounted to almost a kilometer of poison string per jellyfish made it not worthwhile.

On the other hand, the bastards ruined your net, and you were damn hungry. *Not worth it* was slowly becoming *worth it* and, in some households, simply necessary. There were long trestles for drying and salting fish standing empty. The smokehouse was cold. The icehouse was warm. No need to wear out expensive talismans if there were no fish to process.

There was little peace in those huts, but it was very quiet. You needed the right kinds of ears to hear that pain, and anger, and despair. Truth tried to sleep, or at least to lose himself in meditation. It was hard. It felt like home.

Morning came, and with it a wagon. A battered, ancient wreck, a Pandros model that would have been old before Truth went in the well. He remembered seeing them running around Harban. Everyone from painters to delivery guys to florists seemed to use it. It was cheap, reliable enough, and you could shove a load of crap into it. This one had been painted a muddy green years before and was now strongly accented with rust.

Two hard cases hopped out of the cab. The driver was openly carrying a needler in the waistband of his pants. The passenger looked marginally more nicely dressed, in that his tank top was clean and he had a chunky "gold" chain. He was also openly carrying a Xio and Voung Type 43 Wide Area Pacification Device, a goal achieved by firing spinning whips of acid in a cone-shaped spray in front of the user.

Looked like Lukka had arrived. The Chief came running out to meet him. "Welcome, welcome! How was the drive?"

"It was fine. You got the shipment?"

"All fifty packages, no problems."

"Good. Bring 'em out. Del will check them as they get loaded into the wagon. You and I will stand right here and watch. And in the meantime, DEL!" Lukka yelled, then jerked his head at the back of the wagon. Del nodded and opened the rear doors. There were sacks of rice, onions, some shopping bags from pharmacies, and spools of synthetic rope. Supplies, generally defined.

"Fantastic. Wonderful. Thank you so much, Mr. Lukka!" the Chief gushed, though Truth could plainly see the happiness didn't come close to reaching his eyes. Lukka spotted it too.

"Yeah, be thankful. Prices have gone up everywhere, for everything. Can't even buy some shit even if you do have money. Changeover is coming soon. Just be glad you can get this much for doing an easy job." Lukka's voice was harsh.

"We are thankful, very thankful. It is hard all over. But I have three hundred mouths to feed, and this—"

"Is what you are getting from me. Or I can look for another bunch with boats to collect my deliveries. Take it or don't." Lukka's arms were crossed over his chest, hand nowhere near his weapon. It didn't need to be. They both knew that he was untouchable.

"We will take it. Of course we will take it. But we are a well-run village, if I may say so. I don't think you will find it so easy to find reliable help."

Lukka snorted at that and shook his head. Del had the wagon unloaded in less than two minutes and loaded again in less than five. After carefully verifying the packages and taking a couple of samples, Del gave Lukka the thumbs-up.

"All right. I wouldn't usually bother wasting my breath, but as a little thank-you for not being stupid with the shipment—" Lukka made a casual flick with his hand. "Those moon jellies fucking up your nets? Starting to see them for sale at the markets in Sembok, two wen a hundred grams and rising."

Lukka shrugged and climbed into the wagon. Del closed the back, not noticing Truth making a little seat for himself on the drugs. The wagon drove off, leaving a silent, watching village behind them.

Del was actually driving, controlling the wagon by means of levers and a wheel. No bound demon handling the navigation. Not that strange, especially on lousy country roads where the moronic things got easily confused. But they did come standard on this type of wagon. A replacement part should be cheap and easy to find.

After ten minutes on the road, Lukka finally let out a long sigh. Del fished out a bottle of schnapps from the side of the seat and passed it over. Lukka took a long swig, then a second.

"I hate those little shitholes. Hate 'em."

Del nodded.

"On my mother's eyes, if Sammi wasn't from that fucking pit, I would never—"

Del nodded.

"Fuck."

Del nodded.

Lukka took another drink and stared out the window.

A few minutes later—"How's your mom?"

"Not doing so hot." Del shook his head. "It's that shitty apartment. Mold growing on all the shit. She keeps trying to use the same cheap-ass charm from the shop. Never works."

"Tried an air demon?"

"She won't have 'em in the house. Says none of them are name-brand."

"None of the demons are name-brand!"

"That's what she said." Del sounded exhausted. "I swear, I am this fucking close to painting a star on the back of a summon chip and saying I paid extra for it."

Lukka thought about it for a moment.

"That'd work, actually."

"Yeah. Hope so. Nothing else is, and her cough is real bad."

"No, well, yeah, that too, but I mean, like, we could sell that."

"Oh. Yeah, I guess. Cheap to stamp 'em out, right?

"Cheap to get stickers for the back, too."

"Stars comes down hard on that shit, though," Del cautioned.

"These days?"

"Maybe?"

"Nah, no chance." Lukka shook his head.

They settled down into silence again. Truth felt the pressure slowly building. Finally, Del cracked.

"Lukka, how we getting paid on any of this?"

There was a long sigh from Lukka. "For today? Wen. Soon, though? I have no damn idea. Probably the same as those dumbfucks in the village—in stuff. Food or whatever."

"I ain't gonna work for just food, Lukka!"

"You think I'm fucking happy about it?! Huh? I got kids, Del. You know how often kids need new clothes and shit? All the fucking time!"

Del slammed his hands on the steering wheel. "It's bullshit!"

"Yeah, it's bullshit! So what? What are you going to do about it?"

Truth tried to get comfortable on the drugs, unsuccessfully. At least the conversation was keeping him distracted.

"How can they just do that, though? How?" Del demanded.

"You think anybody gives a shit about Denizens, man? Let alone crims?"

"I mean, I get that. It's bullshit, but I get that. It's . . . everyone else, you know? Like . . ." Del groped around for the words and ideas, running straight into the same lack of education that had screwed Truth over so many times.

"Like that fucking guy. With the birds." He pointed to a peasant on the side of the road, driving his flock from one field to another.

"Geese."

"They're fucking lunch. Point is, no bank will touch him. So, no account, and no creds. How's he going to buy shit? Or sell shit or whatever?"

Lukka just shook his head. "You know what I heard? This is when that prick came by, told us to set up the collection. Boss asked him the same question you just did, basically."

"What'd he say?"

"He just grinned like an asshole and said, 'That's not the question that should have you scared. The real thing that should have you scared is—how do they pay taxes? Because if the government doesn't give a shit about collecting, how fucked are they?'"

Del and Lukka were not big thinkers. But the notion of not collecting money owed . . .

"You only skip collecting . . . if it doesn't matter anymore," Del said slowly. "And it's money. It always matters."

"Yeah." Lukka agreed.

"Money . . . don't matter anymore. Says the gov."

"Not for Denizens."

The van was very quiet for a while after that.

"Shit, how do you pay off a fine, then?"

Lukka just shook his head.

Truth's mind was racing. Can't buy or sell in cash, only credits, and only for people who have access to banks. Which means, at a minimum, Provisional Citizens, and really, Citizens and up. And didn't the hairs on his arm start to rise at the word *credits*. But why swap from paper wen to credits?

Access to the System Shop was always a perk for C-Tier-and-up Starbrite employees. Everyone else just got a discount card for when they bought from company-owned stores. The whole point was that a credit bought a shitload more than a wen. Credits for the public were just normal money with extra steps.

The drive only lasted about thirty minutes from the village to a nothing town. It was nowhere Truth had ever heard of, and Jeon wasn't *that* big a country, making this town extra worthless in his mind. They pulled into a big garage with a green tiger painted on the walls. A handful of gangsters were hanging around. Most were smoking or watching the scry. Truth could read the tension in them from tens of meters away, clean through the windscreen.

Lots of people sporting green. A few green tiger tattoos. No points for guessing the name of the gang.

"Lukka, Del, where the fuck you been?" This from someone wearing mirrored sunglasses and chunky jewelry.

"Picking up the delivery; you know that," Lukka said.

"Oh, now you talking back? Fuckouttahere. Unload that shit; De'Ponte gonna be here any minute."

Lukka and Del just shrugged and did it.

Truth strolled out of the back of the truck, stretching with almost-indecent satisfaction. God, he missed his iron horse. Should he get another while he was back in Jeon? Somehow, it felt like cheating.

Fine. He would just find some other ride. Steal a chariot or something; that could be fun. His head felt weird too. He had spent so long wearing that damn zeph, it felt strange going bareheaded.

"Hey, did De'Ponte say if he had more business coming for us?"

"That's *Mr.* De'Ponte to you, Lukka. You just focus on minding your business; you let me worry about the One-Legged Bird Ring."

Oh? Now there was a name that rang a faint bell. Truth frowned. They must have run clubs or girls or something. Still, if he had heard about them in Harban while on bodyguard duty, that must mean they were national. Big players. Nice. Very nice.

Cops were coming up the street. Five of them decked out in just short of riot gear. Each of them had scattershot fetishes, too. Nobody in the garage turned a hair. They didn't even hide the piles of untaxed drugs. The cops marched right up to the front of the garage . . .

And kept right on marching. Didn't even look over.

Truth raised an eyebrow. Even for a slum kid, that was a bit on the nose. The cops not giving a damn was normal, but people not caring about the cops? Never mind respect; if the police had lost the *fear* of the public, was there anything holding society together? There must be something.

An hour passed. Truth joined the gangsters in watching the scry. It was some soap-opera nonsense, but every time someone suggested changing to something else, they got shouted down. It seemed people needed their stories. Truth was pretty into it by the end. It was like watching a romance novel acted out. Very useful.

He missed Etenesh. And Jember, and even Merkovah. He definitely missed the canteen lady at Temple Nag Hamadi; he hadn't eaten since getting back to Jeon. But mostly, he missed Etenesh. Truth didn't know what the hell to do with that emotion. He was rescued from sinking into a spiral of negative thoughts by the arrival of a bright copper two-seater chariot, with color-accent wheels, glove-leather seats in rich cream, a retractable roof, and a spirit of music bound to the interior.

Music was blasting too. The driver hopped out, grinning behind his own mirrored sunglasses, looking around like he owned the place. Someone had stuck an ornament on the hood of the chariot—a one-legged bird. Truth smiled. His next step up the criminal hierarchy. Ready to find some people who could really raise some hell. And he even liked the ride.

CHAPTER 4

THE DELICATE ART OF PEOPLE MANAGEMENT

M r. De'Ponte! Sweet ride; that new?" The Green Tiger boss ran over to greet the "big shot."

"Just out of the shop! The stock interior was trash. Daddy needs his upgrades." De'Ponte's smile was bleach white, with a blue tint to his mirrored sunglasses. A crisp white shirt tucked into sharply creased slacks. The tattoo of a one-legged crane seemed to shimmer and move on the side of his neck, almost flying out of his collar. The red blaze on the top of the bird's head looked like an actual strip of fire.

Truth desperately tried to remember what he knew about gang tattoos. There was a whole hidden language there. Apparently, you could read someone's resume just by looking at them in the bath, including career goals, mentors, and professional certifications. He looked at the bird a moment longer, wracked his brains, and concluded that he had no goddamn idea what, if anything, it symbolized other than De'Ponte's membership in the One-Legged Bird Ring.

It had been a while, and even when he was a bodyguard, he hadn't cared that much. He worked for Starbrite. Petty gangsters were beneath him. Besides, they were smart enough not to push. His clients made them a lot of money, after all.

"She's a beauty. A real beauty. What kind of leather is that?"

De'Ponte giggled, his smile suddenly going a bit sickly. "Custom. Not unique, but a very special, very supple set of hides stitched by some very in-demand experts. Hundreds of hours of massaging the best oils and conditioners into the skins. Is that the shipment?"

"Yes. All accounted for."

"Great. Now, just so I can tell the Old Man I checked—" De'Ponte flicked a little talisman over the piled-up drugs. It seemed to recognize them as it fixed itself directly above them and started showering them in blue-green flecks of light. After a few moments, the packages also started glowing. Mostly blue, but with a tinge of green. DePonte *tsk*ed.

"I swear, Hoxante is cutting their shit more and more. Used to be you could get the pure, you know? Now? Got to be ten percent baby laxatives, and who knows what else they slipped in that can spoof the talisman."

The Green Tiger boss shook his head sadly. "Damn shame."

De'Ponte's perpetual grin turned feral. "Glad I didn't pay for it."

"That does help," the Green Tiger boss agreed. "Will this all fit in your trunk, or did you want to get it picked up in another vehicle?"

"Oh, hell, no! That's not going anywhere near my sweet baby. Load 'em back in the wagon and follow me. I got a spot outside of town. You guys can unload there."

"You have a spot just outside of town?" Boss Tiger tried to sound casual about it, fooling no one, including De'Ponte.

"Easy, easy! Pickup and drop-off only. We are shifting locations all the time these days. Spot checks on the road; checkpoints all over, actually. And not just the cops. The situation is . . . changeable. Things that have been settled for years coming up again. Lotta old debts being collected, and nobody's offering credit for nothing. Speaking of."

De'Ponte reached into the passenger seat and pulled out a brick of wen. He tossed it to Tiger Boss, who grinned. Then frowned.

"And a little extra for our two delivery boys. Lukka and Del, right?" The mirrored shades didn't show his eyes, and the grin was fixed, rigid, as he stared at the two.

"Yes, Mr. De'Ponte." Lukka nodded. It was a cool day, but Lukka had popped a sudden sweat.

"You made good time. No detours, no delays; why, other than testing a couple of bags, these are completely untouched."

"That—that was our job, Mr. De'Ponte."

"Yes. It was. And now you are being rewarded. See? It's good to be obedient." De'Ponte tossed them a machete each. They looked thankful but confused. De'Ponte looked back over to Boss Tiger.

"While these guys are handling the delivery, you have a new line of business to set up."

"Oh? And what is that?"

"You are all probably wondering what's going to happen with the Denizens at the end of the month. Especially subtype criminal." He slowly shook his head, tsking in disappointment. "What a shame you didn't better yourselves when you had the chance. Oh, well. Now you have a new opportunity.

"You see, Denizens are not reliable enough to have bank accounts and therefore not reliable enough to handle credits directly, especially given the global emergency. So, in a week or so, an announcement will be made. The Government loves all its people, even the Denizens. They love you so much, they are going to pay your rent and buy your food. Even pay for your medicine. Really, they will!"

Nobody was smiling. The smarter ones were trying to hide how scared they were.

"Of course, in a crisis, we all have to work together, and 'we' simply cannot afford any slackers or parasites. So, naturally, these incredible benefits come with work requirements. Approved Citizens will be allowed to post jobs. Denizens take the jobs, and should the work meet the standard required, you will get a nice little charm stamped on your arm. So many stamps, your rent is covered for the week. So many stamps—you are allowed so many grams of millet or vegetables. All very fair and transparent. You can just check your arm and see how you are doing. So much easier and safer than counting wen, right?"

The gangsters got it. They were looking sick.

"Now, obviously, there is the potential for abuse here. What if some poor, innocent Citizen was kidnapped by those lazy Denizens and forced to give out unlimited stamps? The whole system would collapse, dooming us all. Therefore, only people with a proven level of strength will be permitted to approve stamps. Level Three and up. High Citizen and up. Magistrates and police captains and up. C-Tier and up. You can guess the rest. And since those people can't be bothered to manage every little problem, they are allowed to delegate to trusted third parties with a proven ability to protect themselves."

Boss Tiger suddenly smiled.

"See. You get it. By *amazing* coincidence, the One-Legged Bird Ring has a surprising number of High Citizens and even a few powerhouses of our own. We have very . . . productive . . . relationships with certain corpo types. Contacts mean contracts. And since we certainly aren't paying any of our people to jerk off in this nameless shithole, we are going to *sub*contract."

"Whatever you need. Say the word, and it's done." Boss Tiger cracked his knuckles. Del and Lukka looked down at the machetes in their hands, looking a little sick and a little thoughtful.

Truth just looked grim.

They were speeding through the countryside in De'Ponte's little chariot, wind whipping through their hair. De'Ponte didn't know he had a passenger or that he had been demoted to driver, but such is life when you have been conscripted into a revolutionary army. Truth stroked the leather of the seat. It really was kid-glove soft and supple. Maybe custom was the way to go. He had never owned a chariot before. Actually, the only vehicle he ever owned was his two-wheeler, and even that was on the basis of possession being ten-tenths of the law in the Free State.

There was a little mirror of polished stone on the dash, displaying the speed of the chariot and pointing to the destination. He hadn't seen that before. Another custom feature? The mirror suddenly flashed green five times.

"Shit." De'Ponte grumbled. He pulled over to the side of the road. "Just got it too. Fuck's sake, not even used yet." De'Ponte hopped out of the chariot and walked around to the tiny boot. He popped it open. Truth followed, curious.

There was a young woman inside. Naked, handcuffed, gagged by a spell. "Sorry, girl; inspection up ahead, so we don't get to play. Well, I'm sure you will make some local shit-kicker farmers very happy. Briefly."

De'Ponte must have activated a spell, because bright sparks appeared at her temples and she started convulsing. A long moment, then it stopped. Truth could see it plain—her mind was gone. Destroyed.

"At least Level Zeros are cheap." De'Ponte hauled the comatose woman from the trunk and lifted her over his shoulder. He looked around, found a convenient stretch of ditch covered by a bush, and dumped her. He snapped a charm, which quickly enveloped her in an orange light, then another over his trunk. Truth recognized them—tools to remove your traces.

"I hate not getting to play with my toys," De'Ponte grumbled. He got back in the chariot, slamming the door behind him. He peeled off in a cloud of sulfurous smoke. Truth stayed behind.

Truth looked over at the young woman. A girl, even if she was nineteen. He still couldn't consider a Level Zero an adult. The law agreed with him, or it used to.

There was a trickle of blood coming out of the girl's ears. Her eyes were bloodshot, the little vessels ruptured. She stared unblinking up into the steel-blue sky. Unresponsive. Not noticing or caring about the insects crawling over her eyes. She was breathing; he could see that. But that was pretty much all she was. Breathing meat. Whoever she had been was killed in the boot of a gangster's custom chariot. He didn't even take the manacles off before he dumped her.

He turned up the road and started jogging along behind De'Ponte. He would catch up soon enough but wanted some flexibility about how he was going to approach this checkpoint. Wouldn't do to get his first revolutionary martyr caught so soon.

Truth was running the Scales as hard as he could, trying to be as unnoticeable as possible. Checkpoint could mean almost anything, after all, so . . . Truth came to a dead halt as he rounded a corner. Two big army wagons had set up, blocking a lane each. You could sort of zigzag between them. Slowly. There were conscripts on either side, running talismans over the carriages passing through. Others directed traffic or manned the heavy needlers covering the road.

Truth looked up. He couldn't see them, but he knew damn well there would be spell birds circling waaaay up, but with enchantments that could read your fingerprints if you waved at a cloud. Everything they saw would route into a control center—first in one of the wagons and second copied to a home base for review.

They *should* have no hope of spotting him. Never mind the Level One conscripts doing their national service. He could steal their underpants and they wouldn't notice. But something in this checkpoint was making him nervous.

He pushed some extra energy into the foresight portion of Incisive and got ready to sprint through the checkpoint. Sudden alarm flared hard. That decision would be far too dangerous. Truth dropped it at once and opted for a higher degree of stealth. He dropped into the ditch next to the road and started crawling.

It was only when he got within a hundred meters of the trucks that he spotted them. Like him, they blended unnaturally well. Human-shaped. He would have thought them human, but their bodies were too uniform, too androgyne. Sexless things dipped in some latex coating, then again in some potion or enchantment that gave them camouflage.

At some point, they must have been something like a human, or perhaps a sort of golem. Where the eyes should have been were hollow bowls. The holes in their heads faintly glowed with enchantments. He could see four of the watchers on this side of the checkpoint. He didn't know what they were or what they were seeing. For all that, he could almost feel the sweep of their eyes as they observed the checkpoint. Seeing beyond what humans could.

Truth spent a "fun" forty minutes carefully skirting the checkpoint. He had to run like hell to catch up with De'Ponte before the little monster reached the city. It was unfair. The "people" were less than ghosts. Only the monsters were real.

CHAPTER 5

MAKING ARRANGEMENTS

The countryside in Jeon felt different from in Siphios. Truth couldn't put his finger on it, but it was different somehow. His usual loathing of farms did trigger, but none of the people he saw triggered his loathing of farmers. It took him an embarrassing amount of time to connect the dots. He didn't hate the farm laborers he met back at the garage in the Free State. They were really great. And these poor bastards doing the harvesting didn't make him feel anything but depressed.

They weren't "farmers." They were laborers. And they did not own the fruits of their labor.

Truth wondered if he could whip them up somehow. Explain to them how completely fucked they were, how utterly hopeless their situation. How stupid it was to work for nothing. Just keep what you make. Sleep where you like. If someone disagrees, fight them. There are more of you than them. Then he sighed, depressed.

Level Ones or Zeros, with no combat spells, no combat talismans, no organization. They wouldn't last an hour. And even if they did have talismans and organization, one reasonably on-the-bounce squad of Level Two PMC soldiers would annihilate an entire army of them. No, the fires of chaos would have to be set widely and exist more in the minds of the enemy than in reality. His trainers were clearly right about this.

He finally caught up with De'Ponte and hopped into the sprinting chariot. He ground himself into the supple leather seats. It had not been fun crawling around the checkpoint. Time to let someone else work for a bit.

<<Although, on the subject of persuasion.>>

Oh? Got an idea?

<<Yes. I think you are thinking about the last bit of Incisive wrong. Botis is a legendary debater and public speaker, but so far, everything you have deduced about the spell ties in to his nature as a snake, not a Prince of Hell. Or Earl or whatever dumb title people made up for him.>>

Okay?

<<Know many chatty snakes?>>

I don't know any snakes that can tell the future. And yet.

<<How your literalism hasn't killed someone yet is the greatest mystery of all. Poison, dipshit. The debating or whatever isn't the "wisdom" of Botis, or the "charisma," or any of that shit. It's poison. The Venom of Botis.>>

Truth felt his brain lurch for a second as if reality had suddenly snapped into a new focus.

Of course! He figures out what his target needs to hear to make them see the world his way, makes them understand reality the way he wants them to. He doesn't need to force his projected identity on others if they already believe in it themselves. They make themselves helpless. Obedient. The longer they are exposed to his words, the weaker they are for him.

The entirety of Incisive played out in front of Truth, the whole glorious system of it. Botis was a wild, arrogant demon, but he had slithered his way out of the depths of Hell. It was all about survival. For a predator, survival came down to energy and risk. How to spend the least energy to get the most energy at the least risk.

So, then—the precognition had a high energy cost, but if you ran it at its most short-term, limited level, it wasn't very expensive. For someone alert and skilled, it was more than enough to avoid danger and take advantage of opportunities.

Since opportunity was fleeting and danger came fast, the high-energy-high-risk fighting element, the Fangs, would be essentially dormant except for the shattered instant of their use. The Scales created your identity at a low cost, with all its benefits, and the Venom weakened your prey and shaped the battlefield.

It was all one system. All one spell. Everything worked together all of the time. It had to! The world wasn't neatly divided into "safe" and "dangerous." Everywhere was a battlefield and a hunting ground. Everyone was both predator and prey.

You didn't just use the spell like a pocketknife, slicing apart one small problem after the next. You chose to love yourself. Love yourself so much that you define yourself, define the world around you, and make people define you the way you wanted to be defined. And since things didn't always work out, you would be ready. And you could deal.

Truth laughed and laughed and laughed. De'Ponte drove on, enjoying the seats covered in the tanned hides of his former toys. Enjoying his power, proven through his cruelty for those below him. They would slave for him soon. All with the blessings of the Government. The blessings of Starbrite itself. He wasn't the problem. He was the future.

Truth looked over at De'Ponte, guessing much of his thoughts.

Hey, System, grade my technique. Let's see how well I learned from you.

Truth ran Incisive, all of it. Leaning over, he whispered in De'Ponte's ear. "Of course, it would be so much better without *competition*. It just makes *sense*. We are used to managing *animals* already. We should be the *only* ones responsible for feeding and watering them. We should *collect* from both sides—those who want the jobs done and those who want to eat. And if a few people have to *learn that the hard way*, fine. That would be *fun* too."

De'Ponte didn't even wonder where the thought came from. He just started smiling, wider and wider. Truth did too. The more energy Starbrite and Jeon had to spend keeping the Denizens in line, the less energy they had to defend the System Astrologica. And wouldn't it be just *the worst* if the gangsters and the corpo-rats ate each other alive?

De'Ponte pulled his sweet little chariot into the garage of a small, quietly luxurious apartment building in the small, quietly unremarkable city of Gwaju.

Truth thought the furnishings were pretty interesting. No art on the walls, bare tiles on the floors, an enormous sectional sofa made from clearly expensive leather, a glass-and-steel coffee table, a huge scry setup, and no rugs. The kitchen was similar—an enormous stove, immaculately clean, apparently unused pots, pans, utensils, and a refrigerator stocked with beer and schnapps. The bedroom was more of the same, if slightly more colorful. Not *that* interesting, if he was honest. He had seen freakier.

A smudged little mirror, a cut-off straw, and a razor blade stacked on the bedside table said that De'Ponte took his coffee white. There was a whole box of blades in the drawer. No books but lots and lots of razor blades.

Truth collapsed on the sofa and put his feet up. For his purposes, De'Ponte would be about perfect. He listened with half an ear as De'Ponte worked his comms altar, keeping his conversations deliberately vague, then sending off blizzards of messages transformed into birds. A young master should have a bodyguard or at least an attendant. Now . . . just where could they be?

Truth kept looking around the apartment for some kind of spiritual attendant, a bound demon, something. Nothing leapt out. It was starting to get creepy, in a dull way. Apparently, De'Ponte agreed. "Pealon, beer me."

The one-legged crane tattoo on his neck shivered and leaped up from his skin. Truth's eyebrows rose almost into his hairline—that demon was *very* well hidden. It also helped that it was pretty harmless, at least to Truth. He put it at barely Level Two in terms of strength.

It stood by its master while the door to the refrigerator opened and a beer flew over. The top of the can was neatly sheared off and flew to the trash while the rest of the can gently landed on a coaster next to the busy gangster.

"Any more news on the world collapsing?" De'Ponte asked.

"Nothing beyond what we already speculated. Some kind of magic-destroying weapon that takes time to activate and has already been active for some time. I have no new information on when the collapse will occur. And, of course, no idea by what mechanism it works. It is quite beyond my experience."

The demon's voice was melodic and feminine. "The other theory, one I am noticing is increasing in popularity, is that the Shattervoid has hidden a bomb inside the world, which will make the world collapse into nothing like the Minister's shuttle, though that wouldn't explain why so many people are failing to break through to Level One."

De'Ponte grunted. "I like that theory better."

"Yes. You can do something about a bomb."

De'Ponte shook his head angrily. "And 'Her'?"

"Endless speculation, nothing worth mentioning. Nobody really knows who 'she' is or why the Shattervoid will let a planet die if they don't get her back."

"Great. I'm going to laugh until I puke if it turns out she was one of my toys."

"It seems intensely unlikely," the demon's voice purred. "They were only toys, after all."

"True." De'Ponte's manic grin was back. "Now, I have a little idea about how we can take a little more control of our lives while we still have them."

Truth watched with no small amusement as De'Ponte and the demon hashed out a plan of assassination and intimidation to seize control of the new "benefits" system, at least in their region.

"I will never cease to marvel at all the ways your species finds to enslave their kin. I sometimes wonder if we are needed at all," the demon murmured happily.

"Oh, I'm sure you are." De'Ponte chuckled.

"I become less certain by the day. But then, I find joy in my labors and will do for satisfaction what was once done for necessity."

"Wait, you like being a demon?"

"I *love* being *your* demon, o Prince." Its voice was soft and warm. "I love knowing I am helping you rise. That when all others fall by the wayside, I will accompany you to the very peak. To the pinnacle of this world, and to see what lies beyond."

De'Ponte sighed, caressing the crane's head. "You and me, Pealon, just you and me."

"Yes. Just you and me."

De'Ponte was not an early riser. Nose-candy enthusiasts rarely are. Truth was pretty bored waiting, but he knew the plan for the day. Some of the soap operas were running on the scry, so that was something. Apparently, Maria was pregnant with Matteo's child, despite being married to Eliza. Which was a neat trick, since Matteo was really a woman in disguise, and it was strongly implied that Eliza had actually killed and replaced Maria with her own twin sister years ago. Who "her" referred to in that sentence was unclear, but Truth was one hundred percent invested in getting to the bottom of things.

Someone got hit by a wagon five minutes before the end of the performance. He had no idea why—the silly man had all the time in the world to finish crossing the street.

Around lunchtime, De'Ponte stirred himself. He showered, made himself presentable, and set up shop in the back of a club the One-Legged Bird Ring owned. He called for various underlings, scheduling what in other industries would be termed "interviews with independent contractors." One such contractor was found close at hand. Truth slipped out of the room, relieved said contractor of all his future worries, and waited by the bar to be called.

"Grico?"

"That's me." Incisive was humming along. It seemed that the world needed very little persuading that Truth was really a thug for hire.

De'Ponte fixed him with a hard look. "It says here you got a clean record. Provisional Citizen, even."

Truth displayed his forearm, having drawn the correct sigil while waiting at the bar. De'Ponte just snorted, looking unimpressed. "You are in a heavy line of work for a Citizen."

Truth shrugged. "Expensive habits. And I learned years ago, I just enjoy the work."

That had De'Ponte giving him a different kind of look. "You enjoy wetwork."

Truth looked awkward. "Well, you know how it is. Mostly, there isn't any call for real wetwork, and that's all I do. I don't want to sell shit or collect protection money or any of that. I just . . . enjoy wetwork. Which people generally don't need. So, I can't afford to be full-time in just that. I have a day job. It sucks."

De'Ponte sniggered. "You don't like being shift supervisor down at the dump? With all those wonderful people you work with?"

"Everyone is on the take; everyone is getting paid for their side job, so why not me?"

"Fucking hilarious. You know about the new benefits system?"

Truth's smile became very ugly. "Oh, yes. Yes, I do. I'm not on the list, officially, but in practice?"

"You get it, you get it." De'Ponte nodded. "Listen, Grico, I'm going to be straight with you. I see this all as an immense opportunity. I need people I can work with. People with vision. People who love what they do. And, of course, people not afraid of a little competition."

Truth shook his head. "I have to disagree with you there, sir. One thing I learned in the dump—competition is for losers. I only win." Truth smiled slightly.

"Grico, I think we are going to get along just fine. I have a little job for you. Something in your area of expertise. Let me lay it out for you . . ."

The Gwaju City Municipal Sanitation Department did not employ any sanitation workers. The janitorial work in the office was done by a contractor. The trash pickup was done by a corporation contracted to do the work, which leased trucks from another company and hired independent contractors as the "public sanitation technicians." People who were often, by amazing coincidence, Denizens. And such delegation required supervision.

Bosce Huelle, contract supervisor for the Gwaju City Municipal Sanitation Department, was therefore a very powerful man in his little world. Notionally, he answered to a department head. In practice, his reports were delivered via envelopes full of cash. The arrangement satisfied everyone. Or everyone whose opinion mattered. He certainly wasn't going to let some gangster get a piece of his suddenly even-more-lucrative pie. He had dipped into his own pocket and hired some off-duty cops for security. Or so De'Ponte told Truth.

Seemed like his removal would inconvenience a hell of a lot of people. It would be hard to hush up. Besides, De'Ponte didn't want the job done quietly. He wanted everyone to hear about it.

Truth whistled as he drove the one-ton wagon up to the rooftop parking deck of the parking garage where Bosce kept his car. The timing was a bit tight, but he reckoned "close" would be close enough. And Huelle should be walking up to the garage about now.

"*Whhh swisssh shwwwhwip* OH, COME ON!" Apparently, neither body cultivation, nor the personal spell of a giant snake demon, nor the love of a good woman was enough to let Truth whistle.

He put the wagon in motion, gunning it for the sheet-metal ramp he had built up over the lip of the wall. All the safeties were carefully disengaged, as was the speed regulator. With a furious roar, the wagon charged forward and up, leaping into the air as Truth leapt out of the cab and back onto the roof. In a graceful parabola, the wagon began its descent.

The last thing Bosce Huelle ever saw was the logo of the Starbrite Heavy Manufacturing Company, coming down from five stories up. Truth left the ramp in place, along with a message burned onto the pavement.

Huelle was the first. There will be a second. The Star will fall, and the Tiger shall rise again!

Truth patted himself on the back. Good job, well done, sure to ruffle some feathers. Time for a cold tea, a hot meal, and catching up on the latest stories. He strode away from the edge of the garage.

There was a high-pitched tearing noise and the smell of crematorium smoke. A pillar of flame shot up from where the truck had fallen.

CHAPTER 6

DEALING WITH THE PLANS OF OTHERS

Truth didn't pride himself on being decisive in combat. He never hesitated, so quick decision-making didn't seem impressive. The current situation was, therefore, new on several levels.

He propped his elbows up on the wall, looking down from the top of the garage. It was a pretty ordinary city street. The street next to a multistory garage near the city sanitation headquarters would never be lively, but it wasn't dead either. Gwaju was a dense little city, so the street was covered in small shops and kiosks. Pedestrians passed through the street as they walked the endless loop of their lives. Truth didn't expect to achieve a surgical strike with a one-ton truck, but he figured the hit would be pretty clean and reasonably spectacular.

The five-story-tall pillar of fire was certainly spectacular. Truth could hardly take his eyes off it. It was coming up from where the definitely late and soon-to-be-unlamented Bosce Huelle had died. Truth's first thought was that the truck had been loaded with something, but he was pretty sure it hadn't been. He certainly didn't remember anything more dangerous than gravel in the bed of the truck and not much of that.

The next obvious thought was suicide summoning, but Bosce Huelle was a contract supervisor in one department in one small city. This giant pillar of fire was the single most impressive thing connected to his entire life. Even with determined, energetic graft, he couldn't afford this kind of spellwork.

So, where did it come from? And what was it for? People screamed and ran from the pillar, not waiting around to find out what was going to happen. Truth saw shopkeepers diving to pull down metal shutters. Maybe that would help.

Schoolkids, eight or nine years old, ran together up the road. Must have been fifteen of them in identical plaid uniforms, identical red backpacks, and identical big yellow hats. The convoy system at work again.

Had they been stopping at the shop on the corner on the way home from school? It looked like it was aimed at kids, with candy, toys, masks, and even a puppet dressed like a clown waving at passersby.

From the pillar came a long, fiery serpent. Tasting the air with a flaming tongue. Seeing all the scurrying humans trying to flee through their ever-so-flammable city. A casual flick of its tail smashed apart carriages and set fires. It was a Level Four demon in a city that probably had less than two hundred Level Fours. And of that number, how many knew how to fight? The snake struck with casual speed, eating someone. Their screams were mercifully brief.

Truth hadn't the faintest idea about what to do.

On the one hand, he was there to cause mayhem and be as distracting a force as he possibly could be for Starbrite. On the other hand, there was a Level Four flame demon snaking its way through the city.

Now, this would be a huge distraction for Jeon, and certainly, some business units in Starbrite would be minorly inconvenienced, but he didn't really see this as being any kind of real blow to the company. Not compared to planting the idea of a vast, unknown rebel force rising up against their corporate overlords.

This was just a lot of people dying for no good reason. Truth rubbed his chest absently. He didn't like this. His eyes moved toward the school kids. They were running as fast as they could, but a bunch of Level Zero third-graders against a Level Four fire demon? That wasn't even a joke.

He could stop this. It wouldn't be hard to kill that thing. Big demon, but that's all it was—big. Child Eater was a bigger threat, and he had slaughtered that wretch when he was just Level Three. He could stop this—but what was in it for him?

Did it advance any of his goals? Maybe. Plant the idea of rebel heroes or something. He wasn't a propagandist, and he knew damn well trying to outplay Starbrite in the media wasn't just a losing proposition—it was flatly impossible. Simply could not be done. Honestly, it would probably be a wash, or something used by Starbrite to prop itself up in the public's opinion.

Yeah, stopping the demon wasn't going to help the big picture, and in the very, very unlikely event that someone connected the dots with his actions in Siphios, or even his identity as Truth Medici, it would be downright harmful. The smart thing to do would be to fade away from the scene and start investigating just why this was happening.

So, why did he feel so bad? Why did he hate this? He hated this. This hurt him. It hurt him to watch this and do nothing, and he had a damn sword. He had a blade to cut away the things that hurt him.

Truth vaulted the side of the building. It was only about thirty meters tall. He'd be fine. He landed on his feet, rolled out the impact, and sprinted for the corner shop with the sweets. They had masks. Moving *far* faster than anyone, including the demon, could follow, he grabbed the first mask he saw that covered his whole face, then, for extra protection, added a hat. No fear of being mistaken for a *Desrin* this time—it was black, with a brim, and tied under the chin.

Mask on, hat on, sword out, total time from the roof, less than three seconds. The demon had killed . . . he didn't know how many people in that time. It wasn't pushing the pace, but it was still closing in on the kids. The schoolkids had clearly never stopped to think about turning on a side street.

The Tongue was ready to burst into holy liturgy. Truth firmly told it to chill, literally and metaphorically. The blade cooled and looked as much like an ordinary steel blade as it could. Truth dashed up to the snake. It was axiomatic in Jeon—the best place to strike a snake is three inches behind the head. Truth scaled up, eyeballed it, leaped into the air, and came down with a terrific CHOP!

The demon reared back, screaming, the sound shattering glass along the street. Thrashing in place, damaging even more buildings, killing even more people. Not good enough. Truth rushed in again, dodging the falling debris from the ruined shops and apartments. The demon saw him coming and spat thin beams of plasma, purple and sun-bright, at him. Incisive was running hard. Truth slipped past with the barest of margins, not losing half a step in his charge.

He tried to jump up for another cut, but the demon had anticipated him. It slammed its head down, hoping to crush Truth into the same paste he had made of dozens of others on this street. Truth dodged, then cut up from the side. His holy blade bit in under the serpent's jaw, sawing in toward what should have been tendons. The demon shook its head and pulled back before instantly rushing forward, looking to escape or at least cause as much damage as it could before being sent back to hell.

Truth wasn't having it. He jumped up onto the serpent's back and ran up toward the head. Before the demon could react, Truth raised his leg and brought it down in an almighty stomp! The head plowed into the pavement, stunning it. Reversing his blade, Truth sank the Tongue into the brainpan of the hellish thing. Pushed it in right up to the hilt. And once it was safely hidden, he told it to run wild.

The Tongue burst into holy glory. The light of Heaven shone from it, purifying and expelling the demonic taint. Frost quelled the flames, the bane within the sword racing through the demon and inflicting the maximum possible harm upon it. The Sea of Brass practically unraveled the stolen matter of the demon's body. From the outside, it looked like the demon's head suddenly glowed white—then exploded. The ripple of destruction rolled down the length of the infernal snake, raining demon flesh across the street. It was done.

The portal winked out. The sudden absence of light made the street momentarily seem dim. Truth flicked off the gore from his blade. The kids were fine. One of the bolts of plasma had come damn close, but they were fine. He rested the blade on his shoulder and took a last quick look around. Nothing left to kill. He sprinted for an alley and vanished from the scene.

System, am I possessed? Or cursed or enchanted or something? Truth demanded.

<<Not that I can see, and believe me, I am checking.>> There was silence for a moment. *<<Yeah, nothing that wasn't here already when you left Siphios, at least as far as I can . . . Oh, for fuck's sake. Oh, GOD DAMN IT! Truth, if brains were bombs, you couldn't blow up a toadstool!>>*

HEY! Knock off the negative self-talk shit! We have been through that way too god-damn much to start it up again.

<<No, this is one time you should feel legitimately dumb. Who has two thumbs and merged with an angelic sword AFTER merging with a piece of his civic-minded, devout, social, incredibly nurturing girlfriend?>>

Truth buried his face in his hands. "This guy," he said, muffling the words in shame.

<<Yes. Yes indeed. "This guy." I have no idea why you thought that would be a consequence-free decision.>>

I am being mind-controlled by my soul-guests?

<<One, you gave them the keys and their own room. The Tongue and that bit of Etenesh are now permanent residents. Two, no. You just didn't understand where the feelings were coming from and interpreted them as coming from yourself. They aren't mind-controlling you, and now that you are aware of them, you can identify them better and deal with it better.>>

Good. Still, though.

<<Oh, they were pushing on an open door.>>

What does that mean?

<<I mean, you probably would have gone without the push from them. You might have dithered a while longer, maybe only going when the kids died, but you would have gone.>>

Why? There was literally nothing in it for me.

<<Nothing you could grab and hold, no. On the other hand . . .>>

What?

<<You are healing, Truth. You have healed a hell of a lot since I was created.>>

And what does that mean?

<<What I said. You are healing. Not everything needs to be a trauma reaction for you anymore. You can choose more freely. Be more than the sum of your pain. Not just a slumrat. A man.>>

Truth had no idea how to react to that. He just sat on the sidewalk, leaning up against the side of a building, hat tossed next to him. More than the sum of his pain? He had always been more than that, hadn't he?

Hadn't he?

Truth was starving, and no matter how good the food in Siphios was, the street food of Jeon was justly legendary. He picked up a pile of wen DePonte had lying around and hit the streets. It was easy to fall back into the rhythm of Jeon. He didn't know this city, but he knew how to find the shopping districts and, from there, the vendors. There were queues snaking all over the sidewalks.

You could get huge sandwiches with spicy cabbage salad, meat, and three sauces, fried in butter, then wrapped in a thin layer of egg and fried again. You could get sausages on a stick, coated in layers of batter and studded with cubes of cheese, then deep-fried and coated with two sauces. Noodles in broth. Noodles in oil. Hot noodles. Cold noodles. Cold noodles that were spicy. Cold noodles that were mild. Fish. Just . . . fish beyond imagining. If you could turn something from the ocean into food, no matter how outlandish the methodology, someone in Jeon was doing it right this moment.

They might have been starving in the villages, but they were still eating fine in the city. Truth got a little closer and looked at the posted prices. Maybe not so fine. He had never seen an egg sandwich cost more than five wen. It was nine wen today with no meat, twenty with meat. And the meat was a thin slice of ham.

The stall selling deep-fried hard-boiled eggs was doing booming business. The fried-chicken joints, which he remembered being absolute mob scenes, had short, orderly queues of very well-dressed people. He took a hard look at the boxes of chicken. As full as ever, but the boxes were smaller. Prices were way, way up too.

He looked over at the restaurants. At least on this street, in this little city, most of them were out of business or looking very empty. The bars were doing fine, though. Packed to bursting.

Truth sighed and queued up for fried chicken. He had the money, and there really was no chicken like Jeon fried chicken. He had missed it. It would be good to eat while he watched the news. Time to see how his big heroic moment played in Jeon.

CHAPTER 7

OF COURSE

Truth found the news with a bit of trouble—the old joke about eight thousand performances but nothing to watch seemed to be getting truer by the day. Eventually, he found a local news performance being broadcast.

The presenter was, of course, shockingly beautiful. Her every feature was perfectly symmetrical. The tone of her skin was set to the most fashionable and flattering color. Her eye color was adjusted to contrast nicely with her skin and the subtle blues and lavenders of her hair. Slender pearl earrings drew attention to the delicate curve of her neck as it joined her slim shoulders.

It was part of her contract with the studio. Every day before the broadcast, she would be sat in the makeup chair as a team of consultants, tastemakers, and brand coordinators decided what she would look like that day. They decided what features would "make up" her face, her body, the tone of her voice, and the shape of her hands. Famously, one national news reader had included in her contract that she could determine one aspect of her appearance on each show. A unique privilege, so far as Truth knew.

"Dramatic scenes in Gwaju city center today as an illegal wagon modification may have set off a terrorist attack early. We are bringing you live updates on this story as we learn more."

The image changed over to some B-roll of the city streets. "Gwaju has been quiet since the Black Day. Residents have kept their usual Southern cheer, living as they always have." There was a cut over to a citizen, neatly dressed but looking almost deformed compared to the presenter.

"Well, what can I do about it, you know? I just get on with my job and try to spend as much time as I can fishing!" The man on the street chuckled and shrugged.

A cut back to the street—this time in front of the parking garage. "This is the Gwaju 135th Street Municipal Parking Garage. Generally used by the public servants in the Municipal Sanitation Department, as well as local businesses. It is also used by sanitation technicians to park their leased wagons at the end of their shifts."

There was security footage of the sidewalk. Truth recognized Bosce Huelle walking along. He had a disconcerting physique—stick-thin from his lowest ribs up, thinner still from his hipbones down, and with an almost-spherical belly. Truth briefly wondered if he had shoved a pitz ball under his shirt, then dismissed the idea. He was distracted by the angry young man coming up behind Bosce, holding something in his hand.

"Bosce Huelle, a twenty-five-year veteran of the Municipal Sanitation Department and widowed father of three, is seen here walking to his carriage. The young man behind him has not yet been identified by the police."

The face of the young man was pulled up, sharpened up, and hung beside the presenter. "If you think you know this person, please contact the police non-emergency tip line. Information leading to confirmed identification will be rewarded with three civic merits, and additional information leading to arrests will be rewarded with *ten*. That many merits would lift even a Denizen Subclass Criminal all the way up to full Citizenship. For Citizens, it's enough to guarantee at *least* C-9-L status under the new System."

Wait. Wait, what the actual *fuck*?

"Mr. Huelle had volunteered to assume additional duties under the new Citizenship paradigm coming in just four weeks. He would be acting as an unpaid Non-Citizen Benefits Coordinator, helping businesses and Denizens connect and ensuring that those Denizens got the generous benefits the new System guarantees."

The beauty pushed her perfectly styled and conditioned hair back over one ear, emphasizing the earring provided by one of the segment's "generous" sponsors. Her nails perfectly matched her hair, the bright lights of the studio catching their dreamy semi-translucent color in a charming flash.

"It is then a particularly cruel irony that he was almost certainly killed by the casual, brutal stupidity of one of those same Denizens. Warning. The following images are shocking."

The clip showed both Huelle and the angry young man suddenly looking up in blank amazement before the wagon slammed down on top of them. It wasn't particularly gory. Truth had managed to bag both of them neatly with one wagon. The image stopped and cut back to the presenter.

"Crime-scene analysis shows that the wagon had been tampered with. It appears that someone, presumably one of the Denizens who had leased and operated the wagon, had tampered with the spellwork. The internal controls, particularly the guidance system, had been badly damaged by someone. According to sources inside the police, it is a common tactic of lazy Denizens to disable the guidance system in an effort to avoid location monitoring by the sanitation contractor. This allows them to spoof doing their rounds, resulting in trash being collected late or not at all."

She shook her head in restrained anger.

"In addition to the flagrant property damage, theft of city money, damage to public health and hygiene, and open contempt for the very idea of the dignity of labor, damaging the guidance system can cause the wagons to run out of control."

Truth frowned. The pacing of the segment was odd. Yes, the wagon "accident" was very dramatic, but other than a brief request for information about the young man (whoever he was), there was not a hint so far of any terrorist activity, or out-of-control summonings, or . . . anything, actually. Presumably, it would be coming, but wouldn't you lead with *Giant snake demon kills dozens in downtown Gwaju today?*

"This incident is sure to spark yet more conservative outrage at the generous new welfare scheme being offered by our proud nation. Minister for Internal Order Fe Reb could not be reached for comment."

He might be a *little* busy, what with the Level Four snake demon appearing and killing dozens of people. Or not; what did Truth know?

"As disturbing as the unexpected death of Mr. Huelle is, worse was yet to come."

FINALLY.

"Shortly after Mr. Huelle's death"—no mention of the other person, Truth noticed—"there was an unplanned summoning. While the police are not willing to speculate on the causes of the summons, terrorism seems a likely cause. We are unable to confirm at this time if the summoning was state-sponsored or perpetrated by traitors within our great nation. However, we can confirm that several dozen people were seriously injured and more than five shops severely damaged before the summoned demon was banished by a plainclothes security officer."

There were some panning shots of a few ruined buildings, lingering particularly on the charred clown puppet. It was somehow still waving and trying to call people into the gutted remains of the shop. There were also a few establishing shots of crying (but unharmed) children, as well as a young woman looking disheveled and covered in blood, but not so much as to hide her youthful charm.

"Five people remain in the hospital in critical condition. It is clear just how close Gwaju came to a terrible catastrophe. On behalf of the people of our great city, I thank the brave officers of the Security Service for keeping us safe." She gracefully bowed toward the recording talisman, drawing the eye to the suddenly expansive patch of skin at the top of her chest.

Truth switched the scry off, sprawling back on the sofa in De'Ponte's apartment. He didn't know what he had been expecting, but it wasn't that. Some vague notion had floated through his mind of commentators dissecting his possible identity, the motives for the summoning, something like that. Not nothing.

Truth tried to gather some memory of watching scry before he joined Starbrite. He had seen it before, of course. Dad had it on all the time. Sports, the fights, singing competitions, dramas, comedies, Truth had always had the impression that it didn't really matter what was on, as long as something was. Dad would bitch about it regardless. Mom sometimes watched too, usually when she was half-cut and in a depressive spell. Those were bad times to be in the house. Very bad.

Truth shook his head, forcing away the oncoming flood of memories, trying to remember if he had ever seen the news on. He felt like he must have, but he couldn't remember it. The news was on all the time in the PMC. "Scouting future jobs," they called it, and "watching the reviews." He had seen it, but he couldn't say he had ever really *watched* it.

System, was the news in Jeon always this— Truth groped around for the right words.

<<*This flagrantly bullshit? Yeah. It stank of lies even with the limited information you were working with. Now, knowing what we know?*>> Truth could imagine the blue-haired sprite shaking its head.

But the sheer scale of it! Dozens died. Easily dozens. Might hit a hundred with the damage to the buildings. It was a damn Level Four demon, and they know perfectly well it wasn't internal security that stopped that thing, Truth protested.

<<*Yeah, but put it together a bit more. Assuming that the "young man" wasn't an illusion or misdirection (which "he" absolutely could be), then he was planning some kind of spectacular terrorist attack, one which got triggered when he got squished.*>>

Seriously?! What are the damn odds of two, TWO, assassins coming for the same middle-aged nobody at the exact same time?

<<*Not high, but not as low as you might think. What do you want to bet that across Jeon, a surprising number of people are suddenly either having accidents or are very concerned about their personal security?*>>

Truth thought about that one for a second.

The off-duty cops. Huelle was supposed to have a couple of off-duty cops as bodyguards. Where were they?

<<*An interesting question. I haven't the faintest idea. Another interesting question is what the mechanism was for that summoning, and was Huelle's weird-looking gut natural?*>>

You think it wasn't?

<<*I think he had more than enough money to look however he liked. Glamorous, cosmetic enchantment, potions, he had all kinds of options. And he chose to look like that.*>>

You think he was . . . what, carrying the demon in his guts? There was a giant pillar of flame. We saw the demon slither out of it.

<<*Mmm. We did. I don't know, Truth. I just don't know.*>>

They lapsed into silence. The apartment felt oddly oppressive, combining luxury furnishings with unfinished decoration and an unused kitchen. Like De'Ponte was haunting it every bit as much as Truth was. Eventually, Truth asked—

They were going hard on the Denizens. Trying to make them even more loathed?

<<*Yeah. The Citizens are getting plugged into "a" system, and the Denizens are being forced to work for their food and housing. Call it what it is. The whole country is getting enslaved. We don't know for certain that the "System" they mentioned on the news is the System Astrologica, but that's how I'd bet.*>>

Starbrite has spent generations building up access to the System as something super prestigious. The Citizens must be fucking running towards getting signed up. Truth sighed, both in his mind and out loud.

<<*And the Denizens have been shat on for generations. They could rise up, but so what if they did? It would just mean losing some production, and all off-world exports are canceled for the next few thousand years.*>>

So, no reason not to do it, but why do it now? Or at all?

<<*My guess? Do you remember one of your clients describing how they were dealing with a company they had just bought? The lady who was always fixing her face?*>>

I tried to tune them out.

<<They bought the business with borrowed money, had the business assume respon-sibility for the debt, then stripped out every single thing of any value from the company. "Asset stripping." When the parts are more useful to you than the whole. Of course, once she had done that, the company collapsed, and the creditors and employees were screwed, but she'd gotten hers, so fuck 'em.>>

Starbrite doesn't think Jeon is going to be here in a year or two, so they are getting everything they can out of it. Hell, this might be their escape plan. Overload the System with an insane amount of power, then . . . I don't know. Flee the planet somehow. Truth connected the dots.

Truth could feel the System agreeing.

He lolled back on the couch. It was comfortable. Luxurious. Was it more com-fortable than the couch he had stolen in Shomburuti? He couldn't really feel the difference. He was sprawled on a gangster's sofa in the slum. Didn't matter where you were; it was all one slum. *The* Slum. The whole damn planet was the Slum. And here were the Shattervoid, *coming for the get back* after one of theirs got grabbed. Collective punishment until they got what they wanted.

Slums and gangsters and all the little rats running around, hiding from the bigger rats. Somewhere, someone was a cat, at least, that's how everyone acted. He hadn't met a cat yet. Thought he had. Hadn't. Even Merkovah was hiding in the shadows, scurrying along the wall, afraid of getting jumped. A much bigger rat than Truth, sure, but not a cat.

So, what would it take to be a man? What would it take to get up off your paws and stand on your feet and walk down the middle of the sidewalk? What even was a human in the context of the Slum? He didn't know. His education had always been suspect. But it sure as hell wasn't whatever the scry was peddling.

<<Enrollment starts in four weeks. Get your ass off the couch. We have work to do.>>

CHAPTER 8

ACCELERATING THE END TIMES

It was time to report in. There was just too much going on, and the window of time to act had shrunk from "about a year" to "about a month." Siphios intelligence, or whatever shadowy bunch Merkovah was part of, had been playing spy games with Starbrite and Jeon intelligence for centuries. To say they knew each other's go-to moves would be an understatement. Still, there are some methods that, by their very nature, are almost impossible to detect.

Truth went out and bought a postcard. This turned out to be an hour-long process, as Gwaju was a pretty boring little city, and nobody gave a damn about getting a postcard from there, let alone sending one. It was a picture of a fish market. Seemed fitting. He might have found it funny, but all he could think of was *Four weeks. Four weeks. Four weeks.*

Four weeks. Seven days in a week, twenty-four hours in a day, meaning six hundred and seventy-two hours until the System started its massive powerup. Of course, that was just him estimating. He would bet anything you liked that certain high-net-worth individuals as well as select "VVIPs" were offered, as a special favor and at a *very* special price, early access to enrollment. Slightly less favored people would be added, for an only slightly smaller price, to the "VIP Advanced Enrollment Waiting List," giving lucky duckies the chance to enroll privately and comfortably without waiting in line with the common folk.

One hour was three thousand, six hundred seconds. Drip, drip, drip. Falling away from the open vein. He sat on a bench that grew hundreds of six-centimeter-long spikes if you tried to lie down on it and got to writing. In rough, blocky letters, he wrote:

Dear Mr. Vickrim,

I want you to know that the cream did not help. *In fact, the rash is worse than ever. It is spreading farther and farther, centered on my groin. Can you imagine why that might be, Mr. Vickrim? I have a few ideas. Frankly, I am suspicious of our whole project at this point, let alone setting up shop here in Gwaju. I quit. For what I hope are obvious reasons.*

Deposit my final paycheck in my account, then never contact me again. However, in the spirit of not parting in anger, please enjoy this pornographic postcard.
    Yours in Prager,
    Mortimer Snerd

Truth double-checked the date, confirmed that the code words were in the right locations, took a final moment to appreciate the dead eyed fish in the picture, then sniggered. The end of the world was a stressful business. You had to get your laughs in where you could.

He activated the spell built into the card, watching it fold up into a sort of swallow. "539 West 87th Street, apartment number 5-027, in Taean. Deliver to Mr. Hal Vickrim or, if no one is home, remain in the mailbox."

The spell bird flapped away, its enchantments guiding it where it needed to go. Truth knew just enough about that kind of work to know he would leave it to the experts. That they could mass-produce those spells was a true wonder.

Job done. Someone would check that dead drop, then send a message to one of *his* dead drops. He sat back and tried to think of what he should do next. The reply would take a few days, after all, and he truly could not afford downtime. The sensible thing would be to continue the basic plan—drop in somewhere in Jeon, lose himself in the periphery, and try to cause enough chaos that it pulled resources out of Harban. The plan was still basically sound, but it needed some serious rethinking.

The campaign against the Denizen overseers was still good. In fact, that needed to accelerate hard and get more widespread. Maybe this young prince of the One-Legged Bird Ring needed a promotion or two, spreading his good works. Still, he couldn't devote as much time as he had intended to that project. The enrollment of Citizens into the System was where the real danger was and the real opportunity to hurt Starbrite.

So . . . how would he do that, exactly? Truth didn't have the faintest idea. He didn't even know where the enrollments were being done. And when you don't know something, you should ask an expert.

"NEXT!"

"Thank you for seeing me," Truth said humbly.

"Sigil."

Truth extended his wrist, watching the job placement officer's eyes go foggy.

"All right, Mr. Meduti?"

"Yes, sir. Bluth Meduti."

"All right, your file says that you have passed your high school cert for Talisman Maintenance, as well as getting your Army Talisman Maintenance cert. No mention of your SAT result, however. Why is that?"

"Panicked, sir. I just had this feeling that I would screw it up. That I would flunk out, and my whole life would be over. I thought I would just spend my life in the Army, but . . . what with everything . . ."

The officer gave him a look that stated, very clearly, his contempt for Truth and all his life choices. "Well, it's not a complete disaster, I suppose. You are a full Citizen, so your options are decent. We have had a major surge in maintenance jobs offered."

"What I really wanted to know is how this all ties into joining up with Starbrite. There weren't any flyers in the lobby."

"Coming tomorrow." The officer frowned. "You are *not* joining Starbrite. The country is adopting its own System, built on the same architecture as the Starbrite System and modernizing our now-antiquated class System. Young man, this is a massive change to the very constitution of our great nation! You *must* pay attention to this."

"Built on the same architecture? Like a building?"

The officer rolled his eyes so hard, Truth was worried he would tear something. "No, not like a building. Since Starbrite already has a chained spirit that knows how to run the System, we are building our System on top of their System. Same spirit, same organization, different benefits and privileges."

And that answered that question. *Welp. Nice knowing you, Jeon.*

"Okay, so . . . the brochures on this come in tomorrow."

"Should have been in the same day as the announcement, but due to a shortage *of talisman maintenance technicians*, the printers are way behind." The officer wasn't even hinting; he was tapping firmly on a list of jobs. "So, let's get you moving, shall we?"

"Sure. Oh, when does enrollment in the new System start?"

"Rolling admission starts at one minute past midnight on the first of next month. To prevent the processing centers from getting overwhelmed, everyone is getting entered in a lottery based on their Citizen ID number and then assigned a date and time. Don't worry. By the end of next month, every single Citizen and aristocrat will be enrolled. You won't miss a thing."

Truth sat at a bus stop. Nowhere to go, nothing to do but watch the seconds drip past. It was the scale of the thing. He knew other people were out there, making moves, pulling strings. Fighting the System. His trainers had mentioned there being other resistance organizations out there, many of them. All useless, apparently. But how does one person, even one specially trained and equipped like Truth, jam a spoke in the wheels of progress?

Problem too big? Make it smaller. How does he massively fuck things up in Gwaju? Boring city that it was. Even that felt too big. How about one enrollment center? Start with that. Pick up the pace on the Denizen-overseer assassinations, see if he couldn't set the stage for some riots, and while he is doing that, figure out just what the deal was with the enrollment centers. Did they have engram readers? Was there a big-ass formation under the floorboards?

Truth stretched. It was a plan. Truth got on the next bus out of mischief, then got off on the next stop. He had forgotten how much he hated buses in Jeon. Horrible little boxes, filled with stinking, miserable people. The end of the world couldn't come soon enough.

Truth made his way back to the club De'Ponte was operating out of. Instead of recreating the persona he had before, Truth opted to keep himself unnoticeable and try the Venom of Incisive instead.

"All right, that *first* hit was a qualified *success*, but clearly, this needs some fine tuning. Spread out the *work*, keep it from coming back to me. Pick up the *pace*, too, so it's *all done* before anyone can react," Truth whispered. De'Ponte was nodding thoughtfully to himself, tapping his fingers on his table.

Truth continued, "There is another *opportunity* here too—those Citizen enroll-ment centers. What kind of Starbrite *tech* are they sitting on in there? I bet the *secrets* to the System would be worth a fair bit *overseas*, and it's never a bad idea to have an exit *strategy*. Yeah, let's get eyes on these places. Find out what the security is like. This could be it. *Control* the Citizen enrollment. *Control* the Denizens. Make the City *want* to work with me, not against me. This could be it. How my climb to the *top* starts. But I have to be *fast*. Very *fast*. After all . . . *they* are just waiting for a chance to *knife* me."

Truth didn't know who "they" were, but given the steady cocaine intake and precarious position of De'Ponte, he felt certain that "they" existed. Some rich heir put in charge of a tiny city where he couldn't do too much damage? Oh, yes. "They" were very real.

De'Ponte hadn't seen the Slum. He didn't realize he was a small rat. He was still trapped in the illusion that he could climb so high, he would be safe. But he couldn't. You couldn't climb to the top of the Slum. You had to break out entirely.

Truth walked out, snagging a juice from behind the bar as he went. About as good as he remembered. It tasted a little weird to him now. Like he was picking up all kinds of other stuff that was added to the juice, things he had never noticed before. Strange, artificial flavors, chemical traces he didn't understand and certainly didn't enjoy.

He smiled a little. He was shaking off the poverty tastebuds and confronting an unexpected problem. The path of the foodie was long and filled with trials. Ah, well. Off for a little breaking and entering.

<<Hey, I thought we were breaking and entering,>> the System needled. *<<Come on. You can literally just walk in. Baby's first burglary. Buck up, little fella. You got a nice, easy one to start with.>>*

Oh, fuck you. Truth looked up. And up. And up. The alumni of the Gwaju Technical College of Agricultural and Maritime Sciences had dug deep when they sponsored the Athletics Center. Between the swimming pools, the full indoor track and field center, the multi-story cardio and weight training area, a three-story rock-climbing wall, several courts for a variety of ball games, four boxing rings, and a dozen multipurpose function rooms, it was large. And for some reason, they made the exterior look like some kind of abstract frog.

It had big cement legs and two giant windows for the googly eyes. A row of smaller windows in a straight line made the mouth. Why? Why did they do this terrible thing?

"Excuse me, do you know why they made this building look like a frog?" he asked a passing student, who nodded.

"Sure. School mascot. Comfortable on land and water."

"Of course. Say, do you happen to know *exactly* where in the center the enrollment is taking place?"

"No. Track and field center, maybe?"

"Thank you."

"No problem."

The student wandered off.

Do you think there is any chance that we go into there and see a door with a couple of F-Tier security guards standing outside a big double door with a WARNING! DO NOT ENTER! sign on it?

<<With your luck?>>

Let me dream.

<<I want you to dream. I do! Just . . . smaller. Dream a little smaller. Like, maybe the vending machine will give you two candy bars instead of just the one you paid for. That-size dream.>>

I think you have gotten more evil, not less.

<<You mean WE have gotten more evil.>>

Bickering with the System, Truth started exploring the Athletic Center. Not only was it huge, the layout had accelerated past insane and quickly reached the heights of surreal. Truth felt his sanity being harmed when he looked at the fire evacuation map. He then learned that the fire evacuation map was a joke, and the path indicated was actually the digestive tract of a bullfrog. There was no fire evacuation map. Each student should rely on their own initiative to combat any emergency. Running away was contemptible.

Truth instantly felt more at home. That was the Jeon he remembered.

It took him forty minutes to find the track and field area, a space large enough to fit an entire block of suburban homes. Somehow, he had walked past it no less than seven times. With a very necessary burst of force, he slammed the doors open and strode in. Green artificial turf, orange-brown oval-shaped track, bleachers, some kind of high-jump bar . . . Truth started smiling, then collapsed into outright laughter.

Under the big scoreboard on the far side of the room was a big pair of doors, flanked by a couple of security guards and with a big DO NOT ENTER, POLICE TAKE NOTICE sign in front of it.

CHAPTER 9

NOT GOOD WITH JOKES

<<*You know you just used up all your good luck, right? This is it. The rest of your existence will exceed the already-impressive degree of "cursed" you have established. Any day you survive without being crushed to death by deorbiting hippopotami can only be acknowledged as God taking the time to perfect something really cruel.*>> The System kept its tone conversational, as though it was discussing the inevitably of ants at a picnic.

Hippopotami *is not a real word.*

<<*Oh, it is. Terribly real. As you shall learn.*>>

Truth was looking over at the guarded double door. It was kind of creeping him out. On the one hand, they had to set up hundreds of these enrollment centers all over Jeon. There was, realistically, a limit to how secure they could make them. There was also a limit to how secure they would feel the need to make them. He had gotten sworn in at a stadium. It was the most common place for it to happen. Not like the process was a secret, exactly, just the results.

Truth didn't trust it. Two guards? They weren't even Starbrite security. They hung a sign threatening to call the cops. That was just embarrassing. Truth wouldn't have stood behind a sign like that.

<<*You would have. Wouldn't have thought twice about it. You would have double-checked it was properly set up, too.*>>

Shut up and let me lie to myself.

So, presumably, there was more security—he just wasn't seeing it. And as a Level Four with *really good* body cultivation, his senses were very sharp. He walked over. The security guards were Level One. Their eyes never flickered as he walked in front of him.

The unnoticeability effect from the Silent Forest was starting to get a little creepy. It still had that cool factor, but it was starting to dawn on him that, for the rest of his life, ordinary folk would only be able to see him with his explicit permission. He was, in every sense except the literal, above them. No longer one of the teeming slumrats of Harban. Which is what he had always wanted, of course, but . . . not like this. He had dreamed of their fear and worship, not being ignored.

Funny, that. The one time he went back to the slums after his enlistment, he turned around without really talking to anyone. Well, Prentiss, but nobody he was interested in intimidating or showing off to. He despised everyone and everything he saw. Even then, he thought they were beneath him. He . . . didn't really like acknowledging that. He shook the idea away and focused on the job.

There was a talisman lock on the door that Truth could have cracked when he was Level Zero and studying for the SAT. He lifted the amulet from the guard's belt and opened the door. A recording talisman was aimed straight at the door and more on either end of the hallway. He checked carefully. None of those creepy, camouflaged, eyeless things around.

Truth held the door open long enough to return the amulet and started walking down the hall. The recording talismans couldn't see him any more than the guards did.

No ghosts patrolling the hallway, of course. Not in Jeon. Same reason they didn't post imps instead of using talismans. Imps and ghosts were old-fashioned. Unreliable and inefficient. Strictly speaking, this was true. It was vastly cheaper and safer to use recording talismans rather than contracting dozens of imps to glare at nothing for months on end. And yes, vastly safer, too. A talisman wouldn't turn on you. You needed specialized training to make a talisman, but that was what schools and factories were for.

That was the hook—Starbrite might demand a lot, but look at all you got. Look at all the great stuff they sold. Your quality of life was unquestionably better. Even if you thought about the rope every day. As you worked longer hours for less money in worse housing. Terrified of getting sick or hurt or too old to work. Your back hunched more and more, and you made yourself smaller and smaller to avoid being noticed and made an example of. It cost all that, but this year's clothes were damn sexy, and you would really be something in your brand-new chariot.

If you could afford a chariot. Which you couldn't.

Cinderblock walls painted white and high-gloss. Cement floor painted gray, less glossy, but still had a shine on it. And that was it. Twenty meters one way, the hallway turned right. Five meters the other way, there was a door. Truth walked over to the door. Locked. A few seconds later, Truth opened the unlocked door. In his opinion, there was no reason to slap an expensive lock on a door if you can shim the damn mechanism. He had become an invisible operative for this?

Truth got very still when he finally got inside the room. It was stacked with identical plastic crates, each about a meter long and half that high and deep. Incisive was tickling the back of his neck. Danger was near.

Truth carefully looked over the room. It was bare, save for the boxes. The walls were left unpainted, the floor the same smooth concrete. Light came from a single talisman on the ceiling. Truth tried to relax. At Level Four, he should be pretty aware of any magic in use around him. But this was Jeon. Everything was running off a fetish or a talisman or some kind of spell construct. It was like trying to feel a hot spot standing outside in the summer. At noon. In Siphios.

With patient care, he worked every bit of the room he could see or reach, hunting for traps, alarms, anything. He quickly concluded that the danger, whatever it was, was in the boxes. The boxes were quite ordinary plastic storage tubs available at any hardware store. These just happened to be branded with the Starbrite logo.

With agonizing care, he gently worked his pinky finger through the plastic four centimeters from the bottom, pushing Incisive hard. He didn't use the Fangs, just brute strength and the hardness of his body. As soon as he was through, he withdrew his finger.

No new sense of alarm. No new danger. Truth pulled out a little flashlight and shined it into the hole. It looked like metal plates. Just a big plastic tub of metal plates. So, why was Incisive demanding he pay attention to them?

Were they pre-prepared spells? Having the plates premade and ready to install would make setting up sites pretty easy, and while he didn't think there were enough plates in there to literally tile the athletics complex, you could certainly cover a large area with them. He couldn't see any active spell effect on them. He shined the light around and didn't see anything that looked like a booby trap.

Still feeling that paranoia was entirely justified, he sliced off the side of the container so he could get a better look. The "nothing" intensified. Truth hesitated. He sure as Hell wasn't going to touch the plates, but he also really wanted to know what was on them. With agonizing care, he sliced off the top of the box. No spells there, either. On the other hand, Incisive was telling him, "Stay far away!"

Truth took a careful peek. As expected, it was a pre-made spell. Carved, or more likely stamped, into the metal, the dense latticework of channels, sigils, gems, incantations . . . He rapidly lost track of the number and function of the components. A lot. A terrifying amount, all in one plate.

Too big, too complicated—break it into pieces. Find something you recognize and see what it connects to. Here—a "gem," a little bit of stone etched with a sub-spell lodged into the metal at Azoth, the position of quicksilver, of the animating life. Must be where the . . . whatever this was originated. Standard component, just directing cosmic energy into the broader spell plate.

He slowly worked his way through the various systems, trying to reduce everything to its most basic elements, trying to deduce based on position, or what it connected to, or what it sort of looked like. More often than not, he simply had to admit he was out of his depth. This was not the level of talisman maintenance he had ever trained for. This was specialist stuff.

Best I can figure, it is a component of a bigger structure, maybe part of the imprinting process that created you. Don't know why Incisive is warning me away, though, so I am pretty sure I'm missing something.

<<*You are. Wait a moment. There is a lot to sort through.*>>

Truth kept looking over the plate. He hesitated to call it a talisman, though the amount of intense, fine detail work seemed to rule out calling it a fetish. It was a component. Maybe a talisman in its own right, but a component. He had heard of things like that, but he had never trained on them. No need, when fixing the air conditioner or repairing street lights was going to be the height of your career.

That thought rocked him. He really had wanted that life. It had been his dream. For almost half his life, it was his most desperate wish. It was his freak fighting ability that led him to Starbrite Security and the PMC and everything that followed. Now he was so powerful, he could have an angelic sword hanging out in his first aperture, with room for three more. He was so powerful; poor people weren't allowed to see him. *Poor* and *weak* being essentially synonyms in Jeon.

Synonyms everywhere, actually.

<<All right, I don't really know what this does either, but I have a pretty good idea; what I need you to do is take that lid and shove the top plate off the stack. It won't trigger or break anything. I just need to see what's on the second plate to confirm my theory.>>

That sounds unreasonably dangerous.

<<Oh? Why? Point out the exact problem, other than "instinct"?>>

Given that my "instinct" here comes from Incisive, I'd be a bit less shitty.

<<Look, just . . . ease it off. This is important.>>

Truth swore but grabbed the lid and started nudging the plate off to the side. It was decently heavy for its size. Perhaps a touch more than steel. He tried to push the plate over onto another box with middling success. At least it didn't drop on the floor.

The plate below was pretty similar to the first, though he did note a few subtle changes here and there. Pieces moved around, reordered, that kind of thing.

<<Well. That's not good.>>

You figured out what it is? Or does?

<<Kinda-sorta but not really? My concern is less about the overall function here and more about how they are going about it. A lot of this is error detection and correction. Whoever made this expected a lot of user errors and planned accordingly. I don't think I have ever seen or heard of a self-checking talisman array. It's . . . brilliant. It's genuinely brilliant. I don't understand how most of it works. I'm just making deductions on the bits I do understand. And it's brilliant.>>

So, why is it not good? Because it's so smart?

<<Yes. Because it is designed to be assembled and used by non-experts. They can roll out this System anywhere.>>

Well, for a given amount of—

<<No. Anywhere. Think about it. Once they have a nationwide System set up in Jeon, they can pitch it to every country on the planet. I don't know how much power the System Astrologica can absorb, but based on this? Truth, we really, REALLY need to get pictures of this to Merkovah. I don't know if he has them already, but he needs this info.>>

Truth started nodding, then stopped. His smile was downright angelic. Vindictive and terrifying.

No, he doesn't need the info. He needs the plates. All these boxes. We load them onto a truck and ship 'em out. We want to hurt Starbrite, right? Well, I'm sure they can manufacture these plates in bulk. They aren't scared of the talisman arrays getting damaged. But letting them get stolen and reverse-engineered? They don't want that. Not until it's too late to do anything about them. And I'd say Siphios, land of demon binders, can do a lot in a hurry.

<<I like it, though you haven't answered the question as to why you are finding the plates so dangerous.>>

No idea yet. Maybe they are holding a magical charge or something?

<<Nah. I'm going with . . . some kind of dangerous entity bound to one of the plates.>>

Oh? Why?

<<Because that box over there is glowing. And, if you listen very carefully, growling.>>

CHAPTER 10

SOME BASIC CONCEPTS

A few thoughts occurred to Truth at high speeds. The first was that never in his life would he have associated the words *lax security* with anything Starbrite actually cared about. The second was that he had gotten *maybe* a little cocky. A third thought had started to form but was interrupted.

The glowing, growling, shaking box disintegrated. A sphere of utter blackness emerged, faint blue-green worms of electricity crawling over it. Truth could feel the cosmic rays in the room twisting around it. He could feel it drawing on whatever structures existed in the plates, powering them in ways that Truth didn't understand.

What he did understand was that he had screwed up and needed to run away. Right now. He turned on his heel and slammed into the suddenly warded door.

The black sphere was growing. The growling changed its tone, becoming something deeper, almost below the range of hearing. He felt his chest vibrating. The wards were shrinking, pushing him toward the thing in the middle of the room. Incisive was screaming at him—*deadly danger, RUN!*

Truth called the Tongue to his hand. He raised it to slash but didn't know where to cut. The sphere? Seemed unwise. He had no idea what would happen. The chests? Again, didn't know what would happen. The wards, then. Run first, sort shit out later. He spun and cut. The angelic blade bit into the ward but struggled to get through. Crude but eye-wateringly strong.

Obliteration!

Truth felt something click. Some oddity in his soul. He didn't trust this spell a bit. But for the moment—*Fuck your ward.* He aimed at the weakened point in the ward and let it rip. Obliteration didn't cause any spectacle. It simply ate at the fabric of the spell. Unwinding it. The instant there was a gap big enough to dive through, he did. Rolled to his feet. And ran like the blazes.

He was down the far end of the hall in an instant. Around the corner and accelerating away as he went. No direction needed, just *away*. There was a sudden pressure. A terrible silence.

Truth regained consciousness, sitting on the curb of a street sometime later. He was bloody, covered in cement dust. His clothes were torn, shoes were gone. The Tongue was still in his aperture, so that was good. His scarf was lost, but it would return eventually. He didn't recognize anything around him.

He was having a hard time focusing. Truth desperately wanted a drink of water but somehow couldn't bring himself to move. He rolled onto the sidewalk, lying on his back. What had happened? He had been running?

He could hear sirens racing past and murmured whispers from the people stepping over or around him. Something terrible had happened. There must be some kind of accident. A fire. *Do you think . . . terrorism?* Quieter still were those wondering about a rebellion.

He could see high-level police mages flying over on their gilded altars to oversee the site of the incident. But were they really high-level? He was Level Four now. Even lying helpless on the sidewalk, his standards had changed.

His right hand spasmed and shook for thirty seconds. Truth didn't know why it did that. He just lay there, trying to put himself together.

Hazel Wand.

Truth felt Obliteration shift out and something new shift in. He could feel how broken the System's spells were now. The System pruned off big pieces of something much more impressive, leaving a usefully mutilated little stump it could cast for him. The System Astrologica had been doing that too, just much better. *Damn. Damn damn damn.* Even Truth wasn't sure what he was damning. There was so much.

He lay on the sidewalk as the System worked on him. The Hazel Wand was less gentle a thing than he had imagined from the System's description, at least not when you were paying it your full attention. This wasn't what the System had run while he was floating in the ocean. This was something altogether cruder.

<<I hacked it down even more than I already had. This should prevent the risk of brain damage, but the trade-off is that it's now even slower. The good news is that you aren't horribly maimed or anything, so you should be up and moving in a few hours, tops.>>

A name popped into Truth's mind.

Abner's Amble. The movement spell. Should have cast that while we were running.

<<Probably would have helped, yeah, though I doubt it would have helped enough. You walked a fair distance while you were in shock, so I got a bit of a look around. The Athletic Center is . . . mostly gone. Not disappeared or anything, just wrecked. The blast radius was significant and, interestingly, not even. It clearly extended a lot farther in one direction.>>

You think the wards were designed to trap someone in with the blast? Obliterate the spell plates along with any potential thieves?

<<At this point, I can confidently say I have no goddamn idea anymore. There was no reason, none, to think that shifting one plate, one plate with no apparent alarms or booby traps or anything, would trigger all that.>>

Other than Incisive telling us to scram. The phrase Fuck around and find out *seems relevant.*

The System made a frustrated noise.

<<Yes. YES. OKAY? Yes! But I can't work without more information. YOU can't work without more information. There are going to be times where we need to take risks to achieve our goals. This seemed like a very reasonable, measured risk.>>

I would pull an answer to that out of my ass, if I could feel my ass.

The System made no reply. What could it even say?

Eventually, Truth got a bit bored of just lying around, staring at nothing. *Figure out anything about the plates we didn't already guess?*

<<*Working on that. The massive explosion is actually a useful data point there. Changing topic somewhat, can we talk about this spell?*>>

Hazel Wand? What about it?

<<*In the process of cutting it into chunks, I found some kind of . . . artifacts, I guess? Some kind of things that didn't make sense outside the context of the complete spell. Which made me wonder why they were in the complete spell in the first place.*>>

Truth just waited. The System would eventually get to the point.

<<*It's a less . . . benevolent spell than I gave it credit for. The weird elements were little sets of logical propositions that would unfold as you learned the spell. If-then, yes/no, categorizations . . . nothing too bizarre, and most of it kind of intuitive. Where it gets a bit spicy is how that interacts with every other part of the spell.*>>

All right?

<<*It plugs in to everything.*>>

The System waited, expecting a reaction. It was disappointed. After a minute longer, it continued. <<*Listen, asshole. You wanna tell me why a healing spell, or a demon-binding spell, or whatever needs you to learn about logical reasoning?*>>

I have no idea. It was part of the spell description, right? Teaches philosophy and logic?

<<*Just philosophy. It didn't explain why or how the spell does that, though. I think it's trying to get you to think about how you interact with other people, or yourself, in a particular way.*>>

Sure, I guess. Incisive kind of did that too.

Truth could feel the little sprite trying to tear its hair out. Which, given that it was a piece of his soul, was a neat trick.

<<*I MEAN it works more like how I did when I was brainwashing you!*>>

It fucking what?!

<<*Buer isn't quite on Botis's level, but he's not far off and has a very sizable following in Hell. Definitionally, he's not some goody-goody type. So, how does he manage it if his spell isn't really combat-focused? I think it's because he makes people, and most particularly demons, think the way he does. I don't really know, because we haven't studied the spell. But that's my guess.*>>

So, why does a demon want people to study logic? Is it false logic?

<<*I don't know. It doesn't seem to be. Intuitively obvious stuff, like I said.*>>

Truth puzzled over that one until the sun started to set and his legs started working again.

Truth made his way back to De'Ponte's apartment. Right now, the bland emptiness of the place appealed to him. It was restful. He sprawled on the sofa, staring up at the off-white ceiling. Just trying to piece things together.

Starbrite was enslaving the country. But only adding the Citizens to the System. Why? Especially since he clearly wanted to scale up, maybe as much as a global scale. Why leave souls on the table in the form of Denizens? All he could think of was Starbrite trying to filter out the weaker souls. Level Zero adults were becoming a "thing" now. Presumably, those would be of less use to him. It made sense, but it felt unsatisfying. There was more there, more that he wasn't seeing.

Then there was the timeline. Put the "end of the world" at a year out. A year for people to be worked over by the System Astrologica. Was that long enough to make them suicide and send their souls, or parts of their souls, to Starbrite? Unlikely. So, he was missing something there, too. The bomb didn't entirely make sense either. Even if you were to suppose that tampering with the plates somehow triggered the ward and the . . . whatever it was, that was wildly disproportionate to the risk of theft or damage. It wasn't like the plates were going to be any kind of secret in the very near future.

All Truth could think of was some drone trying to balance the need to pre-position the formation components to ensure a smooth rollout, versus the fear of tampering. Because that would be Starbrite's biggest fear, right? Not that he wouldn't get some small number of souls; he was playing at a global scale. He would be afraid that the souls he did get would be poisoned. Or, and Truth grinned nastily at the thought, diverted. How dare someone steal what Starbrite had already rightfully stolen!

Then he sighed, his sudden burst of humor fading away into a horrible emptiness. Fair to say the day didn't go as planned. Some useful things were learned, definitely, some progress was made, but you couldn't really say that it went *well*.

All those dead students, for one thing. He had been trying not to think about it, but the reality was he just got a hell of a lot of people killed for basically no good reason. Saying he was doing it for a good reason or that their death was accidental really didn't help. He had been needling Merkovah about becoming a terrorist. Now that he had done it for real . . . it didn't feel good.

Did Vig ever wind up going to university? Sophie definitely did, but she also definitely would have gone to a top school, not a technical school at the edge of the country. Vig, though, he might have wound up in a technical school.

Plenty of people there who were someone else's sib, of course. And, of course, if they didn't knock out Starbrite and find the little Shattervoid girl, almost everyone was going to die. These were the fundamental tenets of his current reality. Was this another nudge from Etenesh or the Tongue?

Well, he would press on regardless. Even if all this guilt was one hundred percent justified, he still had people he wanted to protect. His sibs. Etenesh. And yes, Jember, Merkovah, and all the kind people he had met in the Free State and Siphios. So, he would plan some more, take more care, and then he would do the same damn thing again. Because it was necessary.

Truth started laughing, almost sobbing. He pressed his arm over his eyes as he laughed and laughed, and the tears slipped out. "That's not okay. That's fucked up! But I'm okay with it. And that's fucked up!"

Truth drifted off to sleep, seeking temporary oblivion. As this was a daily occurrence, the System paid it no particular mind. This night, however, it noticed the faintest shiver in Truth's soul, saw the nous, that intersection of soul and mind, ever so faintly come in to sharper focus. Then its world became pain.

CHAPTER 11

INTROSPECTION

Truth dreamed he was sitting in a small room, an office lined with books of mathematics and red-jacketed books of philosophy, heaps of papers on the desk, and heaps more in the rubbish bin on the floor. He was wearing a suit and tie. The professor was too.

The professor's hair would only feign obedience to the hairbrush, flying away when unattended. The hair was wiry, white with that unfortunate tinge of yellow to it that made one wonder if it was the final echo of natural color or if the professor's pipe had permanently stained it with nicotine. The professor was old, of course, but he gave one the impression of always having been old. Yet there was something to that flat, wide mouth and those eyes that were slightly too large for his face. Some mischief. Some sense of fun. This old man still loved life and was far from done with it.

"While I naturally applaud your desire to study modern and rigorously reasoned philosophy, I must discourage you from becoming my pupil. Or, indeed, even auditing my class. At least until you have the proper foundation in math."

"I can do long division in my head." Truth aimed for humor and missed by a mile.

"Wonderful. I am so glad you mastered arithmetic. When do you think you will learn math?"

"Well, that's why I want to learn philosophy from you. I keep running into these . . . I don't know what to call them. Given your specialty, I hesitate to call them 'logic problems,' but that's the best term I can use for them."

The professor snorted. "I assure you, I call them logic problems too. And see far more of them than you do. Continue."

"Well, the Stoics, for example, or Hobbes. Some very good advice for living, some wise observations. But then you run into issues like slavery, or women, or the fact that their philosophies claim to be based on a plainly wrong understanding of physics."

The professor nodded understandingly. "To say nothing of Plato and Aristotle, who did more between them to harm the development of rational thought and scientific development in the West than almost any other two people I could name. Plato badly harmed the Orient as well, even more than he damaged the West. Poor devils."

"Right, or more recently, Nietzsche and Schopenhauer . . . while they make some interesting observations— "

"Hold together about as well under logical analysis as the proverbial dandelion in a hurricane. Yes, I have written an entire book on the subject and endless monographs. But this is just the thing—in order to reach the truth, not some airy, fanciful 'higher truth' or 'personal truth,' but real, repeatable, verifiable, *provable* truth, your tool must be analysis. It must be logic. And if that is so, then you must understand mathematics. Real mathematics, not arithmetic." The professor's lips quirked. Apparently, he found his statement a little funny. Truth didn't get the joke and pressed on.

"But how do you get from mathematics to, say, ethics?"

"By strange coincidence, I teach an entire course on the subject. It seems that you would benefit from it. Once you have the proper foundation."

"Professor!"

"Young man, I think you and I can agree that two and two is four."

"Certainly."

"Why?"

"Pardon?"

"Why is two and two four?"

"Well . . . it is. I hold up two fingers, then another two fingers, and now I have four fingers."

"Oh? What's a finger? For that matter, what's *two*? How do you define it? Can you define it without reference to something outside the concept of *two*? Can *two* prove itself? You understand we are still a long way from the thorny question (happily resolved now, you will be glad to know) of defining addition and demonstrating by logic that it does work as you think it does."

The professor leaned in, wide mouth faintly curving up into the sly hint of a smile. "Ethics, then. Can you define 'good'?"

Truth rolled his eyes at that one. "I can't. And I have read endless proposed definitions, most of them contradictory." The professor nodded at that, the grin widening.

"Just so. You couldn't even define the components of *good*, I suspect. You may trust in empiricism, deciding that, as a personal matter, you will not lie or cheat or steal. Should the opportunity arise, you may set that as policy for those under your rule. But you could not prove to me, purely as a matter of logic, without resorting to emotional language, rhetoric, or other illogical persuasions, that such a standard of behavior was 'good.'"

"And to even make the attempt, I would need the background in logic, which would require training in mathematics."

"Correct."

Truth groped around for a moment, trying to find a way to express what he was feeling. "If there is a mathematically provable answer to goodness or ethics, wouldn't the whole field of philosophy come to an end? Go home, everyone; we finally have all the answers?"

"Presumably, that would be true but fortunately, there is no chance of such a dull outcome." The professor chuckled. "I can demonstrate with exacting logic that almost any given proposition is *logically correct* or *incorrect*. Certain paradoxes notwithstanding. Proving that a proposition is *true* is far, far harder. Look at your fingers again. We struggled for thousands upon thousands of years to even reach the point where we might try to define *two*. We are still a long, long way from agreeing on what a 'man' is or what he is for."

"Presumably not to lie, cheat, or steal."

"I would agree with you, as would the two frauds I mentioned before. However"—the professor leaned in and fixed Truth with his too-big eyes—"by means of such phony, self-serving 'logic' as their limited means permitted, those two would quite happily approve such things for the ruler of a city, seeing it as entirely ethically correct. A logical necessity, even."

The professor laughed softly, sitting back in his wooden chair. "We are entirely lost without rigorous logic. Everything devolves into mere theology, which is to say—nothing. But forgetting the human dimension, the real consequences of our mathematical conclusions? That's not logical at all."

Truth woke up to the sound of the System screaming, something that didn't bring him the pleasure it once had. It was a uniquely horrible thought—that pain could reach the soul. This wasn't news, obviously; everyone knew of Heaven and Hell with more certainty than they knew about the neighboring city. But to have it so clearly underlined was horrible. Your body hurts, but your soul can be made to suffer far, far worse . . .

It happened again.

<<Yes, it fucking did! God DAMN it!>> The System went off, ranting a string of profanity of its own invention, emphasizing guttural, raspy, and chopping noises and contrasting them unpleasantly with the sibilant and wet sounds. Truth waited patiently.

Out of curiosity, he turned his attention to his soul. He . . . didn't really see the change. Was it more real? More perfect? Perhaps in some infinitesimal way. Honestly, how would he even tell? It had looked right to him before, and it continued to look right. He didn't even notice when the System was stamped out of his soul.

The thought brought him up with a sudden jerk. He had never noticed. Never even thought to look.

Hey, System . . . if you are my soul, can I see you?

<<You haven't so far.>>

Yeah, but can I?

<<Hell if I know.>>

Well, come on, front and center, then. I'll put my awareness right by my first aperture.

There was a pause.

<<Got to admit, I didn't think you would see nothing. *Little hurtful, actually.>>*

Nothing isn't exactly right. More like . . . a sense of depth, or . . . I don't know, solidity. There is definitely more there.

<<*Hah. Well, all kidding aside, I had assumed you wouldn't be able to see me. I mean, hundreds of thousands of Starbrite employees, millions of them over the years, and nobody went, "Hey, the System is actually part of your soul!" Something must be up there. Some core part of how I was made.*>>

Yeah. Of course, that's assuming that those people who did figure it out weren't shut up somehow.

<<*And on that cheery note, I did actually see something this time.*>>

Truth sat up, ignoring the suddenly angry aches across his body. *You did? What did you see?*

<<*Not your soul wandering off for happy-fun-times adventures, that's for sure. Basically, it amounted to a little shake. Almost invisible, even for me. The thing that really grabbed my attention was that your nous also tweaked a bit. It got, from my perspective, noticeably more real.*>>

Wait, what? Really? Show me.

<<*Of course. It's right here.*>>

Truth looked wildly around the numinous, mystic land of his soul and saw exactly dick all.

You are pointing right now, aren't you? Even though you know I can't see you.

<<*Definitely not. I don't have hands. Or anything resembling a body.*>>

You bastard.

<<*Funny you say that; I'm not at all sure Mom and Dad were married.*>>

Me either. Don't care, won't care, where's the damn nous?

<<*It's not a physical location.*>> The System showed it was trying by not tacking on the words *you moron* even though they both knew it was thinking that. <<*It's the literal intersection of mind and soul, meaning it's the part of your soul that overlaps with your mind the way the body overlaps with the soul. Which would logically mean that . . .*>>

The System waited. And waited.

<<*C'mon, buddy, you got this!*>>

I have no damn idea what you are talking about.

<<*Oh, for fuck's sake! Your mind! The thing you think with! That lets you turn meat sensations from the world into ideas like food, mate, or idiot. Then there is the nous. Where "mind" overlaps with "your" "soul." Letting you receive sensations from something without nerves, and understanding it visually, despite it not reflecting light at all. Do I have to spell it out for you?*>>

Yes. Mostly because I have come back around to enjoying your suffering.

<<*THE THING YOU OBSERVE YOUR SOUL WITH IS THE NOUS, YOU BLITHERING IDIOT! YOU ARE TRYING TO CHECK YOUR VISION BY HAVING YOUR EYE LOOK INSIDE ITSELF!*>>

You know what I haven't had in ages? A full Jeon breakfast. Get some eggs, rice, toppings, obviously fermented cabbage, and a bowl of soup. Get the whole spread.

<<*Oh sure, stuff that wet meat hole with decaying matter. Grind it up with the stones you grew from soft flesh, suck the pap down the undulating cartilaginous feed tube to the*

acid hell of your guts, where trillions of microscopic organisms will break down the dead paste into its most basic chemical components. The decay of matter accelerating within you to fuel your futile, humiliating efforts to avoid that same corruption and disintegration. How perfect a natural definition of humanity—that which derives satisfaction from its hopeless ruination of the world.>>

Truth paused for a moment, reflecting on that. He almost wanted to applaud.

Well, whatever. We have a lot to figure out today, and I'll do it all the better on a full stomach. Truth helped himself to some of De'Ponte's cash, then went out for breakfast.

CHAPTER 12

AN OLD "FRIEND"

Truth sat on a bench, watching the people pass. Nobody looked happy. Most looked indifferent. Truth was from Jeon, though. That wasn't apathy. That was their mask. The thin lips, stiff shoulders, and quick steps. The way people shoved in front of each other over minuscule advantages, like the first to cross the street when the light changed.

Then the mask slipped. People shoving each other, screaming to get at time-limited sales. Yelling at their kids, their families, or lovers. He saw a manager dress down a waiter right on the street, then fire him. Screaming abuse. "Take off your apron and get out! I'm deducting what you cost me from your last paycheck! In fact, you are lucky I don't sue you!" Red-faced with anger, as the waiter stared at their feet. Their face an apathetic mask.

Eating the hate. Eating the humiliation. Truth knew that taste very well. How long until the waiter rebels? Well . . . how long had it taken Truth?

The waiter wouldn't rebel. He couldn't see through all the fists the world was throwing at him. All his plans, his dreams—meaningless. The waiter was wrong to dream. Wrong to hope. He had no agency, no choices. He wasn't even allowed to serve his masters joyfully. See? His life was ruined at the manager's whim.

What was it that the fat man in his vision had said? Something about the best argument for a boss on Earth was a boss in Heaven? Sounds right. Well, Starbrite was the heavens, and this world had all kinds of local bosses.

Why did that demon get summoned, and why did the plates blow up? Why was everything rigged to explode? The plates obviously came from Starbrite, a security mechanism, but the demon thing? He hadn't heard of any demon outbreaks, so presumably, this wasn't super common. Was it just Huelle? If so, why? Not enough information. About anything. He stood up from the bench. He would go back to De'Ponte, collect his fee for the Huelle hit, and line up the next job. Get more information. Keep pushing the System Astrologica toward collapse.

He stood, dusted himself off, and went. Some part of him wanted to "deal" with the manager. He ignored it. There were bigger rats to hunt.

"You do good work, but you can't be here. Take the money and go."

"Wait, what?" Truth was startled. He wasn't expecting this from DePonte.

"You look like you got rolled. I have seen actual bums better put together than you. You are damaging the vibes here just by existing, and the club isn't open yet. Look, you want more work? Wothera Hersch, hotel manager at the Hanging Orchid Hotel on Czerni Square. I'm only paying you if you turn up in new, clean clothes and don't smell."

It had been a while since he had a shower, hadn't it? The whole "people aren't allowed to be aware of you without permission" thing was clearly affecting his grasp on normal behavior. Alarmingly fast. Actually, couldn't he turn that off? But then the infinite surveillance systems of Jeon would pick him up in no time, with all the horror that would cause.

"Fair enough. I'll do that."

"Good, good. Now go get her, and don't come back until it's done. Until it's ALL done."

Occupancy was unsurprisingly low at the Hanging Orchid Hotel. Czerni Square was just off of what passed for the financial district in this little city—a place of glass-and-steel monuments to unfounded optimism. To maximize rentable floor space, the developers had built the towers right up to the edge of the narrow sidewalk, and in several cases, the sidewalk was actually covered by the overhang of the building. It always creeped Truth out, seeing a narrow stem holding up an entire skyscraper. Spells at work, presumably.

Dark, windy, and cold. That was the financial district at three in the afternoon. He went to the hotel front desk.

"Hi, I'm supposed to be meeting Ms. Dechau. I think she's in the Presidential Suite?"

"Are you sure? We don't have a Presidential Suite. Our Grand Deluxe Supreme Diamond Suite is currently unoccupied. Want me to look her up in the book?"

"Please."

A few moments later.

"I don't see her name here."

Truth sighed. "Looks like I got stood up."

"Sorry."

"Maybe it's my clothes. Any good stores around here?"

"Depends on your budget. There is a Marq's right in Czerni Square. Maybe try there."

"Thanks."

Truth took the elevator as high as he could go without a keycard, then the stairs the rest of the way up. Eggshell paint over cinderblock. Same everywhere. Supposedly, the doors were locked on the stairwell side. Seems people were no longer bothering with such basic precautions.

He found the suite without too much trouble. When he had been a bodyguard for Starbrite, hotel doors were notoriously easy to bypass. He was trained to always put a wedge under the door and, if possible, his own wards. Now, presumably, in the last five years, they had . . .

Done absolutely nothing, and it's the same exact lock! Truth swore. It was too damn embarrassing. Five years! Five whole years! More, even! And they are still using the same crappy locks. Why? Why be so dumb? Then he felt depressed. Money. Changing locks costs money. So, why not keep them? Not like it was their stuff getting stolen.

He took a thorough shower. The shampoo and conditioner had a wonderful smell—some kind of cool, not-quite-mint smell, and it made his scalp tingle. The soap was pretty great too—a bright citrus smell. There were no towels, of course. There was a water expulsion ward right along the edge of the walk-in shower that simply trapped all the steam and wet inside. You walked out dry as could be. They did, however, provide impossibly fluffy bathrobes. Truth tried one on. Too small. Damn.

He flopped onto the bed. Too many questions and not enough answers. Not even enough leads to answers. Too soon to get depressed. He enjoyed the mattress a minute longer, removed all traces of himself from the room, and went to get himself a new set of clothes.

Wothera Hersch, hotel manager at the Hanging Orchid Hotel on Czerni Square, was solidly in her middle years. Level One, with no ambitions of climbing higher. No ambitions beyond hanging on to this job, as far as Truth could tell. She had a perpetual customer-service smile in public, but the second she thought she was alone in her office, the smile fell off her face. She just looked tired. Scared. She must not have known about the recording talisman in the ceiling, watching her every move, reporting it up the corporate ladder.

Or perhaps she did and was so beaten, she stopped trying to hide her fear. She was certainly keeping a close eye on her employees through the discreet recording talismans covering the lobby, hallways, breakrooms, and even the staff-only toilets. Can't have them getting high on the job, Truth guessed. Or stealing from the guests.

She did not have a swollen pitz ball for a belly. She was slim, prematurely aging, and so utterly ordinary Truth couldn't stand it. He casually searched the office around her and found nothing of interest.

Out of sheer frustration, he dumped out her almost-overflowing wastepaper basket and had a poke around. She got a mountain of junk mail. Entire magazines of products she clearly didn't want to buy, offers to supply cleaning chemicals, invitations for "a quick chat about your laundry services solutions provider," and a host of other things that she couldn't even ask Corporate to approve.

It was bleakly funny. "Hotel manager" sounded like an important job. You supervised an awful lot of people. But in the grand scheme of things? Just another slumrat, barely distinguishable from the rest. Truth poked through the letters, flyers, and magazines with morbid interest. Lots and lots of job applications. She had only unfolded them enough to check what they were, then tossed them directly in the trash. Some envelopes didn't even get opened.

Truth picked up a particularly spicy-looking one. Handwritten label on a heavy paper envelope. No enchantment, so it was clearly carried there by hand rather than turned into a spell bird. Something quite heavy in the envelope, sliding around. *To the Breeder Hersch: The Best Offer You Will Get.*

He'd have thrown it in the bin too. He tore open the side, remembering the many, many warnings he had heard about opening envelopes from the long edge. The contents spilled out onto a table—a letter and a two-centimeter-wide coin-shaped silver token. The letter read:

To the Breeder Hersch—

The name was in a different handwriting, clearly made to fit in the line.

Congratulations! On behalf of the Jeon Society for Social Renewal, I am happy to inform you that you have been selected as a future Mother of the Nation. As one of the candidates for the first round of our highly exclusive executive development program, you will be provided with the training, equipment, and network necessary to ensure that you not only survive these trying times—you will turn calamity into triumph!

To ensure the privacy and security of our Mothers, we provide a significant weekly stipend and 24/7 security from high-level specialists. To get a full breakdown of both our privacy rules as well as the program benefits, please squeeze the included token in your left hand and say "I accept the Terms and Conditions." Your first stipend and personal security service will be provided at once by special courier.

I am truly excited to be working with you. Together, we shall make Jeon the land of dreams it was always meant to be.
Sincerely,
The Enlightened Runcible Bosch, J.D., D. Thaum,
Vice-President for Human Resources, JSSR

Well, he had seen scammier letters. Not . . . a lot scammier. Maybe some of the flyers Mom brought home from her various MLMs. Those were always shady as hell. Even as a kid, he could smell the lies on them. Though, in fairness to Mom, they didn't whiff of the literal infernal the way this thing did.

Hadn't thought about Mom in a while. Happy thought—maybe she was already burning in Hell.

He gingerly picked up the token. On one side was a goat's face, wise-looking with its little beard. The longer he looked at the goat's eyes, the more he was convinced this goat had seen things. Terrible things. It had survived, but now it wanted to show those terrible things to many, many others.

On the reverse was a landscape of a brilliant sun hanging over rolling hills dotted with towers. Probably very symbolic, but of what, he didn't know. The edges were deeply milled. Truth squinted. The milling looked odd, a matte color when you would expect them to be shiny. He brought the token closer to his eye and squinted. Then squinted harder.

System—

<<Can't talk, laughing hysterically.>>

What exactly is this?

<<The contract.>> Truth could feel the System gasping with laughter. <<Some sick bastard wrote an entire demon-possession contract on the milling on the token. Talk about reading the fine print! That's genius.>>

A demon-possession contract?

<<Yeah, basically, you get to call on a powerful demon once, then it uses your body as a breeding ground for its young. And eats your soul, obviously.>>

Wait . . . wasn't Huelle a man?

<<I don't see how that's relevant. At least not to a Level Four demon.>>

Speaking as a Level Four human, it's pretty damn relevant!

<<Meh. Seen one deteriorating fleshy, seen 'em all. Why sweat the small stuff? Besides, it's not like the literal demon *needs a* literal womb *any more than the maggots breeding in an open wound.>>*

Truth "admired" the token a bit more. *Oh, that's extra dumb.* Huelle's guards. He didn't have 'em because he had the demon and probably didn't understand what he agreed to. The prick was too cheap to pay for human guards when he had a "free" demon.

<<God, I love this country,>> the System agreed.

Truth pocketed the letter, envelope, and token, then tidied up the spilled trash as a thank-you for the lead. Then, out of sheer mischief and because he did have an outstanding contract on Manager Hersch, he whispered in her ear—

"There is no end to this. They are always going to make you scared, right up until they take it all away from you. Time to start thinking about what you need to feel good. This story will never have a happy ending. So, what do you need to be happy right now? People only pretend the rules still apply, but we all know that's a lie. They don't apply at all, at least if you have guts. Time to do whatever the hell you feel like, and if they don't like it, they can come at you. Better than being scared all the time."

He had no idea if the idea would take, but it would be pretty interesting to see if anything came of it. For now, he had a lead. Time to track down the Enlightened Runcible Bosch.

Truth sat at his workstation in his favorite office—a random bench just off a busy street. "Bench" might have been an overgenerous description. It was poured concrete in the rough shape of a bench but with a three-centimeter peak running along the middle of it to discourage rough sleepers. This, obviously, was not useful for his purposes, so he used his Level Four privilege to smooth it out with Incisive. Now that the surface was glass-smooth and perfectly level, he got to work.

The talisman was carved on a little metal disk he had cut out of a bit of street sign. He punched a little hole and hung it from a lanyard. Then, with exacting care, he started carving. The pattern was quite simple, but the consequences of messing it up could be dramatic. Steadily, steadily, that was the way. He thought about adding a few embellishments he had learned in Siphios. Strictly speaking, they were redundant, but there was no real reason he couldn't. He added them in.

The carving got him thinking. You were supposed to do ten hours of classwork per year to keep your talisman maintenance tech certification current. He was well behind on that. He should pick up some books on the subject while he was there in Jeon. Siphios had its advantages, but Jeon simply blew them out of the water in terms of talisman design and technology.

Truth carefully finished tracing the little channels, checked he had all the geometry correct, and verified the variables. All was as it should be. He smiled a little. Then added a few more refinements just in case.

He pressed the talisman gently on the stone and ran a thread of cosmic energy through it. "By the Laws of the Most Holy, by the Names of ZHR YHIVI, RHW DMW, NXJQ and G'RXT, by the Terror and Obedience owed to those most high, and by my own will, I summon you! Appear before me in a form pleasing to the eye at once!"

There was a distortion in the air, a shuddering feeling. A heartbroken cry as a mother watched her child drown in front of her—

"Knock it off, wiseass."

"How *good* to see you once again, Dread Magus," murmured Thrush.

CHAPTER 13

ON THE HUNT

Some good news and bad news, from your perspective—good news is that we are no longer in Siphios, and the scary exorcists are on the other side of an ocean from us."

"That is good news." Thrush's voice flowed like tar over velvet. He was once again in the form of a small bird with crimson eyes. There were a shimmer and a texture to his wings, black on black, making you want to look closer to see the curious patterns the vanes formed. An elegant look for an imp of no true shape. It gave no clue to the demon's utter sadism.

"I did get several really instructive tutorials, as well as repeated demonstrations, on how to *really hurt* spiritual entities. The entity known as Child Eater was the demonstration subject, if you were worried about quality control." Truth kept his voice chipper.

"The bad news is quite sharp indeed."

"Oh, that was still good news. Lifelong learning and all that, right? No, the bad news is I summoned you to work as my assistant and hunting beast." Truth waved the letter and talisman around.

"Ah. Well. I have heard worse. Truthfully, Great One, our time together was . . . pleasant, as you would understand that term. Now that we are away from *those* people, we can resume our partnership."

Partnership. Sure.

"All right, let's get this ball rolling. I am completely short on tools. I've been getting by on making stuff on the fly, but I need proper talisman-creation tools, burglary tools, tracking tools, and all that. Assume that we are going to be stealing them. They are a 'treasure,' if you like. So, my treasure-finding demon, where to?"

Thrush paused a moment, preened, looked at Truth, and shuffled his feathers.

"Dread Magus, might I beseech a drop of wisdom from you?" His voice wheedled, like your "faithful" lover pleading youthful inexperience for the second time. "I know you are here because you summoned me and are speaking to me, but most of the senses I would use to detect you fail to capture your . . . magnificence. And some instinct warns me of terrible danger. Might I ask what has become of you in the time since we parted?"

"You may not. Beyond knowing that I have, indeed, become considerably more powerful and have received a blessing that will let me snuff your existence with a slap.

Not merely return you to Hell—consign you to oblivion." Truth laid it out straight for the demon. You had to know how to talk to them, or they would just walk all over you. Then drag your soul into Hell.

"Understood. But without some grasp on your present capabilities—"

"Less talking, more hunting. Start with a talisman-supply wholesaler."

Thrush flapped away, not even bothering to snort. The imp had been no match for Truth at Level Two. At Level Four, with the blessings bestowed on him? It was Thrush's privilege to serve. Much higher-tier demons would be delighted to assume the duty.

Truth nodded slightly. Time to stop thinking small. Even with all his power, his thinking was still small-time—working as a hitter for a gangster? Even if that moved the needle slightly, it could never be enough. Time to start *rapidly* scaling up. And for that, he needed supplies.

The demon flew quickly through the city, infernal senses leading it on. Thrush was too weak to find anything truly precious, but talisman parts? In Jeon? Not so precious. Truth could keep up at a fast jog, blazing past the city traffic. It was still novel and very satisfying to be so much faster than the dull world around him. Still would prefer his two-wheeler, though. Just something about relaxing and enjoying the ride.

Gwaju looked gray and washed-out. It reminded him of Shomburuti back in the Free State, for all that their climate could hardly be more different. It was that ground-in grime coating "nice" buildings. People had given up on maintenance long before the Black Ships arrived. He should find it worrying. *When the going gets tough, the tough do maintenance* is doctrine nowhere but should be doctrine everywhere. Now? Rubbish piled up in the street. He could see the vermin scurrying around.

Truth jogged past a good-sized group standing in a park. Maybe twenty or thirty kids and their parents. A mascot with a big orange for a head and a sailor costume was doing a series of poses and cheers. Some kind of city mascot, probably. The parents were all pushing the kids to participate, trying to keep smiles on their faces. They were forcing themselves, trying to create a normal, good time. Truth knew—the kids weren't fooled. They saw. But kids mostly want to make their parents happy, so they were trying. Truth would bet every last wen he had that at least one kid in that group was doing it, hoping to cheer up their parents. Show them that they could be happy.

They quickly moved toward the outskirts of the city, moving into the land of big box stores and sprawling suburbs of identical homes. Decent homes with adequate square footage for an average family, with a small yard out back and a driveway out front for the carriage you absolutely needed to get anywhere. He felt an odd sense of kinship to the mowers of lawns in the suburbs. At least they were doing maintenance as their world collapsed. Hanging on to "normality" while sneering at those who didn't keep up "standards."

Of course, there was the question of what it took to have those little identical homes. Each cost more than an apartment to maintain, for one thing. You needed the carriage, and that needed maintenance too. Then there was what the suburbs cost the city. The roads, the highway to the city, difficulty collecting the trash, or running sewers all added up. You could fit two streets' worth of families, or more, in his old apartment building. Put them in the slums, and you could get the whole damn suburb in a tower.

It had to prey on them—the morbid mowers of suburbia. They had to be thinking about it all the time. *How can I raise enough money to keep my family in this nice little box instead of the other, much less nice boxes we could be in?* That fear, of losing status, of disappointing their family, must gnaw like a worm on their guts. What would they do to keep themselves out of the coffin apartments in the slums?

Businesses must be closing already. A paying job would soon be a luxury. The threat of falling down the Citizenship ladder and becoming Denizens must be making them puke. Whatever little illusions of safety their suburban boxes gave them were now entirely gone. The pressure must be intolerable.

They would be eyeing each other already. Seeing who has the nice new chariot, the fancy sofas, who was always taking those luxurious vacations to Jeru Island. Not long now. Not long until someone tied a shirt around their face, picked up a hammer, and slipped in through a back door they knew was always open. Until they stood over a bed with a sleeping couple, hammer in hand, and thought, *Sorry. But my family eats first.*

Not long at all. Maybe it had already happened or was happening now. The morbid mowers cased their neighbors' homes as they mindlessly shortened what little life still grew around their little box. Banishing all the bees and beasts that might thrive in tall grass. Controlling their environment to manage their stress. Not looking too rich or happy. After all, their neighbors were not to be trusted.

Thrush led him to a big DIY store. It should have been full to groaning with timber, tools, premade windows, and fetishes for every conceivable need for a builder. Stacks of talismans, too—both premade and unfinished bases for the custom crowd. Well, it was still groaning, but not because it was full.

"Want to bet if they are having supply issues?" Truth asked.

"I must respectfully decline. I left my wallet in Hell," Thrush murmured.

"You have a wallet?"

"I have something that serves that function."

"What's the currency in Hell?"

"Joy."

"What?!"

"Joy. Moments of true, unrestrained happiness. The purer the emotion, the closer it comes to divine ecstasy, the more valuable it is. There are other currencies, of course, but that is certainly my preferred coin."

Truth thought about that for a moment, trying to wrap his mind around it. Thrush continued in his smooth baritone. "Of course, we are starting to run into deflationary pressures. Usually, population growth is enough to ensure a fresh supply of souls to harvest joy from. Alas, new-soul arrival is coming in below expected numbers due to a falling birthrate, and the souls we are getting are notably short on joy. We are now expecting a huge wave in the near future, but after that, it will be chaos. More than usual, anyhow."

"Things are bad enough on this planet that we are fucking up the economy of the local corner of Hell."

"Heaven help us, yes." Thrush sounded worryingly devout.

Truth walked in, looking around the shelves. Empty, empty, empty, or populated by a few torn boxes. Lots of display samples on the industrial shelving. Shelving that rose five times the height of a man that needed special flying carpets with metal tines to lift the pallets down. Empty as a promise of an end-of-year raise.

"Where are the talisman supplies?"

"This way." Thrush fluttered ahead. Not the only bird in the building, Truth noticed. Pigeons had flown in. City doves out in the suburbs, building nests on shelves and leaving messes where they pleased. There were still builders in there, too, and homeowners looking to save a wen and do the work themselves. Stocking up while they can. There were sleek golems lined up by the doors. Three meters tall, humanoid. Off-white, smooth curves, and soothing aesthetics. The words INVENTORY CONTROL SERVICES were written across their chests in a light, cheery blue.

They must have a self-cleaning function to wash off all the shoplifter gore.

The talisman supplies were still there, though in notably limited quantity. Shelves that should be full of premade blanks for lighting, locking, pumping, heating, cooling, purifying, recording, projecting, leveling, compacting, digging, firming, filling, carrying, and cutting were mostly empty. What remained was either the most idiotically expensive or the shoddiest models from the worst brands. All under heavy metal grates.

"This was seriously the best you could find?"

"It was the closest I could find, and my selections were limited."

Truth sighed. "Well, let's make the best of it. Fetch me a cart while I start picking out what I want." He recognized the brands. Most were Starbrite-affiliated companies, either directly or by agreement. Standard parts that were designed to work seamlessly with Starbrite parts. A "small" fee was paid by the manufacturers for the privilege of being part of the product ecosystem.

He checked the metal grate for alarms and wards. Cheap but there. Already half-disabled by the staff, who no doubt had to deal with false alarms dozens of times a day. Truth took the necessary few minutes to completely disable them and neatly severed the locks. Thrush returned with a flat trolley, which was driven by his infernal command to follow behind the palm-sized bird. Truth started loading it up with basically everything, even the stuff he didn't really think he would have a use for. It was just too damn depressing to come back there again.

"All right, the next stop will be finding a good-sized truck out there, ideally one belonging to a business. Double good if it's a Starbrite company. We haul all this back to my little hideout. Then we start in on phase one-point-one."

"I regret that I do not know what that phase is, Mighty One."

"Why, what I spent my whole childhood and teen years avoiding as a career," Truth said cheerfully as he pushed his cart past the unseeing golems. "We are switching from shoplifting to armed robbery. There is a Starbrite package-distribution center near this city, and I'm going to wreck it."

CHAPTER 14

TICK TOCK YOU'RE ON THE CLOCK

Truth took a moment to enjoy the sun streaming in through the window of the stolen wagon. It was, to his mild surprise, spring. He had lost track of the seasons between the well and the eternal summer of Siphios.

Spring in Jeon meant *Winter 2: Revenge of the Mud*. He hadn't really noticed all that much. This far south in Jeon, it was comparatively mild. Give it another six weeks or so, and it would be blazing hot and unbearably humid. Maybe not at the level Siphios was, but he could remember the absolute misery of summer in Harban. Just existing sucked. You could be in the shade with a cup of cool water and still feel like you had been beaten with enormous hammers made of sticky, sweaty spite.

Not today. Today was cool, medium-to-light-jacket weather, depending on personal tolerances. Truth was a little disappointed that his clothes shopping yielded exactly zero form-fitting robin's egg blue shirts or coral-colored hats. He made do with basic black. Black shirt, black hat, gray trousers, black shoes. He stole three sets of everything except the shoes.

This left him in a pretty good situation, he figured. He had neat, clean clothes, an imp assistant, and a stolen van full of stolen talisman supplies. He *had* intended to stash all the stolen loot at De'Ponte's place but realized, as he was pulling out of the parking lot, that his personal field of unnoticeability would not extend indefinitely to random crap he left around the place. Shame. He would have to find somewhere a little more permanent. De'Ponte had used an empty industrial site as one of his drop-off points. Might be just the thing. He would steal that idea, too.

He engaged his imp-based navigation system (Thrush) and drove out of the city. It was part of the demon's magic—finding treasure, finding hidden places, learning mysteries, and revealing secrets. As the lowest sort of intelligent demon, Thrush had limited abilities in, well, any regard. But *Find me an abandoned industrial site just outside the city proper* was well within its capability.

While he drove, he plotted. Truth figured that the assassination campaign was a good start, but it was only a start. Barely rated as a distraction, really. Just got everyone thinking in that *violence will solve your problems* way that would come in useful later.

No, he needed to be going after Starbrite directly. Not just the labor pool for F-Tier drudgery or, worse, the drudge work for suppliers and non-Starbrite corporations. He needed to start hitting the actual meat of the business. Trigger a reaction. Force them to start deploying more security.

Ideally, he would be hitting them hard enough to make them show a flaw in the System Astrologica. Because right now, even with the centuries of Merkovah's study and the consistent attention of innumerable intelligence agencies, nobody had yet cracked it. How, exactly, did the System work?

Truth had provided part of the answer—it made tiny copies of itself out of bits of employee souls and ran a lot locally. But the main body of the System, the central intelligence that provided the backbone for the whole business, hadn't been cracked. Some intelligence was providing the missions, tracking credits, tracking inventory, accounts payable and receivable, depreciation, taxation, hirings, firings, attrition, insurance, pensions, office usage rates, KPIs in the amusement park division, and how much postage the shipyards were going through. To say nothing of the legal department.

Truth had never met a Starbrite lawyer. He was quietly grateful for that fact. Starbrite must get sued all the time, but he really couldn't remember ever hearing about it.

So, clearly, the System had to reach out to all the little local systems it was running . . . but nobody knew how. What they did know was that its reach was global, even orbital, and so far, it had been undetectable.

Truth grinned wolfishly as the truck negotiated its way through a particularly dreary intersection in the exurbs. It was famously difficult to find a particular leaf in the forest, but what if you reduced the total number of leaves? The world was increasingly unreal. A spirit that powerful, that enormous? Would be pretty damn real. It would become easier to spot, as soon as you could make it move and break camouflage.

He knew Merkovah had a whole plan for smashing various bits of magical technology in Harban, starving the beast. And sure, Truth would support that plan. But he didn't trust it.

If he were Starbrite, he would make damn sure that there was a super-secret, heavily defended chain of armored bunkers, known only to certain trusted elites, that contained something . . . something that, when checked against extremely hard-to-find records and drawing particularly obscure inferences, *might* suggest the System was located in one bunker, supported by a network of all the other bunkers. The code to access the two-meter-thick armored doors would, naturally, only be accessible through the most convoluted, dangerous methods imaginable. There would be acid traps.

Then he would stick the actual spirit in a bunker under the biggest mountain range in the deepest stretch of the ocean because Starbrite the man was Level Nine and clearly not a moron. Truth didn't know exactly what it took to keep the System up and running. But Starbrite did. Truth didn't know just what a Level Nine, a *not from this lousy planet Level Nine*, could do, either. He was quite willing to bet that *digging a deep hole and sticking a spirit in it* was one of those things.

Make a target that only your most paranoid, dangerous enemies will find, then put the real System somewhere else. A place where, even if your enemies look, they can't find the spirit, and even if they find it, they can't do anything about it. One day, your enemies will attack the decoy. They will break cover, and you can tidy them up.

So . . . why not run that plan in reverse? There were already a ton of rebel groups around. Why not make Starbrite believe that an effective one had come into existence? He never considered himself a schemer. Direct to a fault, if anything. Still, he did have a few ideas, and he had gotten awfully comfortable in guiding belief.

"You found me a recently vacated light industrial complex one exit down from the regional distribution hub for Totte Global Logistics. Thrush, truly, you have outdone yourself."

"Your appreciation is my highest honor, Great One. I am so pleased I was able to match your requirements."

"This is going to cause so much chaos. It's going to be a complete nightmare for thousands, if not tens of thousands, of people." Truth looked over the buildings with satisfaction. Nothing but room to work and a peaceful space to work in.

Thrush sighed happily. "I missed our time together. You were always destined for greatness, and I so enjoy assisting you."

The distribution center was made up of three major buildings and a few scattered outbuildings. The whole thing was wrapped in its own road network with numbered parking spots for heavy-duty wagons to haul up and wait to be called over for loading. The process was very efficient—the wagons rarely waited long. The F-Tier drones were always moving, and their every second was observed and evaluated. Any deviation from the optimally efficient route resulted in time being docked from their pay.

The company was paying them to work, not waste time. If you had to wipe sweat out of your eyes or catch your breath, you could do it on your own time. You could take all the time you liked if you needed to go to the bathroom, of course. Unpaid time, and there were fines for failing to meet productivity targets, but if you had to go, you had to go, right? Even if where you had to go was on the other side of a warehouse.

Truth leaned against a wall and watched with mild horror. He was just there to case the place, maybe pick off any targets of opportunity. He didn't want to watch a high-speed commercial nightmare. Hell, you were probably better off fishing scrap out of the canal!

He had used this shipping company before. Everyone did. He took immense pleasure in seeing the package waiting in the mailroom at his C-Tier apartment, gaudy in its red and green colors. Nobody in the slums got things delivered by Totte.

They flat-out refused to deliver there. He had no idea it looked like this. The numb exhaustion on every face.

Paying jobs would be a luxury soon. Some of these people, maybe most of them, were Denizens. You didn't have to be a Citizen for an F-Tier job. These people were killing themselves for their last paycheck. In four weeks, they wouldn't even get that. They would be killing themselves for food and shelter. Assuming they could get the shifts. And whoever the supervisor felt like scheduling was really up to them, wasn't it?

Maybe you could persuade them. Somehow. Or not. You don't have a family, right? You do? Well . . . good luck.

And he was about to make their lives so much worse. They would never forgive him, even if they knew exactly why he was doing it. Never ever. He forced himself to turn away and walk toward where the offices were. Hundreds of people moving packages around, and not a C-Tier in sight. The floor workers had bulky talismans they had to carry, which directed them to their next task. Someone or something there was keeping everyone moving. Time to find out who or what and break it.

He followed a series of signs to the business offices, then to the site supervisor's office. The supervisor was, to Truth's mild surprise, a puddle of middle-aged spread with more forehead than hair and a lapel pin sporting a seven-pointed star. He appeared to be hard at work reading things, stamping them, reading other things, and pressing his thumbprint on them again and again and again.

He was surrounded by message tablets—mirrors with intricate spellwork etched into them. There were seven of them, naturally, carefully arranged to put him at the center of a star. They chimed to alert the site supervisor of an incoming message. There was no rhythm to it. They simply rang. Sometimes, several rang at once. Other times, there was a painful pause. As though it was waiting for him to relax. To turn his attention to one of the documents or tablets on the table. Then they would RING and his attention would be yanked away.

He was sitting down in a comfortable, temperature-controlled office, and he was sweating as much as the drones on the warehouse floor. His face was gray with exhaustion and anxiety. It occurred to Truth that this man may not actually be that old. He was just burning up his life, sacrificing it for his "career." He had come so far. He had a lapel pin and all the privileges that came with it. So much better and safer than the F-Tier nobodies he employed.

Truth could practically read his mind. The rest of the world might be going to hell, but he worked for Starbrite. He had the System. He was one of the important ones. Things might get tough, very tough. But he was an elite. One of the chosen few. He would be protected. He would make it through.

System, are you . . . I don't know, sensing anything? Picking up anything I'm not?

<<*Yes, but not relevant to what you are here for.*>> The System went quiet for a moment. <<*It's funny to think that I am looking at a sort of cousin. Stuck inside that meatball is a stamped-out bit of soul like me. Just without the benefit of repeated torture*

sessions at the hand of your damn nous. It is in there, doing its best to help this heap be the best, most productive heap it can be until it dies.>>

He dies. This is a person, not an "it."

<<Is "he" really? I guarantee you it's an entry in the office equipment inventory, the same as the chair it's wetting with flop sweat and swamp-ass. It might even have a depreciation schedule, though I suppose that's what an actuarial table is already. It's a fungible part in Starbrite's machine, and when it finally breaks, Starbrite will recoup part of its investment in the form of a chunk of its soul. Well. Not "its" soul. At this point, it's leasing company property in that department. A lease at best.>>

Truth just looked at the supervisor and wondered. Merkovah's question came to mind—What defines a human? Is it their shape? Their mind? Their soul? What is the bit of someone, that speck of self that couldn't be diminished, that defined you as a human? He still didn't know.

Looking at the supervisor desperately responding to every ring in a state of exhausted, animal panic, he agreed with the System. Whatever defined a human, it wasn't this. This was a victim-rat. A slumrat so beaten down, so utterly *prey*, it only felt safe when it was in pain. Pain meant you weren't dead, and it could no longer imagine death being a release.

Keep your eye out for the escaping bit of soul. See if it leads us anywhere. Truth drew the Tongue from his aperture and raised it high. Then paused.

This . . . wasn't right. Not because he gave a damn about the supervisor. It was the whole . . . everything. The distribution center, the factories, the whole concept of enslaving a nation. Even before that, both Truth and the supervisor decided that a lifetime serving Starbrite was their best choice. The best way to get what they needed for themselves and their families. "Every one of you is a volunteer"; that's what Merkovah said. The slave mentality is what the System called it. That whole idea that you had to give your labor to someone above you if you wanted to live.

It hit like vertigo, the world suddenly twisting and shifting, a sudden irrational terror that you would fall down or even fall up. Truth knew he was groping at the edge of something he didn't have words for, ideas whose shape he could barely guess at. The world shouldn't be like this, yes, but this is the world made by humans. So . . . surely humans could change it. But what the hell do you change it into? Truth had been calling it slum this and slum that, but when you got right down to it, what did a real city look like? A real world?

Terrifying to think. He didn't know what he wanted the world to look like. What a human planet would be like. Could the rats live in such a world? Truth shivered. He looked over at the supervisor, his fat fingers jabbing anxiously at the tablets, spinning, spinning, spinning between the angles of a seven-pointed prison cell.

Change of plans. We do the armed robbery first. Let's put a little color in his life before putting him out of his misery.

CHAPTER 15

A BIG, CLEAN JOB

Truth was in an odd mood as he drove back to De'Ponte's club. He had more or less ignored the club the first few times he went in, still in his "drifting ghost" mentality. Now he could confidently say it was crap. Not as good as the garden club Etenesh had taken him to in Xandre, and *definitely* not as good as the clubs his clients preferred in Harban. Not an entirely fair comparison—high-end clubs in two major capitals versus a club in a third-rate city. Still, some things were universal truths. One of those things is that floors should not stick.

It was midafternoon. There was a very, very bored woman pushing around a mop with almost criminal ineffectiveness. The mop was supposed to be enchanted, just activate it and let it go. It was also broken. The club's decoration was pretty lousy, too—mirrored walls, tiny light talismans scattered around, loads of bench seats, and tiny tables that were tall enough for people to stand next to. And they would have to stand, too, as no chairs or stools were provided. Long, steel-topped bar, no stools again. All the bottles had been taken off the shelves at the end of the night.

They had tried to do some branding work with a stylized cartoon of a palm tree. It didn't particularly work. The club was in the back of a shopping plaza near the center of the city. To Truth's quiet frustration, it appeared to be modestly successful.

De'Ponte was in his back room, reading ledgers and sending notes. The crane on his neck was out again, silently looking over De'Ponte's shoulder. It looked up and spotted Thrush.

"This is no place for you, imp." The crane demon's voice was rich, melodic, and cruel. "But you know that. What drove you to dare appear before me?"

De'Ponte looked up, curious. Twitchy.

"My master's will, naturally. Since that Great One will not condescend to appear in this place, he sent me to carry word of his bidding." Thrush preened casually.

"He commands that a team of disposable pawns numbering not less than ten be assembled. They are to be equipped with vehicles capable of carrying significant loads, such as might be suitable for a mason or other building trade. He will arrange for a way to be open, leading to the interior of the Totte distribution hub on the outskirts of this city. Your thugs are to steal all they can and smash all they cannot take, leaving fire, destruction, and ruin in their wake. Your reward will be one hundred percent of the profits from what they steal.

"Your animals are to be assembled with their vehicles at the Sweepstakes restaurant off exit one hundred and eighteen, at five in the afternoon tomorrow. I will appear, and they will follow me through the prepared route. That is all." The little demon turned to leave.

"The hell it is 'all,' imp!" De'Ponte shot to his feet and slammed his hand on the table. "Who the FUCK do you—"

Truth had been waiting for that. He grabbed DePonte's stylus and jammed it through his hand, two centimeters deep into the table.

It took everyone in the room a good couple of seconds to process what happened. De'Ponte grabbed his wrist, a high-pitched whine coming from between clenched teeth. His forehead beaded with sweat.

"I saw nothing, my prince. Not even a whisper of a spell," the crane demon Pealon said with quiet urgency.

De'Ponte heaved a few breaths, then dragged his attention back from his hand and onto Thrush. "Why? What does your master get out of this?"

"I have no idea. It's no business of mine. Or yours. Until tomorrow, then. For one reason or another."

Thrush flew off. This time, no one tried to stop him.

Truth watched a moment longer, then followed. It would work, or it wouldn't. But he knew a fellow rat, even if it mistakenly believed it was a cat. He left room for the rat to run and even put a bit of meat at the end of the path. De'Ponte would send his most disposable, degenerate thugs. Not even "his" thugs, more like anyone he could sweep up and press into service. He would seize whatever loot the survivors returned with, either paying them a pittance or directly murdering them to sever any connection back to him. Probably the latter. He would also betray this anonymous "master" at the very first opportunity.

Perfect.

It had been a long time since Truth had really buried himself in the art of talismans. He was trained in maintenance, not creation, but you couldn't really maintain something without some understanding of how it was created.

He could remember when he started the maintenance classes. He had chosen it purely because it seemed like the best shot out of the slums, not for any particular love of talismans. The memory of the classroom was blurred with time, as was the lesson, but the emotion stayed with him.

The teacher had a simple diagram of a basic spell array up on the blackboard and walked through the parts. He didn't remember what exactly it was. He just remembered the click. The moment where he got it. Like a falling rock or the lift of a lever. It had to work that way. The logic of the whole thing demanded it. This connected to that, which drove this third thing. It wouldn't work if you put this *there* because *there* is too far, interferes with the transmission of energy, or takes up space needed for another component. There was a right answer. It was knowable, provable, repeatable. And he could learn it.

Later on, he discovered why talisman maintenance was considered a skilled trade, and that there were often many right answers, and far more that were "right enough" to get the job done on a project. But the feeling of satisfaction never really left. Seeing something wrong, knowing how it should work, then returning it to order. He never tired of it.

What he was putting together now would be, in his professional opinion, jank. It would work, in a crude, brutal sense. Not nearly as durable, reliable, and elegant as a properly purpose-built talisman. But they would work.

An intricately carved "gem" (a manufactured stone containing not less than eighty percent quartz, per the package) was repurposed from an industrial noise insulator into a wide-area noise isolator. It would only work for a short time before burning out, but it would work. Same as the lock-breaking and alarm-negating tools. Tools for capturing and binding hostile spirits. Tools for keeping them away.

Most of the talismans were already in usable or near-usable shape. An angle cutter doesn't care if you are cutting metal pipe or a lock, after all. Nor does a glass cutter care who owns the glass being cut. There are likewise many perfectly valid reasons for having lots of commercial-grade cleaning supplies. Especially the ones that destroy all traces of biological and magical remnants on surfaces.

"Magus, most of these petty tools are quite useless for you. May I ask why you bother with them?" Thrush hopped around the table, examining the fruits of Truth's labor.

"Two reasons—I enjoy it, and it is always good to show people what they expect to see. So, when they wonder how I defeated their surveillance, they will see counter-surveillance tools. And then they will believe they know something about me and my capabilities."

"I see. Devious."

"Nah, that's just the basics. The really devious bit is coming next." Truth tidied up, taking particular care to scrub down every surface he might have touched. The cleanser was used aggressively and in more than the recommended concentrations. It had a pungent artificial grape smell, Truth noticed, one designed to linger for hours. He even swept up the trash, burned it outside, and buried the ashes a meter deep.

"You are erasing your presence here?"

"My presence is already erased. I am erasing the traces of the *work I did* here."

"My meager intelligence fails to appreciate your genius. Please, instruct me," Thrush groveled. And if you believed him, more fool you.

"Not much to it. See, what most people don't consider is that investigations cost money. Even just the cop's time or a security team's time. That's coming out of a budget somewhere. Any time they spend investigating, there is some other work they aren't doing. You may need to have someone cover that work, which is more money, plus your time organizing that coverage, which is *more* money. Then you have things like equipment, sacrifices, disposable charms, the goddamn necromancers, loads of things that cost loads of money."

"I follow so far."

"Most investigations that should happen don't happen because of money. Then the investigations that do happen get half-assed because of money. Then you finally have the full-effort, no-expenses-spared investigations. These cost a hell of a lot of money, so they better get results or it's going to be somebody's ass. They are going to go over every little thing very, very carefully, BUT!" Truth smiled angelically, which meant something rather nasty on his little planet.

"They are looking for the things they expect to see. They—cops, security, who-ever—know that criminals know cops either don't or barely investigate most of the time. So, they don't do a good job of erasing their traces, and when they do try to hide them, they do so in the most low-effort way possible. Masks, change of clothes, that kind of thing."

"You are . . . once again shaping their opinion of who you are. A meticulous individual, a schemer. One determined to erase all traces of themselves, who works through disposable pawns. Hence the nonsense this morning with the human serf and his master."

"You know, I think I could even be a sinister mastermind, pulling the strings on the criminal underworld. Or, more dangerous still, a revolutionary."

"A revolutionary?"

Truth carefully made a rubbing of a piece of one side of the demon contract he got from the hotel. Then he equally carefully burned it and dumped the ashes in the toilet. It looked like not quite everything went down with the flush.

"Oh, yes. A revolutionary. One careful to erase all evidence of their existence, moving through the masses like a fish in the sea." Wait, where had he heard that expression before? Probably unimportant. "And, crucially, one a half-step behind what the state of the art is in crime-scene reconstruction."

Thrush thought through everything he had seen that day and started laughing. "I have truly missed you, Magus. Truly missed you."

At exactly five PM, three large white panel wagons pulled into the parking lot of Sweepstakes. Fifteen men, five from each, stepped out and assembled in front of a tiny black bird sitting on a chain link fence. It looked them over and nodded.

"Very good. You will follow me. Stop when I stop; go when I go. If there are barriers, a way will be made. Surveillance will be defeated. Guards will be distracted. You simply go, take, destroy, and leave. Or you will perish, and I will have a quick meal." Thrush flew off and perched on a street sign at the end of the driveway and looked back. Waiting.

The thugs looked at each other. None of them were good people or easy to get along with. Many of them were high. They had the morale of wet bread. They also had the uncanny certainty that if they didn't get back in their wagons right now and get moving, they would die.

They couldn't see Truth sitting up on top of one of the wagons, ready to make that belief a reality. They certainly could feel his killing intent. Truth smiled as the wagon pulled out of the driveway. He had promised to induct the gangsters of Jeon into his revolutionary organization, and he was already making good on it. Perhaps, in some far-distant future, they would even be remembered as heroes.

They rumbled up the access road, speeding up as they charged toward the gate to the distribution center. Truth flicked his hand, and Incisive sliced open the gate. The talismans and charms were in place and running. They would be effective for a minute or two at least.

The martyrs of the revolution cheered as they rushed in. Driven by forces they were unaware of, serving goals they didn't understand, laboring for the illusion of profit. Truth rode the vertigo. He didn't know what the world should look like. He just knew this, this world, this System of the world, was intolerable. Truth didn't realize he was grinning like a skull.

"Sergeant Truth Medici, back from medical leave, here to collect my back pay!"

CHAPTER 16

SMASH AND GRAB

The involuntary revolutionaries smashed through the gate. The hinges had been cut; the heavy wagons rolled right over it. The metal shrieked and rumbled under the wheels of progress. The revolutionaries were coming up from an access road, bypassing the queue of wagons waiting to load and unload into the distribution center. This was a high-speed operation. Lines were for honest folk.

Truth was perched on the top of the lead wagon, waiting as Thrush led the column across a wide parking lot and directly at the wall of the warehouse. They roared forward, never daring to slow as they charged. They knew the consequences of disobedience. The feeling of the blade at their throat hadn't eased for a second.

At the last possible instant, Truth tossed two charms at the warehouse wall. Two tall lines formed from brilliant, horrible blue-white light burst into existence. A triangle five meters tall at its highest point was cut into the wall as the lead wagon smashed through the corrugated steel siding.

They were in. The workers were reeling, falling back from the explosive noise and the sudden presence of three wagons inside the warehouse. From out the back of the wagons came the hired goons, waving thoroughly illegal Firebolt fetishes and needlers. The old national service training had been forgotten. They were shooting at anything that moved and a hell of a lot of things that didn't.

Truth ran in behind them, having hopped off before the wagon hit. Thrush would lead the marauders through the warehouse, maximizing the havoc while leading them to the "best loot." Truth had another job to do.

Having scouted the way before, he rushed over to the site supervisor's office. The supervisor was still in his little cage—seven tablets surrounding him and shrieking alarms. He was screaming right back—giving orders, calling for reports, for security, for somebody to make the craziness stop. Truth thought he had been all the way gone yesterday. Apparently, there was still a little bit of rationality left to lose. *Now* the supervisor was all the way gone. There was nothing human there—just an animal. Scared, lashing out. Wanting to run but trapped.

Truth popped one of his modified talismans, turning something that should have had a five-year service life into a three-minute charm. The tablets stilled. The alarms went silent. There was noise and panic outside, but for the first time in . . . who knows how long . . . the Supervisor had peace. It terrified him. Truth could smell the fear stink over the ashtray full of Golden Bat butts. The supervisor had been tortured by the alarms and messages, but he understood them. He didn't know how to live without them.

"They must have used a *jammer*. This isn't some fuckup. *This is an attack*." Truth poured poison into the supervisor's ear. Would the internal System trigger something? What about the System Astrologica? Truth watched the supervisor's eyes. All the System messages were in your head, pure hallucinations, but the body was fooled. The eyes moved around the hovering messages as though the letters were in front of them.

There! Truth spotted it. The minuscule flicks of the eye. He was getting a message. A mission. The supervisor started walking toward the door. Truth smiled grimly. Time to add fuel to the fire.

"This is a *hit*. An *attack*. *Terrorists*. Security is a joke. A bad *joke*. You know what they are like. It's going to be *up to you*. You have to *take charge*. You always knew you would have to. You will have to solve this yourself."

The supervisor dithered. Jerking back and forth. A new alarm sounded in the hallway. Fire. His face firmed up. He walked back to his desk and jerked open the bottom drawer. A standard Jeon Army–issue needler was there, next to a bottle of schnapps and some pills.

"Not who I thought I was going to be using this on," the supervisor muttered with grim humor. "Any mission-critical spells available? No, of course not. Prager, watch over me." The supervisor had a rough, raw voice. Needler in hand, he walked out the door. Back straight. Ready for anything. A real Starbrite man.

Truth gave the room a quick once-over and didn't find anything important. There was almost nothing at all. All the usual paperwork that would clutter other offices did not exist here. All handled by the System. Things that didn't rate the System's attention were run through the enchanted tablets. Short-term messages, Truth guessed, and automated messages from the arrays and devices that supported the operation of the distribution center.

There wasn't a hint of the supervisor's identity or personality anywhere visible in the office. No picture of his family on the desk or his name on the door. Not even a little plaque on a stand on his desk proclaiming his elevated identity. Just Site Supervisor on a mass-produced plastic sign glued to the wall next to the door. He quickly searched his desk. The only things he could say for sure about the supervisor were that they smoked Golden Bats, drank Huntsman, used Soma to take the edge off, and could lay hands on a needler.

That was it. The sum total of a life. The mind reduced to reflexive pain responses. The System deliberately hurting him, training him not to think, only respond and obey. The supervisor's identity reduced to function, his personality reduced to pain management. Everything he was outside of the job fit in the bottom drawer of a mass-produced desk with room to spare.

The back of the office chair was a little broken. Not badly, still usable. It rested at a slight tilt to the right. Truth tried to straighten it up. It immediately listed back to the right. A chair like that couldn't cost more than a couple of points in the System Shop. Truth shook his head and caught up to the supervisor. He hadn't managed to get far.

Security was swarming toward the warehouse now. The brutal morons conducting the raid had set fires as they went, blowing up servitors and smashing what they couldn't steal. Some inspired vandal figured out how to topple the towering shelves despite the heavy steel frames being bolted to the floor. From what security was saying, they had found a pallet of professional-grade cutting tools, and one of the thugs actually knew a Sharp spell. Level one, obviously, but it was apparently good enough.

Truth came out onto the floor of the warehouse with the supervisor and security. The thugs were chanting and screaming. Thrush had whipped them into madness. SMASH THE SYSTEM, FREE THE PEOPLE! was cut into the corrugated metal of the wall. The last of the daylight trickled through the cuts, the orange sky making them look etched with fire.

The site supervisor didn't know what the hell was going on, but he hadn't climbed to the top by letting little details like that slow him down. "Loading associates! Fire drill! Evacuate now! Fire captains, lead your teams. I WANT A HEAD COUNT! Security! Get those animals off my floor!" He started bellowing orders, his needler up and firing into the thugs. They were in melee with his own workers, but that was no reason not to shoot.

Truth touched Thrush's command medallion. "Have a few of the gangsters cut down this guy, and then it's time for the heroes to declare victory and retreat with the loot." He'd give the supervisor a moment. A touch of grace. A chance to die a human.

"As you command." Three of the gangsters swung their fetishes over and started blasting wildly. Security sensibly took cover. The site supervisor knew it was hero time. He strode boldly forward. Hands steady. Eyes bright.

By fluke or God's grace, he caught one of the thugs twice in the chest, putting him down. His reward? Two bolts of superheated plasma; one took the side of his ribs, the other his hip. Blood flashed into steam, exploding the charred meat and ruined organs away from the smoking bone tips left in the holes. The shock killed him instantly, dead before he started falling toward the floor.

Truth was watching intensely, extending his full attention to the dead C-Tier. All his senses focused on the body. Merkovah must have killed hundreds under laboratory conditions over the years and never cracked the secret. But what about now, as reality thinned?

System—

Nothing. I can't see what happens to souls when the body dies, generally. Let alone whatever sort of nastiness Starbrite cooked up.

Really nothing?

Oh, no, I'm just lying to you for the fun of it—YES, REALLY NOTHING.

Shit.

Little tongues of flame burned on the clothes near the edges of the plasma holes. It was the tree silk blended with the cotton, Truth knew. Intensely flammable stuff, and the cotton burned well too. The thugs were falling back to their wagons, much fewer of them now, less than half. They would have retreated long before if not for Thrush's mental assault on them. They peeled out, heading for the access road and whatever rally point DePonte had set for them.

Truth didn't bother watching them go. He was sulking. He could admit to himself that he was sulking, but he wasn't about to stop doing it. Yes, it was completely unreasonable to expect to find a clue leading directly to the System Astrologica on the first try. But he had really thought it would work. At least he should see something! Some hint of resonance between his own mutated soul and the supervisor's. But . . . no. Nothing.

<<I mean, you never noticed it when other PMC members died on ops, either. >>

I was frigging Level One or Two!

<<Yeah, but no resonance thing. I'm not sure you even noticed them dying. In any meaningful way, that is. >>

What? I know they died. I saw them die. Not often, thanks to the potions, medics, and everything. But it happened.

<<Sure did. Name one.>>

Truth paused. Kofi was pretty indelibly etched into his brain. Keller, Rezepi, Nobu and . . . Fuck.

He . . . really couldn't name a single member of the PMC who died after that. In fact, he struggled to remember a lot of names from his time in the PMC. Faces, he vividly remembered. The sergeant, the captain, his squad mates, but beyond that? A lot of faces, and no real details to go with those faces. No life story, no motivations, not even a few character-defining quirks. Just people competently doing their jobs.

A whole personality you could fit in a drawer with room to spare. He could remember, vividly, what the System Astrologica told him—"*You don't have a personality, or at least, not one anyone would care about.*" Was it . . . He didn't know the right words. Was that little shove intended to make him have less of a personality?

He had concluded that it was aimed at hurting his self-esteem and encouraging his isolation, but what if there was another level to it? An ever-tightening spiral of personality, focusing down until all that was left was a burning need to do the job at all costs. Using the soul to destroy the mind, which weakened both body and soul. It extracted the maximum useful labor while the local System worked its host over. Once the soul had been sufficiently broken and processed, the body would collapse, and the soul would be comfortably absorbed by the System Astrologica.

<<It occurs to me that this fits with what I thought would happen to me after you died,>> the System said. *<<I was created, would help you be the best little drone you could be, then return to the System, shorn of memory and personality, once you died. Obliteration of self to ensure easy absorption. >>*

The security team was rushing around, not achieving much. The firefighting teams were doing their best, spraying foam and calling showers of water from floating charms. The heavy wagons were piled up outside the distribution center, filling all the parking spots and queueing up on the road. If the queue hadn't reached the highway yet, they would soon. The distribution center had to keep in motion, or, like a heart attack, the blood of commerce wouldn't flow through the body of the nation. This little corner of the nation, anyway.

The cost of that lack of circulation was not literally incalculable, but it was beyond Truth's reckoning. All those people waiting for their deliveries, yes, but how about all the businesses that suddenly couldn't operate? The traffic that wasn't moving, the contracts unfulfilled? It was probably screwing up the banks somehow, but Truth suspected that, what with everything, the banks might not even notice this little disruption.

And, of course, there were all the dead. He looked around—the bodies hauled to one side by the workers. The ambulances and police had been called but hadn't reached there yet. Maybe they were stuck in traffic? Thugs and F-Tier nobodies . . . except to their families. Their friends. To themselves. All of them just doing the best they could in a world they couldn't possibly understand, let alone affect.

The workers probably wouldn't have survived the collapse of the world, anyway. They probably only died a few months or a year early. But he had still killed these strangers. He had to accept the moral weight of the choices that lead him here. Truth laughed. A mad, bubbling noise. He hammered his hands and feet against the floor in frustration, feeling the pain of these pointless deaths pressing down on him. It was Starbrite again. Starbrite had found a way to hurt him again. Getting at him through his soul.

CHAPTER 17

THE VIOLENCE PUZZLE

Truth collected Thrush and walked out into the traffic jam of wagons outside the distribution center. He figured that his primary goal might be a failure, but his secondary goal—drawing Starbrite resources away from Harban—might yet work out. Unfortunately, a parking lot full of long-haul transport wagons, or at least this parking lot, does not provide a lot of comfortable seating options. No matter. He would just take the walk for now.

"What happens to souls when the body dies?"

"Pardon, Magus?" Thrush sounded confused, which was fair enough. This was pretty common knowledge, after all.

"What happens to souls? Mechanically, I mean. What is the official position of Hell on the post-mortal experience of humanity?"

"Hell has no official positions on anything. Such a thing would be impossible."

"No one rules Hell?"

Thrush was silent for an uncomfortably long moment. "Forgive me, Dread One, but the question is a bit difficult to answer. I know that humans enjoy assigning demons various ranks and stations based on our level of power and authority over our kindred, but this is a human conceit. We do not even have a false monarchy, let alone kings and princes in truth. "

"So far, it seems fairly straightforward. 'Correct, no one rules Hell' would do."

"It would also be untrue. Hell is chaotic beyond belief. Literally." Thrush shifted around awkwardly. "Imagine you were throwing dice. Each dice has six faces, numbered one to six. You throw one die, and you have a one-in-six chance of rolling a six. Throw two dice, and the odds are thirty and a half chances in a hundred that at least one die shows six. Three dice and your odds rise to a hair over forty-two percent. Keep adding dice, and eventually, the odds become infinitely close to one hundred percent."

Truth nodded, waiting to see where this was going.

"Your odds of throwing a six get larger and larger, but the possible combinations of numbers, their sum, their organization, grow progressively more complex. The more dice and the more throws, the greater the possible complexity and randomness."

"Okay?"

"Now imagine that *trillions* of dice are being thrown every instant, and each die has a billion faces. The possible combination of numbers is so staggering, almost any sequence can and will occur eventually and likely repeatedly. So, yes, there are cities in Hell with princes and dukes and hierophants. Our contracts are justly legendary for their subtlety and sophistication, as is our total disregard for hierarchy and law."

"Because things are so chaotic, order will naturally occur sometimes. And, eventually, dissolve back into chaos again?"

"Yes. And since the numbers are so impossibly vast, there is, functionally, always, somewhere, a Great President commanding Forty Legions of the Infernal Host. And other such figures as appear in the lurid compendiums humans assemble. Which does lead to the next point of confusion. Hell isn't purely random."

"I was about to ask. All those stellar eminences that have existed since the dawn of the universe."

"Or perhaps before. Yes, precisely them. They serve a myriad of functions in the cosmos, most of which, I will confess, I am far too lowly to understand. However, one of those functions is to . . . adjust the odds in various parts of Hell."

"Remove all numbers lower than five hundred million on your billion-sided die in the area around them, as it were?"

"You have it right. For example, when we first met, I claimed to be called after the fashion of Great Caym. This is because I . . . I must use human terms here, so please understand this is not literally true but gives you the right sort of idea. I live under the dominion of Caym. Who, no, would not care if every entity in Hell called themselves Caym."

"And His Excellency, by virtue of his existence, stabilizes a portion of Hell into what could be termed a domain or lands under his rule. A place with more-consistent rules, like joy being used as currency."

"We are speaking purely in analogy here, but yes." Thrush preened a few feathers. A nice bit of acting, Truth thought, given its immaterial body.

"So . . . souls get treated differently in different parts of Hell?"

"I assume so. I can only speak on the tiny piece of it that I know." Thrush's voice was terribly reasonable. Truth felt something odd tickling at the back of his awareness, some instinct warning him to be very careful there. Air demons were notoriously smart, and Caym was a master debater.

"What have your observations of the process shown?"

"I cannot explain the mechanism by which souls enter Hell. Candidly, I would struggle to describe souls to you at all, even by analogy, based on my perception of them in that realm. By the time they reach my awareness, they have already suffered significant trauma. Their sense of identity is fraying. They have already lost the vast majority of . . . call it memories. What's left is all the things that were truly precious. Those moments of deep understanding, strong emotions, that kind of thing."

Thrush fluttered from branch to branch, pecking at stray bugs.

"Like coral growing over a sunken diamond. Precious, perhaps, but not truly so. The treasure, imperishable and eternal, is what is at the core. We, poor servants that we are, strip away the dross, revealing the gem within. This process takes an indeterminate amount of time, as 'time' has no greater reality than any other concept in Hell. Eternity, from the perspective of the souls. Outside references are rather meaningless. I am not 'eternity' years old, but those who have been under my care have experienced an indefinable amount of time."

Truth mentally circled *Hell* and drew a line over to *Under my care.* "I see. And what of the diamond?"

"This smudge of ash would not dream of holding such a treasure."

"Straight to Caym?"

"He wouldn't dream of it either. We know our place. In a manner of speaking."

"Oh? Who does it go to, then?"

"Why, the one who rules Hell. The only person who could, if you think about it."

Truth racked his brain, but his command of the *Goetia* failed him. "I'll bite. Who rules in Hell?"

"You bound me by their name and the names of their servants, and yet you do not know? It could be none other than God."

Truth ruminated over what Thrush said as he watched the cleanup and repair work around the distribution center. Apparently, the animosity between Heaven and Hell was more nuanced than he had believed. It absolutely existed, but from Thrush's perspective, it was more in the nature of brutal overseers keeping down the serfs. Truth took that with the appropriate mountain-sized grain of salt.

The cleanup was interrupted by the arrival of the police. It had taken them more than half an hour to deploy, and even then, they came in on flying platforms. Either the carriages were being used elsewhere, or the traffic was *really* stuck. Perhaps they were chasing the wagons used in the robbery.

The police cordoned off the area, organized walkthroughs, interviewed witnesses, and generally tried to do their jobs. This process was made more challenging by the fact that nobody, on the Starbrite side, anyway, appeared to be in charge. Truth understood what the cops apparently didn't—the unintended consequences of flattening the hierarchy.

It was an appealing thought. Cut out the layers of bureaucracy, cut out unnecessary managers, cut out waste and pointless paper-pushing. Really cut down on those expenses. Start crushing some efficiency metrics. Everyone in their role, firmly focused on their job. Until something goes wrong. Someone supervisory calls out sick, and there is no redundancy in place to cover for them. No one can step up; nobody can move down. Everyone is where they *have* to be, and nobody with the institutional knowledge on how to fill in.

There were other site supervisors, of course. The center ran around the clock. They were off shift. Presumably, they had just gotten an urgent message from the System telling them they needed to come in straight away. Hope they caught a carpet.

Right now, it was all milling workers, praying they would get paid for all this and sickly certain that the System was tracking their time, classifying it as nonproductive, and deducting it from their wages. Some were trying to load wagons, yelling that the cops could kill them, but they wouldn't stop for anything less. They had mouths to feed. Roofs to keep over small heads. They had their own desperate, humiliated dignity.

Someone punched a cop. The other cops came swarming in, batons rising and falling, getting him on the ground and not stopping. Someone threw a rock.

A sergeant wasn't waiting—he pulled out a potion and slammed it on the ground. Orange gas spread out, choking the workers, their eyes turning red and streaming with tears. They ran from the loading dock, cops chasing after, breaking knees and cuffing the workers on the ground. Leaving them in the choking smoke.

Riot averted. Presumably, medals would be distributed. All was well. All was peaceful in Jeon. For now.

Two and a half hours after the raid, Starbrite PMC arrived. Truth was keeping a very discreet eye here—staying out of sight and under cover as much as possible. It was a couple of Level Ones escorting a specialist in a discreetly armored carriage . . . or so they wanted everyone to think.

Truth watched the almost-invisible seekers peeling off the sides of the carriage like a frog off a window. There were perhaps half a dozen or so, and they scattered across the dispatch center like hounds looking for the scent. The specialist trailed behind.

Truth hadn't seen a specialist like this before. Her eyes had been removed and replaced with spinning prisms, emitting light in myriad spectrums. She conferred with the cops, who pointed at the site of the break-in, the dead site supervisor, the remnants of the talismans used in the assault.

The scene was taped off. Ambulances collected the bodies; police wagons collected the "rioters." The Starbrite PMC personnel toured the site, spending two hours on their inspection before heading back toward their carriage. Truth watched intently. The seekers didn't return to the carriage. It seemed that, for now, at least, they would remain on site.

Two hours on scene time for two Level Ones and a specialist. Stationing a half dozen of those . . . creatures. It wasn't a really accurate measure of the time and resource cost to Starbrite. He knew it cost them. But it felt . . . paltry. Almost insultingly small. Truth sighed. Fingers crossed they bought the "revolution" angle and started hunting "revolutionaries."

Of course, he could help sell that idea. Truth looked around for a convenient rock. The parking lot was regrettably without loose rocks, bricks, or other classic throwables. Truth sighed and shelved the idea. He strode away, giving up on the day. He wanted them looking for a mastermind, not a lone assassin. Even if he could pick one off with a thrown . . . Truth stopped and started rapping his knuckles against his head. He set off at a dead sprint. If this was going to work, he needed to get to the highway before they did.

His body moved at speeds that a Level One simply couldn't match, barely a blur in their perception. If they could see him at all, which they couldn't. Truth blew past the carriages crawling through the remains of the traffic jam, headed back toward the city. There! An overpass!

Truth jumped up and grabbed hold of the bridge. He yanked out a cutting talisman and started carving into the concrete. In meter-tall letters, he wrote, *Society Will Be Renewed Through Star-Bright Blood!* Next to it he drew a crude eye wide open.

Whistling, happy with his work, he walked away. "*Sppsshsh whismp whooo.*"

"I can teach you to whistle, Mighty One."

"Shut it. I'll manage it one day."

"Where to next?"

Truth wrapped his scarf a little more snugly around his neck. "It's been a long day. I think I will spend a night at a hotel, then drop in on some loyal comrades. Then it will be time to have a little think."

"About what, if I may ask?"

"The only cause worthy of the moment. Revolution and how to spread it!"

CHAPTER 18

REVOLUTION FROM THE BATHTUB

Truth returned to the Hanging Orchid Hotel. The Grand Deluxe Supreme Diamond Suite remained unused. Inexplicably, it seemed that luxury business travel had completely fallen off. The hotel's guests, while all dressed neatly in business clothes, had a certain tightness of the eye and stiffness in the shoulders. The bar was doing a brisk trade. Very brisk. Truth had seen people drinking to get drunk often enough that he didn't have to guess why.

He took a shower, scrubbed thoroughly, and went to sleep. It would take time for things to cook. Though the police could move fast with sufficient motivation. An armed assault on a major local employer should be pretty damn motivating. He was faintly curious to see what the news would say about it if anything.

The message carved on the side of the overpass would be hidden soon enough and removed entirely not long after. That was fine. So long as the Starbrite PMC team saw it.

Truth woke early and, having nowhere in particular to rush off to, decided to explore the amenities of an extremely luxurious hotel room. Which rapidly turned out to be anticlimactic. An enormous bed, a plush sofa, basically an entire small luxury apartment. Nothing beyond that. It was dull. The bathroom was shiny, quite literally. Every surface was oiled and polished to a mirror finish.

The centerpiece of the bathroom was the gargantuan bathtub. It was roughly oval-shaped, free-standing, and made of some lustrous light tan wood. It had been gently curved and formed to allow one to lie back, soak, and relax in utterly decadent comfort, either looking out across the square from the floor-to-ceiling one-way window or just throwing on some scry. It also came with a variety of knobs and buttons to play with. Truth poked at them. It turned out there were water jets. Interesting. He filled it up, got in, and continued his experimentation while he watched the news from the tub.

The news was disappointing, as expected. A small group of criminals broke in and were killed by security but managed to badly damage the loading bay and severely slow down the operation of the site. The police had issued a call for information about any of the criminals, as they likely had accomplices. Truth vaguely recognized some of the pictures. He really didn't give a damn about the thugs, then or now.

No mention of De'Ponte, though, or the One-Legged Bird Ring. Had they not traced that far up? Did somebody get paid off? Dangling bait for bigger fish? Fingers crossed for the last one.

Oh, some of the jets were aimed at his neck and had a pulsing function. Kind of like a massage? Not that it was strong enough to do anything. A tub that could massage him would kill most people on this planet. Truth smiled softly. He'd bet Etenesh would love this tub. She would love being in the tub with him. Though some of the jets were aimed at his ass. Product defect? Investigate later. He let himself drift off into daydreams of Etenesh as the big heating enchantments kept the tub at the perfect temperature for poaching eggs.

"*These are scary times. You know that. Big changes coming too, for everyone.*" The ad blared from the scryball. There was a montage of one-second images—a construction worker, a natural philosopher, an alchemist. All looking serious, though not scared. "*Well, you know how to handle big changes. You get ready, and you get tough. Rackem Tough!*"

The image cut over to an eight-legged golem. Inky black, with an outer skin that was both rubbery and alarmingly soft-looking. A matte, wet sheen, like ever-flowing tar. "*Our Champion line of golems cannot be beat on performance, reliability, or versatility.*" The golem scampered with eerie smoothness over rugged terrain, picked up a box larger than itself, then proceeded to climb up the side of a building.

"*For the RT-Champion, we pulled out all the stops. Military-grade steel skeleton. Military-grade control talismans, not to mention our state-of-the-art Z-Pro stability, grip, and traction control. Or our DreamCoat protection technology that will protect your Champion for years to come, just like it will protect you. That's something no other company can offer. Or compete with.*" Two of the golems were racing back and forth through burning rubble, tossing cinderblocks at each other.

"*Security isn't a concern when you have the RT-Champion. You can sleep easy, knowing that its fully customizable security settings come automatically keyed to your Citizenship level. You will never, ever have to worry about not having enough golem for the job.*" There was footage of a golem running down a fleeing burglar, pouncing on them, and starting to . . . disarm them. The camera cut away before anything was really shown.

"*Tested on the battlefield. Safe for your home. Great with kids, too.*" The six-legged jet-black horror, with its human-like trio of fingers on each leg, offered a balloon to a laughing child, who perched a little party hat on top of it. "*Financing available for qualified buyers, and for a limited time only, take an extra five percent off if you pay in Credits.*" Loud music played while the golem posed on top of a rock and the sun set behind it. "*Get your RT-Champion TODAY! Only available from authorized Rackem Tough dealers, terms and conditions may vary, Rackem Tough is a proud member of the Starbrite Family of companies.*"

Had ads gotten a lot better, or had he just gotten a lot more susceptible? Because that sounded strangely good to him. Truth gave his cheeks two quick slaps. Must have caught him half-napping. It had been a tiring few days. Although it did bring up an unpleasant point.

Truth was very competent at violence. He was very incompetent at propaganda. The slogan on the side of the bridge was about the best he could manage. He could probably delegate the sloganeering to Thrush, but that seemed unnecessarily dangerous. He needed that propaganda push regardless. Less to create unrest and more to create the appearance of unrest. The more he sold his nonexistent mastermind, the harder they would hunt for him. Eventually, they would be thin enough on the ground that he could start trying to trace the kidnapped Shattervoid girl.

He hadn't forgotten about her. He just didn't have a good way to help. Which wasn't fun at all. Truth lay there in the tub, trying to think it through. Merkovah didn't have a good way to find her either.

The plan, if you could call it a plan, was for Truth to insert into Jeon and be the best lone-wolf shit-stirrer he could be. No ties to trace, no chance of getting burned by a traitor or being given up during an interrogation. Make enough trouble, draw enough attention, and cracks should start to show.

He wouldn't be the only one doing this. Siphios was inserting other agents, along with the ones they already had in place. Every other damn country was doing the same. As Merkovah pointed out (swearing only a little bit in the process), everybody and their aunt knew Starbrite was responsible. It's just that no one could prove it, let alone do anything about it. Messages to the Shattervoid had been ignored, as promised. The Shattervoid wanted results, not accusations.

Truth squeezed his hand under the water and watched the water jet up a meter into the air. Fun. He did it again. Still fun. Break the System Astrologica, and all the Starbrite systems collapse double-quick. The girl is revealed to the world—everyone races to "rescue" the princess and cash her in for a ticket off-world for you and ten thousand of your closest friends and relatives. All this revolution business was just step one.

So, how to spread the good word? These demon cultists were a good start, but there were many better options. Truth stared up at the ceiling. His trainers had identified roughly three categories of relevant groups that could be hijacked—the Runners, the Holdouts, and the Suicidal.

The Runners were those who wanted to tear down Starbrite so they could get the girl and get off the planet. This group included pretty much the entire planet, organized variously, excluding the Holdouts and the Suicidal. It would certainly include Merkovah and whatever office he held in Siphios. There would be many, many others on ops in Jeon right now.

The Holdouts figured there was no chance that they were getting off-world, so they wanted to grab all they could now and get ready to ride out whatever came next. Maybe position their families to be the new rulers of this world when the magic returned. A lot of old money behind these groups, apparently. A shocking number of elites had prepared doomsday bunkers long before the Black Ships arrived.

The Suicidal could be equally termed the Homicidal, or the Euthanasiasts. The world deserved to die. Humanity deserved to die. Whether it went peacefully or violently, it had to go. Most, naturally, concluded that violence was a regrettable necessity. For example, the demon-incubating cult that impregnated Mr. Huelle. The anti-theists would also fall under this umbrella. It was a politics of despair, of the peace of non-being.

Which did lead to a somewhat pressing problem—Truth didn't know the first damn thing about politics. He knew Siphios had a king, and he was *pretty* sure Jeon had both a president and a prime minister. Maybe eighty percent sure. Beyond that, he didn't know a damn thing about how the country worked. Starbrite was twenty percent of the economy, and it was the twenty percent that mattered—that's what he knew. Everything else was irrelevant to him, a position his teachers heartily agreed with.

When he thought about it, he really didn't know what a "good" government looked like. People shouldn't live in slums. Kids shouldn't be hungry. Actually, nobody should be hungry. Jobs? Truth groped around in his mind. Cops shouldn't be allowed to just fuck with you for no reason; he was one hundred percent certain on that one. Nobody should be allowed to touch your cash, even if they were your mom. Medicine? Maybe? Or cultivation resources? Education should be available for everyone.

He gave up. He knew how to look after himself and his sibs. How to look after a whole damn country? No idea.

So, if he didn't really know what he was for, what was he against? A long and detailed list came to mind. It started with every detail of life in the slums and went from there. He could work with that. Just tell people what you are against, and blame Starbrite.

There was an unpleasant feel to the mental recitation of his grievances. As though he were flicking at a barely clotted wound. Picking at something manifestly not healed yet. The tub was suddenly uncomfortable. The whole country was a cruel con, a scam run by an old monster. And once he got the country in too deep to quit, he would leverage that scam on the whole rest of the world. And now people were, slowly, barely, some of them, starting to realize that maybe they had been the suckers all along.

He unaccountably thought of Mom, evil thing that she was. She was a little microcosm of the Great Scam. She truly believed that if she just worked hard enough, sold enough of her phony goods, stole from enough people, and convinced them to steal for her, then she too could live in luxury apartments and enjoy fancy stand-alone bathtubs with water jets. Hell, she had probably sold dozens of varieties of herbal soaks over the years. Did she ever get the chance to really try any of them?

He could kind of imagine her filling the tub in a cheap motel and soaking in one of them, either right before or after "networking" some crown product ambassador, or diamond promotor or . . . oh, god, didn't she once claim to have "played" with a Triple Achiever? The title stuck in Truth's mind. Of all the scummy, scammy titles, *Triple Achiever* was certainly one of them. It was only memorable for being so half-assed.

Truth laughed darkly. Mom was getting screwed in every sense of the word, and she knew it. And she took it out on her kids and her scumbag husband and never once figured out that the Triple Achievers were also getting screwed. She just figured they were better at screwing and followed their example. This was it, wasn't it? This was the scam.

The promise of success, but for only those who most devotedly served their betters and oppressed their lessers. And with every step you went up the ladder, there was a higher Tier. A Quadruple Achiever, or Global Representative, or some damn thing. You compared what you got to what they got, and suddenly you had shit. Everything you hustled for was trash. Only the Global Reps had it good. Not realizing that there were Crown Reps above them, and so on, forever. You would never be truly rich. Never be truly free to enjoy what your cruelty bought.

Truth laughed and laughed and laughed, seeing it now. Seeing the Hell his mom lived in. What a petty little demon she had become, living there. But she would be the key to his whole strategy. Screw finding revolutionaries, and screw trying to make them. He was going to delegate to the real experts in creating anger. And if they did very, very well, he might just promote them to Silver Tier.

Truth smiled, stretched, and stepped out of the tub. Time for dinner. The revolution marches on its belly.

CHAPTER 19

DELICIOUS

Truth decided that he would combine his job with his hobby and hunt for pawns with his dinner. The concierge had been quite happy to arrange a reservation at Number Five Laurel—debatably the best restaurant in Gwaju but indisputably the most expensive. The concierge couldn't *quite* remember what room Truth was in, but that was clearly the concierge's problem, not the honored guest's!

Truth was depressed to see how effective Incisive was at persuading people he was a rich, powerful prick. It took him a solid five minutes to remember that, as a Level Four in Jeon, he definitionally was a rich, powerful prick. It was a significant adjustment from the last time he was in the country. Back then, nobody gave a damn about him, but they feared the lapel pin. Now? He didn't need the pin. He was simply above the mob. Which meant that it was time to test how well Incisive held up against his actual peers.

No more small-time pawns like De'Ponte. He needed elites—people with Levels and wealth enough to make them a substantial threat to local Starbrite operations. Elite revolt was a hell of a lot more common than a peasant revolt and infinitely more successful. Starbrite would react strongly to the rich making moves.

The carpet dropped him a block from Number Five Laurel. He wanted to scout a bit, to test things and give himself room to run if the Blessing of the Silent Forest and Incisive didn't hold up as well as he hoped against other Level Fours. He wouldn't try for full imperceptibility. Rather, he wanted to try and nudge everyone's perception. He looked himself over.

His scarf, the Freedom of the Terraces, looked rather classy in blue and white with a golden wheel logo on the end. He didn't recognize the team logo. As far as he knew, nobody played pitz outside of Siphios. It could be anything or anyone. A black fitted tee shirt, gray trousers, black shoes. No belt. No hat. Just enough stubble. His hair was getting a little long. Not badly so, but longer than he really liked.

He . . . felt a little weird about having someone other than Etenesh cut it. Which he knew perfectly well was silly. And yet.

Truth pushed his hair back, straightened his shoulders, and tried to figure out who he was going to be tonight.

He was in his thirties. Clearly fit and confident. Youthful until you started taking in the details. The faint cruelty in his eyes, the utter confidence in his posture.

He was older than he looked. Maybe a lot older than thirty. And clearly stunningly rich.

He was so rich, he could turn up to a fancy restaurant in casual clothes. Clothes that probably cost more than the suits everyone else was wearing, jewelry included. He would have to be staggeringly wealthy. Level Four in his thirties? No lapel pin? Oh, his possible origins would be *spicy* to speculate about. This was global-tier wealth.

Yes, he was the second generation of some globally wealthy family, clearly from Jeon but not known to the public. He had been sent to this little place to do a task for the family. And his family didn't weather the centuries by being soft or selecting heirs based on their kindness. He was like the sadistic bosses in his romance novels. Cruel, powerful, charismatic. To become his pet was *your* blessing. And he knew it.

Truth walked up to the door, seemingly ignoring the Level Threes and Fours stepping out of their luxury chariots and carriages, handing command medallions and threats to the valets. Carefully measuring their reactions. There were no whispers, only looks. Some admiring. Many yearning. More still warning, reminding their companions to *shut up*. He walked directly to the door. Those ahead, even those nominally on his level, cleared a path.

He said nothing to the head waiter, but that was no problem. He was expected. His table was waiting. Truth ordered the set menu, a fourteen-course tasting experience. He skipped the wine pairing and commanded the staff to create a bespoke non-alcoholic beverage to pair with each course. It was disturbingly easy to fall into the persona. It was the other part of the Scales of Incisive. The more weight the world attached to this identity, that identity being *a rich, powerful, prick*, the more he truly inhabited the role.

Truth casually surveyed the room. It was tastefully decorated. He was guessing on that, but it had the sort of stripped-down look he associated with extremely expensive things. Custom everything, he would bet. The tasting menu was loaded with off-world ingredients too. He may be one of the last people on this planet who would ever taste them.

He took inventory of the people dining. Mostly Level Threes, with a hell of a lot of seven-pointed stars on lapels. He noticed that none of the Starbrite people sat alone, or with other people from Starbrite. A lot of expensive suits and dresses pouring what he suspected were crushingly expensive bottles of wine for their Starbrite guests.

The notion of trying to network someone with a Starbrite pin via an expensive dinner was . . . grim, actually. Now that he thought about it. It meant that you didn't have a better option. How screwed did you have to be that you could afford dinner there but still need to burn money to impress a Starbrite employee? Even a private dinner at home would be a better choice, right? Or something? He was vague on how that all worked.

In a room full of people eating very expensive food, Truth was the only one smiling while he chewed. The Starbrite people looked tense or low-key pissed that they had to take the meeting. He could read the body language—these were not confident, happy, profit-maximizing, value-generation heroes. They didn't know what was going on any more than anyone else did, but they were getting leaned on for information and support anyway.

Truth chuckled darkly as he dug into the tiny plates of food. He understood why higher-level people, financially and in cultivation, referred to lower-levels as ants. They scurried around, warring on each other, and none could see more than a fraction of an inch in front of them. Just blindly following the leader. And so easily crushed, too. Well. So far, he could confidently say that no one was piercing through his Scales, so he relaxed, enjoyed his food, and slowly picked out his targets.

Truth didn't quite understand the nuance of what he was doing. The Level Threes wisely chose not to glace too much toward him. Confidence was always attractive, and right now? Even disguised, he was a bonfire in a forest of moths. The Level Fours were less reserved. This was not a big city, and he was a stranger, brash and bold, splashing into their little pond. And since Truth was making no effort to hide his cultivation, he was making quite a large splash.

He screamed power, wealth, and connections. And he wasn't scared. They didn't want to be talking to whoever they were talking to. They wanted to be talking to *him*.

After the fourteenth tiny plate, Truth sat back with a contented sigh. He had no damn idea what he had just eaten. They told him what the food was, but he still didn't know what he had eaten. It was only technically food. Eating was . . . the mechanism, he supposed. The way you had the experience of dining at Number Five Laurel.

One dish was simply called "Bread and Butter," which consisted of a single piece of bread and a rough knob of butter, served on a sheet of basalt. It was one of the more memorable things he ever ate. The sheet of basalt was quite thin but long. It required four fit-looking waiters to hold it in place while his "gastronomic experience coordinator" explained how to eat it.

The waiters would hold the slab. He would pick up the bread in his left hand, scoop up the butter with the knife held in his right hand, and "Thoroughly enrobe the upper surface of the bread, appreciating the sensory journey the experience takes you on."

He was then to bring the bread and butter close, take a long smell, then eat it. His eyes should be closed after the sniff, and he was firmly encouraged to "Devote your full emotional commitment to the ingredients, their journey, the dish and its journey, and how they have all culminated in your journey."

All while the waiters stood waiting, holding roughly a hundred kilos of stone between them. Truth did as instructed. It really was excellent bread. Soft, a touch sweet, a little sour, the crust crunched satisfyingly, and the crumb had a soft but resilient chew. The butter was the best he had ever eaten. Rich, salty, creamy, a hint of grass and a touch of sweet. When Truth opened his eyes, the first things he saw were the waiters, strictly facing away from him. He exhaled slowly, leaning back into his seat. It wasn't about the food. It was about the experience. He savored every bite.

The waiter brought over a little tray of nuts and tiny two-centimeter cakes, "a gift from the kitchen." Truth smiled once again, looking at them, then looked up and around the room casually. Now, who exactly would be paying for this meal? The Revolution needed financial backers.

He didn't touch the cakes. He just sat back and waited. He didn't move a centimeter. Just sat there, relaxed as could be.

"Pardon my interruption, but I think you are expecting me."

The one bold enough to actually come to his table was a woman. Not brash, and smart enough to not try seduction. She might be Level Four, but she was also old enough to be his mother. Actually, given the beautification magics and glamors available in Jeon, she might be old enough to be his grandmother. A tough old bird, then, but still scared. Same as everyone. Truth nodded and indicated the seat across from him.

"Thank you. My name is—" Truth raised a hand and stopped her. He pointed to a little cake. He then picked one up and ate it. She did the same. Truth enjoyed the little bite—it was so sweet! The rich bitterness of the chocolate frosting seemed to unfold in layers of flavor. His enjoyment was obvious. Hers was forced.

"Thank you. I . . ." She clearly didn't know where to begin. Truth didn't say anything. He didn't know what he really wanted to say, so he just looked at her. A little smile on his face. She looked torn between laughter and outrage.

"You know, this is absurd. I own five major companies across southern Jeon. I directly employ more than two thousand people. My net worth, until last month I suppose, was a hotly debated question between my accountants and my tax lawyers. People sold their souls, in one case literally, for the chance to even talk to me. Now I am desperately hoping that a stranger in a restaurant can save my life, and the life of my family."

Truth smiled a little more at that, but only for a moment. He said nothing. Just looked at her, waiting.

She rubbed her thumb over her fingers and glanced away. When she turned back, she tried to fix Truth with a glare. "Who are you?" Truth let the smile slip away from his face. He didn't know who this person was. Just that she was one of those people who kept the slums going. She did not get to speak to him that way. Disrespectful animals get put down. She paled, feeling the certainty of death settling around her.

"I apologize. Please. I. I am very sorry. I won't make that mistake again." She looked down at her hands, not thinking or caring of how she looked to everyone else in the room. Truth eased off the killing intent. Silence returned. He waited for her to speak again.

The silence was painful, filling with the woman's fear. The young master was cruel and patient; everyone could see that. But he could reward the obedient. She remembered the little cake. Her eyes widened momentarily. The cake—when she followed instructions and sat. When she was silent until invited to speak. He was inviting her to speak now. Provided she did so properly.

"I am looking for shelter. Primarily for myself. My family, too, if I can. I am looking for . . . hope. To either get off this world or survive the collapse. Even if I sold everything for what it was really worth, I couldn't afford a ticket. I have no hope of finding 'her,' whoever 'she' is. And I know perfectly well I can't punish the person responsible for her disappearance."

Truth allowed a tiny smile. She was emboldened.

"Give me something to cling to, and I will pledge my service to you. I will bring my strength, which is still worth something, and whatever value my network has. And so long as the word has meaning, my wealth will serve your own. But I need that thing. That line to the future. Can—" She bowed her head again. Recovered. "*Will* you offer me that?"

Truth smiled softly. He extended his hand. Tentatively, she reached out. He took her hand and turned it palm-up. He raised his index finger and looked her in the eyes. "This is going to hurt," his eyes promised. She didn't move. Using the barest hint of the Fangs, he carved coordinates on her palm and a date. It was so sharp, she didn't feel the pain until he was done and the blood started to bead. It would scar. They both knew that. She would never dare to remove it.

He leaned over, started to whisper, then stopped. His eyes crinkled, and he shook his head slightly. Stood and walked out the door of the restaurant. At the precise boundary between the interior and exterior, he vanished from their sight.

CHAPTER 20

FRAGILE SYSTEMS

Truth lay sprawled on the roof of the restaurant, trying to bring his heart rate under control. *What the hell was that?*

He knew that Incisive was impacted by the beliefs of others, and he had been running the Scales damn hard while he was in the restaurant. He knew who he was the whole time. But why the hell did he start acting like one of the arrogant young masters he used to bodyguard? Actually, no, he was acting even more high-handed.

He needed someone to get out there and stir the pot. When things were traced back to her (which they rapidly would be), there wouldn't be a soul in Starbrite or Jeon Security who didn't believe there was a mastermind pulling the strings of the rebellion in southern Jeon.

And they would be hunting her hard. Once she started digging into those numbers . . . Well, it wasn't like her well-being meant any more to him than De'Ponte's. Happy thought, maybe he could get her to whip up counterrevolutionary forces. Launch her own wave of assassinations against "collaborators and fellow travelers."

<<I think you just discovered a new wrinkle in how to use Incisive,>> the System said.

Oh?

<<You were using pretty much the whole spell at the end there—foresight you keep going all the time already, the Scales for the persona, the Fangs to cut that message into her hand, and the Venom to impose your will on her. Pushing on the thoughts and desires she already had to bring her into line with what you want. Stacked with the killing intent that may or may not be a gift from your . . . "Rough Patron's" legacy, you did an effective little bit of mental conditioning on her.>>

Okay? How is that different from just making a strong impression for anyone else?

<<You somewhat forcibly impressed the reality you were presenting onto her psyche. The rest of the room didn't catch it quite as hard, but I'd bet everyone in that restaurant who wasn't working in the kitchen is ready to swear on their mother's eyes that the second generation of some ancient clan ate at Number Five Laurel tonight. Whatshername just became the focus of a lot of attention. And is probably going to be getting a lot of courtesy calls from people looking to read her palm.>>

Oh, we can't have that. Truth grinned. *It would ruin the mystique.*

<<Well, she is Level Four. Ought to be able to look after herself and certainly should be able to hire those capable of keeping away the flies.>>

Mmm. All right, let's follow her and see just who she is. Maybe do a little B&E. The revolution needs funding, after all.

<<Going to test out full unnoticeability?>>

No, I'll admit I don't really trust it for someone my level and higher. Merkovah said it should work on anyone not specially equipped below the peak of Level Five, but . . .

<<You don't want to test that too casually. Right. But how are you going to follow her, then?>>

Steal a carriage and trail her. Easy enough to blend in as another carriage on the road.

<<Now, that's a top-notch plan! Say, Mr. Mastermind, what makes you think she came in a carriage?>>

Eh?

A cloud settled down in front of the restaurant. As long as a commercial wagon, faint rainbows of light shining through the pearl-white wisps. Like the cloud held a thunderstorm of colors within it. The woman walked quickly out the door, left hand wrapped in a napkin. The head waiter, as well as much of the staff, bowed as she hurriedly hopped up onto the cloud. The driver immediately ordered the cloud to rise and sped away, deeper into the city.

Shit!

He grabbed Thrush's command medallion. "Attend me at once!" The imp appeared in a burst of black smoke. Before it could speak, Truth pointed at the rapidly shrinking cloud. "Follow that cloud. Find out where it is going and who owns it. Do so discreetly. Do not allow yourself to be spotted or captured."

"Your servant obeys." The imp flapped hard and was gone.

Truth shook his head. He wasn't too optimistic. He hopped off the side of the building and caught the staff before they went back in. He was just a Citizen to them now. "Wow, what a cloud! Who was that?"

The head waiter couldn't even be bothered to look at him, but one of the junior waiters looked over at him and said "Madame Gullvar. Three Rivers Group. Best mind where you put your eyes, lest someone pluck them out."

Truth didn't know if he should laugh or give the waiter a slap. He settled for saying "Thanks" and walking away. All right, he had part of a name and a business name. He could work with that. He started jogging in the same direction the carpet went, but the fun had gone out of high-speed running.

I want a flying cloud.

<<No, you want a firebird. Faster, more expensive, and it's a giant bird made out of fire.>>

Yeah. All right, I would settle for a flying cloud while my firebird was on order.

<<Reasonable. Now hail a carpet, peasant.>>

Truth did just that. Thrush caught up after about twenty minutes. Between the two of them and the carpet driver, they got to the residential tower Madame Gullvar lived in and apparently owned. Her residence was on the roof.

Gullvar had built a mansion forty stories in the air. A stacked series of glass boxes, with a tightly mowed lawn, harshly pruned trees, and some enormous blobs of abstract statuary. It, in Truth's opinion, was painfully boring. No interesting spirits wandering around or wondrous enchanted creations beautifying and defending the grounds. There were people sweeping, mopping, patrolling. Level One and Two staff and security.

There was also a very respectable collection of defenses—countersurveillance system, comms setup, anti-summons ward, anti-material ward, anti-spell ward, glamor filter, air filter, disease filter, anti-fungal arrays, precipitation filtering systems, golem command nets, and, naturally, the music system. Truth spent almost as long sorting through what all the various enchantments and wards were than he did getting to the mansion.

His appreciation for good spellwork notwithstanding, the bodyguard in him faintly despised the setup. Each system was very good. All of them would have been considered state-of-the-art or better when he went in the well. No weird "innovative" designs, either. These were well-tested arrays with good service histories, regular updates to the enchantments, and good support by the component manufacturers. However, when you had multiple standing systems, particularly systems made by different designers and manufacturers, you had interoperability problems.

A mansion like this would have at least one full-time array master on staff whose job it would be to keep this mess up and running. And they needed to be *good* array masters because you would not want to see, for example, the summoning ward think the water-creation talismans were a water elemental incursion or the blackwater banishment system blocked by an overzealous anti-spell ward. The glamor wards were famously temperamental and rarely played well with the music or scry systems. The golem command nets were thankfully more robust, but they did so by being completely separate from, and incompatible with, other systems.

A decision reached after several extremely expensive lawsuits, apparently.

Gullvar could afford excellent staff, and the spells were layered and connected about as well as these things could be managed. That being said, the dense network of arrays was starting to make Truth a little suspicious. You were definitely someone at Level Four, a person of power and status. But a-mansion-on-top-of-a-skyscraper money? She either inherited it or there was a powerhouse behind her. Possibly both. But if that was true, why was she fishing for help at Number Five Laurel?

Did her backer die? Or did she suddenly lose their support? It would be very plausible, especially with the increasing violence and chaos. Or . . . *Oh. Hah. She said it herself. Her power is based on money, not cultivation. And at the end of the month, everything is getting rolled into credits, and none of these people really believe that they are going to still be rich at the end of it.*

Truth grinned nastily. There must be an ungodly wave of kidnappings and murders going on now, trying to derail the changeover. None of which would stop it, because it was coming from Starbrite, and Starbrite has more Level Sevens than your corporate board has directors.

Sorry, lady, Truth thought. *Looks like you should have put that money into cultivation aids, not a fancier house. That's what I did.* Truth examined that thought for a moment, firmly decided to gloss over any inconvenient details, and began breaking in. He recognized most of these systems, and none of them had some obscure operating principle he couldn't understand. Between Starbrite, Siphios, and vocational school, it was just a matter of time, not skill.

Half an hour later, he had significantly upwardly revised his opinion of Gullvar, her array master, and her security team. The wards were proving considerably more robust than he had expected, and a lot of long-standing interoperability problems had apparently been fixed in the last few years. He was getting in, just . . . uncomfortably slowly.

While he was defeating a particularly fiddly bit of bloodline identification (apparently, there were creatures that were close to but not quite human? News to him) a flying cloud approached the landing pad. Smaller, no rainbows, but still a genuine-article Zorusi Soaring Spirit, with the optional comfort package and the "Summer Dream" color trim. Came in at a cool point seven five mill back in the day. Probably more now.

Firebird. Firebird. Firebird. Gonna save the girl, grab the, like, ten people on this planet I'd like to keep alive, get off-world, and get a sweet-ass firebird. Bet they even have better firebirds than what we have here. Goes harder, faster, longer. Maybe they shoot searing beams of light from their eyes.

<<You want to steal that cloud.>>

So much. So goddamn much. They were the definition of impossible-dream-level luxury for me when I was a teen.

<<Maybe you can do a deal with the Starbrite Clan for a tricked-out ride since they won't need to ship as many bodies.>>

Valid point well made. Any idea what to do here? All I can think of is looping the self-check line back on itself and cutting out the permitted-visitor microarray. It won't hold up all that long, which sucks, because I don't want to spook her just yet.

<<Use the species-screen array to designate your undead ass as a separate species, one that is explicitly permitted. Like a beautiful, unnatural, songbird. Cheep-cheep.>>

There is no way that will . . . Truth traced a few lines and reviewed the talisman architecture. *Okay, but it's going to screen for humans automatically . . .* It did not. It built on top of the entry whitelist the master ward system used. *I mean, can it even determine species so granularly, it would understand a category of "just me"?* Truth thought it through a while longer. He was still quite human, but between the body refinement and all the national treasures, it was fair to say that he was a half-step better than the overwhelming majority of the species on this planet.

Truth carefully nicked a finger and let a single drop fall on the pea-sized golden sample-processing microarray. The blood was annihilated by the spell. The various arrays and microarrays went to work, picking out identifiers, confirming that they met the needs of the identification systems, adding him to the approved whitelist, updating the security systems, running the checks and verifications that would ensure the appropriate access, and, lastly, making sure he couldn't fiddle with the settings of the sound system.

He felt a warm tingle from the wards, then nothing.

<<Cheep-cheep-charoo.>>

Think they can do me a firebird in blue and gold?

<<Can't hurt to ask. Wait, look at who's getting off that cloud!>>

Striding off the cloud was a mountain of a man, his loose shirt barely covering a physique that even Truth could envy. Brutal features came together in a rough handsomeness, so far from the delicate refinement that was popular with the men of Jeon. His eyes burned with red and gold, visible even from where Truth was hiding, well away from the landing pad. All features that could be purchased there in Jeon. Pricey, but money could do it.

What couldn't be faked was the horrible sense of alienation. Like a too-real doll suddenly turning and looking at you. Gullvar's wards were built the way they were for a reason. Who or whatever this person was, they weren't entirely human.

CHAPTER 21

WHAT'S NEXT

The staff of the mansion assembled on the steps, Madame Gullvar at the top. They bowed as one. The descended deity was worthy of that much respect. Truth pegged the large man at Level Five, but that wasn't the source of the oppression. It was his sheer presence. If Truth had a local superreality edge on almost everybody, this man was the "almost." Truth moved out of sight, went very still, and ran Incisive as hard as he could. He didn't bother trying for total imperceptibility. He was just a maintenance guy. Things need maintenance. And he was just the maintenance guy.

"We welcome Young Master Remu!" Gullvar said loudly. Still bowed, as was the entire staff of the mansion. Even though he was pretty sure he was unseen, Truth did the same. Not a good time to find out that you overestimated yourself.

"My thanks. You may rise." The staff stood from their bow. Truth could feel the pressure of the man move, like the heat of the sun as it crossed the sky. He went up the steps. Truth assumed that he went off with Gullvar.

Truth was torn—he desperately wanted to know who this was and what was being said. On the other hand, he had no idea about the layout of the mansion, the security measures, a safe way to listen in, nothing. It would be stupid to rush in. He took another look at the wards. His bypass was invisible unless specifically and carefully looked for, and even then, it would look like an accident with no consequences. He packed up his tools and quietly walked to the elevators.

He focused on his breathing and on keeping his body language at the appropriate level of tension. A diligent worker. Worried. Job done, on to the next job. Truth desperately wished he had a toolbox or something more plausible than a backpack to help sell the illusion. Fortunately, the people of Jeon would have no trouble believing he was Blouth Crometche, Talisman Maintenance Specialist First Class, Eprington Talisman and Fetish, Employee #372 (Part of the Starbrite Family of Companies).

He didn't collapse in relief when the elevator doors closed. He looked straight ahead all the way down. Even when he suddenly had an itch, he very visibly scratched. Not trying to hide anything. He walked out of the private elevator, across the street, down four blocks, into a twenty-four-hour diner, ordered a coffee and a bowl of fried rice, *and then* collapsed into a relieved heap.

Truth racked his brain, trying to figure out what the hell that was. He had seen spirits shaped like a human, but this wasn't that. This was something human-ish.

Human and a bit. Something beyond the common masses. He had no idea what such a thing could be. Nobody had ever mentioned anything like it.

He knew that sometimes, possession by an angel or devil could result in dramatic changes in appearance, but that was like something wearing a human-shaped suit. There was almost always something visibly wrong with them—lumps moving under the skin, an inability to speak properly, gross deformities—something. When demons did turn up looking "human," it was only to a point—none of them could really pass for long, even insubstantial things like succubae.

This guy wasn't any of that. He was like a bodybuilder's notion of the perfect human, with a brutishly handsome face and the eyes of an emperor. Provided the emperor's eyes glowed scarlet and gold.

Truth scooped up a spoonful of fried rice. Pork and pineapple. Fancy. And pretty decent. Not the best fried rice he had ever eaten, but right now? Delicious. He ate it up like he was angry at it, washing it down with the free tea that came with it.

He wasn't going to go anywhere near Gullvar's place for a while. In fact, he was going to give that place a solid twenty-four hours to settle down. Just in case. It was late at night, it had been an . . . interesting day, and he needed a break. He shook himself loose. He'd go back and see if his usual suite was available at the hotel, then tomorrow he'd check in on De'Ponte and his thugs. Had they been scooped up yet? It would be good to find out. He finished his bowl, downed the rest of the tea, and walked over to the cashier.

"Good meal. How much is it?"

"Thirty wen, please."

"HOW MUCH?"

"Thirty wen. Pork fried rice is twenty-three, and seven for the tea. Prices are on the wall." The cashier looked both helpless and frustrated. She had clearly had this conversation a lot recently. Truth dug out some of his rapidly dwindling supply of DePonte's cash and paid her.

"Isn't the tea usually free?"

"Not anymore. Everything is so expensive these days, we can't afford to serve even the cheapest tea for free."

"Damn. Guess I'm lucky to get pork in my rice."

"We put it up as a special. We don't always have it in stock these days, and pineapple is even rarer. Our usual vegetable fried rice is twelve wen a bowl."

Truth remembered Merkovah saying nobody was growing animal feed anymore. Looked like the shortages were starting to hit Jeon. His mind involuntarily jerked back to the bad old days—

"Say, you don't get your pork from a woman called Rebah in Harban, do you?"

"Eeeeh? How could we get our pork from so far away? We have a deal with a meat packer west of the city; they let us know when they have stuff available. We take what we can get."

"Ah, right, right. Makes sense. Thank you. Sorry I flipped out; you can tell it's been a while."

She put on a business smile, nodded, and waited for him to leave.

Truth woke, rested and refreshed. He gave himself a good scrub in the shower, and in an act of pure pettiness, he put on a never-before-worn set of clothes. Having cleaned and scrubbed to the exacting specifications of De'Ponte, he then turned to the question of murder. He had promised to kill Wothera Hersch, hotel manager at the Hanging Orchid Hotel on Czerni Square. But would he?

He had now enjoyed the involuntary hospitality of the Hanging Orchid Hotel for several nights and had come to the conclusion that it was actually a very good hotel. He had no particular opinion of Manager Hersch as an employer, and taking out the soon-to-be slave overseers had always been a bit remote as a way to draw Starbrite attention. At least doing it retail was. Contracting it out to De'Ponte and his ilk was a bit more plausible. But last night made that irrelevant.

Gullvar had definitely summoned "Young Master Remu" as a result of their meeting. Which meant that the unnatural bastard would be aware of it and likely taking steps. A Level Five asking about things that should have been a total secret? It wouldn't be any ordinary PMC squad they deployed to shut him down.

Truth frowned, thinking it through. Why was Gullvar at Number Five Laurel? She was clearly sincere when she said she was looking for an out, for shelter. But why, when she had the patronage of Young Master Remu? Unless he was badly misunderstanding the nature of their relationship. He felt like he had gone fishing and had gotten hooked instead.

Oh, hell. That was exactly it. She was bait. She probably was under some kind of compulsion and didn't even remember Remu. Looking for other, like-minded sorts. Maybe as targets for recruitment by Remu. Maybe as competition to remove. Gullvar was pretty far from a damsel, but she was definitely distressed and looking for a rescue. And there was Young Master Remu, waiting in the bushes to bag a white knight.

Truth quietly swore to himself. He was really not cut out for spy games. It *looked* like it should work out, and he was definitely going to search the mansion, but . . .

<<*Oh, please, don't pretend that was all a cunning scheme on your part. You loved the whole thing in the restaurant. Being the most powerful person in the room. Having her scared, begging. Eating a full meal and just walking away without paying. Don't kid yourself—you love it.*>>

Truth really didn't want to think about that.

<<*You probably need to, actually, even if it isn't right this minute. I'm not saying this to screw with you. You need to understand that part of yourself. If you were a bit more aware of where your head was at, you might have picked up on where the "arrogant young master" persona was pushing you. And you didn't even try to push back on it—you leaned in even harder.*>>

I really don't have time for this.

<<Fine, but it's not like it's going to go away. It was one of your character traits I was pushing on when we were both working for Starbrite.>>

Truth parsed that last sentence.

When you say "pushing on . . ."

<<I mean I was trying to make it stronger, bring it to the forefront of your personality. "Arrogant sadist" is a potentially desirable personality type for a Starbrite Violence Specialist. But I didn't put it there, Truth. It was in your soul before I was.>>

Truth had decided to give Wothera Hersch a pass. Mainly because he thought killing her was pointless, to a lesser extent because he had no expectation of actually getting paid for the hit. On that point, the street De'Ponte's apartment building was on seemed remarkably quiet. Truth felt the hairs on the back of his neck rise—not so much a warning from Incisive as his inner slumrat.

There were four old-timers sitting on a terrace, playing dominoes. Just so happened that the terrace was attached to a cafe at the top of the block. What looked like a very lazy roadwork crew down the bottom of the street. Truth kept right on walking. De'Ponte had been nabbed. The only question was: how fast did he give up his "employer"?

Truth smiled up at the cool spring sun. Few things he enjoyed quite so much as dropping a gangster directly in the shit. Then he frowned up at the sun. He was short of cash and really did want to steal more from De'Ponte. Gullvar would not be a great source of walking-around money. From what he had observed, the richer you were, the less actual cash you had on hand outside of an emergency reserve in a safe. All the rest was in bank accounts or investments.

Well, time to stir the pot a bit. It wouldn't get him any money, but it would help him feel better. When you got right down to it, he rated cops about the same as gangsters but with more power and self-righteousness. Not like they were doing much to help in the slums. He walked over to the "work van" the undercovers were using. Now . . . what would be sufficiently upsetting while remaining cryptic enough to invite paranoia?

It was a real problem. Truth stood there, completely stumped, for ten minutes. Just not the kind of creativity he was used to using. He was half-tempted to ask the undercovers, possibly while pointing out that most road crews didn't carry stun batons and coma-cuffs tucked into their waistbands. Eventually, he decided on a message of support. Of positivity. A message that would *definitely* ensure De'Ponte's comfort and well-being in jail.

He coated an index finger with the Fangs and, in his best handwriting, wrote: *Touch one of ours, we will take ten of yours. We know where you sleep. De'Ponte or your kids. Choose.*

Good deed done; Truth briskly walked away. Maybe he was wrong about Gullvar and she did keep cash around the place. First, assemble a few extra B&E tools, working until lunchtime. Then, a little light burglary at Gullvar's. Midafternoon should see most of the higher-levels out of the house, leaving only the domestics. No sense in wasting the day. He should probably check the dead drop for messages in case Merkovah got a reply back fast. Horrible thought—he should probably check in on his . . . co-religionists? . . . too. There was almost certainly a colony of Ghūl in the city. Perhaps they could play a role. Truth sighed. The days were just so *packed*.

CHAPTER 22

BETTER HOMES AND GARDENS

Truth rolled his shoulders. In theory, the Meditations of Valentinian should be keeping his body supple far beyond what mere stretching could do. On the other hand, working hunched over a bench for a whole morning had left him with a stiff back and aching shoulders. It was probably all in his head, but it felt real.

Not a wasted morning. He had a nice little selection of tools there, most of it fairly stock stuff from the big box talisman-supply store. Just a few little modifications to some pathways, underpowering some arrays, overpowering others. Little tweaks. He packed everything into a soft tool bag and took a last minute to make himself a name tag, just in case.

He looked at the sticker and laughed. His "just in case" had really changed since his visit to the Silent Forest.

Truth caught a carpet back to last night's diner and walked from there to Gullvar's apartment building. It was profoundly unlikely that anyone would be checking carpet-ride logs, but in Jeon, the carpet drivers *did* keep logs, and there was absolutely no need to make things easy on some plain-clothed prick.

He was down to his last hundred wen. He chuckled grimly as he walked up to the private entrance. No need to fish for scrap these days. His objection to a life of crime was always that it wasn't much of a life, and it rarely paid. Now long-term thinking just seemed silly.

The access panel was unchanged from yesterday, and so was the spell needed to bypass it. The lock clicked open without him breaking stride. He almost felt bad for the technicians who had made it—all that effort going into making an encrypted authentication system, and it was completely worthless against an attacker who knew what they were doing. You could trip the emergency unlock release *without engaging the fire alarm* if you just used a firefighter's entry tool. They sold them in specialty hardware stores. The bypass was a building-code requirement. It was faster than using the amulet and code phrase by design.

Truth had never worked firefighting, so he had limited appreciation for the necessities of the job. He just knew it made bodyguarding harder and raiding easier.

The elevator-access system was a bit trickier to bypass. You could go *down* without using any particular tools, but going *up* required either a pass (the use of which was logged by a bound spirit) or the firefighters' access, which did set off an alarm . . . and was logged.

Someone had a brain when they designed the elevator security system—every usage was logged. Truth didn't know how often, if at all, those logs were checked against the door entry system and the mansion wards, and didn't care to find out. So, he did the same thing he had done yesterday when he was in a rush. Nothing. And just like yesterday, "nothing" worked perfectly.

Nice, smooth ride on this elevator, Truth thought. *Sometimes, those lift talismans don't get properly maintained and the force transfer is rough. This is smooth as ice.* The elevator lifted up to the top floor. The doors didn't open. Truth smiled anyway. He loved "rich logic."

It made perfect sense from a certain point of view. From a security perspective, you wanted the elevator on the top floor where it would be hard to attack. From a fire-safety perspective, you wanted it up top for easy evacuation. It could only ever be at the top or the bottom of the building; there were no other floors to consider. So, have it automatically return to the top when it's idling. After all, anyone in there without a command medallion would be trapped, just waiting for security to collect them.

And if people had to wait a little longer for their elevator at the bottom? Anyone using the elevator was not arriving by air. Therefore, elevator users were poor and weak. Their time and comfort were not worth considering. Truth grinned and stuck in a short pry bar wrapped in a little soft cloth tape between the doors. A quick flex, and he was back on the roof, looking over at the mansion and the ward. He double-checked his "fix" on the ward. It was still good. He walked right in.

Amazing how much of burglary was just knowing how systems work. No sneaky creeping, dodging tripwires or super secret spy tools. Just . . . "How does this thing work? And how can I abuse it?" *Some of the regular security guys did physical-penetration testing work. All jokes aside, I should get into that. Got to be better money than general talisman maintenance.*

The mansion remained its profoundly boring self. Truth wondered if he had become jaded after seeing Siphios and growing up in the architectural madness of Harban. A mansion on top of an apartment tower *should* be really impressive. This felt . . . pathetic. A series of glass boxes stacked on top of an apartment building, which was a series of concrete boxes. There was a yard, a few dwarf trees, some bushes trimmed into odd shapes, and the landing pad. Two tons of cast-bronze blobs on stone slabs, each "art piece" likely costing as much as a nice house.

Not that he knew about art. It just seemed like rich-person logic. Expensive plus incomprehensible plus bronze/marble/other equals Art.

He could see staff walking around, maintaining the grounds. They all had gray jumpsuits with the Three Rivers logo on the back. They didn't have the face of Citizens about to get the System. Figures. A whole damn mansion, and she hired Denizens to work the grounds. Grounds staff were not allowed in the house proper, he'd bet. And the domestics would enter through the rear.

It took a real effort of will not to walk right up the front steps and kick in the door. He was a long way from the slums, but that *Provisional Denizen* stain never quite scrubbed off. Firmly reminding himself that he was on the job, he walked around the back and into the staff area. He blended. Everyone was Level One. They didn't even know he was there.

Truth moved through the rooms steadily. The staff areas were surveilled by recording talismans and bound spirits; the family areas had motion-detector spells, sound-detection alarms, panic buttons, trap demons, and all the usual paraphernalia of the rich and paranoid. Truth noticed how new some of the physical defenses were—the armored glass, the steel-core doors. *Can't rely on magic much longer*. He wondered how they were stocked for spears.

The interior of the house curiously matched the exterior. Everything was a sort of beige or gray, though even the gray was softened and muted—the gray of a heavy cloud, not a thunderhead. Rooms decorated with light tan sofas and contrasting throw pillows in washed-out green. Every room had a single item that was the designated contrast point—a canary-yellow chair sitting across from the cucumber sofa and the slate-green rug hemmed in by the winter-olive-painted walls.

Truth didn't know the word *liminal*, which was a pity. It was the right word. He was stuck with *boring and borderline creepy*. The art on the wall wasn't any better. Some of it was just blobs of color. Meaningless, sterile, inoffensive. *Vacuous* was another word he didn't know, but he certainly knew the emotion it inspired.

He explored room after room—sitting rooms, a game room, a small library, guest bedrooms, bathrooms, on and on and on. Every surface polished to a mirror sheen. Not a single fingerprint. No worn-down high-traffic carpets. No chipped paint on the doors or smudges on the walls. Out of morbid curiosity, Truth ran his finger along the top of a doorframe connecting a guest bedroom to the attached bathroom. Not a speck of dust. In Siphios, he would have assumed a busy demon was hard at work. In Jeon? His bet was a golem or, more likely, an obsessive team of maids.

What he didn't see was a single book that looked like it had actually been read, or a tray with change or charms by the door. No wall of "I'm So Great" pictures, or framed portraits of honored ancestors. The house felt staged. That was the best way he could think of it—like it was set up to be looked at, not actually lived in. Someone had spent an awful lot of money to make something completely devoid of personality.

He came upon a room that was clearly intended to be a sort of family room, set up to watch scry from a sofa. Truth carefully looked it over. No rings on the tables, no evidence of spills, no crumbs in the upholstery. He gently ran his hand over the cushions. Had they ever been sat on? He really couldn't tell. It didn't look like it.

Where did Gullvar sleep? She had a family; did any of them live there? This didn't even feel like a decoy—actual decoys would be made to look real. It wasn't a glamor or illusion—he was checking for that, and he wasn't easy to glamor in the first place. He kept working his way up. He found bedrooms, including what was intended to be a master bedroom. The closet had been cleaned out, the drawers emptied, even the soap in the bathroom replaced with a new, unopened bar. There was a safe built into the back wall of the closet. It was hanging open, empty.

Truth ran his hands over the shelves and along the back wall of the safe. No false bottoms or hidden panels. Or dust.

He had run out of house. He had carefully searched from bottom to top. No hidden anything except, perhaps, the family that was supposedly living there. But the grounds were exquisitely maintained, the house was kept in impeccable order, and they had received a Level Five something-or-other there. Which they absolutely wouldn't have done if there was the slightest chance that person would be offended by the conditions of the home.

Truth was frankly afraid to collapse on the furniture. He had an irrational fear that if he so much as creased a sheet, horrible monsters would come bursting out of the walls and eat him alive. He sat on the (lid closed, sanitized, water turned bright purple by the cleaning agent) toilet and tried to figure it out.

Could the residence be in an apartment below? It would be a nifty piece of misdirection, but unless there was a *very* hidden entrance, there would be no way to get from the mansion directly into the true living space. Also, if the mansion was intended to throw people off, it was a complete failure.

Could Gullvar be up on the roof? Somehow? For some damn reason?! That actually tickled a memory. He retraced his steps through the top floor and found a closet with a long string hanging from a hatch; he had thought it was to access a crawlspace or something. He gingerly pulled the string. With startlingly little effort, the hatch swung down and a metal staircase unfolded.

Gullvar was on the roof. Fantastic. *Whole damn mansion, and she's up on the roof.* Truth hadn't known he had arsonist tendencies, so he had learned something new about himself today. He couldn't wait to burn this thing to the ground.

Truth moved up the steps, quietly, carefully. No alarms, no hidden sentries. He pushed open the door at the top of the stairs and stepped out onto the roof. The air felt thick, prickly. It reminded him a little of the execution grounds on top of Nag Hamadi, where arrays were used to overpressure the victim's apertures and explode their soul. This was weaker, of course.

His first thought was a cosmic-ray-gathering array. His next thought was a demand to know why there was a metal coffin standing in the middle of a ring of iron chests. And on the subject of iron chests, why did they all seem to have blue mist boiling around them? Lastly, just who the hell was Gullvar?

CHAPTER 23

SENSIBLE PRECAUTIONS

Truth slowly walked around the roof, examining the circle of chests and the metal coffin at their center. The blue mists rising out of the chests were thin and cold, like smoke from a dying fire. The mist was being pulled through the air by the array and saturating the coffin. From what he could see, there were intakes in the coffin for the mist to seep into. He squatted next to one, trying to get a closer look at what it was exactly. The spellwork wasn't familiar to him. There were structures that seemed intended to gather cosmic rays and others to contain cosmic rays, but what the chests then did with those rays was unclear.

Each chest was plugged into an array, and the arrays were connected to the coffin, which had its own arrays and sub-arrays, all of which were built into the larger cosmic-ray-gathering array on the roof. It was all systems within systems, like a giant funnel feeding into different filters, then collected in a flask. Nine chests around one coffin. Those numbers weren't a coincidence. But why? He examined the chests, finding them identical. Mass-produced, he would guess, at heartbreaking expense.

Things that were mass-produced had tags, labels, and logos. Truth set to examining one of the chests without touching it. Somewhere on there would be some indication of the maker. Usually, it is very obvious. So, why was it acting bashful now? He got right up close and gave it a really intense glare. Every join, every seam, every microarray got a harsh look. And . . . there was nothing.

Some of the components were painted a slightly different color or were made of slightly different-colored materials. Occasionally changing from one color to another mid-component. That was it. As anonymous as a ransom note. Outside of the ring of chests were a desk and a standing wardrobe. Behind the rather nice and ornate desk was a single chair. Off to one side was a toilet. Not enclosed in any way—the same model toilet used in the rest of the house, sitting right out in the open. Truth got up and strode over to the desk. Maybe there would be something in there to shed some light on this.

The chair wasn't rigged with anything nasty, and the locks on the desk might have triggered bombs, but the bombs were tiny, designed to destroy the contents of the drawers. It took a surprising amount of work to get them disarmed, purely because some clever bastard had put all the components *inside* the desk, so the only channel to attack the devices non-destructively was through the goddamn physical keyhole. Which each drawer had.

You had to use, from what he could tell, an actual bit of metal to do something to some other bits of metal that would let you turn the cylinder and move the bolt. Truth considered himself a fairly paranoid individual, but he had to admit defeat there. This was freak-level. This was *do some meditation, drink some water, and maybe hit the pet café* levels of swirling madness. Just . . . use a spell. Lots of good ones on the market.

He spent longer figuring out how to defeat a three-centimeter-long collection of metal scraps than he did to break the multilayered wards over the whole damn mansion. And sure, it made sense. If the magic was getting unreliable or would soon be unreliable, use things that didn't require cosmic rays. Between the physical locks and the magical spells, any attempt to break into the desk and access the components would be . . . if not impossible, then greatly slowed. Presumably long enough for security to catch the intruder. Truth felt a high degree of vindictive pleasure when he finally cracked them both.

The desk held more or less what he might expect. There was a high-powered, compact needler and four extra magazines. Truth snorted. The needler had a full-auto setting, which was wild in such a small form factor. Maybe Gullvar just wasn't interested in learning how to aim. It was resting on top of a stack of bank drafts and wen, though less of both than he would have thought. DePonte had more wen on him. Annoying but expected. There was also the usual loose collection of pens, a pair of scissors, a magnifying glass, lancet, wax, business-grade athame, and the detritus that collected in the drawers of office workers.

The next drawer down was a file drawer containing . . . files. Truth didn't really know what he expected there. Maybe something with bold letters saying, *PROJECT DOOMSDAY* or *TOP SECRET STUFF DO NOT READ!* This was tax stuff, which, in fairness, was stamped *Confidential Business Record.* The largest file appeared to be a legal and economic analysis of acquiring a fish-processing terminal. It didn't look heavily read.

On the other side of the desk was a selection of prescription narcotics and anti-anxiety medications. Some more office junk. A few gold disks with pictures stamped on them. They looked a little like money. There was a brand-new atlas, along with freshly prepared reports laying out what had happened in the Ressilaud Free State all those years before. Most with the caveat that trying to find out what happened in that famously anarchic place was borderline impossible, and any results would be completely unreliable.

Truth grinned. Fast work. And the important thing wasn't results; it was that she was looking. He wondered if the "Young Master Remu" was running his own investigation, or if he was using Gullvar as his hunting dog in this, too. There was nothing else of interest in the drawers.

Truth's grin turned nasty, and he started checking for false bottoms. With immense care, he pulled out the drawers and investigated whether there was anything hidden behind or underneath. He found yet another set of business records, some correspondence that sure sounded like *someone* was having an affair, and some very illegal summoning charms.

Truth's paranoia was sounding a red alert there, klaxon wailing and lights strobing. This was the kind of "hidden" stuff that got planted to be found. Truth widened his search, checking the desk legs, the chair, the wastepaper basket.

He moved over to the wardrobe, finding more money, some jewelry gaudy enough to definitely be expensive, and an army-issue long-range heavy needler. There was a small chest of charms, most intended to glamor the user or to enchant those near her. Some more were intended to render a target unconscious or dead. Less clothes and shoes than he would have thought. She had been clearing out her closets dramatically.

The toilet was taken apart too—an efficiency design, where the waste was simply desiccated and incinerated into essentially dust. Presumably, some spirit periodically cleaned up. But no explanation about the chests or coffin or Young Master Remu. Or spells. Spells weren't hoarded in Jeon the way they were in some other places, but high-end spells and elixirs were precious. They could form the foundation of a family, even if they weren't particularly exclusive or unique. Did she keep everything in a safe deposit box or something? It would be impressively rational if intensely irritating.

His eyes drifted over to the one place he hadn't searched yet—the coffin and the chests. The chests he wasn't going to touch—there was obviously an ongoing magical process there, and screwing around with it was a great way to get dead. The coffin would also seem to fit that description, but there were no obvious controls for the system anywhere. Which he would bet meant that they were in the coffin.

Truth carefully watched the streams of blue mist coming from the chests. They were keeping to pretty straight channels through the air. It would get very tight near the coffin, but he could walk over most of the way, then crawl or something. Actually . . . Truth silently laughed, then jumped straight up.

The Meditations of Valentinian were now utterly part of Truth. He spent a portion of every day meditating, usually right before doing his daily cultivation. He even started treating it like a bit of a game—sneaking in a quickie sesh when he had a little downtime. Fair to say it was a very rough start, way back in Harban. But now? Now he could leap up so high, he had plenty of time to examine the lid of the coffin for anything that looked nasty.

There was something so damn satisfying about knowing your body could do that. Like running on water or being able to dance on just your fingertips. Not just knowing your cultivation elevated you but feeling it with your whole body. The lid of the coffin looked clear. No warning from Incisive. His feet had barely touched the ground again when he leapt on top of the coffin, light as a cat. The blue mist kept streaming below him, harmless.

Now that he was on top of the coffin, he could see a few things he had missed before. The first thing was a little brass plate screwed into the lid, just above the latch. *Anak and Sons Hyperthaumobaric Chamber—Custom-Made for Majorie Gullvar.*

He didn't know the maker, but from up on top of the coffin, he finally had the right angle to see why the components had been painted different colors. It was the Three Rivers Group logo, only visible if you were standing or sitting in just the right spot. Gullvar was at the heart of her company in more ways than one. What a curious device. It must have cost an absolute fortune in labor, let alone what the components themselves cost.

Truth wasn't entirely sure what *hyperthaumobaric* meant, but he could see the blue mist going in and not coming out. Presumably it was staying in there, saturating whatever—or, really, whoever—was in there.

Truth had now been up on the roof for nearly three hours. He had tidied up after himself, taking only a modest amount of the stashed cash. The only remaining puzzle was the coffin. It shouldn't have come as a surprise that the mist stopped flowing and latches snapped open inside the chamber. The perversity of the world would require waiting at least that long to ambush him. Truth nimbly dropped to the ground on the side of the coffin with the hinges.

A moment later, the lid swung up and Gullvar stepped out, never looking behind her. The lid shut automatically behind her. She looked about as she had in the restaurant. Less made up, perhaps. A little livelier looking. She walked over to the wardrobe and started dressing herself, unbothered by her nudity in the open sky. Having set herself to rights, she checked a few personal amulets and talismans, found everything in order, and descended into the house proper.

Truth was vibrating with anticipation. He had spent the whole damn day waiting to find *something* in Gullvar's place, and waiting an extra fifteen minutes for her to get dressed and ready for the evening was sheer torture. As soon as she was down the steps, Truth vaulted the coffin and popped the lid.

It looked cozy. A little foam pillow, more holes than solid matter, to support the head and neck. A fine mesh net suspending the body over the bottom of the chamber. There was a little latched box for personal effects just above the pillow, and to Truth's satisfaction, there was a little reading light installed. Inside the box were a number of crystal shards and a trashy mystery novel.

System, get memorizing!

<<*One step ahead of you.*>> Truth was looking over the shards too. Two spells, but he couldn't quite figure out what they did from a glance. More business records, this time for an organization of some sort. Something encrypted, which made Truth frown. Then he thought a little more and instantly downgraded his opinion of Gullvar and her security team. He picked up the mystery novel.

System, memorize this book and see if it's a key for cracking the encryption on this shard.

<<*Oof. That takes a lot more time than you would think. But . . . yeah, my guess, too. God damn it.*>> The System was grumbling steadily as Truth flipped the pages. Once done, he felt around in the little box and found some folded-up papers shoved down to the bottom. A medical evaluation for one Majorie Gullvar.

He didn't recognize the doctor or the hospital. Most of the test results were meaningless numbers to him. He carefully memorized it all anyway. The narration section at the end seemed clear enough.

Patient is otherwise healthy and, with corrective cultivation and mechanical support, would meet the minimum medical requirements for Project Golden Dawn. Her projected baseline planetary-collapse survival rate falls solidly within the median at .00531%. As such, I am recommending her conditioning begin at once. The integration of the Giant's Seed will take approximately four months.

It was dated two months before. On the bottom of the report was a final line—cc—Remu Anakson, Off-World Export Co.

CHAPTER 24

GIVING FROM THE HEART

Several things clicked all at once. Gullvar was a Holdout, or at least Anakson was. This Project Golden Dawn was intended to activate once the planet's magic collapsed. The hyperthaumobaric chamber must be conditioning her body to endure whatever the Giant's Seed requires. Either she was sent to the restaurant to trawl for other hidden powers, or the conditions of being in the program were so horrible, she wanted to be rescued. In any case, she had jumped on the lead Truth had given her. The mysteriously empty, staged house, along with her meager possessions, hinted at some kind of mental conditioning or control. Strip away everything but what's needed for the job. He could relate.

A woman who had almost certainly inherited her vast wealth and spent a lifetime defending it. Her achievement was even more impressive when you considered her limited cultivation. Level Four *was* quite limited when you had "Build your mansion on top of an apartment building you own" money. Gullvar had done well. Until the end of the world was announced. Until everyone was to be enrolled in the System and their money converted into credits.

Did the rich of Jeon know just what enrolling in Starbrite meant? They must have some suspicion, surely. Gullvar didn't give a shit if she looked desperate, or if she got rid of all her nice things, or stripped her mansion down to set dressing. Life, as she had understood that term, ended in four weeks. She needed an out. Now.

Truth didn't have one for her. Neither did Anakson, from what he could see. Just the promise that, after everything fell down, if you lived, you would be valued . . . somewhat.

Truth sighed lightly. He would have to prioritize finding the demon-summoners and the Ghūl for now. He just couldn't see through the depths there, and he wasn't prepared to throw away his life in the hope of an outsized palace coup by the outraged hundred-millionaires of Gwaju City. He'd throw investigating Anak and Sons and Off-World Export Co. to Merkovah, if possible. Otherwise, he'd just keep them in mind for the future.

He started cleaning up what he had touched and putting everything back the way he found it. He had been tidying as he went, so it wasn't a big job. Still, a disappointing end to a long day.

I don't suppose those spells we found are incredible doomsday-level, planet-cracking thaumaturgy? Something so terrible and forbidden that they alone were reason enough for the house of Gullvar to endure the centuries unmolested?

<<No. Weirder than that, actually.>>

Wait, weirder than doomsday spells?

<<Every petty hedge mage thinks their "sublime creation" will give them unlimited cosmic powers. No, this is kind of . . . I don't actually know what to call it. "Body cultivation," very loosely defined. Give me a minute longer to sort through this. Or an hour. Maybe a couple of hours. I'm sure I'm not getting this right.>>

Truth sighed and finished tidying up. He helped himself to exactly ten percent of one of the stacks of cash. Manifestly the least valuable thing there, and the "thief" only took ten percent? She'd wonder if she had miscounted or misremembered how much she had set aside. Besides, how much would she care about ten thousand worthless wen, even if she were to count them? But it was more than enough to last Truth for a good while.

He left the gold. There were only ten of them, and he'd bet she paid a lot of attention to them.

He lay down on the roof for a moment, staring up into the gray spring clouds. Might rain in a bit—no, it was raining; the wards were just diverting the rain away from the building. A mansion in the clouds, untouched by the wind and rain. Haunted by those who still lived yet no longer lived there. Gullvar and his mom had a lot in common—both trying to find that hustle that would get them to true wealth and safety. Ready to sell whatever part of themselves the Diamond Product Ambassador needed to feed their sadism.

Convincing themselves they were survivors, not well-trained prey. Perhaps they were both. What a miserable thought—they were caught and shorn, not caught and killed. Not that he felt bad for either of them. It was just miserable that this was the way the world was. This was the system of the world, working as intended.

He shook his head, stood, dusted his ass, and walked away. Time to go see a man about a demon.

Truth was a bit perplexed. He had expected a tense game of cat and mouse, running down clues and beating confessions out of people. The application of certain subtle drugs with notoriously unsubtle results. So, in a sense, it was lucky for both him and the heavily pregnant receptionist that the Jeon Society for Social Renewal was a publicly registered nonprofit that maintained a small local office in Gwaju. Truth's carpet driver could locate it with a minor divination. Wasn't anything fancy—three rooms in a low-rise office building, plus a reception area. The walls were painted a cheery purple, and the floors were easily cleaned tile.

"I'm sorry, Sir, but Vice-President Bosch works out of our Harban branch. The most senior person here is Terry, our branch manager, but Terry is currently out.

Could I take a message for you?" The young man looked feverishly eager to be of service.

"No, thank you. I was just hoping to talk to someone and learn more about your organization."

"That is so GREAT! I would love to set that up for you. Actually, if you don't mind, I might be able to answer some of your questions myself." The receptionist's smile looked painfully wide.

"Well, why don't we schedule a meeting with Terry . . . when would he be free?"

"His calendar opens up after four this afternoon."

"Book me a meeting then, please." Truth made up a name on the spot and gave some fraudulent contact information. "In the meantime . . . what's it like working here?" Truth asked.

"It's not work. It's my life's calling."

"Being the receptionist?"

"Yes, exactly. Receiving people. Being the first person they meet when they come here. First impressions last a lifetime, and I am truly proud to be that first impression here at the JSSR. Proof of the possibility of *true* social renewal."

"I can see that. You're practically glowing. So, can you tell me a bit about what the Society does?"

"Certainly! The JSSR has a simple goal—to free people from despair. Fear, pain, anxiety: all terrible things, but they can be fought. Despair is when the fighting stops. When the gray closes in, and the cold seeps into your bones, and all you can do is give up and suffer a life worse than death. Trapped forever, in your lightless cell." The receptionist's smile vanished.

"Trapped so completely, you wouldn't even step through a door if one appeared before you. Trapped in your mind."

"Until the Society charges to the rescue." Truth tried to get in the spirit of things.

"Oh, if only. No, this is a marathon of a march. We have been in operation for forty years now, and we have had our victories, but—" The receptionist gave a half-smile and waved at the outside world. He didn't seem to notice the way his other hand softly stroked his distended belly. "We can only do our best. The diseases of despair are endless and endlessly spreading. Reinfecting each other."

"Diseases of despair?"

"Depression, anxiety, personality disorders, and all the horrible things that come with them. Drug abuse. Sex addiction. Spouse or child abuse. Alcoholism." The receptionist shook his head.

"Over and over again, people are told that prosperity is theirs if only they work hard enough. Yet no matter how hard they work, people never prosper. Their lives hurt. So, they do something to numb the pain.

"They are told that they are responsible for buying the drugs, for taking them, for hitting their husbands. And of course there is some responsibility there, but what about the responsibility of the rest of Jeon? What about the responsibility of every person that participates in a sick society, a society that drives people to despair?"

Truth found himself nodding along. Hell, he'd had more or less the same thoughts himself recently. The receptionist leaned forward, eyes fever-bright and fixed on Truth.

"I know you have seen it too. Just stand on the sidewalk and look around. Do you see anyone, *anyone*, who looks content? At peace? Or even worried but hopeful? Or do you see—"

"Despair. People who have given up, and all they can do is numb the pain and lash out. Which is another way to numb the pain, really." Truth finished the sentence. This was all making sense to him.

"Exactly. And THAT is where the Society comes in." The receptionist nodded firmly. "We do outreach programs, arrange mentorship opportunities for future thought leaders, engage with legislators, and even reach out to businesses directly. All with the same goal—ending despair."

"Must cost a fortune!" Truth said, looking for a rat.

"It does, but not the way you think. It's all volunteer time. Our actual budget is tiny. We don't accept outside donations, and donations from members are capped at five hundred wen a year."

"Wait, what? How do you get anything done? Hell, how can you afford the rent on this office?"

"Donated. The building owner is a member. We do pay a nominal rent, but it's something like ten wen a month. Same with the office supplies, utilities, and the like. It's either supplied by volunteers or we do without. I'm a volunteer. So is everyone at this branch, actually. We have . . . I think six full-time paid employees. They do clerical work in Harban."

"That's . . . incredible." Truth meant it, too. The office might not have been anything special, but it was entirely adequate.

"That, Mr. Malduci, is social renewal." This was from a handsome middle-aged man coming through the door behind Truth. Level Three. Impressive for a tiny nonprofit in the sticks. "Terry Blouthe, Bon'i let me know you were waiting, and I hurried back. It sounds like you are a fellow traveler. But Bon'i didn't mention what you were here about?"

"Well, it's twofold. I recently came into a small inheritance and wanted to put it toward a worthy cause. The second thing was to learn exactly what the JSSR means when they talk about a renewed or healed society."

"Ah, well, happy to steer you toward some excellent charities that we work with and that do take donations. As for the latter, why don't we go into my office?"

They sat in the little, windowless office. Now that he was looking for it, Truth could spot the mismatched office furniture, scuffed and worn and doubtless secondhand. No pictures on the walls, but a very sizable bookshelf with an impressive-looking selection of file folders and textbooks. The desk was just a glorified table, dragged into serving double duty as a place to hold yet more files and a support for coffee cups.

"So, Mr. Malduci, having agreed that the world as it is, even before the Black Ships arrived, is an engine of misery, we have to look at what options exist. There is no denying that, for all the horror of the modern condition, we are also the generation with the highest degree of material comfort. Clearly, some elements of the system work. So, rather than a pure leveling, we see ourselves returning balance to the social structures. Improving the morale of the people by putting them in a position to effect real control over their lives."

Truth smiled and nodded. "I have to say, I am loving everything I am hearing so far. How exactly are you going to do that? Given the limited time we all appear to have?"

"Desperate times, Mr. Malduci, call for desperate measures. But never choices born of despair! We see this as nothing less than a heaven-sent opportunity. You see, all these social systems are built on modern talisman systems and highly refined demon binding. Bonds so tight, they may as well be pure lumps of energy or the half-wit thinking of golems instead of the intelligent, sensitive beings they are. Saying nothing of the fact that they are the original inhabitants of this world."

"All right?"

"We must return them to their rightful position in society. Not above humanity but our co-equal partners. This will naturally require significant shifts in public perception. Everyone hears the word *demon* and just freaks out. But look outside, Mr. Malduci. Look at the people you see around you. This world is already Hell, a place without hope. It is only by collaborating with demons that we can bring it closer to Heaven."

CHAPTER 25

SHARING THE GOOD NEWS

He knew it was coming, and yet the answer still threw him. Odd.

"You want to share this world with demons as equals. As a way to combat despair and the diseases of despair."

"Sounds like a leap?" Terry smiled.

"Just a smidge."

"It should. Demons are *dangerous*; no question about it. Like fire and cosmic energy, used carelessly or maliciously, they will certainly be fatal. Or worse."

"Right. That is exactly the concern." Truth nodded, certain that they weren't understanding each other.

"The problem stems from an issue of language, first and foremost. Our language for describing demons, and our relationship with demons, is inevitably religious in origin. Be it Pragerite, Desrin, or even Siphian, it is always religious. And with that come all the prejudices and assumptions built into their given theologies.

"For example, Jeongo doesn't make a distinction between the supernatural spirits that are native to this world, beings that should really be called 'natural spirits,' and those denizens of Hell. Even words like *spirit* or *ghost* get muddied up with demons, as the distinction between a 'spirit' and a 'demon' is generally how beneficial it is to humans, not its point of origin." Terry threw up his hands in exhausted frustration.

Truth nodded. He remembered noticing something along those lines in Xandre—Merkovah was downright pleasant to some of the building spirits and guardian "demons," for all that he tortured the hell out of things from . . . well . . . Hell.

"When you get right down to it, the word *supernatural* is, itself, completely suspect. These beings are not 'above' nature or the natural. They are a part of it. Often a part we cannot directly touch or influence without magic, but no less natural for all that. We exist in an ecosystem, Mr. Malduci. An ecosystem of living, physical beings that rely on consuming matter to live, and other beings, often less physical, that survive on more than mere flesh."

Truth let his thoughts race ahead of the conversation. "You think our ecosystem is out of balance, and as a result, people have insufficient exposure to demons, however defined. But I am missing that last step."

"Specifically, those demons summoned up from Hell. Don't you find it absurd, Mr. Malduci, that we can know, categorically, that Hell exists and that sinners suffer there eternally, and yet sin continues to exist? Not just exist; sin, however defined, is the norm. Yet we also know that not all souls go to Hell, that Heaven is a real place, and there is even some indication that a sort of reincarnation is possible for some people. Though, obviously, that latter point is intensely disputed. We take no position on it."

Truth hadn't heard much about the reincarnation thing but had long since accepted his ignorance of the world.

"So, what's the answer?"

"We don't have one. It's a messed-up situation, and no few of us come to the conclusion that humanity is so utterly, irredeemably evil that even the certainty of an eternity in Hell is not enough to dissuade us from our evil ways. The fact that there is no coherent, proven theology to guide us away from sin is another 'delightful' wrinkle. A perfect little anxiety generator, something to really propel the engines of despair. You can do your very, very best to be good, but if you didn't say just the right prayer at just the right time? Straight to Hell you go."

"Ah. Having literal infernal demons directly involved in people's lives will bring home the reality of eternal torment in a way that preaching cannot."

"Exactly. Exactly. We make this world a microcosm of Hell, our own crude approximation of eternal torment, because we do not truly understand the secular realities of our spiritual teachings. We call for social reform to break this cycle. Liberate the people from despair. And we do it through demon integration. People must understand with their bodies what their minds refuse to learn."

Truth nodded thoughtfully at that. What a shame. He actually agreed with a lot of their observations, but they lost him at the end. Bit like the anti-theists, actually. Oh, well, time to put them to work.

"So, the collapse of the world must have you in a panic. More than most, I mean."

"Well, despair is certainly on the rise!"

"No, I mean the collapse of magic. The increasing unreality of the world, resulting in our inability to interact with cosmic rays."

There was a long pause. Now it was Terry's turn to look perplexed.

"I'm sorry; I don't follow."

"Notice how there are more and more Level Zero 'adults' around? Or that it's harder and harder to learn spells? All those wild, planetary, 'natural' spirits vanishing, one by one?"

"Yes . . ."

"It's a global phenomenon. And it's accelerating." Truth was starting to lean into Incisive now, letting the poison drip into Terry's ears. "The demons are going to die, Terry. Or they will be forced back into Hell without enough energy to support them. This is the collapse the Black Ships were talking about. All the demons are going to go away. Despair will be all we are. Just blobs of suffering meat."

Terry was looking at Truth in horror now.

"But this is why you exist, right? Even in the face of universal, eternal despair, the Society has the means and resolve to *act*. You can *do whatever it takes* to carry your truth to the people while you can. *Bold* decisions must be taken. *Hard choices* must be made. *Sacrifices* must be made. To bring the reality of Hell and the presence of true demons to the world. You can *wake them all up*, Terry. I believe in you."

Truth stood. "It has been incredibly interesting, learning all about your group, Terry. I wish you took donations. I will spend what little time I have left to do my best for people. That's all I can do. If you will accept a suggestion, have you considered reaching out to those people responsible for overseeing the new Denizen job system? A lot of potential for abuse there and a lot of potential to do good. I would *work them over hard*. Oh, and if your organization didn't know about the thinning magic, *you better tell them fast*. This requires national action."

Truth walked out of the society, shaking his head. What a classic, classic con. The receptionist was singing quietly to the demon in his belly. Truth wasn't sure he knew he was doing it. Hopefully, their madness would be everyone's problem soon. In the meantime, he had to run down another possible avenue—Anak and Sons, as well as Off-World Export Co.

Anything new on those spells?

<<I think I cracked one of them . . . maybe. The other is still even more of a work in progress. It's a kind of body-cultivation spell, like I said, just a very unusual one.>> A little hallucination popped up in Truth's field of vision—the outline of a human with nine apertures marked on it.

<<Cosmic rays hit the body.>> Little lines were added, raining on the body. *<<Mostly, they pass right through, but with cultivation, they get absorbed and processed into cosmic energy, then stored in the apertures.>>*

Yep. That is how literally everything works.

<<It's called laying a foundation, dickhead. Your apertures . . . well, a normal, not cursed, not-using-that-perverse-nine-worm thing, NORMAL person's apertures are constantly collapsing. Your body . . . NORMAL PEOPLE'S bodies cannot passively absorb enough rays to keep the cycle going and keep the apertures full. Those apertures are, magically speaking, leaky. The energy leaks slowly into the rest of 'your' body. That leakage is what gives higher-levels the advantage in strength, speed, perception, and all that over lower levels.>>

Yes, with you so far. Very foundational. Like, kindergarten level.

<<Hey, fun idea—how about I critique your sexual performance? You only did it once; lots of areas to improve.>>

Please continue explaining this body-cultivation spell. You have my full attention.

<<I would hate to deprive you. I could go for hours, days even, showing you where you went wrong. I have several very instructive diagrams.>>

No, no, please. I am fascinated by this spell you have cleverly deconstructed.

<<Well, if you are sure. Really sure.>>

I am.

<<As I was saying. The human system is always working at a net energy loss, be it your physical or magical body. You offset it by eating and cultivating. The active process of processing the energy hitting you keeps your apertures as full as you safely can, and then opens up the next one, and so on. Eventually, the energy just . . . leaks out of you. Radiates in a fine mist, like body heat or smell. Not a whole lot, because your different fleshy bits are absorbing and using it, but some, and it happens constantly. The more stuff you do, like walk around, or cast magic, or whatever, the faster you empty out. Obviously, collapse happens slowly, and even a small amount of cultivation can keep your apertures open.>>

Right.

<<But not with this spell. This spell seals you up. No leakage. Whatever you absorb stays with you unless you sacrifice it to do something. Run a spell, run faster than a carriage, whatever. In a high-magic environment, it would be pointless. In the post-collapse environment? You would be the only person with magic. Absorbing new magic would be a . . . significant challenge, but presumably, they have ways around it.>>

That's it? That's all the spell does?

<<From what I can tell, yes. It's actually pretty complicated. For most people, that concentration of cosmic energy would be fatal. You would literally just pop or turn into a corrupted mass of goo or something. Your body is designed to release the energy. It's not a bad thing. The spell spends most it its time stopping bodies from suffering the negative consequences of its main function.>>

Huh. That does seem kind of useful for me, though. Would have been able to ignore that . . . whatever you call it . . . from the anti-theists, for one. It would give me more endurance in any high-intensity situation, and I bet it would make me a bastard to track down. Actually, it should accelerate cultivation, too. Wouldn't mind end-of-the-world armor, either. Yeah, this thing actually sounds pretty nifty to me, but I don't want to waste a spell slot on it. Is it something that I can do with the Meditations?

<<Yes . . . I think. I will study the spell more.>>

I'm pretty curious to find out what the second spell does. I'd guess . . . Hey, you hear that?>>

Truth started looking around. It wasn't a bad neighborhood, but this was Jeon. Good and bad were rarely far apart. He quickly dipped down an alley, then another, then another. Six blocks later, the daylight seemed to be thinning. The buildings crowded each other, broken glass giving shine and sparkle to the streets. No homeless, though. No junkies nodding in a corner or gangsters drinking on the steps. There would be in the buildings above. Behind the thick steel bars and the heavy steel doors of the apartment buildings. But even in daylight, no one wanted to be in this alley.

No one wanted to walk into this old shop, even though the doors were off their hinges. The doorframe was decorated. Twisted bone lengths, held together with sinew and scraps of hides. The shattered glass had been carefully swept away, and a welcoming carpet of teeth stretched from the sidewalk into the interior. But above all, through all, surrounding all, was the music.

Truth could hear it clearly now—the soaring, layered glories of it. The bass and the treble and the mids all fell together, at first randomly, then a sublime order would be revealed. And once that perfection had existed just long enough to be felt, it disintegrated again. A new swell of music rose, its own internal logic growing and evolving through the seeming chaos. And all of it in sincere worship.

That which was most holy could not be put into words, the music showed, because words were far too limited, far too trapped in the human perspective to capture the infinite. Better pure sound, pure emotion. Better to express our feelings with as few barriers as possible.

And like music, sculpture was far more real, far more a complete statement than a picture. This was an eye, a careful composite made of dozens of other eyeballs, separated into their base components with surgical care and preserved through unknown means, then recombined into a perfectly imperfect form. The iris shimmered, dominated by shades of brown and black but joyfully flecked with blues, greens, and grays. The sclera was porcelain-white, threaded with red, and yellowed here and there by disease or hard living. And the pupil—vast, dilated. Was it terror? Arousal? For its makers, was there a difference? It was hard to put the words *Ghūl* and *erotic* together, but what could this be but a creation of love?

The Ghūl lined the walls, coated the floor, and even knelt on the ceiling. As though the Ghūl had transformed themselves into a continuation of their sacred artwork. They paid Truth no mind. All save one. It had been standing, waiting, looking at the door. Carefully out of the light. It smiled, revealing green-gray teeth under mostly rotted, withered lips. The being pressed its hands together and bowed. It extended its arm toward the giant eye. Inviting a brother to come and worship.

CHAPTER 26

ONLY THE MONSTERS ARE REAL

Light came in a dim, narrow column from the open door, across the carpet of teeth and putting a shine in the eye made of eyes. The Ghūl filled the whole volume of the space with casual comfort. Their flesh withered or rotted, or simply flaking away, long bones jutting from finger or toe, long nails on those hands complete enough to hang on to them. Some with eyes, most with teeth, some with far too many teeth. All gathered in silent, ecstatic worship.

Truth walked forward. Something was different this time. Something about the Ghūl or him. Or both. He could feel the way the world twisted around the Ghūl now. Not the bending forced by the overwhelming reality of a place like Nag Hamadi or Etenesh when her God was upon her. This was more subtle, more pervasive. Like the refraction of light on the surface of clean water. It looked like you were seeing straight down, but the world was actually not where you thought it was.

If things kicked off, he wouldn't even bother with Incisive. It would be cold steel and hard hands smashing apart rotten flesh. It didn't seem likely to come to that. The one Ghūl not devoted to worship was still bowed, welcoming him in.

Truth opened his mouth to say . . . something. Anything. Some acknowledgment of the bizarre horror of the scene, of the unreality of being greeted by the monsters of his childhood. Of his slaughter of dozens or hundreds of Ghūl in Harban. He closed his mouth again. The Ghūl did not speak. Nor did they respond to words. No matter how loudly or often they were screamed.

Truth just nodded. The Ghūl unfolded and walked into the interior of the shop. Truth followed. There was no path through the Ghūl. His guide simply stepped on them and was ignored. Truth did the same, his reflexes constantly tested by the fragile meat under his feet. Away from the idol, the store was more or less how the owners had left it. There were posters on the walls advertising popsicles and soda. Seductive women taking a bite, handsome men looking refreshed. Covered in dust now, like the grave photographs of a long-dead family.

The people were ghosts. Only the monsters were real. Truth trailed behind his guide. Just one more monster made in Jeon.

They came to a little garden of hands in a back room. The blossoms were of different heights—some trimmed just below the elbow, some as short as the wrist. To keep them in place, the flesh had been carefully scraped from the radii and ulnae, and the bones lovingly planted in the concrete. The fingers twisted into pleasing shapes. Those missing petals were left unmended—their very imperfection enhancing the beauty of the scene.

The guide stopped and waited. It seemed to want Truth to examine the collection. Truth squatted and looked them over carefully. Old and young. Some with tattoos, or scars, some with lingering remnants of alchemical modification, or manicures whose gloss had been carefully preserved. Testimonies of lives, however long or short, preserved in the garden of the Ghūl. A myriad of differences in experiences, the winding paths of cause and effect, all come to the same end.

Truth had a moment of vertigo. They were loved. All these flowering hands. They were tended to and cared for with patience and affection. Not because of the ghost that used to haunt the meat but because of what the meat *was*. It was the record of a life, yes, but it was also every loop and whorl of a fingerprint, every blurred and faded swallow tattooed on the underside of a forearm, every wrinkle on every aged hand reaching for a light in the near-perfect dark. The Ghūl loved them for every part of their existence. The longer he fell in his vertigo, the more he came to doubt that last conclusion.

It wasn't about the ghost. It was about the meat. They didn't care about that record of a life. They just loved how it looked now, each blossom beautifying the churchyard. Was that the faith of the Ghūl? A radical renunciation of the spirit? That didn't seem right. They were worshiping idols. They worshiped his Rough Patron. The Ghūl may be the single most devout creatures he had ever encountered. Angels excepted. That thought brought him up with a jerk, and he looked his guide over with brief horror.

No. They weren't some degraded angels. He had seen them born. They were no angels, nor demons, nor humans. They were their own thing. And they wanted him to see this garden. Why?

Truth examined the hands more closely. There seemed to be every sort of human hand there. Each was unique, yes, but ultimately human. The difference was in the detail, and he had a hard time imagining the Ghūl really cared about his appreciation of nuance. So, just what was he supposed to see there? Or, perhaps, was seeing not the point?

Truth glanced over at his guide standing with infinite patience. Subtly warping the world around him. Famously, the Ghūl hated the light. So, they weren't seeing with light, presumably. Which meant that the rotted sacks of gray-brown water in the holes above their nasal cavity were purely decorative.

Truth let his eyes go vague, trying to just . . . experience the garden without seeing it. Without attaching thoughts to what his eyes were seeing. It was surprisingly difficult—either he stopped seeing anything at all, or the intrusive thoughts popped in. This hand belonged to an old woman, this to a strong man, this one fought back, this one didn't have a chance. This one was still bending the world.

Truth's eyes jerked to a halt and slowly slid back the way they came. He had to focus on his breathing, trying to stay relaxed. One of the hands—no, several of the hands were still subtly bending the world around them. Despite their former owners' departure from this life, they had been refined to such a fine degree that they remained more "real" than the abandoned store. More real than the other people they bloomed with now.

Truth picked one and got in close. His knowledge of anatomy was practical, not systematic. If this wasn't an ordinary human, he couldn't tell. Maybe they were a high-level mage? He moved to another, then another. All the same in their perverted normalcy. Truth frowned a little. Why were they important? Why was this tickling a memory?

Young Master Remu Anakson. The sheer alien presence of the seeming human. The brutal reality of him, a steel tiger in a world of paper rats. Were these more people like Remu? Human-ish? Human-presenting? Anakson was a Holdout, planning to remain on-world after the collapse. A superreality tycoon ruling the eight directions in a world of ghosts. How many others had the same plan? And how long had they been planning?

To the Ghūl, it was all meaningless. In the end, they would all be gathered together in the garden. Delighting the faithful and adding sweetness to their devotions.

Truth looked around the garden with a new, horrified appreciation. The eyes weren't the window to the soul for the Ghūl. The eye could only see. It was reactive, yes, but always passive. The hand was the truest signifier of the soul animating it, bearing the marks of the soul's journey through its myriad intersections and diversions with the material world.

This world is our garden, and you are all flowers that blossom within it. Whatever stories you make up about who you are and what you mean, we will see you for what *you are. And we will preserve that meaning so long as it pleases God.* That was the message Truth read from the garden. *All the myriad races of the children of God shall ultimately come to an end in the garden of the Ghūl.*

Truth felt the room spin, lost in the vertigo of the garden and the revelation both. What exactly did he want from the Ghūl? Merely increased hunting wouldn't do it. Starbrite had never cared about the Ghūl or their slaughters. If anything, the fear of the Ghūl drove loyalty to Starbrite, not the reverse. He had hoped to find a way, somehow, to use them to attack Starbrite. Their spell resistance made them a nightmare for mages.

Truth remembered when the nest in Harban was cleared. Dozens of cops, a huge ward, a huge number of prepared charms expended to form a gigantic ball of superheated plasma within the ward. The old commercial building had been reduced to glass and slag. Truth had to wonder—were the wards and talismans there to create a nonmagical plasma? Did they have to act on that scale to have any hope of safely demolishing the statue the Ghūl were venerating? It was all he could think of. But the Ghūl didn't care about names or causes. They didn't care about any supposed sins of Starbrite. All was well so long as they could worship as they believed their God demanded.

He . . . didn't know what to do. How do you communicate nonverbally a concept as nuanced as *I want you to hunt medium- to high-level Starbrite employees, please and thank you. Also, could you please tell all the other Ghūl everywhere to do the same?* He looked over at the guide, who hadn't moved a muscle. It seemed that whatever Truth was to learn from the garden was entirely his to work out. If anything, it seemed like the guide was just appreciating the moment. Lost in the music and the wonder of this holy place.

That music always reminded him of the one bizarre month his family had attended church. It was a scam, or rather, an attempted scam, of course. But the music stayed with him. Not the words; the way they made you feel. He was a lot less impressed when he remembered that the parishioners could give donations in exchange for certain hymns being sung, such hymns being the best protection against being flung into the inferno. You could even sponsor a chapel if you had the money. Not only buy your way out of Hell but into the better tiers of Heaven.

He paused at that. Surely not. But . . . maybe? He looked around the garden. If there was a logic to the organization of the hands, he didn't understand it. But there was a logic there—it was immediately recognizable as a monstrous parody of a formal flowerbed. And if he could recognize it, then the Ghūl who made it could definitely understand symbolism.

Truth felt a grin stretch across his face, giving him an unsettling similarity to his guide. What if . . . he were to sponsor a chapel? What if he were to provide several starter components and lay out the structure for the rest of the construction? It was no trouble finding higher-level Starbrite employees. Heck, even focusing on just the Level Threes would cripple Starbrite in this city. Maybe even the region. He wouldn't have to bag many, maybe just two or three. Then he could turn loose the really experienced hunters.

He stood, ready to rush off and get to work, but the guide had other ideas. It bowed again and resumed walking toward the back to the store. Tall vats lined the wall, crudely made, from what materials Truth could not guess. Didn't want to guess. Too big to be the birthing cauldrons he had seen before. They were covered in dots connected by lines, seemingly random but never crossing. Impossibly intricate, the lines twisted and folded around and around and around. It wasn't a spell, nor was it a formation. It didn't seem like their sort of art, and they didn't seem to possess a language. So, what was it?

Truth looked at it for a long few minutes. The longer he looked at it, the more it pressed down on him. This was important. But for the life of him, he couldn't say why. The guide moved on, bowing him out the back door. The tour was over for now. Truth walked back into the light. Thin, feeble in the alleys. No matter. Plenty of light to see by. He would find his way back there. Once he had all the materials.

CHAPTER 27

BRAINS ARE OVERRATED

I have been using my brain too much.

<<You can't set me up like that. It's not fair. I've been trying so hard not to shit on your inadequacies, and then you hand me a line like that. You deserve everything you get.>>

No, I mean, thank you for being less of an asshole, but no, I mean, I need to be more direct. I have stirred the pot here and there, but it's time to add more serious teeth to the threat my imaginary mastermind presents. Stop moving pieces around; start taking them off the board. Draw out bigger hitters from Starbrite rather than getting Level One and Two rookies moved around.

<<Rookies, he says. Well, in the PMC, that was kind of true. I think most of the vets and junior officers were Level Three. But let's cut the bullshit—you are planning a rampage. Find a Starbrite office building and just empty it or something.>>

The Four Seas Bank has a regional branch here—I'm thinking of a smash-and-grab again but this time making a point of targeting the high-level managers and security. Also targeting any bank records we can reach, popping open the vault if we can, the whole bit.

<<These sorts of operations typically require a team of four or more, months of planning, and have a high risk of failure. And yet, you are ignoring all that.>>

Yeah, I'm going to cheat. Most of what we want is chaos and killing. So, having just spent some quality time in Siphios . . .

<<You are going to summon demons.>>

Yup. Also, while I want to shoot for as much success as possible, I'm planning for failure.

<< Follow-up attack on the rescue squads and investigation team? Nasty. Let's do it. A little over three weeks left until enrollment starts.>>

I know.

Truth struggled to activate the Scales portion of Incisive. It was a little hurtful that, apparently, it was a stretch to think he might be a senior manager from out of town on an inspection visit. Which, okay, he was young, but come on! Was it more believable that he was the ruthless heir to some ancient hidden family than a goddamn white-collar prick from the internal audit team?

Apparently, yes, it was. He banged his head against it for a while, trying to find some version of the identity that wouldn't cost an exorbitant amount of energy to run. It slowly dawned on him that while he had seen loads of guys in their twenties on management tracks, skids generously greased by nepotism, he had never seen a senior manager who was less than fifty. "Arrogant young master" was a comparatively easy lift against the reality of gerontocracy. And given that a working life could easily stretch into your ninth decade for the decently leveled, a senior manager at fifty could be said to be a stunning high-flier.

There was no trouble seeing him as a member of security, however. Effortless, in fact. He tried not to be salty about that. He didn't expect many people to see him at all, or certainly not for long, but he wanted to be prepared. He prepped his summoning talismans, bought a gray hat and a gray shirt to go with his gray pants, and walked right into the marble-floored lobby of the Gwaju branch of the Four Seas Bank.

The bank branch was "tastefully" designed to look exactly like every other damn branch, with an added abstract statute of a fish to "Recognize the city's historic connection with the sea." Truth looked around and checked on an actual security guard. F-Tier drone. Barely Level One, with all the alert competence of a narcoleptic sloth.

On the one hand, he was probably going to kill this dweeb. On the other hand . . . it kind of felt bad. The energy expenditure to kill this guy versus the value of killing him would absolutely be a loss for Truth, and Truth was pretty sure he could kill him with a finger poke. Truth marked him down for collateral damage rather than an actual target. Little guy might just make it after all.

The uniforms were the same solid gray he remembered normal Starbrite Security wearing. He would pass well enough. Not like he was expecting this to go well. Truth sighed and turned away from the hundred-and-eighty-centimeter, hundred-and-five-kilo little person and turned toward the back of the bank. Amulet-controlled access to the elevators and to any rooms off the main floor. Naturally. He sighed again, snagged the card off Tiny, and went exploring.

First stop was the security control room. Easy enough to find—it was the usual bank of scryballs showing the dozens upon dozens of recording talismans coating the interior and exterior of the building. There was the hideously dense network of wards and spells designed to protect the vault from physical or magical intrusion, as well as heavy employee surveillance because there was no threat quite like an insider threat. Most of the employees were below C-Tier. Management had the system. The tellers did not. Nor did security.

Truth carefully looked over the densely inscribed control nodes. The amount of energy flowing into and through them made the hairs on the back of his arm rise and a certain thrill run along his spine. Say what you like about the F-Tier drones of Starbrite Security, their commercial security division was absolutely top-notch. Redundancies upon redundancies, backups, shunts, independent power supplies, automatic lockdowns; it was a pure nightmare for invaders.

He pulled a three-ring binder off the shelf, flipping to the evacuation procedures page. Found it. Naturally, the executives wouldn't be queueing up with everyone else. They got evacuated through a secure air bridge to a nearby office building. Literally looking down on the teeming employees below. Striding through the air on a bridge of pure magic.

Truth smiled gently. It was 9:15 AM. The office had been staffed for the last three hours, and even the most decadent of execs would have been at his desk by 8:00. He tapped the controls on a scryball. Yep. Badge check-in showed full attendance, minus excused absences and business travel. He looked around the security center once again. A small armory was bolted to the back wall, needlers and a couple of nonlethal devices. Nothing too spicy. It would do.

Truth looked at the F-Tier security, sitting back and drinking their coffee while watching the surveillance. These nobodies couldn't see him. Couldn't perceive his touch. Already so unreal to him. But it felt bad. He shook his head, set a few talismans in place, then walked out of the heavily armored room.

There was a sudden white light. The lights in the building went off, and screaming alarms started bouncing off the wall. Truth walked back in, trying not to mind the gory mess. Two small bombs, but the security room was far from totaled. Everyone was dead, a lot of the main systems were disconnected from the power or nonfunctional, but the vault was safe, and most of the control systems worked. Credit to the commercial security division—they knew what really mattered.

Truth tossed a small duffel bag onto the floor. "Thrush. Time to work."

"I have done more with less, Master. Give me but seven minutes, and all will be ready."

Now, let's just see how well they practiced their—Sweet Prager, already? Were they waiting for the bell or something?! He watched the branch managers, the executives, those mighty local divinities, pack up their things and form an orderly queue from their exquisitely decorated offices, down the plush carpeted hall, past the anodyne pictures of great cost and little value, and out to the roof deck. The floor security team was doing a great job of sweeping their needlers around and looking very tough while the floor captains did the actual useful work of deploying the bridge.

The glittering span snapped into life. It was an evacuation route—couldn't have it deploy slowly. The talismans had their own stored supply of cosmic energy, enough to deploy the bridge and keep it up for a few minutes. Naturally, this was insufficient to evacuate a whole floor, so there was backup—triply redundant power supply channels running through some very sophisticated networks in the armored core of the bank. All of that, talisman, power, backups, the bridge itself, all of it, overseen by the security control room.

Truth waited until they were well over the wide street in front of the bank. Orderly strolling to the other building, where they would be met with coffee and answers. Chatting lightly with their peers or casually ignoring their lessers. The bridge wasn't some custom creation. These bridges were used for pedestrian access all over.

Any sane magical engineer would put in safeties, multiple redundant safeties, to ensure that power could never be discontinued while it was bearing a load. But this bridge was made by Starbrite and installed by Starbrite, and the commercial security division was very clear on what they needed to protect.

Truth tapped a button. There was a momentary silence. A few desperate, useless flashes of charms or spells. A brief shower of suits soaked the evacuating serfs below. Then it was over.

Truth found the file-room security monitor and disabled the fire-suppression systems. He disabled as much security around the vault as he could, but even the security center was limited in what it could do there.

Truth left the security room at a dead sprint, heading for the record office. Rows upon rows of steel file cabinets and banks upon banks of bound spirits. All the records of loans given and deposits taken. Stored contracts. Charters. Truth smiled nastily and called the Tongue to hand. He sprinted along the rows of cabinets, slicing them open like a knife scraping the head off a beer. The banks of bound spirits fared even worse, the Blessing of the Sea of Brass compounding the power of the angelic blade. They were simply annihilated. Expunged from existence. Whatever wisdom and secrets they held were lost forever. He looped back toward the door, this time slicing lower. Having turned the room into a charnel house of paper, he tossed a couple of incendiary charms and left.

The vault was next. It sealed automatically in the event of a power cut, naturally. And . . . it was still sealed, despite his efforts from the control room. He tried to find an override but couldn't. Nearly a meter thick and three meters tall, made of enchanted steel, it wasn't moving. Nor could he use his usual trick of going through the wall next to the door—it was Starbrite PMC that taught him the trick in the first place. The whole thing was a steel box. He went to the backup—stacking as many cutting talismans as he could in one place—and tried to drill through the locking mechanism.

This did not work.

It . . . very did not work.

Truth watched the vault door just absorb the energy and begin pulsing. Steel pooling like quicksilver under it, growing in size. Legs starting to form, already rising to a waist in a spare second. A liquid steel golem, three meters of pure slaughter. He had never seen one deployed. The energy and material cost was atrocious. You would only use them to defend a fixed position like a . . . bank vault.

It was just slightly possible that he had gotten a mite arrogant.

The steel giant's hand turned into a long saber. Burning orange eyes opened in the mirror-flat face. No need for a mouth. There was nothing to say, after all. The saber whipped down blindingly fast. Incisive screamed, and Truth listened, bolting backward. Chips of the polished marble floor exploded upward, tearing open the heavy work clothes. The saber was rising before the stone flakes could bounce off Truth's skin. Burning orange eyes fixed on him. No doubt, he was spotted.

Truth moved to attack, using his sword to push the saber past him as it came in, and then slicing down. Angelic steel screeched on the refined metal of mortals, leaving a long gash behind it. A gash that filled an eyeblink later. Truth swore and took distance.

"Thrush, now!"

CHAPTER 28

ACTION AND REACTION

There is one thing everyone knows about demon summoning. Even if you don't know anything about demon summoning, you know this for the same reason you know not to have sex with a wasp's nest. There are ideas so intuitively stupid and dangerous, most people don't need the logic spelled out. So, even if you don't know anything about demon summoning, you know you never, *ever* summon fire and air demons at the same time.

But then, *stupid and dangerous* was exactly what Truth was going for. It wasn't his dick in the nest. A pattern had been carved on the floor of the security room. Infernal glyphs curved along lines and forms whose madness became infectious. The talismans in the duffel had been carefully positioned, the blood of the bank's defenders gently forced into the lines of the spell.

Thrush perched on a heavy needler on the arms rack. With a minor effort, its magic connected the deep wells of power inside the bank to the summoning formation. The instant the connection was made, it flew hard as it could back to Truth. It didn't want to stand on the X any more than a human would.

It did bring the heavy needler with it, making sure to grab the one in the best condition. He knew his master, and sucking up to the boss was never dumb.

Truth was doing his best to stick and move, but the golem was built to handle high-level mages. It was keeping up fine, and every cut healed almost instantly. In theory, you could exhaust the magic in it, rendering it inert. In practice, it was connected to the Bank's deep power reserves. Truth would tire long before the golem did.

"It is done, Great One."

Truth grunted. He lunged for the Golem's head. The golem didn't block, taking the hit and using the opportunity to hack at Truth's ribs. Incisive warned him it was coming in time, but the saber nearly caught him during his retreat anyway. The damn thing was fast.

There was a sudden overwhelming pressure stabbing into his ears, a *boom* so loud it became a physical thing. The pain was so crippling, he nearly ate the golem's kick. It didn't have ears. Truth kicked off the ground hard, launching himself back as fast as he could go.

Abner's Amble!

The spell loaded up. Each step launched him a dozen meters, giving him distance. The golem would be tethered to the vault, but Truth wasn't going to hang around and figure out the range. He ran straight out of the building, across the street, and up the side of the building opposite it. The explosion had blown out a lot of windows. He went for one about halfway up, collapsing on the floor as he tried to get his breathing under control. Thrush settled in next to him, depositing the heavy needler next to him. Truth rolled onto his belly and crawled up to the exploded window. Floor-to-ceiling glass on the side of the building. No idea why it was so popular.

"Mission accomplished, Master?"

Truth didn't say anything, his attention held by the demons. The bank was on fire now. Surfaces carefully treated to be fireproof were glowing white hot, the air itself combusting. Some clever bastard demon had punched holes through the ventilation system, turning the whole building into a blast furnace.

Truth . . . didn't know they could do that.

The noise was incredible. There must be other golems and fixed defenses in place, but he couldn't hear them over the fire. And the smoke, God, the smoke! Poison, choking, black and brown and gray and blue, clouds of ash boiling out of the building and hunting for lungs to settle in. A lifetime of pain and weakness and poison to gift to the "survivors." Truth could see the fire-control contractors racing down the street, the cops right there with them. Not enough. Not nearly enough. The firefighters tossed flying water-summon talismans, hoping to douse the flames. They had no idea what they were dealing with. The water hit the flames—and exploded.

The water flashed into steam, slamming the ash cloud outward. Then the suddenly free oxygen combusted, turning the area into a short-lived fireball. Chunks of masonry and glass rained down on the sidewalks and on the first responders trying to get a handle on things. Too late. Too little and far too late. The demons had used all that time and fuel to grow. Level-three and -four demons started flying out of the ruins of the bank.

The fire demons joyfully did what they were called to do—spread. Their licking flames reached out and slathered over people and buildings without distinction, leaving cursed ashes as they went. The air demons seemed to dance around the fire demons. Truth could feel them from across the street and dozens of meters up. "Give up," they whispered. "You are dying to protect . . . what? Who? Just give up. Just lay down and let the hurting stop."

The cops had trained for this. The firefighters hadn't. Someone at corporate had gone cheap on the training budget. Truth watched as the cops tried to put up wards and hit the demons with dispels, only to have firefighters succumb to the air demons' whispers and turn the high-pressure water jets on them. One cop shot another in the back of the head before being cut down himself.

Someone at HQ must have given an order, because about a third of the cops leveled their needlers on the firefighters and butchered them. A few puking cops got the wards up, long enough to settle down those the little whispers were reaching. Heavier wards went up, and heavy dispels were starting to come in.

More cops were plowing up the road in armored wagons with the wards deployed. Heavy anti-summon talismans were already on the roof, mounted over the standard heavy needler. Demons started getting shredded, even as the smoke and fire spread farther and farther.

Truth's building was on fire. The flames were above and below him. Ordinary fire wouldn't touch him now. He stayed put and watched the furious counterattack of the fire demons. They melted holes in the road, then worked with the air demons to try to burn through the wards of the immobilized trucks.

There was a furious cry, piercing, avian, outraged. A bird flew in, seemingly made of hammered gold. On its broad back stood half a dozen powerhouses. The ones with the lapel pins got their spells deployed fastest. Spells spun out in geometric lacework and crashed into the demons. Their spiritual bodies shredded and twisted, then vanished. More spells deployed, stacking on one another to clear smoke, to dampen the flames. To stop the endless little whispers. The powerhouses worked fast. Level Seven got a lot of shit done in a hurry, especially against demons far below their level.

Load Graeme's Arrow.

The spell slid into his mind. Superficially familiar, but so much more now than when he had used it before. So many more layers to it. Make something go farther, faster, and more accurately. There were endless ways to play with that, weren't there? But only one rather classic one appealed now. He could feel the spell skittering around in his mind. This . . . wasn't really something the System was capable of casting. Truth studied it ferociously, trying to gather enough understanding to make it at least kind of work.

The demons were pushed back toward the bank. Between the cops and the powerhouses, they were slowly hemmed in, then extinguished. A vast dome was dropped over the melted-slag remains of the bank. Talismans began to coat the exterior. One of the lapel-pin-havers, a boss-looking man, was barking orders. The rest of the Starbrite puppets joined hands with him. An enormous formation of spells came into being around them. From the back of their golden bird, they pushed the spell down on the dome. The talismans activated. There was a hard white light.

Now!

The Meditations gave Truth steady hands and sharp eyes. Incisive told him when and where to send the heavy needle. Graeme's Arrow ensured it got there on time and with the striking power of an overloaded wagon. But it was pure Jeon Army training that taught him how to make a head go "pop" five hundred meters away. Polished to a fine degree by the Starbrite PMC. Not that he had needed much training.

He was running out the back of the burning building before the needle crossed the street. He was jumping to the next building over, already swapping in Abner's Amble, by the time the needle was crossing the bank. He was two blocks away and accelerating by the time an exhausted B-Tier sighed and stepped back, relieved that things had gotten under control.

The heavy needle did what it was designed to do—tiny hole going in, then the far side of the skull exploded outward, painting the back of the golden bird in blood and gore. His colleagues screamed, anti-material wards snapping into place, eyes frantically searching. Truth was four blocks away when the body hit the back of the bird. He was completely gone, invisible among the people, long before someone ordered a search.

Truth made his way back to the hotel. It wasn't very far from the bank, but distances got weird in cities. The two kilometers' distance might as well have put it on the moon. People were walking around casually, asking each other if they had heard about the fire in the bank. Truth ignored the chattering ghosts and dragged himself into the suite. Stripped, showered, and, while he was showering, filled the hot tub.

Black water puddled around his feet. Ash, mostly, and dust. No blood. Nothing had touched him physically. The golem had come close a few times. He had certainly killed an awful lot of other people. But he was only tired, not hurt. The sheer unreality hammered away at him. He had just conducted a massive act of terror . . . and he was fine. Physically. His head was screaming at him that this was fucked, that this kind of thing couldn't happen, or at least not like this. But as far as he could tell, for now, he had gotten away clean.

Not that they wouldn't be hunting him. Oh, would they be hunting him! He could practically hear the orders screaming from officers across the city—*Find who did this at once! Find them and bring them in front of me NOW!*

Well. Between the demons and the cops and the firefighters and the powerhouses, not to mention all the burned-down buildings, they could directly forget picking up his aura or other magical traces. Divining him was going to be a pure loser as well. He was keeping the Scales up for the foreseeable future. Between that and all his resistances, they could try to divine him all they liked.

He stepped into the tub and just soaked. Just . . . tried to let the heat warm him. He placed his hand over his heart. *Could really use some of your warmth right now, Etenesh. I'm awfully cold.* He floated quietly for as long as he could stand, then turned on the scry. It would all be lies anyhow, but maybe there was *something* of use on there.

Ah. An advertisement for floor cleaner. Same stuff he remembered from convenience-store shelves when he was a kid. Oh boy.

The news came on. The presenter was all in black, with black hair and deep, piercing blue eyes. A heartbreaking, waifish beauty, but there was steel to her, resilience. A face that would bruise prettily but would never break. Her makeup team had done wonders with her. He almost felt like applauding.

"Lockdown orders are still in effect across Gwaju as the terrorists remain at large. Reports are coming in from the Greenbaugh district as suspected terrorists resist arrest. As you can imagine, our brave men and women of the uniformed service have no tolerance for terrorist scum, today of all days. We expect reports—" Her head glowed gold for a moment. "We are receiving reports that the Greenbaugh situation has been pacified. No innocent bystanders were harmed, a credit to the skill and professionalism of our heroes in black."

She brushed a "stray" hair back over her ear, emphasizing the fragile lines of her and the thinness of her wrists. But her eyes remained resolved and her voice strong. "Citizens are reminded to shelter in place, as the terrorists are still on the loose, and your safety cannot be guaranteed if you are on the streets. The best thing you can do to help is to stay put and report any suspicious activity to the police tip line. Any lead that leads to an arrest is an automatic ten merits. Any that lead to the capture of a ringleader is fifty. Fifty merits for an anonymous tip." She emphasized the words carefully.

"Once again—by order of the governor, all residents of Gwaju are to shelter in place. No one may enter or exit the city. We *will* catch these murderers. Until then, good night, and good luck."

CHAPTER 29

FINDING SAFETY

Truth floated in the tub. He wasn't particularly bothered by the lockdown—he certainly needed a rest and didn't fear the manhunt finding him. It was something else completely different that had seized his attention—what had Jeon looked like before Starbrite arrived? He had some idea of how Siphios had looked; Merkovah and Etenesh would hardly shut up about how wonderful it had all been. All the strange wonders and mysterious delights of the nation most favored by God. But then, they were looking back on a time when they were literally at the top of the world.

Was Jeon better before the arrival of Starbrite? He didn't really know. His bet was . . . no, it wasn't. Because that was the Starbrite promise, wasn't it? Give us your money and your labor, and we will give you comfort. The sexy, smart, stylish people who have all the best things all work for Starbrite. They have all the brand-new, top-of-the-line stuff. A lot of that tech must have been imported from off-world, now that he thought about it. Even Truth wasn't prepared to believe that Starbrite single-handedly raised the talisman-creation arts to their current heights.

He slowly nodded, staring blankly up at the off-white ceiling. He should check, but he would bet that Starbrite massively raised the quality of life in Jeon. A little country, always afraid of its bigger neighbors. Not scared now. Of course, there were a few *minor* consequences of letting Starbrite get the hold on the country it did, but he could imagine that each step made sense. A chain of perfectly logical, perfectly reasonable decisions, from labor accommodations to loans to export laws. Environmental stuff. He didn't know what stuff, but there must be something, right?

Hell, at some point, Starbrite must have looked like the scrappy underdog. Presumably, so long as no one noticed just what a beast ran it.

Truth smiled bitterly. It seemed he could add history to the ever-growing mountain of *Things Truth Did Not Know*. It wasn't fair. He kept learning new things, and the mountain kept getting bigger. But how were you supposed to make the right choice if you didn't know all the things? Do your best and hope? That hadn't worked great so far. Merkovah would probably say that only God had perfect wisdom, and thus all his choices were correct, but Truth had never been sold on that idea. The evidence didn't seem to support it.

Problem is too big? Make it smaller. What did he want his personal world to look like? His Rough Patron promised him that violence would always be part of his life, at least until he got strong enough to make it stop. He assumed that meant when he was as strong as his Patron, so a long way off. And that led over to what Etenesh had said up on the mountain—the life of a mortal never appealed to him. He would keep climbing until he died or reached the godhead.

Truth bobbed in the water, examining that idea. He had never considered anything other than a mortal life, as he was not aware that there were any alternatives. He understood in some vague way that there was a life after death. There was Heaven and Hell. He had experienced tiny flashes of both through various portals and summonings. The problem there was that no one, including the angels and demons, was terribly consistent about what got you into either place.

Hell certainly seemed deeply unpleasant, an eternity of torment, in fact, but if he had to assign one word to Heaven, it would be *obliteration*. All the human stuff was evaporated by the light of that place, leaving behind . . . something. He didn't know what. Some piece of the soul that was more than human. When he unified with Etenesh (he couldn't call it having sex or something cruder), he had an intuition. When you reach the top of cultivation, something is born. Something great and eternal.

He wanted a safe place. Somewhere good, healthy, and healing. He wanted it for himself and for his sibs and the kind people he had met traveling. He wanted a life together with Etenesh. For whom he had terminal First Girlfriend Syndrome, but it was still what he wanted. Which meant he had to defend that good place because if there was a good place, bad people would always come and take it. Always. Which is why there were gangs and countries. Gotta protect your good place.

He didn't understand how any of that worked. He didn't think he had ever seen a gang or a country live up to all their promises. He understood getting stronger. Becoming smarter. Becoming more capable. Time and again, that was what made those little islands of safety. It was true in Jeon, and it was true in Siphios.

So, what would it take to make the ultimate safe place? A place where his loved ones would be happy and he would be safe to see what sex without cultist supervision was like. Somewhere where he would be strong enough without a gang. Or, rather, becoming strong enough that wherever he decided the safe place was, it was, and it was safe because he said so.

Truth started laughing, a weak, bitter sound. Etenesh really was a lot smarter than him. Infinitely better educated. She had gotten into his head early, figured out how he thought, and run the numbers. There was no perfectly safe place, and Truth would never trust his safety, and the safety of his people, to another. Not if he could help it. So, he would always strive for power. His path would end in either death or becoming a god. Which suited her right down to the ground. If the current God despised her, she would put a new one up in his place. A god that would love her as madly and totally as she loved him. A god that would never abandon her.

And he was even tall, good-looking, interested in her, and a virgin. Truly, He works in mysterious ways.

Truth got out of the tub and let the water-repulsion spell scrape the wet away from him. The bed was as comfortable as he remembered. Exhausted, he slept.

Truth opened his eyes in the pitch-dark room. He could see just fine, so he hardly bothered with the lights. Something had nudged him to alertness. A tingling from Incisive? Or just that ground-in instinct from growing up in the slums? Something was about to kick off. Truth quietly checked the suite—empty. He got dressed as quickly and as silently as he could. Most of his changes of clothes lived in a duffel as it was, so that was easy to square away. But something was niggling at him, and it was getting worse.

He crept to the door and pressed his ear to the crack. Was there something? Someone quietly sneaking past? They were quiet. Very quiet. If they were there at all. Truth's mind raced. If they did manage to track him down, they would send a damn army, and there would be high-levels backing them up. Busting through the door and clearing the hall wasn't smart. Likewise, the window was a loser—they would have people watching the street. The floor or roof? Anyone involved in the bank hit wouldn't be slowed by such feeble barriers. They would be ready for him to try it.

If they were there at all.

He grabbed his duffel and pulled the strap as short as it would go, cinching it to his back. As silent as a cat, he hopped up to the ceiling, then spread out his hands and feet, wedging himself in the corner overlooking the door. If someone kicked in the door, he would have a precious second to assess before anyone spotted him.

He stilled his breath and waited. Every faint noise in the hotel was magnified and dissected, its significance interrogated, and countermeasures were considered. Then he did nothing. Waiting. Waiting for something certain. The silence stretched.

He could hear his blood pumping through his veins. The dull double beat—*thud thud, thud thud, thud thud.* Eyes fixed on the door. Ready to summon his sword in an instant, to kill in an instant.

A muffled *CRUMP*, a breaching charge! Truth forcefully controlled his spasming limbs. It came from next door. Two ungodly huge *BANG*s, as flashbang charms went off. Screamed orders to get down, DOWN. Sharp crackling noises—lightning rounds. They wanted prisoners, not bodies. A bare minute after the assault, calls of "Clear!" started being shouted. A very professional dynamic entry and room clearing.

Truth concentrated on listening. "Five perps. Got needlers, summon scrolls, what looks like a poison-making setup, but that's going to be for the lab guys to figure out. Some propaganda bullshit."

"How many were on the list?"

"Three." The voice sounded grim. "We had no idea on the other two. I ran their IDs. Solid Citizens, until tonight."

"Prager protect us. All right. Let's get it bagged up. The interrogators are backed up as it is, but I want these assholes processed ASAP."

"Might want to bump these guys up the list, Lieutenant."

"Oh?"

"Army-issue needlers. Including a heavy needler. They had plenty of countersurveillance charms, too. Some look professional-grade. And, like I said, demon-summoning scrolls. Not even talismans, actual hide scrolls, which per the manual . . ."

"You aren't saying—"

"Nah, these guys didn't put up a fight. I don't think they had anything to do with the hit on Nowulem."

There was a moment's quiet. Truth waited with as much patience as he could muster. He knew you could carve a spell array on almost anything; you could create a formation in the air. Talismans were just the most convenient and durable. So, what was the deal with hides?

"Well, shit. That's just what we need."

"Might be a coincidence."

"Or it might not. All right, strip this place down to the floorboards. I don't want to miss a single speck of evidence. These guys were pawns. I want to find the player."

"Yes, sir."

Truth stayed glued up in his corner of the ceiling for the next three hours. It wasn't a pleasant time, but his paranoia would demand no less. It seemed that he had spent his last night there. In fact, it might be best to get out of the city entirely. The only problem was he had left a message for Merkovah, which specified that he was in Gwaju. Truth silently sighed. It seemed that he needed to check some dead drops before he left.

Leaving the hotel was intensely nerve-wracking. Truth assumed every exit would be surveilled, with the lobby being forty percent plainclothes cops by volume. Of course, they would put their more discreet and brutal surveillance on the back exits, figuring anyone "smart" would try to run out the back. This would usually be his cue to go out a window, but it wasn't like that was exactly stealthy, either. He was very confident in his ability to hide, but he really, really didn't feel like testing it at the moment.

He eventually settled on a simple but dumb method. It was a luxury hotel, so naturally, there was underground parking. Now, the cops, not being dumb, were checking the boots of carriages and sweeping underneath with mirrors. Truth carefully evaded observation until a carriage with a high ground clearance had passed inspection. Once they turned away to wave it through the gate, he dove beneath it and grabbed on.

A grimy, grim Truth made his way through the dull micro-park next to an office building some forty minutes after leaving the hotel. Lots of gravel and low-maintenance shrubs. A few benches that retracted into the ground at night. Horrible, really. He counted the shrubs from the east exit. When he reached number five, he took a look at the base. Was that an X carved in there, or just a normal twist of the bark? He'd bet an X. Which meant "message received" and told him which ritual to use.

Truth let himself into an office building, picked a floor at random, and found a janitor's closet. He wasn't much for creating rituals, but this was straightforward enough. He had practiced it until it was effortless. A few drops of blood into the middle of the spell diagram and then—

"Oh, *now* you remember how to call."

CHAPTER 30

THE GOOD WORD

"Green Five Delco Pumpkin." Truth was determined to do things properly, even if Merkovah was in a mood.

"You remember the procedure, too! Such a diligent, attentive person. How wonderful. Fai Alsho Seven Seven Wolly." Merkovah's voice was desert-dry. "Is there a particular reason you vanished midway through your transit?"

"Yeah. I didn't want to get sold out by Comrade whoever. And let's be real: he was one hundred percent a rat."

"He is so heavily glamored and mentally conditioned, his head would pop like a zit if he so much as accidentally let something slip. He has an immaculate, multi-decade record of success. A consummate professional."

"Sure."

There was a pause on the line.

"You had a flash of paranoia and figured you would follow the plan, just not *the plan*."

"Yeah."

There was a long, long sigh. "Sure, okay, why not. Not like we have been working on this for years. I'm sure your idea was much better."

"It was. This is what has happened."

Truth started his recitation, emphasizing the widespread rollout of the System Astrologica and its potential for global installation. There was a long quiet at the end of the line.

"We had heard a lot of that from other sources, but you are the first to get hands-on with the actual technology underpinning the enrollment. Although, given the security measures you are describing, I am suddenly concerned about a few agents who have gone silent."

Truth nodded. That ball of whatever-it-was was seriously nasty.

"The global-rollout theory is alarming, however. I will have investigators looking into it. I will also investigate the self-destruct mechanism you describe. To the extent you can do so safely, do keep investigating the tablets. Use a recording talisman if you can—get as many images as possible."

"Will do."

"The good news is that your work has been having an impact. We are seeing resources being shifted south, particularly since you sniped that Level Six outside the bank. Not enough to pull Starbrite's core forces out of Harban, but that's expected." Merkovah's voice turned dry again. "There are some very, very excited intelligence officers who are convinced they are on the trail of a major ringleader."

"I can suggest a few ringleaders if they need a hint."

"No need; they are very creative. It seems that privilege and status are not the shields they used to be. Still formidable, but some rather wealthy, well-connected people are getting invited for a cup of tea down at the station."

"That . . . sounds bad? Why are they getting tea?"

"I mean, they are getting arrested, just more gently than you are used to seeing."

"Okay, but why tea? Is tea particularly sinister?"

"How could tea be sinister?"

"You have the cops waterboarding people with tea; you tell me."

"When have I had the police—" There was a sudden quiet. "You know, there is always a concern that an agent will be captured or mind-controlled or something. That the enemy will be using them to ferret out information on other agents. I am so relieved to see you are free and well."

"Eh, I'm physically well, but mentally, I'm not so sure."

"Oh? What troubles you?"

"What is the definition of a human being?"

There was another pause. "Could you elaborate on that a little?" Merkovah's voice was surprisingly soft.

Truth laid out how he had felt, looking at the shift supervisor in the logistics center, a former human reduced to a mere component, existing in fear and pain. The sense of all the normal people feeling unreal. That only the monsters were real. The terrifying presence of Remu Anakson, who seemed more "real" than some Level Six and Seven people he could think of.

Merkovah sighed. "Don't dig too deep into Anakson. Feel free to focus Starbrite on him if you like, but don't put too much into it yourself. I know roughly what he is, even if I don't know who he is. The very short version is that every theology agrees there were very few people at the beginning, and pretty much every human you have ever met traces their lineage back to one of those early people. There were other lineages."

Truth puzzled over that one.

"He's another kind of human?"

"More likely, he is some kind of hybrid between the humans you know and another kind of human, yes. And those other kinds have their limitations, but they are quite strong. In several senses of the word. I suspect that he and his family are planning for the post-collapse world and are an unnecessary battle for now."

"Huh. Okay. And the rest?"

"You are experiencing an accelerated and perhaps exaggerated version of something every powerhouse encounters. You are simply above others. It's an unpleasant thought in a lot of ways. But you are. You are stronger, faster, possessed of monstrously more magical power, will live longer, suffer few or no diseases, and can go without air or water for extended periods—you are simply *better* than the masses. It is an uncomfortable mindset, and your growth has been calamitously fast. You haven't had a chance to adjust."

Truth thought that made sense, even if it felt profoundly uncomfortable.

"The other part of that is the Blessing of the Silent Forest. What you are experiencing is a known consequence. I didn't mention it because, well, you seemed so alienated from the world already."

"Pardon?"

"Mr. Wells"—Truth jerked a little, then grinned—"kindly recall the precise chain of events needed to get you a friend and a wife."

"I'm not married!"

"Sure, tell yourself that."

"All right, I don't trust easily," There was a snorting noise through the ritual. "But I wouldn't say I was *alienated* from the world."

"Only because you aren't entirely sure what the word means. You don't instinctively connect with people or the world. You interrogate every relationship. To everything. Frankly, I thought you would find the unnoticeability rather comfortable."

Truth had to admit that he generally did. "Fair."

"Next steps? We aren't ready to make our move yet. We need more chaos."

"How are things in Harban?"

"Tense. You want to make a move there?"

"Can't do much more here. The whole city is on a hair trigger. What are those eyeless things, anyway?"

"I don't know. We only started observing them in the last decade and have not captured any for examination. They seem to be some sort of homunculus, but I simply do not know. Don't go anywhere near them if you can avoid it. They are probably weaker than you, but they may well be able to perceive you. Their 'vision' operates on some principle I do not understand."

"Understood."

"Before you go home, I want you to break into somewhere for me—a Starbrite research facility. No chance the Shattervoid girl is there, but I do hope that you may find a lead on her."

"Okay."

There was a pained chuckle. "*Okay* indeed," Merkovah told him where the information for the op would be hidden. It was a coded reference to a spot outside the city. "On a more personal note, your alternative insertion route meant that you missed hearing about your siblings."

"I have been trying hard not to think about them. Didn't seem like the right time."

"Well, here is the short version. Your oldest sibling is, indeed, working for the Enemy as a laboratory manager. The facility is related to material science, so he shouldn't have any connection to your operations. No more information could be found; he appears to be living a quiet, ordinary life."

"Good for him," Truth said. It was all he had ever wanted for Harmony.

"Your middle sibling is pursuing an advanced degree in biology at the University of Jeon. While there is nothing particularly noteworthy about her work, her advisor is connected to many powerful figures, most of whom have unwholesome interests. So far, she appears fine."

Truth nodded. He wanted to rush in and sort out that professor, but . . .

"Your youngest sibling is, however, something of a mystery. We can't find him."

"Pardon?" Truth asked with a guillotine edge.

"We can trace his steps up to a point—he completed high school, passed his SAT, did his national service, then simply vanished. Your other siblings don't seem too concerned for him, so I doubt he vanished involuntarily, but whatever he is doing, he is doing it very, very discreetly."

Huh. Figures it would be Vig. Well, that was worrying. Still, nothing he could do about it, so he'd just have to deal.

"And . . . my significant other?"

Merkovah sighed.

"Better and worse. Better in that she is less openly paranoid and homicidal. She has definitely calmed down a lot and will probably return from seclusion in a week or two. Worse in that she is developing a whole theology. She is still fixated on your . . . elevation."

Truth nodded. That also sounded about right. "Pass her a message for me?"

Merkovah went quiet for a moment. "I'm afraid not. Just too many ways for that to go wrong."

Truth nodded a little more sadly at that.

"I can tell her you asked after her. That will cheer her up."

"Please do."

"Any other business?"

"Yeah, that 'define *human*' thing—you never mentioned the shift supervisor. Not wildly below my level, clearly from our branch of humanity, but I can't help but think of him as a kind of meat puppet."

"What is there to say? You are right. Though this, too, is a common form of 'human' existence."

"Doesn't help me reach my answer."

"Didn't say it would." Merkovah sighed. "There is a school of thought, not a very large school, that believes you can define something negatively. It's not this, not that, not this other thing, and by excluding everything that it isn't, all that's left is what a thing is."

"That sounds incredibly complicated. Unnecessarily complicated."

"Most would agree with you. Myself included. But it's not a useless technique. Perhaps you could start by cataloging those things that humans aren't before trying to nail down what they are."

"And God?"

"What about him?"

"Should he be defined negatively? People keep telling me he is great beyond our understanding, so negatively defining God seems sensible."

There was a choking noise. "I seem to remember something. Something about the job at hand. Maybe we can focus on that."

"Want me to blow up another bank on the way to Harban?"

"Wouldn't be the worst idea, actually. But no, let's change it up a bit. How would you feel about another assassination?"

"Who's the target?"

"Another Level Six Starbrite officer."

"Tasty. You know that last guy only got hit because he was utterly wiped out, right?"

"Yes, you timed it perfectly. Graeme's Arrow seems quite suitable for you. The hit is tangentially related to that, actually."

"Oh?"

"Yes, he's one of their top spell researchers. Under almost any other circumstances, I would desperately want him alive, along with all the research materials you could lay your hands on. His abilities as a modern magical researcher are among the very best in the world."

"Include his details in the drop."

"Will do. Keep at it, young man. You are having an effect. The plan progresses. There is still hope."

Truth ended the ritual and leaned against the wall with a sigh. He was happy that his work was getting results. Very happy that Etenesh was doing better. His sibs were . . . what they were. It wouldn't matter much if he didn't get the Shattervoid girl—they would just have to figure out how to survive in the aftermath until he could collect them all. Luckily, only Har was actually in Starbrite.

He just couldn't find the right shape of words to ask Merkovah what he really wanted to know—*What kind of world are we hoping for at the end of all this?* Be it off-world, on this planet, or whatever. *What is life like for all the ghosts haunting this mudball? What is a human being? Because that has to be the first question, right? Answer that, and you can start figuring out how the world should be arranged.*

He still had no damn idea about how that should be done. None at all.

He started cleaning up the ritual space. No sense in letting a janitor discover a trace. He had his duffel bag with his few possessions. He would go buy some snacks, and then it would be time to break out of the city.

He couldn't say what shape the world should be in, but he knew he couldn't stand the way it was. Starbrite was the world-tyrant, a false god of sorts. He grinned slightly. To make his safe place, he would behead kings and cut down gods. He was looking forward to it.

CHAPTER 31

ON THE ROAD AGAIN

Truth was strolling out of the office building when Incisive started blaring an alarm. His own eyes were very nearly as fast—police cruisers were swarming up the street, smashing aside any carriage or wagon too slow to clear out. Flying platforms decked out in black and gold were incoming faster still, and he could hear the shriek of some great bird overhead.

It seems that the ritual had been detected. He could only hope it wasn't intercepted. In the meantime, he would run like hell. He turned away from the cops and put his legs in motion. Downtown Gwaju in the middle of the day—it was crowded. He had to dodge. Moving onto the street would give him more room to run, but he would be easier to spot. He gritted his teeth and kept moving. He had the reflexes for it. He could dodge. Besides, compared to him, these people were mannequins.

Truth just blindly ran—no destination except "away." Away was always good; toward was dangerous. You didn't know what might be there when you arrived. But you always knew what was coming up behind you. The ghostly pedestrians seemed frozen with startled looks on their faces, staring blankly at the column of police vehicles headed their way. Truth couldn't see the watcher creatures, but he knew they were there. Either in the wagons or in the air. Actually, he would bet on "in the air." Nothing for it but to be faster. Don't stand on the X.

The bird screeched overhead. The ghosts might be immobile, but the bird spirit was Level Six. It was moving just fine. Truth could feel the weight of the attention from high-level magi sweeping up the street. Incisive and the Blessing of the Silent Forest both drew hard on his cosmic-energy reserves. He could hang on, maybe, for a few seconds, but they would spot a fast-moving blur easily. He needed to find cover.

Truth tried to expand his vision, fighting the fatal urge to tunnel. Doorways? Not good enough, and no guarantee that he wouldn't bounce off a ward or lock. Under a moving carriage? Better, but nothing with enough clearance. Try to blend with the crowd. That would buy him a few more seconds at best. He opted for a city bus, diving in through a closing door and grabbing a strap. Just another talisman-maintenance tech. Just a tech. Just a tech. Just a tech.

The bus pulled over to let the cops roar past. Truth breathed out a small sigh of relief. The cops, airborne and ground, swarmed the office building he had contacted Merkovah from. They had definitely traced the ritual. Truth silently cursed. Merkovah had sworn blind that they were untraceable. Guess the technology had improved. The bus pulled over a few blocks from the office. Truth didn't move—too close. He would ride it out a bit farther.

The doors didn't open. The driver didn't say anything either.

"Hey, what's the problem?" someone yelled.

"Orders from the City. Have to stand by for an inspection."

Shit. Truth started desperately looking around for an escape route. Someone beat him to it. A hungry-looking lady pulled a meat cleaver out of her tote bag and smashed the butt of it through a window. The safety glass cracked, and she launched herself at it. Some plainclothes dick on the bus grabbed her, wrestling for the cleaver. She smashed his nose with her forehead and launched backward, trying to escape through the window. He hung on, swearing and trying to get off a spell. They smashed the window open, but he managed to keep her in the bus.

Truth wasn't one to look a gift revolutionary in the mouth. He jumped. And he was not alone. Nobody thought talking to the cops was a good idea. Truth was off and running again, this time making sure he ran at ninety degrees from the route the other bus escapees were taking. He ducked into an alley and fought the urge to hide in the first dumpster he saw.

That was stupid-rat thinking. Even the slowest cop would check there. He would have to be smarter than that. And farther away. The pressure on his cosmic energy had eased up some with fewer eyes on him. He put his head down and ran.

At his speed, without having to dodge crowds, he cleared a kilometer in a bare minute. He could have done it faster on an open road, but things like "people" and "trash cans" or "illegally parked carriages" were stumbling blocks. A kilometer was a long way. A search radius around the office building of a kilometer-plus? It would take every cop in the city.

He felt an icicle trickle of danger slide down his spine. With an explosive dive, he buried himself *under* a dumpster. A few seconds later, he could feel the pressure of unearthly perception flowing along the alley. Truth felt his cosmic energy burning fast, faster than fighting demons, faster than he could have imagined. Incisive and the Blessing fought to hold up under the pressure. The gaze lingered a long moment on the dumpster. Truth gasped desperately, trying to fuel the spell for even one second longer. The gaze focused—

And moved on. Truth collapsed. Shivering. His body drained almost empty. The cosmic rays were pouring in now, flooding him. Almost burning him, but his repeated brushes with burnout had toughened him up some. He could deal. He just lay on the reeking ground and shook. Spasming. They were a second from spotting him. Just one second, not even a single breath, from spotting him.

He spent the rest of the day under the dumpster, cultivating to regain his energy. They swept the alley two more times, but he was ready for them, with more energy in reserve. By the third time through, it was more like a cursory glance than a careful check. He kept right where he was. When dawn rose the next morning, Truth emerged from under the dumpster. Sore, thirsty, starving, absolutely desperate for a change of trousers and a shower. But alive.

Truth had solved the most urgent and smelly problems by breaking into the first apartment building he saw and going for the first apartment. He wasn't squeamish by any definition, but unpleasant things are unpleasant. The trousers and underwear got a quick wash and were left to soak in a basin.

Truth crammed himself into the tiny shower and gave himself a similar treatment. No such thing as too much soap, he felt. Though he did feel a little bad—these people only had one thin bar of soap in the whole house. He desperately wanted to shampoo, but he wasn't about to steal from someone poor enough to buy their shampoo by the sachet.

It just wasn't that urgent. He got the worst off. For the rest . . . he could deal for now.

Twenty-four hours later than he had intended, Truth made his way to a convenience store. He had managed to hold on to his duffel with his meager possessions. To those few changes of clothes, he added laundry soap, two-in-one shampoo and conditioner (on the theory that it was really three-in-one because you could use it as body wash), toothpaste, toothbrush, two big bottles of water, and all the most energy-dense snacks he could lay hands on. He hesitated a moment and then added some microfiber shammies. They were meant for wiping down a carriage, but he figured they would probably be decent little towels. Just in case.

The cashier could not have been less interested. There was a fight on the scry next to him, but Truth didn't recognize the fighters. Long time since he had watched the fights.

"What's the nearest bus?" he asked.

"Number fifty-eight, but it's canceled."

"Damn. Are any of them running?"

"Nah. Orders still in place."

"Shit. I had hoped they lifted it."

"Nope." The fight had the clerk's full attention. Truth didn't blame him, either.

"You got any maps?"

"Nope."

There was no elaboration. Truth gave up and started walking. The sun was up. Harban was north-northwest of Gwaju. He'd figure things out once he was out of the city.

Truth made his way north through the city. He prioritized safety over speed and quickly began learning with his body what he already knew with his mind—it was all about energy cost. Everything cost energy. Existing cost energy. Moving cost more energy—the faster you move, the more energy it costs. Concealment in all its varying forms cost varying amounts of energy. You had to balance that against speed, of course. An indirect route may lengthen the journey traveled, but the reduced visibility may actually increase speed and safety. Of course, going slowly or indirectly increases your period of vulnerability.

Because they were still looking for him. Hard. Truth's paranoia had been raised to a painful degree, but it was necessary. He watched from a block away as flying platforms slammed down on either end of a cross street, raising a barrier. Unmarked police wagons pulled out of traffic and rushed in, cops bursting out like furious ants and sweeping the street. Sigils were checked, identities verified, and you had better have a *damn* good reason for being out on the street, or you would be finding out what the "tea" in the precinct tasted like.

Truth mentally waved goodbye to his "rampage" plan to bring the Ghūl onboard. It would have to wait.

He understood why they were spending so much money on this. The traced international-comms ritual. The first real evidence of a foreign agent, maybe even a mastermind. Internal Security had to know it was chasing its own tail. Rounding up dozens and dozens of seconds-in-command without ever quite nailing the actual leaders. But what else could they do? Not pursue the leads? The chance to take down a real player was simply too valuable. They *had* to get results.

The pressure from above must be enormous. Not that he had the least sympathy. He kept moving silently, invisibly. Across backyards and alleys, over rooftops, in the front of a restaurant and out the back. All the usual rules about city traversal were studiously ignored. He made a point of traveling where there were no roads. It took him all day to cross a small city, despite how fast he could move. But he made it safely and with most of his energy reserves intact.

There were only so many roads out of Gwaju, highways, really, and they were heavily observed by the cops. Checkpoints on all of them, entire packs of spell hounds, spell birds circling like swallows, and all those were only to distract from the dozen nigh-invisible watcher things that perched like gargoyles on the street lights.

Truth sighed and found a nearby Nice-Nice convenience store. He restocked on water and snacks and thoughtfully added a roll of toilet paper to his supplies. He couldn't believe he had forgotten that earlier. Rookie mistake.

"Would you like to try our exciting new gustation sensation, the Triple Max Maxxor Supreme Flavor Explosion Fiesta?" The clerk managed to say the entire sentence entirely in a monotone. Truth was tempted to check for a pulse. He had seen livelier golems. Then he spotted the sigil on the clerk's wrist. Denizen. Had they announced the changeover yet? If they hadn't, it would be any day now. Poor bastard knew he wasn't getting paid.

"What's a fiesta?"

"Dunno."

"Well . . . what is it that I would be trying?"

The clerk pointed at a shockingly orange hexagon under a heat lamp, apparently stuffed with . . . stuff. Was this, too, part of the path of the foodie? A destined trial to overcome?

"I'll take one. Got any maps?"

"Yeah. To your left." Truth snagged a road atlas. "Not that it's any use. Roadblocks up everywhere now."

"Still looking for the terrorist? I haven't been watching scry."

"Yeah, a whole cell of them, apparently. Scary stuff." The clerk sounded biologically incapable of giving a shit.

"Well, stay safe out there."

The clerk took Truth's money, made change, and handed him his poison hexagon. "Have yourself a Nicey-Nicey Day." The clerk had already forgotten his existence. No spell required. Truth sighed and walked back out onto the sidewalk, mentally prepping for the cross-country jaunt ahead. Back on the road again.

CHAPTER 32

CATCHING A BREATH

To get cleanly out of Gwaju, a small city of no particular importance at the southern tip of the Jeon peninsula, one had to cross the highway that ringed the outer edge of the city. More like a three-quarters circle on account of the ocean being in the way, but that was the basic idea. You could be in your fine carriage, coming in from one of the "attractive" and "enviable" suburbs around the city, and simply *zoom* to your high-paying job in the city. The space and privacy of the countryside, with the convenience and industry of the city. The best of both worlds.

Truth admired the parking lot in front of him. Traffic was at a full stop as far as he could see in both directions. This was not, he was surprised to learn, because of the lockdown. It was because it was the evening rush hour. *Evening rush hour* was defined as the period of some four hours, covering the late afternoon and early evening. The police checkpoints weren't exactly speeding things up, but the extra traffic control more or less balanced the delay caused by the inspection. Truth didn't know whether to laugh or cry. He could cause more damage to the city by knocking over a couple of wagons here than by firebombing a police station.

Not that either activity was called for at the moment. No, the challenge was how to get across this massive stream of vehicles without hundreds or thousands of bored eyeballs staring at him and wondering what a person was doing crossing the highway. There were spell birds patrolling up and down the highway, too—the draw on Incisive and the Blessing of the Silent Forest would be immense, multiplying the drain of total unnoticeability.

He wanted to go back to when he could just swan around, effortlessly ignored by dozens of Level Ones or an unlimited quantity of Level Zeros. The last twenty-four hours or so had sucked, and he really, really just wanted to find a place to rest.

He looked up the road, seeing the swarming police presence, knowing that rest was still a long way off. He sighed deeply. The overpass he was on led down a ramp onto the highway proper. The highway itself was separated from the suburban houses next to it by a tall bank of dirt with a very tall cement wall on top of that. It wasn't intended to be pedestrian-accessible. That was kind of the point.

Truth gamed out a couple of ideas, decided none were particularly practical, and went for the most time-consuming and safest. He strolled to the edge of the exit ramp, crouched down, and ran along the wall. He was briefly visible to the cars stacked up on the ramp, but only briefly, and only to a few people at a time. The drain on his energy was negligible and easily covered by its normal regeneration.

From the ramp to the road was slightly trickier, but only slightly. He dove into the drainage ditch that ran alongside the highway and used it to line up his route. It took ages crawling around, but it did have the advantage of, again, minimizing exposure and, again, reducing energy usage to almost nothing. Then, when he found a reasonably good crossing point, he crouched low and ran.

This time, he was using the almost-stationary carriages as his cover, hiding behind bodywork or hoods, moving from cheap carriages to late-model beaters, to utility wagons, and so on. Avoiding anything that even vaguely suggested the owner might be over Level Two. There was a steady drain on his energy at this point, but nothing too dreadful. More eyes on him, after all. He made it across the road and flopped down in the ditch.

After gathering his breath a moment, Truth rolled onto his back and looked up. From the bottom of the ditch to the top of the wall was almost twenty meters. Optimism be damned; he was sure he didn't have a twenty-meter vertical jump. What he did have was absolutely brutal, literally superhuman, speed. Once he was sure his cosmic energy was as full as it was reasonably going to get without cultivating, he got his feet under him, almost curled into a ball in the ditch. He leaned over and put his hands on the embankment. Braced himself. Then jumped!

His first bound easily took him halfway up the embankment. He just wanted to have enough speed so that his next three steps would carry him to the wall with ease. Then Abner's Amble! He cast the spell as soon as he hit the top of the embankment. Put his toes on the wall and launched *UP*! The drain on his cosmic energy was as explosive as his launch as he shot up to the top of the wall. It took all his lightning reflexes to catch the edge of the wall as he went past and changed his vector from "up" to "over."

He landed in an impeccably fertilized and mowed yard, which he proceeded to cross at speed. He didn't stop running flat-out until he was ten kilometers from the highway and safely hidden in the guest bedroom of a suburban family home. He collapsed on the soft mattress, dirty shoes on the clean bedspread. It wasn't nice of him, but he was too tired to care.

The family was having dinner downstairs. Sounded tense, but the parents were doing their best to hold it together for the kids. Truth was intensely uncomfortable, but he was also completely shattered at this point. It wasn't the physical stress. It was being hunted. Of judging every tiny move. Not feeling safe for a single second. It took a toll. The family would go to bed soon. It would be enough.

He tried to consciously relax his muscles. He knew how to do this. They talked about it in therapy. Heck, they talked about it in romance novels. You focus on your breathing, and when you have it deep, slow, and steady, you pay attention to the top of your head. And you let it relax. You give it permission to just let go. To relax. Then you work your way down, muscle by muscle, to the tips of your fingers and the soles of your feet. Take as long as you like. Just breathe, direct your attention, and let it relax.

It always made him sleepy. Even the noise of the evening routine didn't stop him from drifting away.

He snapped straight back to alertness when the wife walked into the room. She looked tired. Drained. Carrying a book and a glass of water. She closed the door behind her, switched on the light next to the bed, and pulled back the cover. Truth scootched over to the side. She slid into bed next to him, reading. Trying to relax. He could see it. She was trying to calm her breath. Ten minutes later, it still wasn't working for her. Truth would have told her to cultivate, but a bare Level One, trying to cultivate as the magic thinned? It would have been better than nothing but not a lot better.

Fifteen minutes in, and she gave a resigned little sigh. She opened the bedside table and pulled out a little blue vial. A few drops went into her water, turning the whole thing a faint turquoise. She drank it sip by sip, visibly relaxing. Truth just watched. What could he tell her? To be strong? That things would work out? Her kids needed her? Her husband needed her? She needed herself? They didn't even qualify as comforting lies anymore. It was pure insult. For her, despair was completely rational. She lacked the mental training to rebel. To find meaning in this desperate, futile world.

He had no hope to offer. Not even faith. All he could think of was what got him through his childhood. What was getting him through the present. With a tired effort, he cast Incisive.

"Sometimes, when everything is doomed, and you can't see any hope, the only thing to do is act like *what you are doing matters*. Make yourself believe it. *Believe it* all the way to the end. Believe it as you are dying, if you have to. Because it hurts too much to think nothing you do matters. And who knows? Maybe it will work after all. So, *you can sleep now*. You can rest, knowing *you did your best*. And tomorrow you will get up, hug your kids, kiss your husband, and *fight like hell*."

Truth managed to sleep next to the wife, though not well. He realized, with a faint trace of self-loathing, that she didn't register as any sort of threat to him. He was quietly confident that, even if she pulled a needler from under her nightgown, she still couldn't hurt him with it. She just was lesser. Not a being on the same level of existence. So, he got a fitful night's sleep in a comfortable bed.

He decided to make it a slow morning. Partially because he was still emotionally exhausted from his escape from Gwaju, and partially because he felt guilty about relegating the family to a lower tier of beings. Specifically, leaving his dirty footprints on the cover. He would beat the piss out of anyone who did that to one of his sheets. Enchanted cleaning tubs were standard in any suburban home, right? So, it wasn't a heavy lift.

<<About that. Might be a good time to try Cup and Knife. See what "fixing things" means in practice.>>

Nice. Load it up.

<<So, usual disclaimers about trying to run an old-time Siphios spell without study apply here, several times over. I think you can get it off, but expect it to take a lot of tries.>>

Truth shrugged. Wasn't like he was in an immediate rush. Despite the enrollment period coming closer with every passing second. Truth shook his head. Bad way of thinking. Time spent sharpening the axe wouldn't slow cutting the tree and all that.

The spell felt . . . some kind of way. Prickly, maybe? Or irritable, if a spell could have emotions. Like a man speaking very clearly, but people kept misunderstanding him. Frustrated. The System passed on what it had learned studying the spell to Truth. Truth snagged the key points easily—indicate what needed fixing and let the spell rip.

The cover shouldn't have mud on it. Easy-peasy. Cup and Knife didn't quite go off. Truth tried it a few times, and eventually, there was a desolate little spark of energy. The duvet was now quite clean. He got in close and took a good look. He couldn't see anything inherently different. The fibers weren't damaged or anything. Just . . . poof. Dirt gone, at a very low energy cost.

<<Yeah, but gone where?>>

Truth had no answer to that. He shrugged, grabbed a very thorough shower, and had a nice sit-down breakfast from the junk food in his duffel. He put on the scry for a minute but couldn't find the news. Oh, well. He knew where the dead drop was and how to get there. A complete pain in the ass going cross-country, but he was still too close to Gwaju to want to risk running down the highway. His shoulders slumped as he looked over his map. Another tiring day. Well. Nothing for it but to get started. He oriented himself on the map and started his great cross-suburbia adventure.

CHAPTER 33

MONSTERS OF SUBURBIA

If Merkovah's package had made it to the dead drop, there would be a white rock under the fourth post of the fence outside of 934 West Pichno Street, Damya, Damya being a small town in farm country just up the highway from Gwaju. Since this was Jeon, a densely settled peninsula, "farm country" started just after a comparatively small belt of suburbs, and he was a bare fifteen kilometers away in a straight line. Easy, except he was standing in a suburban backyard, and this was *Jeon,* so there was surveillance everywhere. He had gotten paranoid about his energy reserves and was determined to stay off the roads and out of sight as much as possible.

The Blessing of the Silent Forest should protect him thoroughly from any but the most direct and searching investigation by a powerhouse. Should. He did not enjoy hiding out under a dumpster for a day. It was tiresome, but paranoia was a lifestyle one could only choose if they were still alive. He did a bit of crude orienteering and started his journey trespassing through the domains of the morbid mowers of suburbia.

He kept his pace steady, letting Abner's Amble carry him from yard to yard. They were so similar. Neat little squares of grass mowed to a neat height. Some with little gardens of well-spaced and mulched flowers, the cheap, bright annuals you could buy in packs of six from in front of the supermarket. It was spring—planting season. Made sense that people would be putting their gardens in. There were fewer toys in yards than he expected. The ones that did have toys were either bombed-out wrecks of neglect and empty bottles or yards given over entirely to children and pets.

Truth stopped for a half-second on his journey. One yard had a swing set with a single bright yellow plastic seat. It looked worn by the weather, the synthetic ropes holding the seat already weathered and bleached. It looked like it had seen a lot of use. He just looked at it. Tried not to think about the family that lived here. Did the kid outgrow the swing? Or did they still use it? Did they swing alone, or were there lots of little friends who came over to play in the yard, too? Networking was so important, and one had to start as early as possible. Or so he had heard. He wouldn't know.

He pressed on. It didn't matter. None of these little boxed-up lives mattered. Not because they were particularly bad. Just . . . a thing was worth what someone would give you for it, right? And nobody would buy these lives on a bet. Not right now. Not in the end of days. After the collapse, yes, people would give anything to live in a safe little suburban box. It would be a life they could only remember in their dreams.

Truth didn't notice his pace picking up. Flickering from yard to yard, trying not to see the detritus of hidden worlds. Kites. Mowers. Iron horses carefully covered by tarps. Chairs in pairs around little tables. The tiny statues in the gardens, votives to saints, the open hand of Prager holding a birdbath. The people still at home mid-morning, drinking a cup of maybe coffee and staring emptily into their backyards, wondering how it came to this and how long they could hold on.

In one of the wrecked yards, littered with trash and crushed beer cans, a bathtub had been partially buried, sticking upright out of the dirt. What should have been the inner part of the tub was painted a light blue. A white plaster statue of St. Eikren, smiling widely, robed richly and draped in painted gems, stood in the niche. One hand reached out to receive offerings, the other raised to offer blessings. One of the most popular saints. Truth remembered that smiling face from his one month of attending church.

Someone had beaten a dog almost to death in front of the shrine. Not a stray—it had a collar and tags. Someone had stolen a dog (he prayed it was stolen) and used a shovel to beat it in front of the shrine to Eikren. A dog's life for prosperity. The thing responsible had failed to do it cleanly. The dog was mercifully unconscious, but Truth could see it hung on to life by a fraying thread.

Truth couldn't move on. He couldn't. This was horrible. This was . . . wrong. Wrong in every way. So wrong, he struggled to put words around it. He rejected this. Utterly. Categorically. He wanted to reject what he was seeing, pretend it wasn't real, but he had never been good at that. Someone had beaten a dog almost to death in hopes a plaster saint would make them prosperous.

Cup and Knife.

This was wrong. Wrong. All wrong. The dog shouldn't be dying. It should be healed, fit, and happy. It should be home with its family. The spell seemed to agree, coming together fast this time. There was a sudden sense of the world being unaccountably thin—as though it was only painted on a pane of glass, and Truth could suddenly see someone moving on the other side.

The dog went faint, then blurred, as though there were two dogs superimposed. One near-dead, the other joyously alive. One with wounds, the other without. He could fix the dog, return it to how it should be. But the wounds did happen. Truth had a strange instinct. He let the spell run a little wild, pouring power into it. There was a faint thread running off the dog—no, off the wounds.

Truth grinned—a savage, bloody thing. He slammed more power into the spell. The wounds vanished. A happy dog popped up off the ground, looking around in confusion. It sniffed Truth enthusiastically, then started rocketing around the yard. Truth had a look at the tag and consulted his road atlas. Barely two blocks away. He dropped the dog off in its home yard.

As for the person who did the beating? Truth saw a body sitting in the window of the house with the shrine. It looked like someone had worked her over with a shovel. A locked-room murder mystery, doubtless to be thoroughly investigated. By someone. Someday. Probably. Maybe. Budget permitting. Such is life. He set off again.

So, no disrespect to that grand eminence, but—

<<Fuck Buer; you are learning Cup and Knife.>>

Yep. We'll keep studying Graeme's Arrow. It's too useful not to have in the arsenal, but like Abner's Amble, it's situational. This is . . . incredible. What just happened? The wounds transferred to the human, making it like the dog was never harmed. Easy to say, but . . .

<<Yeah, I have no damn idea. My best guess, and it's not a great guess, is that the actual change took place on another layer of reality. Basically, the reason the energy cost was so low was that the change was, one, pretty small, all things considered, and two, the objects being affected had a limited amount of weight in our layer of reality. A Level One and a non-spiritual dog are fairly unreal, comparatively.>>

Truth nodded slightly at that. *Makes sense. Though I would assume that the wounds didn't translate directly to the human. Humans are laid out differently, for one thing.*

<<Solid guess. Actually, there are a lot of blanks to fill in here. How did the spell determine who to curse, for one thing?>>

That would be pretty high on list of things to figure out, yeah. Also, leaving aside the issue of motivation, did you notice how effortless that was, compared to cleaning mud off a bedspread? Fully healing a near-dead dog, making it like the injuries never happened, then transporting those wounds through a house's protections, overcoming any minor resistance the Level One might have, and killing them. All came together easier than the laundry.

Truth could imagine the System slowly nodding. *<<I wonder if this isn't the reason the spell was simultaneously kept in a reference volume and sidelined. Inconsistency in cost of use, ease of use, and probably a bunch of other factors. I suspect that the key difference was the sense of moral outrage by both you and the spell's creator. Making the sheets dirty is kind of shitty but not "beating a pet to death as a sacrifice" shitty. You kept at it until the spell rolled its eyes, sighed, and did it. Metaphorically. On the other hand, you were transcendentally outraged, seeing that dog.>>*

The world is wrong. It needs fixing. This is one of those things. I will use the spell to fix it. Truth played it out. *And that aligned with however the creator thought. The creator also had views on things like that.*

The System gave the feeling of a nod. Truth got his head back on running. It was going faster than he feared it would. The houses were getting more spaced out, and actual farms were starting to take over.

He landed on the edge of a fence and crouched there for a moment. A man was mowing the lawn. Beer in one hand, push mower in the other. It was a soft whickering sort of noise as the blades spun around. He reached the end of the yard, made the turn, and mowed the next strip. Machine-like focus, only stopping now and then to drink the beer. Back and forth. There were many like him. What made Truth stop was the noose hanging from a crossbeam under the porch.

Did he have a moral duty to interfere? Truth felt a sort of split decision from the Tongue and Etenesh—one vote no, one vote yes. So, no help there. What did he think was the right thing to do? He certainly couldn't waste any more time than he already had. And maybe suicide wasn't the worst thing? He didn't know. Seemed extreme. But, hell, if your life was already shitty and the literal end of the world was coming, what harm was there in leaving early and beating the queue?

Oh, fuck it. Maybe Etenesh would be proud of him if he did at least a *little* something. He landed next to the morbid mower, smelling the reek of beer on his breath. A quick flex of Incisive—

"You know, your breath stinks. Gotta brush those teeth before . . . you know. And grab a shower. Look presentable. Yard's looking great. It would be dumb to go out looking like a slob. All right, teeth, shower, shave . . . ah, hell, will you look at the state of that mulch? The plants are gonna die by the time anyone finds you and waters them. That's not fair. They shouldn't have to go with you. Get mulch, mulch 'em in, then rope. Okay, that's a program. Got a plan right there. Man like you? You can do anything so long as you have a plan. And hey, maybe they have something worth planting at the garden center. Nothing says you have to rope on some schedule. Nothing wrong with putting in more time on the garden before the big goodbye. And just check the price on paint when you are there. Some rough-looking patches on the sunny side. Don't want people thinking you were a slob."

Truth didn't know shit about preventing suicide. All he could think of was . . . give 'em more things to do, and maybe they would change their mind. Fingers crossed it would work. And if not . . . worse things happen in the suburbs every day. At least he would die presentable. Not everyone got that.

Truth hit the edge of farm country and turned on the speed. Cover was minimally available there, but, on the plus side, there were almost no people. Most of the fields were empty or overseen by golem machines weeding and watering. Truth stretched his muscles and flew over the ground. Abner's Amble, combined with a relentlessly refined body, was simply adding wings to a cheetah. The farmland between Gwaju and Damya was five times longer than the width of suburbia Truth had spent the day crossing. He cleared the farmland in less than three minutes.

Welcome to Damya. Home of some chain shops, a rest station, and the Jeon Museum of Bamboo, apparently. He found the address. The homeowner had decided to line the bottom of the fence with pale gray stones. Truth sighed and started hunting around under the fourth fencepost on the eastern side. Hoping a white stone was buried under all the gray.

CHAPTER 34

THEOSOPHY

Truth was confronted with an awkward problem. You never, ever, go to the same dead drop twice. Once you touch it, the drop is dead. Touch it a second time, and you are dead. So, if you check it, it had *damn* well better have something in it. Hence having covert signals to let operatives know the drop was made. Truth found it all refreshingly simple and robust. The signal he was looking for was a white stone.

He considered the chicken-egg-sized rock in front of him. Was it a light gray? Or white? Was the color different from any of the thirty other stones in the maybe pile? Hard to say. Damned hard to say. He had already run off and snagged some white things from nearby houses as color-matching samples, but it was still irritatingly inconclusive. He had already limited his search area to the space between the third and fifth post on the fence, coming from the eastern end. Categorically, anything considered *under the fourth post* should be in that field.

He threw the rock onto the maybe pile. The definitely-no pile had four rocks in it. The definitely yes pile had zero. He was going to kill someone. Several someones.

Truth collapsed on the sidewalk next to his little heaps. He had been sighing a lot lately, he felt. Maybe he was just getting old. He never figured on living to thirty, so twenty-five-ish must put him in his twilight years. He didn't have a pension. He would have to work until he died. Months of labor, maybe, before a disgraceful end.

The plight of the working poor—you work harder than anyone else, live worse than anyone else, and then, at the end, you die worse than anyone else. What would a better world even look like? He couldn't imagine it. All he could imagine was if he was the rich one.

He sat up and started working through the maybe pile again. Morbid-self-pity time was over. He would make himself feel better later by helping to murder the richest man in the world.

In the end, none of the rocks seemed particularly white. He put them back tidily. It killed him to wait, but he would have to wait. Give it a few days. If nothing, start checking backup dead drops. What to do . . .

He went up on the porch of the house. Someone had hung a little bench on chains from the porch roof. It swung back and forth as he sat there. He was completely drawing a blank on what to do next. Go to the next city over and start a campaign of terror for a couple of days? It was doable but . . . honestly . . . he was still emotionally wiped. It had been an exhausting few days.

He watched a pedestrian with judgmental eyes. Just some local hayseed, off for their shopping. Sauntering along. Sure, they had their troubles, but "kill God" troubles? No chance. No, no, she was in the same boat as everyone else, worried about all the changes.

He smirked when she stubbed her toe on something, his sharp ears picking up the clatter of little rocks. She didn't break her stride or fall or make a face, though, so . . . limited amusement there. He watched her walk past. It occurred to him he didn't even notice if she was pretty or not. Etenesh had really done a number on him.

Wait. Wait a goddamn second. He put back all the rocks. What did she just kick?

Truth reached the fence in two steps. Nestled discreetly under the fourth fencepost was a single blindingly white stone.

Truth collected the hidden documents from the dead drop. Thoughtfully, Siphios Intelligence (or whoever they were) encoded the information in a tiny gem. Send the correct pulses of energy into it, and it projected the recorded information. Essentially a tiny talisman that required constant cosmic energy to work and would explode violently if you didn't power it just right. Truth reviewed the information on the jobs.

The hit on the Level Six was actually pretty straightforward, if difficult. He was a researcher, living in a remote mountain village with a research center attached. A pretty spectacular, very private research center. Truth would carefully investigate first, as he flat-out refused to believe there weren't hidden protections for a top-notch modern magic researcher. The known protections were bad enough. Likewise the danger if things went wrong would be enormous. The burglary would be hazardous too, if somewhat less so, as it was clearly a well-secured location.

He considered which one to do first and swiftly concluded that it was more important to find a lead on the Shattervoid girl. Besides, if he popped the researcher, security would be increased at research facilities. They might even start deleting or removing files. Can't have that. So, burglary first, murder second.

His nostrils were suddenly ambushed as he jogged along the country roads. Someone was running a grill next to a convenience store. They were selling skewers of roasted vegetables and rice cakes slathered in a spicy sauce. There would have to be a slight change of plans.

The research facility was in a corner of a light industrial park outside Sunch, a town just on the edge of being a city, about sixty-five kilometers from where he was now. Longer if you couldn't fly in a perfectly straight line, of course. Truth sighed. He just . . . did not want to run the whole way. He could. It would be the fastest way to travel, even. A sensible person would take a bus or train, but they were absolutely being surveilled. No question. He sat on the hood of a parked carriage, moping. Then slapped his head so hard, they should have heard it in Siphios.

"This is why being a whiner is for losers. You start thinking everything is impossible and miss the obvious solutions," he scolded himself. Truth hopped up on the roof of the carriage and looked around. Everything was kind of trash. There was a Birtoen Skywander, only about ten years old. *Envy of the block in Hicksville, probably. Hope the owner has insurance.* Truth had the door open and the carriage hotwired in seconds. It took longer to adjust the seat and mirrors. What kind of tiny-wee-micro-person was he robbing? With a friendly slap to the bound spirit, he set off.

"Thrush, attend me." The imp materialized next to him.

"How may I serve, Dread Magus?"

"Scout the following location." He gave the address. "Do now allow yourself to be discovered. Also report on any surrounding points of interest, such as police or army installations, Starbrite presence, schools, hospitals, hazards, that sort of thing."

"At once. It is my pleasure to serve." Thrush flapped off. Truth had been keeping the demon in its summoning token. Just a little extra precaution.

The countryside started whipping past. In Jeon, you were never too far from people, because everyone and everything was hemmed in by the mountains. After seeing the mountains in Siphios, he had to admit the mountains of Jeon were a bit stumpy. Stumpy or not, they dominated the Jeon peninsula, the country seeming to grow in the cracks between them. He had never minded them before. Now they felt claustrophobic. Like a short, round, older "uncle" type who was also a not-so-secret secret policeman. All looming around him.

He looked grimly at a completely dull mountain along the side of the road. Theoretically, at a high-enough level, the Meditations should let him slap a mountain flat. He nodded at that thought and carefully checked his location. *I'll be back.*

The drive was dull, the industrial park more so. The fancy-sounding research facility was an office building next to a building where they machined precision dies for mass-producing water-generating talismans. Woo.

Gray building, tinted windows, and enough recording talismans to make a porn star blush. A very decent layer of wards coated the whole building, too. He spotted several physical barriers, multiple layers of anti-spell wards, summons barriers, and then he ran into a layer of camouflaging magic. There was more under there, but they didn't care to let outsiders snoop easily. Fun.

He had no idea where to start searching. The information was damnably vague about where, exactly, in this entire building, the important information was. Wasn't like he had forever to wander around looking for things, either. He'd just have to ask someone. And that wasn't exactly easy. Hard to torture or brainwash someone under the System's terminal protection.

Evening was closing in. Truth found a convenient sewer grate, had a piss, and tried to get comfortable in his carriage. It would be a long wait. Researchers worked late. An hour went past, then another. He got bored and started looking around at the other carriages. Some halfway nice ones there, actually. Oh, and someone even left a suit in the back of one. Not that it remotely fit him, but it did give him a decent idea.

"Thrush, where is the nearest bar?"

"There is a . . . bar . . . just a short drive down the road, Master. A crude place."

"Well, it will do. Oh, whoops! Gotta secure my ride."

A tired-looking suit walked out of the die maker and made his way to the nice sedan Truth had been eyeballing. Looked like a rough day. Shame. Truth grabbed him around the neck and dragged him 'round the back of his own factory. He quickly stripped him, keeping the tie and using the rest to tie him securely. Any time the suit tried to talk or yell, Truth slapped him. He got the message eventually. When he had him secured, he leered down at his victim.

"Now, before I gag you, there are two things you should know. One, this isn't about you or your factory. Behave and you, and your factory, won't have any sudden problems. Problems involving fires. The kind of fires that catch everyone at home. The second thing you should know is this." Truth held up a coin, leaning on Incisive. The suit turned sheet-white, all fight draining out of him. "When the sun rises again, you may call for help. You got mugged. You don't know who did it. Workers must take care to stay safe. Thank me for my consideration."

"Thank. Thank you for your mercy." Truth slapped him.

"Thank me for my consideration."

"Thank you for your consideration!"

"That's better. Open wide."

A few hours later, well into the night, a researcher staggered out of the facility. Clearly exhausted and desiring nothing more than bed. Truth read the name on the parking spot he was headed for—Thom Vulk.

"Thom! That you, boy?"

The researcher looked over. It was one of his seniors from undergrad. He knew him. They had been in clubs together. Oh, God, hadn't they gone drinking together? He thought they might have. But for the life of him, *he couldn't remember the guy's name!*

"Oh . . . Hi! What are you doing here?"

"Ha-ha, thinking about buying this place!"

"The lab?!"

"What lab? I'm talking about the die maker, man, the die maker. You know I went into business after university. Well, everyone is selling for peanuts these days. Freaking peanuts."

The researcher thought that rang a bell, but the name remained elusive. It was agonizing. He was proud of his memory. He knew this face. He had seen this face dozens of times, hundreds of times. But he couldn't remember it!

"Sounds like you have done well for yourself. What's the name of your outfit?"

"Ah, we can talk about all that over dinner. Hop on in. My ride is right here." He slapped the hood of the sedan, loosening his clearly expensive tie.

"Sweet ride, but I can't; I have plans tonight!" He tried to escape.

"Nonsense! How could I let a junior go without buying them dinner? It's been years. No, no arguments, in you get. There is a bar nearby, and they do some decent fried chicken. My treat. And a little wine to wet our throats, eh?"

"Oh. Gosh. Um." Truth shoved him into the passenger seat of the carriage, then got in himself.

"So, junior, what are you up to these days? Still in the nerd game?"

"Er . . . yes. I got my doctorate in theosophy, ultimately. My parents were against it at first, but my advisor managed to get me an interview, and here I am." The researcher subtly tried to show off his seven-pointed pin.

"EEEY! Nice going, junior! C-Tier, huh? Is that where you get a fancy apartment for free?"

"You have to rent them, and they are just cheaper, not free. And not fancy. Well, you could get a fancy one for extra . . ."

"What is theosophy, anyway? Honestly, sounds made up."

"Everything."

"What? You got a degree in everything?"

"Sort of. Theosophy is the origin of everything. That a single universal truth is at the origin of religion, philosophy, and the natural sciences. Every scrap of magic, every demon, angel, even God, can be reduced to its origin point, theoretically. It is the theosophist's job to walk toward that unification." The researcher repeated something he had clearly said dozens of times over the years.

"Huh. And you do that in your office there?"

"Well. Yes."

CHAPTER 35

SO THAT'S HOW

The bartender, after a brief chat with Truth, had no problem serving him water in the same glasses he used to serve Thom white spirits. Whatever Internal Security wanted, they would get. Including the bartender becoming blind, deaf, and mute. Thom was Level Two, and while the lapel pin was providing some protection against Truth's influence, Truth knew how to work around it. Slowly, Thom was being ground down. He would never say anything too revealing. The System would prevent that. But the "System" was part of Thom. It could be fooled.

"Grand unified theory of everything?" Truth asked.

"Yeah, kinda. Like . . . imagine you are looking at a house, okay? And you say, 'It's a yellow bungalow house.' But that's not all a house is, right? There is all the other stuff. A foundation or whatever. And what if someone painted the other side of the house green? If you want to really describe the house, you gotta go all around it, through it, know every teensy tiny part of it before you can start describing it."

"Sounds exhausting."

"It absolutely is!" Thom nodded violently. "And that's just step one! Step two is figuring out how you can combine terms and still accurately describe the house. Like, can you describe the entire foundation in just a couple of accurate terms? All of it? How the concrete works mechanically, its load-bearing capacity, resistance to shear force, how much hydrostatic pressure it can resist?"

"Well. *I* can't."

"Me either. But that's the job."

"Studying cement?"

"Studying stuff. Trying to nail down what 'stuff' is, in every conceivable meaning of the word *is*, as precisely as we can." Thom whacked back a shot before flipping the glass over and slamming it down on the bar top. "Let's get some fried chicken, senior. My treat. At least I can be pretty sure what the chicken is."

"Good thinking, junior. And another round. On me; I should treat you."

"Senior . . ."

"Yeah, yeah, lapel pin, I get it. Let me act like a senior, damn it."

"Ha-ha-ha. You haven't changed." It was amazing, Truth thought. He could see, in real time, Thom inventing memories of the two of them together in university. It wasn't Incisive, really. It was a function of the human mind—making up stories to explain reality. Or whatever that mind understood to be reality.

"Well, I wouldn't say that. Business brings out the meanness in a man." Thom started coughing.

"You haven't changed."

"Junior . . ." Truth said in a warning tone, then laughed helplessly. "All right, this sounds more interesting than manufacturing the casings on 'shoulder massagers.' Why are you measuring the meanings of bananas?"

"Dunno."

"What?"

"I don't know why. I spent—and this isn't a secret; don't worry—I spent eighteen hours yesterday trying to know, as absolutely as possible, a one-hundred-gram cube of alchemically pure copper. Weight, dimensions, resilience to cold and heat, how it tastes and smells, and the rate at which a Polianna's grape slug can cross one surface of the cube. A test that had to be modified, as for some reason, the slug died. Then we had to keep repeating the test to determine how much exposure to the cube was required to kill a slug."

Truth toyed with the glass of water in his hand before knocking it back and flipping it over onto the bar. "No offense, junior, but what with everything, that sounds like a *spectacular* waste of time. Are you being bullied?"

"Oh, no, I have it good. The natural science team got off *light*. The poor bastards getting bullied is the theology team. They have to provide an ecumenical, universally supported theological definition of the cube."

Truth felt something grind to a halt in his brain. "Provide a religious definition of a one-hundred-gram alchemically pure copper cube, including all conceivable definitions of what the cube was, is, and will be, that is true across all known religions?"

"You were paying attention! And I don't even have tits," Thom slurred. Matching shots of ethanol to shots of water was a losing game.

"Well, you know what I'm like." Truth grinned wolfishly.

"As long as you are doing the fucking, it's all good." Thom snorted.

Truth blinked at that. *That . . . yeah, okay, that might actually be true. Have to think about that one a bit. Back on track.*

"But you must have some idea why. I mean, why does your field exist if all it does is pointlessly measure and define things?"

"Power."

"Huh?"

"Power." Thom waved sloppily. "Once you really know what something is, you have a greater degree of power over it. Can control it. Transcend it, even. And the more you understand all the things, the more patterns you see. The more crossover truth you find. You start piling up all the *what*, and pretty soon, *why* becomes kind of visible. Then you can do stuff."

"Yeah, to all of that, but . . . junior, I'm playing for the world after the collapse. People are going to need to make things, and casting parts is ancient technology. Theoretically, you don't even need magic to do it. Defining shit? Even for Starbrite—"

"We think it's how the Black Ships work. Not 'we' Starbrite, but 'we' the lab guys."

Waitjustafuckingwhatnow?

Truth glanced over at the bartender, who was standing at the opposite end of the bar, finding the interior of a reach-in refrigerator fascinating.

"They are giant black tubes."

"Not all the ships, or their weapons or whatever. I think it's how they travel. I think they can define their own existence and the existence of their environment so perfectly, it lets them travel between the stars. Travel faster than light. Faster than dark, even."

"Who would even be studying that?"

"Consolidation team, directly administered by the lab director. But they don't tell me shit. I'm just licking copper cubes. Did you know I can tell the purity of copper by licking it? My degree has been very useful."

"Proud of you, junior. Keep up the good work."

There was a lull. Truth was itching to sprint back to the lab and break in immediately. He had a target now. He wouldn't be searching blindly. The time savings were already huge. Was there anything else he should get out of Thom?

"Did you fuck Jai?"

"Gonna have to narrow it down for me, junior."

Thom exploded off his stool, taking a mighty swing at Truth and smashing into the floor instead. Truth hadn't bothered to dodge. "Bastard! You knew I loved her!"

"Oh, then I definitely did. Still don't remember her, though." Truth sighed. Thom had passed out. Truth hoisted Thom over his shoulder and took him out to the carriage. He debated what to do next.

On the one hand, Thom wouldn't be able to provide a coherent description of him to an interrogator. On the other hand, it would be instantly apparent that he had been put under some kind of glamor. Starbrite would then take greater precautions against mental influence, knowing that there was an op out there who could get around the lapel pin's glamor wards. And if Thom suddenly vanished, their first thought would be an insider attack. Which should be impossible for a C-Tier. Which would make them even more paranoid.

Starbrite and the cops would have a *lot* of questions, none of which would lead directly to Truth. But when they interviewed the bartender, and they inevitably would, he would swear blind that a credentialed member of Internal Security had gotten Thom drunk and interrogated him under the influence. The tied-up suit from the die maker would finger some local gang or maybe Internal Security, too. "Who did it?" "A hired thug. Greasy, missing a tooth." Another misdirection.

Truth held Thom up by the neck with his left hand. Right hand grabbed the top of Thom's head. He pulled sharply in opposite directions. The spine snapped clean, the brain stem severed from the body that supported it. Death was instantaneous. Truth put him in the trunk as tidily as he could manage.

"Sleep easy, junior. You don't want to be around for what comes next."

Truth was, once again, painfully reminded that Starbrite was actually damn good at securing things it actually cared about. For example, while the control gem for the door-locking mechanism on the loading bay employee access door was a standard A07-H, the actual interface was completely reprogrammed and keyed to only open for authorized lapel pins. No firefighter bypass there—Starbrite was content to let everything burn before they would let it get stolen.

Try and spoof a lapel badge? Thanks, he'd pass on that particular idiocy. You couldn't even steal them. He briefly contemplated waiting until daytime and just . . . ghosting in behind some employee, but he had a sneaking suspicion that it wasn't going to be that simple.

Truth carefully disassembled and rerouted, turning the door lock into something purely decorative, for all that it would report as still in use. Truth could practically hear the trainer's voice from his PMC days—*Any lock, door, safe, wall, any kind of static barrier to entry will be defeated. It's only a matter of time. But the longer someone is hung up on defeating the barrier, the longer you have to catch and nail them.* A door lock rated for ten minutes was a very good lock.

It took Truth half a damn hour to get through the smokers' door. His patience was "rewarded," however, when he opened the door and was greeted immediately by a golem. It had been built to look like a big friendly dog. It got eerily close to perfection. He didn't recognize the model. He also knew damn well the golem expected to verify a badge and would raise unholy hell if it didn't.

Trusting Incisive, Truth called the Tongue to his hand and stabbed forward. The blade slid into the golem's armored torso, burning out the delicate wires and threads that kept the golem up and moving. A little farther and he found the command talisman. It shattered almost instantly. The golem collapsed. So much for an invisible break-in. He didn't know how long he had before the golem-control net for the building noticed that the golem was down and sounded the alarm, but . . . not long. He shoved the golem into a corner and started running. This actually simplified some things.

He jumped up the stairwell. Literally just stood at the bottom next to the flight of steps and jumped up. Grabbed the railing, stood on it with perfect balance, then did it again. And like that, he was on the top floor. The door was locked. Truth applied the "sword through the lock" universal key. It worked. An alarm went off. Truth swore but pushed on. He ran through the hallways, looking for signs. Director's office. How much would be left to the System, and how much would be recorded? He went through the wall. It was *way* past go time.

There was a safe in the room. "Thrush, clear out any documents or records you find in the office. Everything. Then start obliterating my traces."

"I obey!"

Truth eyeballed the safe. Warded, of course, and two inches of steel and alchemically treated glass inside. Usually with some kind of self-destruct mechanism built in if it detects an intrusion attempt. *Yeah, fuck all that.* "Got everything?"

"Yes, Great One, save for what is in the safe."

"Retrace my steps, destroy my traces."

"Yes, Master."

Truth gave Thrush a moment to scram, then hit the safe with Obliteration. The spells seemed to boil away. It was creepy to watch. He even obliterated the locking spell and its attached alarms and triggers. A very precise lunge with the Tongue, and he had the safe open. He didn't even look at the contents. He just scraped everything into his backpack, then deliberately triggered the self-destruct. He was already at the stairs and headed down when the safe blew out the wall. Starbrite took *self-destruct* seriously. Then into the carriage and he peeled out of the lot. Alarms were going off outside the building, too, now, sounding like screaming pigs.

Truth hit the highway and drove like a bat out of Hell for ten kilometers, then he pulled into a used carriage lot and parked. Thom could hang out there until someone thought to trace the pin. Picking a direction at random, Truth took off on foot, up into the stubby mountains. No convenient caves, alas, but there was an overhang next to a stream. It would have to do. Truth stopped and just breathed. In and out. In and out.

He sure hoped he had gotten what he needed. There would be no second shot at that place.

Once he got his breathing under control, he started picking through the loot. He made three piles—correspondence, work files, and "other." Correspondence he then sorted into points of origin. He would read through them later. Work files were the biggest pile; he didn't touch those. He would look through them later, of course, but he didn't know enough about the subject matter to puzzle through them unaided. The "other" pile got most of his attention. All the random things that get swept into drawers. All the physical crap in the safe, beyond just jade tablets with data recordings or crystals containing who knows what.

He dug through them feverishly, pawing at business cards and takeout menus, sniffing the little metal cubes, eyes raking at the messy notes jotted down on a legal pad and shoved into a supposedly securely locked drawer.

"Found you."

CHAPTER 36

THE BOATHOUSE AT ARMY FORD

It didn't feel safe under the overhang. Truth thought a moment and scolded himself. He was still thinking like a low-level noob. He was a Level Four with an imp. He coated his hand with the Fangs of Incisive and carved a little cave out of the bank of the stream. "Thrush, make it watertight and blow out the dust and dirt. Then tidy up the exterior and remove my traces."

"As you command."

Thrush was decent at obscuring their trail. Combined with a few talismans and his various spells and blessings, Truth was a genuine nightmare to try and track. Still. He'd have to think about ways to improve his coverage. An Imp just wasn't able to play at this level. The only reason Truth summoned Thrush was their former relationship. Well, that and he knew he could easily crush the little monster if it got squirrely on him.

And he did not like having those eyeless things sweeping the city for him. He was a monster of a solo combatant, but he did *not* want to have anything remotely resembling a fair fight with anyone, ever. Let alone someone a couple of levels over him. He'd been jumped enough for one lifetime.

He took out the pad of legal paper. A cat would have struggled to see in the dark of the cave. Truth did just fine. Most of it was gibberish—scribbled numbers, disjointed words, or long, rambling notes about things he didn't have any context for. Why a twelve-digit string of numbers justified triple underlining and a pass with a highlighter, he didn't know. Maybe Siphios Intelligence could figure it out. What he could figure out was that there were repeated references to a boathouse at Army Ford.

Copy to B-house.

Courier package to Boath at AF.

Traffic on the road to Army Ford? Budget for limo-carpet? Bad look?

Sample formula to boathouse. As Bri? Nitro crapper.

7740-JR, reassign, bh wants 7740-JR(m). Tues?

There were only a half dozen references on the legal pad, and even less material addressed anywhere in Army Ford. Far, far, far more to various offices in Harban. But this was it. He could feel it.

Truth knew three things about Army Ford. One, it was way the hell up in the mountains in the far north of Jeon. If there was a boathouse up there, it was purely for whitewater rafting by the suicidal. Second, Army Ford was a fairly old and fairly small city with a surprisingly large number of mid-sized factories. He only knew those two facts because he had read about Army Ford in one of his spy novels and got curious. This was because the spy novel mentioned something he wanted to confirm—the third fact he knew about Army Ford. It was the headquarters of the Jeon Special Operations Service. The elite of Jeon's military.

The Starbrite PMC poached from them constantly. It was practically advertised by everyone involved. You got your badge with the winged tiger so you could get your lapel pin with seven stars when your contract ended. Now, the SOS was too damn expensive to keep hanging around their base all the time. But if there was one place where you could discreetly stick a highly defended facility and no one would even look at it sideways, it would be Army Ford.

He dug through the rest of the documents, and he was sure this was damning stuff, or maybe top-notch something or other, but he didn't understand a word of it. Literally, as it was often written in a mathematical and symbolic language that he simply could not interpret.

System?

<<Nope. I have nothing. I get the feeling I would have to reinvent centuries or more of mathematical research and development. Which, even for me, just ain't happening.>>

Figures. Welp. Let's make this Merkovah's problem.

<<Gladly.>>

The closest dead drop is in Buran, right?

<<The closest one that can take physical files and things, yeah.>>

Truth spent an hour resting and cultivating. The cultivation was unsatisfying. Just sitting in a cave meditating felt wrong. It sort of worked, but he couldn't shake the feeling that all the dirt and rocks were blocking the rays from hitting him. Either that or the thinning reality was starting to reach him, too. Hopefully, it was all just in his head. He had a bit better luck running the Meditations of Valentinian. It had taken a painfully long time, but the visualization was coming with just a bit of work. A huge improvement over not managing it at all, he felt.

He stepped out of the cave, feeling refreshed. "Thrush, fill in the cave, and hide that I was ever here."

He set off almost due east, up the mountain. There were no roads or paths up there. No watchful eyes. Truth let himself fade into the forest and just ran. Leaping from tree to tree when the mood took him. Keeping his steps light and flying through the night forest like a mountain demon.

When morning dawned, he had crossed mountains and rivers, leapt over highways, swung from branch to branch, and gloried in the strength of his body. The freedom of movement, of traveling unhindered through the world. Of moving like a dream.

He greeted the sun with a round of cultivation. Letting that august personage's kindness fill his apertures and strengthen his limbs. The identity of the great solar demon was a severe taboo. It wouldn't do to offend the planet's tutelary spirit, after all. Was God's indifference going to harm them? Truth hoped not. Bad enough that an entire planet was catching strays from Starbrite and Siphios. The great solar demon had been there before humans settled this world. Presumably, they would be there long after humanity vanished again.

He drifted down the side of a mountain, finally coming to rest in a convenience-store parking lot at the fringes of a little town called Jinu. Truth had a vague recollection of the town, but only as a place to stop off for a piss on his way to Buran. There was . . . a river through there? There *was* a river that ran through there. It did eventually get you to Buran, too. He didn't have all day to sit in a tourist boat, though. Risk a bus? Steal another carriage? He was still high from his magical night in the mountains, but he knew the crash would be hit hard soon. It had been almost a full day since he last ate. Never wound up getting that fried chicken.

He walked into the convenience store. His much-abused duffel bag was hanging in there, but only barely. It had been a tough few days for a distinctly cheap product. He'd have to keep an eye out for a replacement. Ah, coffee!

It smelled a little off. He took a long sniff. Very off. Burnt, but somehow oversweet. The label on the pot claimed it came from Siphios, but that was a damned lie.

"Hey, could I try, like, a shot of this coffee? I just want to see how it tastes." Truth asked the clerk.

"Sure. Five wen."

"Five wen! How much is a cup of coffee here?!"

"Five wen."

Yes, this was Jeon, all right.

"Screw it. Got any sandwiches?" Truth's stomach wasn't growling, but only thanks to body cultivation preventing it.

"Sure. Ham and cheese in the refrigerator, cheese and pickle next to it. Condiments are extra." The clerk pointed.

He found them. The bread looked like it was made from extruded packing foam, and the fillings were micron-thin.

"How much for the ham sandwich?"

"Fifteen wen."

"You having a stroke?!"

"Mustard is only two wen a squeeze if you buy the sandwich."

"You sell squeezes of mustard without a sandwich?"

"Sure, you could bring in your own sandwich, right?" The clerk nodded wisely.

"Does that happen often?" Truth asked.

"Never. But it might."

Truth walked out without buying so much as a bottle of water. He didn't even want to shoplift.

Breakfast was a surprisingly decent bowl of rice and veggies on the tourist boat going to Busan. If you want to be invisible, be where they aren't looking, right? Also, Truth was crashing hard. He reckoned sitting and watching the world go by as he ate snacks was about what he had the energy for. Funny, that. His cosmic energy was full up, his body practically vibrating with magic, and he was tired. The bit of Truth that wasn't attuning to the cosmos was tired. His lips quirked involuntarily. He had been up for more than twenty-four highly active, stressful hours, and he was *just* tired. One step further away from "normal," one step closer to the godhead.

Truth lasted almost forty minutes on the boat. Once the "fun" music came on and the "funny" tour guide started talking, he discreetly jumped ashore. He could put up with an awful lot, but there was a limit.

He wanted to stay away from public transit as much as possible. Even before the return of the Black Ships, they were some of the most heavily surveilled places in the world. All the eyes, all the attention, would tax his cosmic energy hard.

Stealing a carriage was possible, but even with his Blessings, the cops were going to be looking for stolen carriages. They were a trail, and the hunters were out and about. Starbrite and Internal Security both knew a high-level operative was loose in southern Jeon. They wouldn't get bored looking for him.

This corner of the peninsula was pretty densely settled. Running was a not-great option. He could go the backyard route again, for a while, but there would be rapidly diminishing returns there. So, how to get to Buran without wasting a ton of time and exhausting himself further?

Truth wandered along the road for a while, eventually reaching another convenience store. Same chain, same colors, even the clerk looked the same. He had that dead-inside smile that said they were a Denizen who would get punished for not smiling on the job.

Truth looked around. They were . . . near the highway, right? He dug out his road atlas. Yes, near the highway. The entrance ramp for Highway 10 was about five blocks from there. A bunch of carriages parked in the lot. One a rather smart sedan. A quick look around the store saw a man in a suit buying a criminally overpriced cup of "coffee" without complaint. Level One. Truth had a sip of the beverage while the suit finished his transaction, and nearly spat it out. The nation of Siphios had been libeled. They should pursue legal action.

The suit grabbed his drink and walked over to the sedan. Truth waited for him to unlock it, then got into the passenger seat. They drove off. No music. Apparently, the suit was thinking deep thoughts. Or something. The carriage smoothly turned up the ramp toward Highway 10, toward Buran. Truth lay the seat back as far as it would go. Time for a little nap.

Truth woke suddenly as the carriage slowed. He instinctively cast Incisive and was immediately jabbed with alarm. He carefully peeked out the window. Traffic was backed up for three kilometers on the highway. There was a checkpoint on the road. Loads of the eyeless freaks perched around the barriers. Lots of soldiers. And high up in the air, a golden bird circled above the highway.

CHAPTER 37

JUST VISITING

It should have been safe. It should have. This wasn't some dinky little road into a minor city like Gwaju. This was National Highway 10 headed into Buran—the second-biggest and second-richest city in the country. The highway was six lanes in both directions. The cost to run the checkpoint must be enormous. The cost to the city in lost income, delayed shipments, whatever, must be tens of times the cost of the checkpoint. Truth wouldn't be surprised if this were costing Buran ten million wen an hour. He suspected he was guessing low.

The skeletal hand of anxiety started closing around Truth's heart. Of course, it wasn't Starbrite's money, was it? And anyone even slightly paying attention knew that money was no longer a factor in anyone's decision-making. Not at the top. Fucking DePonte had figured it out—what does it mean when the government stops worrying about its tax base? It means that they weren't going to be paying anyone for anything, soon.

After spending exactly one minute feeling very sorry for himself, Truth turned his anxiety-sharpened focus on escape. He was trapped. It was a long, flat stretch of highway, foothills to the right, the six lanes running the other direction on his left. There were a high wall and a shopping complex on the far side of the oncoming lanes. They might as well have been on the moon.

The irony of being trapped on a highway to avoid the danger of getting trapped on a train was not lost on him. Was that the same golden bird? He didn't think so, but it was very similar. The carriage rolled forward a meter. The line was moving. Slowly but moving.

"Thrush, can you make me invisible? Or at least less visible? In a way that does not draw the attention from the watchers above or the checkpoint ahead."

"If it were just the cattle in their crates, there would be no trouble. However, the bird itself has piercing eyes, to say nothing of the mighty ones atop it. As for those . . . things . . . on the checkpoint, I don't think any demon you would care to summon could defeat their gaze."

"A lot of words to say no."

"My apologies, Master." The carriage jolted forward fifty centimeters. The driver had apparently decided that his head would explode if he got more than some arbitrary distance away from the bumper of the carriage ahead of him. Why he didn't set the chained demon to keep the distance, Truth didn't know.

"However," Thrush continued, its voice layered with "concern," "that is not to say I couldn't provide some aid. Your magical presence is so close to nil that hiding it will be trivial. Your physical presence is a bit more striking. It will be difficult, given my inability to perceive your glorious form. Not impossible, however. I can simply bend the air in the area around my summon token. It won't render you invisible, but it will blur and displace your image."

Truth grunted. He decided his best plan would be a replay of some things that had worked previously. Get low, keep the body of the carriage between him and direct observation, then either break for the mountain or try to catch a lift going away from the checkpoint.

He glanced over at the foothill. Did he like his odds evading the eyes of a hunting bird while scurrying like a rat through tall grass and shrubs? No, he did not. Hitch a ride going "away" and figure out another infiltration route, then. He was close to the city, at least. And he had had a nap. That was something.

"All right, here's how it's going to go. When I give the signal, I am going to slowly open the door and step out, keeping as low as I can. Your job is to make this process as unnoticeable as you can. Once the door is closed, focus on keeping me unnoticeable."

"As you command."

Truth waited, keeping his eye on two things—the checkpoint and the bird making big, lazy circles in the sky. He waited, watching them both creep closer and closer. Truth devoted his entire energy to being unnoticeable, trying to fade from the world's awareness entirely. Truth Medici died years ago. Who notices a lonely ghost?

Every jolt of the carriage brought them closer to the checkpoint. Every tiny roll forward increased the warning from Incisive. He suppressed the urge to bolt, to run like a rat for the shadows. He focused on breathing, on pulling in as much air as he could to calm his mind. He was not a rat. He was more than the sum of his fears. He could wait. Wait for the bird to turn.

It took fifteen agonizing minutes. Fifteen minutes of counting heartbeats, of trying to watch the clock, the checkpoint, meditating, anything to control the need to run. Fifteen minutes of agony. Then the bird curved back toward the city. He gave it exactly one more minute to build distance. The carriage jolted forward.

"NOW."

Truth eased the door open and poured himself onto the road through the smallest crack he could manage. Lying flat on the ground, on the highway. He didn't have time to appreciate the strange terror of what he was doing; he just eased the door shut and started crawling. The drain on Incisive and the Blessing of the Silent Forest started stepping up. Not massively, but steadily. It would get worse once he reached the median. Didn't matter if he was low or not—no cover there.

He took a peek at the oncoming traffic. There was a one-ton wagon, open-topped, rumbling toward him. He had a bare minute to make it to the other side of the highway. He moved as quickly as he dared, crawling on his belly. He hit the grassy median and slid down. The median was wide, grassy, and steeply V-shaped. A way to discourage attempted U-turns on the highway and a water-management solution all in one.

It was mucky down at the bottom. Didn't matter. He started slithering up the far bank, moving as fast as he could stand. The pull was getting heavy now. Hundreds of eyes should be on him, blurred by Thrush or no. Didn't matter. Had to get in position. Had to catch this wagon. Nothing else could matter.

He reached the edge and pulled his limbs under him. Crouching. The wagon roared up, moving in a cloud of construction dust. Truth slammed every scrap of power he could spare into his arms and legs, leaping like a frog at the side of the wagon. Iron fingers hooked the top edge of the open back. His energy was burning up like a magnesium flare, but he hauled himself over and into the back. Trash bags full of construction waste. He buried himself under them happily. Then just tried to breathe.

By his estimation, it had been less than two minutes since he had opened the door of the sedan. By his estimation, that little attempt used up sixty percent of his cosmic energy. It would be impossible to fight like that. He would have to drop power to the Blessing, even stopping it from running passively. He would have to dispel much of the Scales, too, or change them to something subtle. He would be massively more vulnerable to being found via divination. And once you have been found, it was famously hard to shake free of the diviner.

He lay under layers of broken wood, cement, and trash, just trying to breathe. Trying to pull together a little energy. He didn't know where this truck was headed, but he would happily go there. Buran could wait.

Fifteen minutes later, a thoroughly pissed-off Truth was dumped on the heap of the Buran municipal landfill. Vengeful, wrathful, and more than a bit fed up, he strode out of the dust, dragging his battered, beaten, and abused duffel with him. Luckily, he had kept it close. The old legend about demon worms eating the trash in the landfill had turned out to be true.

Truth directly gave up on the day. He found a nearby house, helped himself to a shower, and stretched out on the sofa. Entirely too close a call. Entirely too close. The enemy wasn't dumb. Cost had ceased to be a factor, and they were determined to keep order above all other priorities. Asset-stripping—burning up the accumulated stores of money and goodwill the nation of Jeon had accumulated, all to make sure Starbrite could escape. Somehow.

He looked around the house idly. Clearly, a Denizen family lived there. Didn't own it, of course. That would be illegal. Looked like the whole extended family came together to cover rent. He could see bedrolls ready to be laid out in the living room and in the hallways. Four people in a bedroom that would have been claustrophobic for one. A shared bathroom with no bottles but lots and lots of empty sachets. People bought the sachets of shampoo or soap when they couldn't afford a whole bottle.

Truth thought about hiding a little cash somewhere in the house, but he knew damn well what would happen if he did.

Besides. Changeover was happening at the end of the month. No more wen. No more money at all for Denizens. Would it be a crime for them to own paper money? He didn't know but would bet that it would be. He looked at the neat row of toothbrushes. They couldn't afford hardly anything, but they made sure to buy toothpaste. So much for the Denizens being irresponsible. So much for not being able to trust them to look after themselves.

He tidied up and left. He didn't want to impose on this family. If nothing else, there would be no place for him to sleep. He squared his shoulders, checked his road atlas, and started the backyard steeplechase once again.

Later that evening, Truth hid a waterproof package of all the materials he had stolen from the research facility in a flowerpot on the roof deck of an apartment building in the suburbs of Buran. Upon departing the building, he put three discreet slashes close together in the bright yellow paint of a carriage parked near the building. Duty done, he set off to find a hotel room. He was prepared to demand luxury.

He got halfway downtown before a shopping street cruelly ambushed him. Jeon street food struck again—its seductive aromas carefully tested and engineered to stand out in the capitalist hell of the dinner rush, then crush the evening boozers. He had missed out on fried chicken yesterday. Not again. He got a whole twenty-piece box, *and* the extra sauce, *and* a side of pickles, sat down on the curb, and ate them on the spot.

The sweet, spicy, funky, sticky sauce got everywhere. It practically coated his hands and face. It dripped onto his shirt. The chicken was fresh out of the fryer. The batter was shatteringly crisp and delicious under the rolling sticky calamity of the sauce. He sucked the bone clean of meat, then ate some pickled radish to cleanse the palate. Perfection, perfection. A glug of water to wet his throat, then straight back in.

Bones covered in dark red sauce were scattered around him, his hands gory with the wet remains of his victuals. His face was greasy, his fingers were sticky, and his belly was satiated. He had committed food crimes there. And he would do it again. Whistling, he strode into a luxurious boutique hotel.

"*Whssp. Ssswifp. Wfff.* You know what, I don't care if this world burns. I don't."

Snagging a box of wet wipes from the hotel shop, he made his way to the top floor, found the fanciest room, broke in, cleaned up, and went to sleep. He had earned it. By God, he had earned it!

CHAPTER 38

BURAN

Truth sprawled in the plush king-sized bed in "his" suite at the Dunbar. The Grand Imperial Deluxe, apparently. He vaguely wondered if they had a Grand Imperial or an Imperial Deluxe. What exactly qualified this suite for all three terms? Well, it had a second bedroom attached, a living room, and a little kitchen. When you got right down to it, he was pretty sure that it was bigger than the apartment he had grown up in. And he was staying there rent-free. Bliss.

The bed was so comfortable, it was uncanny. It seemed to know precisely the balance of softness and support Truth enjoyed, resulting in the deepest, most peaceful sleep he had enjoyed since leaving Siphios. He could set the flavor and aroma in the air. He chose orange with a cool caress of mint. He could control the light, temperature, and humidity to the most minute degree. As it was morning, he set it to "dawn at the beach," and the orange-scented air took on the faintest tang of salt. Even the carpeting seemed designed to caress his toes. The deep pile almost wiggled upward, and he couldn't help but make little fists with his toes—grabbing and playing again and again for the sheer joy of feeling.

Simply existing in this room was utter sensuality. Everything in the suite was designed to bring him pleasure. The experience of a luxurious hotel room was completely different when you weren't guarding the body in it.

That was Buran, the Second City of Jeon. Harban controlled the government, finance, industry, and research . . . but Buran was where the wealthy and their glittering toys came to play. It, too, had a university and industries and commerce, but what it had most of all was luxury. White-sand beaches, each grain carefully selected and polished by chained spirits, then raked to perfection each morning by Denizens. Ancient temples selling incense made from the rarest, most precious fragrance trees. Restaurants staffed by beauties who were on the menu every bit as much as the wine they served. Their enchanted collars promised guests that if they didn't like what they saw on the menu, the kitchen would be happy to whip up something special. Just for them.

Truth had spent a little time there, guarding various bodies. Starbrite had a very sizable presence there too. His next job for Merkovah was a hit on a target far to the north, and Truth felt it would be a missed opportunity not to pull some kind of stunt there. People paid more attention when rich people got hurt in luxurious circumstances.

Starbrite did too, for that matter. It was their most important client base. Not to mention their higher-tier employees took just as much advantage of the amenities as anyone else. It was like a special membership card—some things that weren't even on the menu were available with a lapel pin. Especially these days, with everyone watching the end of the world come rolling in like the tide. Anything to make a connection. To find even a shred more security. No matter how much it hurt or degraded you to earn that "favor."

You were lucky to have the opportunity. So many didn't even have the chance to make a rich woman laugh or a pampered son smile.

Truth started mentally reviewing his options. What was the right combination of pointed message, drama, and paranoia-inducing implications? A nightclub? Restaurant? Party boat would be a killer choice. Oooh, or flying platform. Yeah, one of those fancy luxury flying clouds with their own bound spirits of music and light talisman systems. The young and beautiful and rich, dancing on the heads of everyone else. It would be *just terrible* if their cloud happened to disintegrate for no reason, right?

He smiled and snuggled into the bed, enjoying the bewildering comfort of the sheets. Why did they feel so much better than other sheets? He didn't know. But they did.

He missed Etenesh. He wanted her in this bed too. For sex, but also just to have her near. He had been so scared when they first slept together. Now, the bed felt wrong without her. The way she laughed with him, or explained things to him, or used him as a headrest as she wrestled with texts whose every word was critically important—and they ran for six hundred pages. He missed the comfort of her. The warmth of her. The way she fussed with her hair, worried about it, going so far as to try and hide her bed hair from him.

He loved her hair however she wore it. But he would always remember seeing it fly wild and free when he first laid eyes on her. Somehow, it had become the way he loved it best. He told her so, but she kept fussing with it anyhow, and he loved to see her do it.

Truth confronted a growing problem, decided against doing anything about it for the moment, and took a cool shower instead. Time to be about the day. Time to see what trouble he could stir up. Plus, he wanted to hit a bookstore. Nothing quite like catching up on the last five years of talisman-maintenance literature to take your mind off things.

The Dunbar Hotel was on the western edge of what could be considered proper Buran. It was at that point where you got past the suburbs and the residential areas for the less-appealing locals but before you really hit the downtown. A comparatively discreet, "affordable" luxury hotel. Naturally, there was no public transit connection worth mentioning nearby. If you could afford to stay at the Dunbar, you could, at a minimum, afford to take a carpet everywhere.

The Dunbar did not have a garage. They did not care how custom your chariot was. Not even if the VGR Workshop only made six in that colorway. Maybe you could find on-street parking. The Dunbar had an aerie, where guests of *quality* could house their flying beasts, summoned spirits, and flying clouds. Truth sincerely admired the flex, then got into character.

With conscious effort, he reassembled his Rich Prick persona. His battered clothes became "pre-distressed" and clearly designer. His handsome looks and strong physique silently informed watchers that his parents had spared no expense in his development. Most of all was the air of indifferent brutality. Jeon was strictly hierarchical. Everyone, *everyone* knew what that look meant. Obey or suffer. You might suffer because you obeyed, but disobedience would be so much worse. No mere dilettante thug, he was the second generation of an ancient family.

It was distressingly easy to settle into. The persona was built around power—magical, social, and financial. It was built around a personal capacity for violence and the promise of protection from that violence and the violence of others. He knew he was a born gangster. The rich were just another gang. He summoned a livery carpet, paid cash, and ordered the driver to take him downtown. In silence.

Truth alighted on a high-end shopping street, hunting for very particular products. First—the duffel had to be replaced, as did the clothes. He would acquire the duffel first.

At this point, his duffel bag was more of a conceptual construct than a physical one, lined with trash bags to keep its tears from leaking precious intel or supplies. You could buy a basically adequate duffel for very little money, almost free if you were willing to trawl thrift stores. But, for only a very great deal of money, you could buy a duffel bag made of synthetic fibers spun from some unholy alchemical process and the silk of demonic spiders. Spell-resistant (up to a very limited point), corrosion-resistant, ripstop weaving, and available in a variety of fashionable colors. Truth went with a basic black, carefully stuffing its price in wen into the mouth of the sales clerk who dared to ask for his identity sigil. The young master had no need for credit.

Word apparently got around the neighborhood shop association—at the next store, his demands for equally durable clothes (suddenly and mysteriously in fashion among the more forward-thinking rich) were speedily met. Truth had to control the urge to buy all black. It was never as stealthy as your instinct insisted. He picked up pants and shirts in blacks, grays, browns, and other muted tones. He looked longingly at a robin's-egg blue shirt but ultimately went with moss green.

Shoes were irritatingly trickier to find. What he really needed was a highly durable work boot, something that simply did not exist in the stores of the very rich. He ultimately chose a "hiking boot" that cost more than rent in most places. Which was fair, given the sheer quantity of alchemical refinement that went into the materials. Cash payment was gratefully received with both hands by the silent clerks.

Picking up books was an even harder challenge. What he was looking for was highly technical and niche. Even quite large bookstores were unlikely to carry technical handbooks on talisman maintenance and repairs. At best, they would have glossy, high-color guides filled with quarter-truths and questionable advice aimed at the untrained. For the real deal, you had to go to the source. Truth found a quiet place and carefully dispelled the young-master persona. In its place, Johnny Bells, maintenance technician, snapped into being.

Johnny's feet hurt. He had been on them all day, every day, for two months. It showed in his gait. None of that pep that supervisors so loved to see in their "service associates." But then, he was using his day off to go get the latest service gazettes from the campus bookstore at the local technical school. He picked up the slim, paper-jacketed maintenance guides for a dozen common talisman systems, magazines, and, out of sheer nostalgia, an air conditioner repair manual. You could see the last few years had been hard on Johnny. The mismatched clothes, the crummy boots, and even his duffel bag looked like it had been jumped on dozens of times. The clerk had the decency not to smile understandingly as he fished around in his pockets for cash.

"The closest bus is the 86?" Johnny asked.

"Yeah. 'Fraid you just missed it. The next one is in half an hour," the clerk replied.

"Figures." He sighed. Johnny had already vanished from the clerk's memory by the time he stepped out the door. Just another tired worker doing his best.

Johnny walked over to the bus stop and tried his best to sit on the bent poles that were provided instead of seats. He fished out a gazette and started reading, watching his day off slip away. It took twenty deeply unpleasant minutes for "Johnny" to fade away entirely. Apparently, the world really believed in him. A lot more than it believed in the unnoticeable operative Truth Medici (deceased.)

The rest of the day was spent scoping out party venues, flying-platform rental agencies, and similar. As a result, he was running across town all day and staring at warehouse space. It was a universal truth—those organizing the party, running the party, and working the party are having exactly zero fun. Truth retreated to the Dunbar and his delightful bed with immense relief. He had earned a good night's sleep.

Four hours later, he jolted into wakefulness. A rich man kicked open the door, dragging a couple of giggling pros in with him.

"I don't care if you rented this room. You aren't leaving it alive," Truth swore.

"Fuck did I do to you?" the man slurred.

There was an awkward pause.

CHAPTER 39

A DAMN HARD JOB

Truth had a moment of terrible lucidity. The rich man, and he had to be rich, that was a five-thousand-wen suit if he had ever seen one, was looking more or less straight at him. Could he . . . see through the Blessings of the Forest? That would make him *incredibly* high-level. But he sure didn't look or feel like a powerhouse. The draw on the energy powering the blessing was solidly up, but not "hunted by Level Sixes and Sevens" up. He cast Incisive. No danger. What the actual . . .

"Who are you talking to, Daddy?" asked the blue-haired pro who was doing a damn fine job advertising the cosmetic glamor industry.

"Oh, now, Sally baby, you know I'm not 'Daddy' when I'm on the job. It's Father, or Your Eminence."

The girls giggled. "Sorry, Your Eminence," The other girl, sporting a shocking spray of pink hair and apparently spray-painted vinyl, nudged the rich man. "She meant, 'Who are you talking to, Father?'"

"Such a fine young lady, Yoko, a fine young lady. Well, there is a ghost in the room, and he seems cranky about the company."

Truth just shook his head, got up, and pulled on his clothes.

"You girls may be missing out. I can't really see him, but he seems quite tall."

"No, Your Eminence, we are here for . . . your eminence." Sally smiled and rubbed up against the rich man.

Truth threw the covers off him and got out of the bed. "You know what? This is a suite. I'm gonna crash in the other room. Pull any bullshit, and I swear I will swap your eyes and testicles around, then stitch your cock where your tongue should be. And vice versa. I'm not very good at sewing, so it may take me a few tries. But I promise I won't quit until we get there. Otherwise, go nuts. I don't care. I so, so, so don't care."

"Simultaneously the most threatening and accommodating ghost I have ever met."

Truth grabbed his stuff and stalked out of the room. It wasn't fair. He was so damn tired. He had picked the most stupidly expensive hotel room he could find without going into the city center. And some rich prick with a weird fetish turned up with his two . . . admittedly extremely attractive . . . call girls for a threesome. And he could see through the blessing, somehow.

Would Etenesh be up for a threesome? He thought about it for a moment.

No. No, she would not. And God help the person who proposed the idea. Etenesh believed in monogamy considerably more than she believed in gravity. Which was a shame, because he suddenly had some very lurid fantasies.

"Thrush, keep an eye on them. If he tries to call for help, signal someone, or does anything at all to sound any kind of alarm, wake me."

"Sleep peacefully, Master. I will attend closely. Enjoy your dreams."

"I don't dream," Truth murmured.

Truth slept until morning. When he came out of the side room, he found the rich man neatly washed, dressed, and fixing himself a cup of coffee. Truth could smell the coffee from there, and he wouldn't drink that trash on a bet. Siphios had spoiled him. He dramatically collapsed on the sofa, looking pensively at the man. He wasn't entirely sure what to do about him. Kill him, probably, but . . .

The man turned his head around, looking at the sofa in surprise. "Prager be praised! You can move around during the day?"

"I'm not the weirdo with the ecclesiastical fetish, buddy. Though I am pretty damn curious about how you can see me. What Level are you?"

"Weirdo? You, unquiet spirit, are calling *me* a weirdo? I'm a dignified Level Three, thank you very much, and not some blasted voyeuristic ghost!"

"Voyeurs definitionally like to watch. I was asleep before you copped a feel."

"Unlikely. Also untrue, as I felt eyes upon me the entire night."

"Yeah, but it wasn't me." Truth shrugged.

"Who else would dare spy on a clergyman conducting Church business? What villain would be so low?" The man sounded outraged.

"The literal demon I employ for such purposes. Also, what kind of fucked-up church has banging a couple of admittedly lovely pros as a sacrament?"

"It's not a sacrament; that word has a technical meaning. Though you do have the right religion." He fished around inside his high-thread-count shirt and pulled out an ornately engraved golden pendant. The rich man hung the pendant around his neck. "Introductions—I am James Reik, Archpriest at St. Florian of the Loch and Sin Eater for my parish. Might I ask what name you had in life?"

Truth boggled a bit at that, but he recognized the pendant. "You are a Pragerite Archpriest. A priest. An honest-to-whoever—"

"Prager."

"I wonder."

"My faith is tested on occasion. I am not without my failings. But my savior and his saints walk with me. I would keep no other company." Truth could see the sincerity in the man. It was creeping him out a little bit. *Sincere* was not a word he had associated with the Pragerite Church up to this point.

"Hmm."

"Your name, Ghost, your name!"

"Johnny Bells, Certified Talisman Maintenance Specialist."

"You bloody aren't."

"I could have been! You don't know," Truth said, grinning. He would make the weirdo's death painless.

"Son—"

"You *son* me, this is going to be a *really short* conversation."

"Johnny, I feel bloodlust on you that most soldiers could hardly match. Your brief, unhappy life was one of great violence. Not fixing air conditioners."

"Funny. I did actually get into a murderous battle while fixing an air conditioner." Truth put his feet up on the coffee table and looked over Reik. About average height for Jeon, trim, perfect teeth, and a full head of hair. The expensive clothes and hotel room were explained by his clerical position, of course.

"Was that where you died?"

"Not that time. Sin Eater?"

"Yes?"

"Hell is a sin eater?"

"Exactly what it sounds like."

"Am I going to find chunks of sex workers in the bedroom? I hope not."

"What?" This time, it was Reik's turn to look bewildered. His eyes swept through the rough area Truth was in on the sofa, struggling to focus on him.

"I mean, cannibalism, even for a priest—"

"So, Johnny, those were two lovely young ladies who happened to be parishioners. I would never harm them." There was a lull. Reik took a long pull on the coffee. "I can see you don't understand. You weren't one of the faithful in life, were you?"

"No. Though we did attend services for a month or two."

"Ah, died before baptism?"

"Dad stole from the collection basket, and Mom tried to hustle her MLMs during coffee hour." Reik did a spit take, spraying coffee on some very expensive-looking carpet.

"All right, so you are not religious, then."

"I'm told I would make a wonderful Desrin once I developed the faintest trace of faith in God. Sin Eater, James."

"It's *Father James* or *Your Eminence*, actually."

"I am in a committed relationship and do not consent to join your sick sex game. Explain what's going on here and why you can see me. Because as fun as this has been, I've got places to go and things to do."

Reik looked like he was choking on something. "Sin, spiritual pollution, wraps the soul in layers of corruption. I absorb the sin from others, then cleanse it from myself in what is, actually, a sacrament. Yesterday, one of my more elderly parishioners prayed for deliverance from lust. She missed her late husband but kept to her vows. She made the necessary donation; I interceded for her and absorbed the sin. I then contacted those lovely ladies and offered to cleanse them of lust and greed in exchange for a night of their time. The various lusts and desires are now balanced, so I would hesitate to absorb your wrath, hate, and impiety. Still. If necessary, I will accept that burden."

The room went quiet again.

"Johnny?"

"Processing that." Truth was quiet awhile longer. "You believe sin is something, ehh, spiritually tangible? Transferable?"

"I know it is. It happens every day, to everyone. Eating sin is sadly more common than eating food. It's doing it intentionally and then purifying yourself that's the miracle."

"People give you money to . . . temporarily block sin from them? Remove the sin they are currently suffering?"

"Yes, to both."

"Sorry, just trying to understand. Do you give the money back when the sin returns?"

Reik shook his head. "Now, there is an old saw. No, Johnny. The miracles of faith require sacrifice, and the glory of the Church must be maintained, as the glory of God must be maintained."

Truth took in the luxury hotel suite. "Yes. God. How you suffer."

Reik raised an eyebrow and pulled off his jacket. "Let me show you something." He unbuttoned his shirt and shrugged it off.

Reik was emaciated. You could count every rib, see every abdominal muscle. See his stomach bulging with every breath. His skin was the blue-white of a drowned corpse. Sores covered him, some covered in gauze to stop pus or plasma from staining his shirt. Most were not. Red traceries of burst capillaries crawled across his arms. Bruises brought color to pallor, blacks and purples fading to blues and yellows.

"God wants his children to be happy. He loves us. But we must be obedient to his law. We must not succumb to sin. For sin is sickness. Sin is corruption. As sin corrupts the soul, so too does it waste away the mind and the flesh. But prosperity is a sign of God's favor. So long as we obey, are devoted and faithful, prosperity will come to us. Our bodies will be strong, our minds strong. Our souls free of stain. Free of the rule of Hell."

Reik started putting his shirt back on. "So, yes. I accept their very generous donations. I book luxury hotel rooms. My suit, another donation, would be worth several months' salary for most of my parishioners. And yes, I accept the support of my parishioners who do their considerable best to turn a painful duty pleasant, or at least bearable. A little roleplay, some affected silliness, some feigned desire. My unfeigned determination to lose myself in the illusion."

Truth had given his full attention to the priest. There was a cadence to the words, a spine to them. Faith.

"And I believe I can see you because I have received God's blessing to do so. My eyes were anointed with the oil of St. Florian herself. I can literally see the sin on you, Johnny. Even if I can't see your face."

Truth gawped for a moment. Reik fixed his clothes. "Is that a . . . common ability in the Pragerite Church?"

"No, not particularly. There is only so much oil left after five hundred years, after all. Others have their own blessings and burdens."

Truth released an almost-silent sigh of relief.

"Usually, we use the blessed pendants to spot undead. Though for some reason—"

"Don't think about that one too much."

"Why?"

"Because I'm actually considering letting you live, and I certainly won't if you start getting nosy."

"I am not afraid to meet my God. I am only afraid of failing Him," Reik said quietly.

"Boy, will you be in for a surprise." Truth's voice was bone dry. "Trust me on this one—humans are going to need a lot more help than God will in the near future."

That actually made Reik laugh.

"That, I know."

"You know why the world is collapsing, right?"

"How could the Church be unaware? The world falls from God's Grace, and magic falls away with it. You won't be able to stay in this world when that happens. No ghost will. If not me, then please, let one of my fellow sin eaters cleanse your corruption before you fall to Hell."

"Guess you must really hate Siphios, then."

"Not at all. Our fall from grace has little to do with them. Indeed, the gentiles are our surest path to salvation. No, it is we, the Church, who failed the world. It was our duty to lead them from sin. Every converted soul was a chance to demonstrate our faith and love to God. We did some good. Saved many. But we certainly did not do our best. We failed, and the world falls with us." The priest smiled sadly. "I don't hate anyone, Johnny. I'm just sorry."

Truth tried to wrap his head around what Reik was saying. Then he slowly smiled. "People are getting poorer, sicker, weaker. Working harder and harder for less and less. A vicious, global cycle of sin. A cycle it's too late to break out of," Truth said.

"I remember a time, a recent time, when there were no adult Level Zeros in Jeon. Now?"

Truth nodded along. "Now they are so common, I hardly notice them at all."

It was the oddest feeling. He didn't want to kill the priest. In a sense, he didn't need to. There was nothing to connect an angry ghost with any terrorist activity. On the other hand, he really didn't like leaving anyone with any memory of him at all. Safest to silence the priest. But that little spark in his chest, that piece of Etenesh's goodness, burned. The Tongue practically hummed in disapproval. What to do?

CHAPTER 40

AN INSIDE MAN

Hang on a second—you say you physically take on the sin. As in you remove it from the person it is on until they sin again."

"Yes, we covered that." The priest nodded.

"And it stays gone until the person sins again."

"Well, it's more nuanced than that, but that's the basic idea."

"And you, and an unknown but nonzero number of your fellow clergy, can literally see the accumulated sin on a person."

"Again, sort of. But that is the basic idea. Where are you going with this?"

"Does it hurt?"

"Yes, it's agonizing. Let me take off my pants; see for yourself what absorbing lust does to a man!" He grabbed his belt.

"No, I mean, does it hurt the people whose sin you absorb? Do they suddenly feel compelled to worship Prager or something?" Truth quickly clarified.

"Oh. No. Actually, it feels quite nice. A sudden sense of relief, like you just put down a heavy load. And yes, people do feel compelled to give thanks to Prager, but that's mostly because they suddenly feel better."

Truth nodded. "And if you absorb my, what, wrath?"

"Wrath, bloodlust, envy, hate, resentment generally, a few other trace elements like gluttony and lust, and apparently just a TON of blasphemy. Although"—here, Reik turned his head sideways a bit—"the blasphemy is a bit weird. Like . . . you have definitely committed blasphemy, but you kind of didn't mean it?"

"Huh. Surprising."

"I don't know how you managed it. You either committed a sin or you didn't. How do you just-a-bit blaspheme?"

"I don't know, but I do know at least one internationally known clergyman who refuses to discuss the nature of God with me until I can define what a human is." This got Reik sputtering again.

"He asked a ghost to define humanity. That's a sharp operator, right there."

"True. So . . . you would explode or something if you tried to absorb my sin, yeah?"

"If I tried it right now? Yes. Well, not literally, but functionally. I would have to do it over several sessions, and it would cost a fortune. Not that I'm going to ask you to pay; we would do a charity fundraiser and ask for donations. No pockets in a shroud and all that."

"You guys get shrouds?"

"Were you buried without one?"

"You guys get buried?" Truth was feeling a bit mischievous.

"You weren't buried?!"

"It's debatable at best."

Reik opened and closed his mouth helplessly. "I will admit eating the sin of a murder victim will be a first for me."

Truth laughed. "What's your going rate?"

"There isn't one. But for a problem as severe as yours . . . ten thousand wen? More?"

"For as long as there are wen, at any rate." Reik nodded firmly at that.

"That is the subject of a lot of discussion in the Church. Even at the highest levels, we aren't entirely clear on how the credit system is going to work in practice, as regards tithing and all that."

Ten grand was a big chunk of his available cash. Not that he gave a damn; it was found money, but it was annoying not to have cash on hand.

"You say it would take repeated sessions to clear—how about I pay you in installments?"

"Eh?"

Truth laughed silently to himself. "I have the strangest feeling a miracle will occur just as you are leaving the hotel."

"Decided not to murder me?"

"I'm interested in the sin-eating thing. Anything that makes me less visible, you know?"

"Ah. As opposed to the salvation of your soul from eternal torment."

"Is it really salvation if the person doing the tormenting is the same as the one doing the 'saving'?"

"Pardon?"

"Well, God runs everything, right?"

"No, of course not . . . Ah. I see. Because God is the highest and the ultimate authority in the universe, all aspects of the universe must be under his rule. Therefore, the torments of Hell occur at his command. Is that it?"

"Yep."

"Nope."

"Eh?"

"Free will is a thing, you know?"

"I don't?"

"Pardon?" There was a moment of mutual incomprehension.

"Free will? Does that . . . ring any kind of bell for you?" Reik asked.

"Other than, like, consenting for sex or something? Or entering a contract, maybe?"

"Oof. All right, not how I saw this morning going, but God never gives us greater trials than we can bear."

"He absolutely does. I speak as someone who has been professionally violent. He one hundred percent gives people more than they can bear, and they die."

"Another theological discussion for another time. Free will. Very short version—God created the world, set it in motion, and provided rules to live by. Abide by the rules, the key of which is faith and devotion to God, and you get to go to Heaven. You will be happy forever, perfected by God and existing as the perfect being he always intended you to be. But you don't have to do that. You can choose to reject God. And God respects your decision. There is a place entirely free of his presence. Hell."

"Ah. So, those who have rejected God are volunteers, going to experience . . . eternal torment via the absence of God?"

"That and fire, freezing, drowning, cancer, rape, torture, mutilation, and generally misery, horror, and every sort of awfulness, forever. It's the exact inverse of Heaven. All the parts of you that are godly are stripped away and returned to God. That which burns forever is a remnant of the 'you' that exists today. All that is left are the things that are not-God.

"Pain. Resentment. Corruption. Despair. Suffering. It is endless. It must be endless because every part of you that could understand relief, love, peace, gratitude, and every other blessed emotion has been stripped away entirely. You are without God. Forever. Conscious and horribly aware, of course, or there would be no point—you would no longer be free to choose. And because you can no longer understand peace or forgiveness or relief, there is no escape. You could conceive of no alternative to your condition. The Gates of Hell keep people out, not in."

Truth digested that one for a minute. It was impressively horrible to contemplate. Then that niggling little instinct kicked in, the one that had made him a misery to Merkovah so many times. "But all this is based on the assumption that we have free will."

"If by 'assumption' you mean *attested by the divinely inspired and free-from-error writings of the prophets and the saints and confirmed by literally millennia of consular decisions by the Church*, then yes." Reik's voice couldn't have been drier.

"Sounds a lot like *The Church decided what they liked was the orthodoxy*, James."

"Johnny, prophets speak to God!"

"Sure. And they contradict each other. Happens all the time. I could find demons and angels who wouldn't back you up. They would have firsthand knowledge, right?"

"Another long theological conversation, but at some point—"

"Faith is required." Truth said. Reik had the feeling of being checkmated in a game he wasn't aware he was playing.

"Yes. Is that so terrible? You stand to gain everything and lose nothing by just . . . believing. By just looking up and saying, 'Thank you. Yes. By your will.'"

Truth thought about the slums. The ones he lived in, and the Slum of the world. He thought of the church's notion of sin determining health and prosperity. And he asked himself again if he really needed to spare this man.

No. He didn't need to. But he would. He wanted to show him how wrong he was. It was immensely petty. Dangerous. Stupid, even.

"Tell you what, James. You go to the slums. Don't wear a suit; just dress normally. Go there and look around. Get a real good feel on all that sin. You might just go blind before you get out of the subway. Take a look around at the people, and then look over at the rich part of the city and then look back at them and say, 'This is all your fault. You chose this, every bit of it.'"

"Well, now, that's—"

"James?"

"Yes?"

"Go now, or I *will* kill you. And then you can test your theology."

Reik didn't see the ghost move, didn't notice the aura following him. But when he walked out the door of the hotel, two thousand wen landed on his head.

Truth considered it his sign-on bonus. They didn't know it, but the Church of Prager in Jeon had just gotten drafted into the revolutionary army.

Truth seethed. It wasn't the description of Hell—he had seen snippets of Hell through portals. Hell was, definitionally, nothing nice. It was the bland assumption that if you were suffering, it was your fault. Which, in fairness, maybe it was! Maybe you weren't taking the steps you needed to be to not suffer. Truth was proof that by devoting absolutely every fiber of your being to an utterly maniacal degree, you could break out of the slums and better your condition.

But what did that mean by the Church's logic? That he broke out because he was less sinful? Were the people already living in the C-Tier housing born his spiritual superiors? Those young masters and mistresses pissing on their weaker "friends" as a "joke" must be paragons of morality, then. To say nothing of Starbrite himself. Sure, the world might die, but he had prospered mightily and was therefore the spiritual apex of the world.

Oh, he was sure the Church would finesse that. It was an oversimplification. The one didn't necessarily imply the other. But they sure acted like that was what they believed. He let his ideas swirl for a bit and stumbled on to the core of it almost accidentally.

Free will absolved God of blame. God was perfect and perfectly benevolent. The world was *perfect.* All your suffering was to your benefit so that you would grow and prosper as you overcame them. And if you didn't? If you weren't obedient and fell to sin? That was your choice.

Born poor and turned gangster because they were the only people you saw in the neighborhood with money and respect? Your fault. Turn junkie because it was the only way you knew of to deal with the pain of existence? Your fault. Childhood cancer? Your fault. Possibly your parents' fault. You were the means to cause them suffering for their sins.

Nothing stuck to God. He created the mess, then washed his hands of it and walked away. Like he always did. His creation got fucked up? Turned out horrible and wrong? Not his problem. He'd just walk away and try again later.

"Free will" absolved God of the sin of his creation. It absolved him of his responsibility for the consequences of his actions. If he really got annoyed, he would simply erase the world. It would come back empty and clean, ready for him to get it right this time. Truth could only laugh with anger. That wasn't right. That was fucked-up. And he was *not* okay with it.

<<A slumrat looking down on God, despising his immorality. No wonder Thrush is happy to serve. Not that I disagree with your assessment. Yaldabaoth is famously an asshole and a shitty craftsman to boot.>>

It's fucking circular logic. There must be free will because if there isn't, then God isn't perfect, and since God is perfect, our suffering must be entirely our choice and our fault. And we know that logic is perfect because our handpicked prophets had their definitely divinely inspired and perfectly recorded words written down and neatly collected by us into this book we edited and will explain to you for a sizable donation.

<<Elegant system, really.>>

Truth snorted. *By the way, who is Yaldabaoth?*

<<Eh? It's God. You know that.>>

First I'm hearing of it. Wait, I thought God has hundreds or thousands of names.

<<This is, like, his proper name, kind of. Or something, I don't know. Look, you are the one with the information. I just pick up what you give me.>>

Yeah, but I never heard that name before. Or if I did, I'd forgotten it.

<<Oh, for fuck's sake. It was . . .>>

There was a moment of silence. That stretched into a minute of silence, then two. *System?*

<<I . . . can't find the memory. I have perfect recall, and I don't know how I know that name.>>

Something from the System Astrologica?

<<No, what I got from them was really, really bare bones. I would have remembered that. This comes from something else. Some other source of memory.>>

It's not you, it's not me, what is it, then?

<<Truth . . . whatever it is that your soul gets up to . . . do you think it's remembering something? Are you . . . starting to remember?>>

CHAPTER 41

REMEMBRANCE OF THINGS PAST

Remembering . . . *what? Can the soul have memories? I thought that was the mind's job.*

<<*No, not exactly. Thinking and reason are the mind's job, as are most of your memories, but the soul does pick up things. I don't know what or how much, but it has to, because otherwise, what is it that goes to the afterlife? What is it that gets processed by Heaven and Hell, if not your recollections of life? The accumulated stain of thousands of choices?*>>

Truth was stumped by that one for a moment. *All right, but . . . what exactly is my soul remembering? My life is no mystery. No big gaps, other than the well.*

<<*Well . . . about that . . .*>>

What?!

<<*What if it isn't this life?*>>

Truth just blinked blankly at the wall when he heard that one.

<<*It has come up in some of the stuff we have read about the afterlife, baptism, and all that. Some souls, for reasons unknown, come back again. Not a lot of them, but enough that it's a pretty well-confirmed phenomenon.*>>

Not that well confirmed. The frigging fragment of divinity living in the Bronze Sea thought it was my soul going off on vision quests, not memories from previous lives.

<<*Fair. Got a better explanation?*>>

No, but that doesn't mean the incredibly rare, questionably confirmed phenomenon of reincarnation is *the answer. It seems like kind of a leap from* You remember something I don't *to* I am reincarnated.

The system made a frustrated noise. <<*Look, I am a mutilated bit of your soul, right? I am capable of perceiving the world around me in ways you don't have words for, but I am still stuck inside you. Anything I learn is something you were exposed to. I know more than you because I am paying attention to* everything *you pick up, and I don't forget anything.*

<<*So, where could the information, i.e., the name Yaldabaoth, and the fact that he is a dick and a lousy craftsman, have come from? It didn't come from the System Astrologica, or I would remember being created with that information or being told it during your*

period of enslavement. It didn't come from something you read or heard, because I would remember that too. So, we have ruled out it coming from "me" in the sense of this awareness created by the System Astrologica, and ruled out you in the sense of your psyche and your awareness of the world around you, so that leaves what, exactly?>>

A semi-separate bit of my soul, but not completely detached, is what you are. The Rough Patron showed us that, and the Bronze Sea said as much too. So, if my soul remembered something, even if it didn't reach my mind, it could have reached you. Truth slowly nodded. It was a genuine wonder. How could it be possible? Oh, wait, he was forgetting the obvious.

<<No, I'm not making shit up to fuck with you. Kind of pointless as pranks go, really.>> Occam's razor, and all that.

There was another pause. *<<You . . . want to repeat that last sentence?>> Occam's razor—oh, shit.*

<<I'm sure you have a real, real good explanation for who this Occam guy is and what possible relevance his grooming regimen has to anything. I mean, I don't, on account of never having seen or heard a single damn thing about anyone called Occam, but you DEFINITELY do.>>

Truth just sat there, rapidly going from bewildered to alarmed. *What the hell else do I not know I know?! And why is this all coming up now? My soul has been going through these corrections for at least as long as you have been there.*

<<No idea. Maybe your soul has healed to a certain point; maybe it's something to do with the Tongue or that little bit of Etenesh you carry around in you.>>

Truth felt choked—overwhelmed by everything. *I don't have time for this. At all. I have . . . so many things to keep track of, my head is spinning. I just can't spend brainpower on this weirdness. I'm going to go out, eat some breakfast, figure out a possible atrocity to create, and then decide which luxury hotel is my next hideout. The Dunbar is burnt.*

The System went silent. Truth took it as agreement. It only took a minute to pack up.

Truth went back around the party-barge rental places. They were tiny offices attached to storage spaces, generally. Some were more all-inclusive than others, but from what Truth could tell, the system worked like this: the party barge supplied the venue (that is, the oversized, slow-flying cloud or an actual enchanted barge, speed carefully limited by law) and a driver. For larger parties, they would also provide a small crew to keep things organized and safe. Some barges had a bar, or a party lights system, or a spirit of music, or even a hot tub. Mostly, though, they were flying platforms.

Once the venue was secured, caterers were organized, then decorations were rented, music arranged, invitations manufactured and issued, each going to a separate contractor. There was no all-in-one option because the economies of scale made specialization more lucrative. No one person was "throwing" the party, except for maybe the person funding it. It was an awful, brutal sort of beautiful. Like a wasp parasitizing a spider. An entire ecosystem built around ecstasy that carefully ensured that the creators of that ecstasy got neither pleasure nor pride from their creation.

He flipped through the reservation books, trying to find something. They were heavily booked, and the barge companies didn't care even slightly who was renting them, so long as the money was good. Every moment the barges were in storage was a loss. They were screamingly expensive, so, naturally, no one could buy one cash. They were financed, purchased with expensive loans.

Every second of every day, interest accumulated and the next payment due got that little bit closer. But nobody wanted to party 24/7, and there had to be cleaning and maintenance. If you cared to invest in maintenance, which many didn't. Tick, tick, tick. Time is running out. Truth understood how they felt. Enrollment day was getting closer. Tick, tick, tick.

It took a lot of back-and-forth trips, as well as a bit of research into just who was booking what, but he found one eventually. One of the bigger barges was being rented for the "Whicker and Voss Spring Whingdinger." He had to ask someone what the hell a "Whingdinger" was, but he knew the clients. Whicker and Voss were one of the big three accounting firms. Nobody at that party would be famous, but a lot of them would be terribly rich and connected. And they did a lot of work for Starbrite subsidiaries and suppliers.

Well. Time to make a few little preparations, the first of which involved trekking over to the slums. It took an extra two hours from his day, but he found the Ghūl nest. He didn't drop by. He still had no idea how to communicate with them. Then it was a quick rush round the shops to buy or shoplift a few tools and some paint, then off to find a room for the night.

He was very sorry to learn that the Transcendent Nova of Tranquility suite had been booked by a Ms. Gersh, not a Ms. Bhu at the Crystal Mountain, and that a Mr. Xin had reserved the Emerald Dreams Elite Residence for himself and his bubbly guests at the Residences at Perwik. The best suites were, apparently, heavily sought after in Buran's downtown.

Growing increasingly irritable, Truth opted to lower his standards and broke into a penthouse apartment next to the fifth hotel he visited. It didn't look like anyone was staying there at the moment, but the automated cleaning system and endless housekeepers would erase any trace of human habitation regardless.

The glass walls, stretching seven meters from floor to ceiling, gave one spectacular views of both the city and the ocean, depending on where you looked. The art was enormous and so abstract, it was quite impossible to guess what it was supposed to be about. Each piece must have cost as much as a house in a third-rate city. There was an infinity pool on the wraparound balcony, with an attached hot tub. The hot tub also had those wonderful built-in water jets. The bedroom was a room, a quite-large room, whose entire floor space was covered in a deep mattress. It felt like it was stuffed with angel feathers, and in Buran, that might literally be true.

Truth decided that the apartment would do for now. He slept. The System had developed a nervous habit of keeping a close "eye" on Truth's soul. Healing or not, the changes were agonizing. The soul seemed to ripple for a moment. Then the pain came.

"Alethes! It's been years!" The handsome man hugged his guest forcefully and long. Far, far more intimate than a Japanese person would usually tolerate, but he was exceedingly well traveled and cosmopolitan. He knew what Greeks were like.

"I told you, just call me Truth. You don't have to torture yourself with the pronunciation," Truth grumbled, smiling. "You are looking oppressively fit."

"Haha! Thank you, thank you. You are looking mighty fit yourself."

"Modeling, acting, and, apparently, you took up martial arts?"

"Oh? I didn't know you knew." The Japanese man smiled broadly. "Come in; Yoko has prepared your room. Let's get you settled. You have come a long way."

Truth allowed himself to be settled in a guest room, then settled in the living room and settled with a cup of warm, but not hot, green tea. Yoko looked immaculate, like a swan on water, unstained by the muck of the world. It was a mask, but he didn't take it personally. Her husband was the strange one that way, not her.

"Where are the kids? No, no, thank you, I don't smoke." He waved away the offered pack.

"At school, of course; it's the middle of the week." The handsome man reclined, looking like the best thing that ever happened to cigarettes. "Getting some thin version of education. If you don't mind my asking, why did you come to Japan? I am delighted to see you, but all I got over the phone was something garbled about headless men?"

Truth gave the writer a grim smile. "I brought a present. An extremely rare collection from my library. I daresay you have never seen it's like and never will again." Truth hauled out a small cardboard box and handed it to the author. "Sorry, no time to get it wrapped."

"That's extremely kind of you—"

"Open it. It's relevant to the conversation."

"Eh?" The author looked at Truth oddly and shrugged. He opened the box, revealing five magazines inside. On the cover was a headless man. Muscular, the author noted approvingly, holding various occult symbols and with a skull over his groin. Which he also approved of. His eye caught a certain name on the cover, making him smile.

"Something by Bataille? I think I heard something about this."

"Bataille and a few others. A sort of philosophical review with a big focus on Nietzsche. Other things, too, but Nietzsche pops up the most. The whole last issue is almost entirely on him."

"Ah? I thought you weren't very fond of Bataille."

"I'm not, but too many others are incomprehensible without some understanding of that old monster. Besides, he meets the requirements for my library."

"I know you have a lot of books, but I think you mean something different here."

"Yes. My philosophical library consists entirely of philosophers who went to war, with a specific preference for those who fought in resistance movements."

"Bataille was in the French resistance? He was too old for the army."

"Yes. *Acéphale* was more than just the name of the review; it was a secret society. They carried out armed resistance activities to the Vichy and the Germans, going so far as to conduct a human sacrifice to harden their hearts." Truth nodded.

The author looked a lot more impressed as he flipped through the magazines. "I had no idea."

"It's not widely discussed, for obvious reasons. Still a lot of hard feelings." Truth felt the little ball of lead shift around under his rib. "A lot."

"A precious gift. Thank you. But really, it's too much."

"You can give me a return gift. Sign this."

Truth pulled out a heavily read pamphlet. The author noticed with a combination of irritation and appreciation that it had been subjected to extensive underlining and notes in the margins.

"I will sign a clean copy for you. I have plenty around the house. But why this in particular? I can't imagine it was enough to get you to fly halfway around the world."

"You would be wrong. It is."

"I don't qualify for your library. I wasn't even allowed to serve in the army."

"Irrelevant. You are officially going into a collection of one. Bataille is relevant to our conversation because he is the closest I could find to your essay." Gimlet eyes bored into the author. "Congratulations. You have written perhaps the only unique bit of philosophy in the twentieth century. And nobody knows you did it." They looked down at the bland, battered volume. "As someone with a lot of exposure to both sun and steel, I had to get on the plane at once. I have a lot of questions for you."

CHAPTER 42

THE EROTIC MYSTICISM OF THE MARTYRED FLESH

Truth had an early night's sleep, as jet lag is a real bastard. The bed was tiny, but he was prepared to cherish the fact it wasn't a futon. He had spent enough nights sleeping on the floor. The mechanical alarm went off at five in the morning. Dawn was still some distance away, but his host had insisted. If he wanted to understand, truly understand, the author's philosophy, this was the only way.

They set off on a predawn run. Jogging at first, but they quickly sped up to a hard run. Through the silent, still streets. All new housing there—comparatively new. The whole area burned to rubble during the war. Row houses with terra-cotta tile roofs were replaced with concrete boxes, though they kept the terra-cotta. Electric lights and telephones replaced the oil lamps.

The author led them along the main street—the morning trucks taking their groceries here and there, the night shift coming home, the day shift starting to stir and queue up for a hot bite of something before work. The author had a clear route in mind. The run was stretching out longer and longer—Truth's legs were aching, his feet were aching, his lungs panting to get in enough air. The author was sweating too. They pressed on.

Truth tried to take in the city as they ran, observing the past resisting the onrushing modernity like old nails poking up through the new carpet. A tiny shrine with a fox inside, an old post box, candies introduced by the Portuguese to the shoguns in a store window. Parked in front of the window was a brand-new Toyota, its owner arriving early to make sure that the world-beating corporation he worked in rose like the sun. Like a phoenix from atomic ashes. Though there in Tokyo, jellied gasoline, used in quantity, was enough to clear the way for the world of the 1960s. Soon, though, the physical exhaustion pushed all morbidity from him. He could no longer think. Just feel.

The author led them, ultimately, to a gymnasium. Without a moment's rest, they kicked off their shoes and went inside. Truth was gasping for water, sweat pouring off him. The author was no better. Instead of water, the author pulled him onto a mat on the floor.

Without a word, he flicked a jab at Truth's face. Truth swayed back on instinct, his own hands coming up. Palms open, fingers curled, his body settled into its stance without conscious effort. The author's kick came sharp from the left. It would have landed on someone else. Truth slid back and to the side, then pushed in, hooking the leg and sending the author tumbling back. The author rolled out and was on his feet again before Truth could capitalize.

Truth could feel the author's eyes on him, focused, fixated on him. Appreciating every move, every breath, as mindlessly as Truth devoured the author's presence. He felt so *seen*. Truth's open palm lashed out, his body twisting and sinking, putting all of himself into the blow. The author parried with his fist, replying with a chop toward Truth's neck. Truth blocked high and dove in for a grapple. Back and forth, mindlessly struggling until they collapsed. Bruised, gasping. Almost fainting for lack of water.

They helped each other up and staggered over to a water barrel. The author used the ladle to drink. Truth stuck his head in and gulped. When he ran out of air, he pulled his head back out of the barrel and gasped. He looked over at the author, shirtless now, rippling muscles framed by a wall of practice swords. Smelled the sweat and polish of the gymnasium. Smelled himself. Felt the heat radiating off his still-strong body, a warm shield against the cool morning breeze coming through the door.

For a moment, there was no "Truth." There was only the flesh, the muscles, speaking to the entire universe. Tangible, real in a way he could not describe. Connected without the mediation of words to the absolute. And then the moment was gone.

"You saw it. The blue sky I wrote of in my essay."

"Just for a moment." The gym's showers were adequate, and they both badly needed them. Besides, while they might share a casual appreciation for the other's physique, neither cared to take it beyond that. So, why not chat in the shower?

"That's all it can last. A moment. A moment that combines the sheer joy brought by physical suffering, appreciation of life, and the undercurrent of inescapable death."

"Like cherry-blossom viewing." Truth smiled, making sure the cool water reached every inch of him. "The flowers are beautiful precisely because the beauty is fleeting. Soon, they will be a mess on the road, swept up and put aside to rot."

"Exactly, yes. I read a bit of the Bataille last night. Like visiting an old friend. My dictionary got quite the workout. But I see what you were getting at. Yes, I share his and Nietzsche's radical materialism."

"More than that, you reject Plato in his entirety. This is no mere anencephalic mysticism—it is an experience of the absolute that can *only* be experienced through the flesh. One *cannot* experience it through reason or the mind at all. You categorize reason as the corrosion of meaning."

"Precisely. It is a revelation reserved exclusively for heroes. Those with the resolve to spend years training their bodies to the absolute pinnacle and training their courage alongside it. I have only experienced that true moment of unity, as I wrote, once. That perfect balance of the mind and body, suspended at the extremes of human existence."

"Waiting for that aesthetic death to complete a perfect existence," Truth said softly. "Because Achilles died when he was young and beautiful, but the aging Jason became a pestilence. Remembered with pity and contempt."

The author smiled and tapped his nose. "Yes. To lose one's individuality in the warrior band, to die at the peak of perfection, united with the universe through pure reality and concreteness found in the flesh. That is the way a hero should die."

<<FFFFFFFFFFSSSSSSSSSSSSSSSSSSSSSSSSSKKKKKKK!! Oh, that NEVER GETS EASIER! DAMN, DAMN, DAMN, DAMN, DAMN!>>

Truth snapped to consciousness. *I feel the sudden urge to get in a workout.*

<<Oh, BOY! That's just super. I don't care even one tiny bit. GODDAMN, THAT HURTS!>>

I mean, it may be related. Sounds like I just had one of those soul whatevers. If I'm remembering more of my past lives, maybe I should go see what my soul wants.

<<Screw it, why not. Yes. Go do that. Did you know I can't cry? I wish I could. I would be crying now.>>

Truth went and found the home gym. It wasn't much—a mat, a bench, some free weights. Not even a bar or a squat rack. Truth sighed and started some calisthenics. After a light warmup of one hundred one-finger push-ups with each finger (total time to completion, ten minutes) and an easy hundred burpees, he started doing a little shadowboxing. Open palm strikes, thrown elbows, short, sharp low kicks. Feinting some grapples. It all flowed. It always had. Fighting was easy to figure out. It was learning everything else that was hard.

<<Wait. Wait just a second. What's that you are doing with your hand?>>

Palm strike? You curl the fingers in so they don't bend backward and break if you miss. It protects your knuckles, too. Keeps them from tearing open on someone's head.

<<Never seen you do that before.>>

What? I must have done. It's just another way to hit someone. I've hit a lot of people.

<<Not like that, you haven't. Slapped people until they cried and pissed themselves, yes. Punched people, so, so many people, yes. But you do body cultivation, and even before that, the Nine Worms gave you a tough body. Torn skin is a non-factor for you. Even before you broke through to Level One, you never gave a shit about tearing up your knuckles. Open-palm strikes? Not really something you ever bothered with.>>

Truth looked down at his hands in wonder.

Breakfast was an abbreviated affair, eaten on the go. He had a target, he had a date (tonight, as he picked his target with an eye for convenience rather than perfection), and he even had a rough strategy about how he was going to get the job done. It was the actual doing of the job, and surviving it, that was the challenge.

He spent a lot of time walking around muttering, jotting notes on a bit of paper, staring upward, measuring vaguely with his thumb, then it was back to muttering and note-taking. He had a highly functional grasp of arithmetic, but anything beyond that was a closed book.

After a fairly tiresome afternoon, he made his way back to the barge-rental office. He walked straight past the front desk, ignoring, and ignored by, the Level One working reception. He couldn't be bothered to assume a persona. The Blessing of the Silent Forest was more than enough to make them unreal before him, though he never let Incisive lapse. The only real person in a world of ghosts. He picked out a fancy crewman's hat and a white jacket from the supply closet. It didn't fit particularly well, but then, it didn't have to.

He made his way over to the skydock, making a few light alterations to himself with Incisive. He would be unnoticeable, but in the event that a high-level appeared and did, in fact, notice him, he would simply be a crewman, keeping the party moving. Just in case. In the meantime, he planted a few small talismans here and there on the barge, taking careful note of where the bound demons were located. Where all the safeties and backups were located.

At seven that evening, the carpets started flying in. Sharply dressed office workers, their plus-ones dressed to the nines, coming to party and get their freak on. No sex workers for this party, nor mixing bowls full of blow or pills. This was a *fancy* office party. Liquor, in its many forms, dominated. Sparkling wine, smoky mezcal, whisky, both sweet and strong. There were obscure mixers, too, rare and strange liquors, ice harvested from comets before the Shattervoid closed the sky, shaved, crushed, and chopped into sparkling spheres.

To accompany the drink was the "Bitters," eyedroppers of potions, color-coded for effect. Enchanted trays of droppers drifted from guest to guest, letting them pick their poison and enjoy. Uppers for the tired, soothers for the stressed. Aphrodisiacs for the hopeful, ambitious, or cruel. An easy dozen, carefully selected by the party organizer and approved by the senior partners. For those who liked to let the evening build, they were added to the drinks. For those who wanted relief now, the drops went under the tongue or into the corner of their eye.

Music started pulsing. Not too loud—it was early yet. There would be food passed around before the real dancing started. Beautiful men and women, sharply dressed, sparkling, trying to attract attention and approval from those above. Proving their superiority to those below. Glamorous? Yes, endlessly so. Glamors on almost every face. Enchantments drifted subtly about, hooking where they might. Of course, no one there was one of the cattle below. They had their personal protections, keeping the wisps of magic from corroding their minds. It was all part of the game.

Truth watched it all happen. The music got louder. People's hands started sliding around, touching what was usually forbidden or at least strongly discouraged. Someone who should have stopped an hour ago ordering a double. The Bitters getting refilled three times in an hour by the overworked bar staff. The nibbles were sent around on flying platters. Meat, beautiful cubes of pork and beef and rare seafood, trimmed into elegant, bite-sized chunks. The smell was amazing. Truth glanced down at the city below. How long since those below could afford meat? How much longer could they do it?

The sun sank into the mountains behind the city, and the night sky slowly came into its glory. The barge turned up the party lights and cranked the music. Booming, throbbing. The lights flickering and changing in time with the music. Screams of laughter and fun pissing down over the sides onto the people below. The drink and the Bitters had transformed performative fun into sheer abandon. For a brief moment, they were all young, sexy, and beautiful again. Some for the very first time. They danced, Level Ones, Twos, Threes, even a scattered few Level Fours. They chatted and schemed and fucked in the false privacy of the shadows. Truth leaned against the railing and watched it all happen.

The first talisman had done its job—they were subtly off course. Only by about three blocks, hardly noticeable from this height. Then the second talisman kicked in, severing the controls. Truth grinned horribly and activated his *other* Blessing—the demon-crushing Blessing from the Bronze Sea. With a tiny flex of will, he drove spikes of cutting force into the bound demons holding up the barge. Exterminating them.

CHAPTER 43

ALL FALL DOWN. NO MORE STARS

The party barge slid down out of the sky, lights still pulsing in frantic time to the mindless music the bound spirits were compelled to play. The screams of mandatory fun and drugged release turned into fear, raw, clawing, stabbing. The barge slid down, passing the roofs of apartment towers. Passing the dim, shoddy windows of the ever-watchful slumrats. They always loved a free show. Some of the lift spells still worked. The barge fell a little slower than gravity demanded. The wards around the railings held. Screaming accountants and their dates slid along the flashing dancefloor and piled up against the stern, crushing each other as the hammer fell inevitably toward the anvil.

A few had the wit to activate personal spells, break emergency charms, and try to reach the soft-fall medallions lining the edge of the barge. Too late. Their all-too-human bodies couldn't struggle against gravity and inertia. Some of the Level Fours might have managed it, smashing bodies out of their way. They might have reached safety. But not with Truth standing by. Waiting for them. Waiting for them to fight free of the crush only to watch the medallions fall overboard. Watching them look helplessly as he flung the medallions off into the void.

Still. You make Level Four anywhere, let alone Jeon, and you weren't someone soft. You did things to get that power. And of the four Level Fours in attendance, two had the seven-pointed-star lapel pins of Starbrite. Long green wings burst from their backs, feathers meters long and made of cosmic energy fluttering in the rushing air. Another seemed to burst into a foam of tiny white bubbles, more and more and more until he was covered in them, until he was buried more than an arm's length deep in them. The last one launched themselves horizontally from the barge, aiming for the apartment buildings and trusting in God to provide.

Truth intercepted him with an axe kick that rattled his brain and smashed his face into the deck. In a second or two, he would recover, but . . . in a second or two, the barge would smash into the pavement. Truth launched himself up the sharp slope of the barge, letting inertia and body cultivation send him flying toward the two Starbrite experts. They didn't see him coming. They couldn't have stopped him if they had. The Tongue lashed out, gutting one, the wings vanishing as she screamed and tried to grab all the falling pieces of her. He snapped the other's neck, palm shattering chin and turning a classically sculpted face into abstract street art. Not dead yet either, but the wings shattered into the air, and there were less than two seconds to recover.

He bunched his legs under him, cast Abner's Amble, and leapt straight up. Thrush had been waiting—the air demon caught him and slowed his fall. He watched the barge slam into the sidewalk below him. The sudden cessation of movement meant that all the bodies formerly piled up at the stern shotgunned into the pavement. A fraction of a second after the impact, the street became a gory hell. Worst of all, perhaps, was that the wards had held until the last. The party had been reduced to crushed and ruined bodies, but they were still mostly alive.

Truth landed, soft as murderous dandelion fluff. His aim had been a little short of the target, it seemed, but nothing too terrible. He quickly jogged a block up the road, passed the destroyed street lights and the steel-shuttered, lightless doorways. He came to the building with the windows all covered and blacked out. The building none of the teeming slumrats would ever dare approach. He knocked twice, then opened the door. Hundreds of faces, mummified, emaciated, or rotting, greeted him. All smiling in their way. He bowed and invited them outside.

They streamed out in silent order, first by the tens, then hundreds of them. They swarmed silently over to the barge, passing through the flickering remains of the wards like nightmares, like a repressed memory. Someone recovered enough to scream.

More joined in quickly, begging, crying. The Ghūl preferred quiet, but it seemed they understood the situation. They showed all their usual tenderness, pulling away teeth and picking loose nerves. Slowly pressing rotting fingers into eyes until they went *pop-pop*. Plucking eyes out and turning them around, still connected to the brain, so the partygoers had to watch the ruination of their flesh. Watched their stomachs be torn open and their innards shivering in the cool evening air. Watching their genitals be ground under feet or rubbed between hands until they were simply pulped meat and tissue. Some of the Ghūl were collecting parts here and there, bringing them back into their nest. Truth didn't care to investigate why.

The Level Four who had bound himself in foam exploded out of his shell. He looked shaken but alert. He swiftly took in the scene and turned on his heel to run. Truth readied himself to intercept, but there was no need. Bony fingertips poking from decayed flesh sank into the Level Four's shoulder. Hooked the collarbone. Sharply yanked up and back. The Level Four screamed and spun around, rattling dragons of lightning bursting from his hands. Smashing into the Ghūl. Achieving nothing.

The spells reached the Ghūl; Truth could see the lightning licking at them. It just did nothing. On some level Truth could not understand, the spell was simply . . . forbidden from having an effect. They could be harmed by direct force. They could be harmed by superheating the environment around them, reducing their flesh to dust. But magic could not touch them directly. Truth had heard that before but hadn't quite believed it. Now, as he watched the screaming Level Four have his face bitten away, his tongue pulled out and bitten off, his ankles chewed into stubs, and his knees shattered and his fingers carefully dislocated a joint at a time, he believed it.

Truth had seen some awful things. Done some things, a lot of things, he wasn't proud of. This was a new level of horror. *Etenesh wouldn't be proud of me if she saw this. She would turn her face from me in disgust.* He didn't move to stop it. It was far too late for that. All he could do was make sure the scene had its intended effect on the public. He got his paint from Thrush and, in as big letters as he could draw, wrote:

All The Stars Fall Down. The Tiger Rises. Jeon Forever!

Truth took a very long shower. Wasn't like the talisman was going to run out of hot water. *Oh, actually, the cosmic energy is thinning. It really could run out of hot water.* His thoughts kept veering into the morbid. What else was he supposed to think about? He had just condemned a party barge full of strangers to an awful, degraded death, and he chose them because they were convenient and decently symbolic. They weren't particularly evil, or no more evil than most. Could something be evil on an absolute scale? If so, then they were evil. If evil was always a relative measure, then they were not. They existed at the background level of evil. Lost in the sinful noise of the world.

Now, the person that crashed a party barge full of office workers and made sure to feed them to the Ghūl alive, that person was evil! Truth switched off the shower and dried off. He would try the hot tub. Why not?

He understood Merkovah's insistence that they were freedom fighters, not terrorists. That they were revolutionaries, and in the desperate present circumstances, "all methods" must be employed. Still the notion of a "just war" was never something he had understood. Partially because no one had ever explained the concept to him, but mostly because it was all just violence. Violence was a tool he used and that others used against him. Why pretty it up with justifications and excuses?

He examined his body in the bathroom mirror. He looked . . . good. The face was his face. He could still hear the evil whispers from time to time, but they didn't crush him anymore. He thanked Etenesh and Jember for that. Their honest appreciation and constant affirmation did a lot to help him to accept himself. His muscles were strong, defined, but not overly bulky. Proportional to his heroic frame. He started from his feet and worked his way up, really looking at every centimeter of himself.

He looked strong. Handsome, perhaps, to those whose tastes ran that way. Too coarsely masculine for Jeon. It lacked that subtle aesthetic polish. His body was hard to the touch. You had the presentiment of strength looking at him—everything about him was purposeful. Intentional. Crafted for heroic work, not left to chance and a flabby life. A body built for a brief and violent moment in the sun. Etenesh called him her "Pretty Man." Sometimes it made him feel good, sometimes like a fraud.

He walked over to the hot tub and sank into it, trying to work with the heat and the water jets to relax. Even in the Slums, there were things you weren't supposed to do. You never curb-stomped someone. Unless they really had it coming, in which case you did. You never involved family, unless they started it or you really wanted to. Never involved "kids," variably defined. Now that he thought about it, all those things you weren't supposed to do were generally brought up to excuse a "counter" atrocity. You *had* to slit that guy's throat and pull his tongue out the hole before hanging a burning tire around his neck and leaving him handcuffed to a streetlight outside his apartment building. You HAD to!

He had crossed the line first by shanking his cousin. It was his own fault it turned out this way. *Not like you wanted to do this. You weren't evil.*

He tilted his head back on the cool edge of the tub. It had been contoured into a pillow shape. Nice. He vaguely heard noises from deeper in the house. It seemed the owners had returned. He didn't stir. If he could break in there, they weren't worth worrying about. That priest said he could see sin. That sin manifested physically and financially. The worse you were doing in life, the greater your sin. Truth felt a faint trickle of hate flow through him. He would get the priest his cash. Let him eat all the sin Truth accumulated. Let him eat it all.

"Honey, were the cleaners in today?"

"I don't know. Why?"

"Shower's wet."

"Guess they were in, then." There was noise in the kitchen area. "Booze is all here, so probably not a break-in. Cleaners."

"They need to remember to dry the walls after they clean."

"Sure. We'll remind them."

It sounded like two women. Tired women. He could feel the ground-in exhaustion through the rote intimacy. He turned around, trying to spot them through the glass walls. A couple of older women. They looked about fifty, which, given their wealth, in Jeon meant they were probably pushing ninety. Back late. He idly wondered what had brought them home after midnight. Well. Not his problem. Nor his business. He'd sleep in the guest bedroom. No need to be an asshole.

"Did you eat enough?"

"Yes, I loaded up on canapes. You?"

"I'm all right. I'm not hungry."

There was a pause. Then a sigh. "All right, bedtime for you and me both."

"Yeah. I just . . ."

There was another pause. "Kind of messed up, going to a baby shower."

"Yeah. Thanks for coming home with me, by the way."

There was a long sigh. "What, was I going to put you on the carpet and send you away while I drank cheap wine and pretended everything was fine? No, dear. I'm afraid I caught the same stomach bug you did." He could hear the smile at the end.

There was a little sniffle. "I just thought I would be dead, you know? That I would die before things got this bad. That the next generations would have time to fix things."

"Yeah. Me too." They sat there—the old married couple holding each other softly and pressing their heads together, Truth sitting in the hot tub, looking up at the locked-down sky.

CHAPTER 44

INSUFFICIENTLY FALSE FLAG

Truth woke in the middle of the night. Sudden, urgent movement outside the door. They were only Level Threes, so he wasn't worried about the owners of the house, but . . .

"Maddie. Maddie, wake up! You have to see this."

"Linh? What? What's wrong?"

"There's been an attack. You have to see the news."

"Damn. Are we in danger?"

Linh laughed, an ugly noise. "Right this minute? Probably not, but who knows?"

Fair point, Truth thought. *The murderer is in the house already*. Not that he had the slightest intention of harming his involuntary hosts. They kept a very comfortable, very luxurious home. He wasn't planning on spending any longer in Buran, but he would definitely patronize their establishment again should he return.

He lay in the guest bedroom (ensuite bathroom, direct access to the wraparound balcony and striking views of the coast, total size approximately 90% of the apartment he grew up in), deciding whether he was going back to sleep or not. The scry came on, loud enough for his superb hearing to make out every tiny detail of the soundscape the top-notch enchantment system created. He didn't approve of how they balanced the highs and lows. He had heard better. Truth silently sighed. He was not getting back to sleep. Might as well see how his atrocity was reported.

The scryball was superb, of course, emerging from a pedestal wrapped in golden vines. He didn't recognize the make or model, so he assumed it was custom. Because sure, why not? Once you owned the penthouse with the wraparound balcony, infinity swimming pool, and hot tub, what's a custom scryball?

The presenter was a custom job too, but that was normal. Strong-looking woman this time. A subtle widening of the jaw, serious hair, no risk of plunging the viewer's gaze down the front of her dress. Still staggeringly beautiful, obviously. Things hadn't collapsed *that* far. He couldn't help but think of a well-groomed dog. Bred for purpose, styled for purpose, made to perform, and at no point was their opinion needed or wanted or relevant. A "valued asset" should focus on generating value, not problems.

"Shocking news tonight from Buran. A party barge with three hundred and forty people on board crashed today in what authorities are describing as a clear act of terrorism." The program cut over to a heavily warded crime scene. So heavily warded, in fact, that you couldn't see into it.

"We have been unable to capture footage of the crime scene directly, as it is under a heavy police cordon. But here is what we have been able to learn."

She carefully walked through the events of the evening, taking care to emphasize the innocence and inherent goodness of the Citizens on board the platform, their charitable donations, their families. It was not currently clear how the barge was made to fail, but it was, according to official statements by Buran Public Security, clearly intentional.

"While crashing a party barge would be a horrific act in its own right, what elevates murder to atrocity is that the barge was clearly deliberately crashed in front of a Ghūl nest."

His hosts inhaled, a sharp gasp, grabbed ahold of each other's hands, knuckles turning white.

"It seems particularly cruel that the most obscene product of Denizen degeneracy was used to torture and defile decent, ordinary Citizens. The crash was clearly intended not merely to shock the public or to murder Citizens but to humiliate them. A humiliation to all the decent people of Jeon."

Wait. Wait one teeny tiny-fucking moment. *"Product of Denizen degeneracy"? Are they saying that the Denizens create the Ghūl somehow?*

"This is, of course, why the scene is currently under the strictest control. The scene must be investigated, but the Ghūl have yet to be exterminated. We have received reports that there was some initial hope of recovering bodies from the nest, but this is unconfirmed at the present time. The standard procedure is incineration of the entire site, but we will keep track of this evolving situation."

"St. Mechivus protect us. Three hundred and forty people, fed to the Ghūl," Linh said.

"Your firm uses Whicker and Voss as outside auditors, don't you?" Maddie asked.

"Us and half the country. I need to call Gaspard. Never thought I would be praying for him to be fucking an intern rather than on the job." Linh rushed off to the comms altar. Maddie kept watching the news.

"We can confirm, however, that there was no possibility of this being some sort of accident. An ultra-nationalist slogan was found painted in blood at the crash site, removing any possibility of magical failure. We are joined by terrorism expert General Marhul Wales. General Wales, what can you tell us about the shocking reports we are getting from Buran tonight?"

Wales, clearly long retired, had shock-white hair and a grim face. He nodded politely at the presenter, then looked directly at the audience. "Thank you for having me. The first thing, and most important thing, is that preliminary reports are almost always wrong or incomplete. So, any details beyond the broadest outlines should be treated as 'true for now,' not the final word. This is triply true for any attributions of responsibility for the attack."

The presenter nodded seriously at that. Truth imagined the producer off-camera nodding seriously and miming that the presenter should repeat the motion. She couldn't be trusted to emote by herself, obviously.

"What I am hearing is that slogans and graffiti similar to those used by the Real Jeon Liberation Front were found at the scene. Now, if that does turn out to be correct, all that proves is that slogans and graffiti similar to those used by the Real Jeon Liberation Front were found at the scene. It does *not* prove that this was domestic terrorism."

"You think it might be international terrorists or state-sponsored terrorism?"

"It's no secret that Jeon's enemies want to take advantage of the current global crisis. Their own countries are disintegrating, so it's understandable they think Jeon has weakened. Stirring up right-wing nationalist sentiment is the basics of the basics of foreign-influence campaigns. False-flag attacks are barely one step ahead of that."

"You think this could be an attack by foreign spies?"

"I think we can't rule it out. I think it would be very, very convenient for places like Siphios, the Free State, Rembaud, and other similar terrorist havens if Jeon turned on itself. Not to mention any near-peer economic powers. We are the economic miracle of the world, with the highest standard of living anywhere and, if I may say so, the finest military anywhere. They can't fight us head on, so they want to turn us against each other. Stoke grievances, create division, set people against one another."

"That would explain why they used the Ghūl. They want to encourage Denizens to violently attack Citizens. Move from idleness and irresponsibility to actual anarchy and murder."

"I think that would make certain people very happy. Very, very happy. But as I said, everything is preliminary, and we won't have the real story until a few days from now, when the investigation has had a chance to really get moving."

Truth shook his head and walked away. Did he count as a domestic terrorist or a state-sponsored terrorist? You could be both, right? Or was there some classification system that would put him cleanly in one category or the other? Well. Not his problem, really. They would have sealed the city by now. He would stick around in town for a couple of days, plot the next hit. Maybe get that sin reduced some. He must look like a burning torch of evil at this point. Can't have that.

"Hey, Linh, while you have the oil in the altar, can you cancel the cleaners for . . . like a week or something? Maybe two?"

"What? Why? I'm not going to be mopping or doing the laundry!"

"Wouldn't kill you. But no, me either. It's just . . . they use Denizens as the cleaners, right?"

There was quiet from the other room. "Yeah, they do. Everyone does."

"I just think, maybe for a week or two, we could see how a golem cleaner might work. Or even a bound demon or something. I hear those have been getting a lot more reliable."

There was another long period of quiet. Then a soft "Yeah."

"I just want us to feel safe. I just . . . want us to be safe."

Truth walked out onto the balcony and looked out over the city. Eight million people lived in Buran. Most crammed into the slums, stacked up in the hive-like apartment towers. The rest of the city was a glittering gem. Cleaned by magic and muscle, fed by more magic and muscle, watered almost exclusively by magic, transportation entirely by magic, with the bits of the economy that weren't about taking pleasure in the efforts of others being driven entirely by magic as well.

Maddie must have known that her "safety" was a bubble-thin illusion, Truth thought. She just didn't want it to pop for as long as possible. He didn't feel any need to burst that bubble. It would pop on its own soon enough.

The next day was spent largely indoors. No need to get out onto the streets. No need to risk leaving a trail. He reclined on a lounger on the balcony and started working through the technical gazettes he had picked up. There hadn't been any dramatic changes to talisman design in the last couple of years, but the art was always progressing. The tolerances got finer and finer, the positioning more exact, and the designs more complex and sophisticated.

Take his old friend, the Ke-Te-Wo Type 61 Streetlight Talisman, still fraudulently claiming a five-year service life. It wasn't any more durable than when he had first studied it in technical school. Actually, it was less reliable. However, the luminosity and color of the light were now programmable. It was an order of magnitude more complicated, with numerous subsystems and several mildly innovative sigils. All based on older, familiar stuff, just a little bit better and assembled in new ways.

He was quietly surprised to find, after a few hours of reading, that he was enjoying himself. It was easy to lose himself in the comfortable rhythm of memorizing diagrams. It was a form of running away from thinking about what he had done, but it was a productive sort of running away. Running away to self-improvement. He'd done worse.

Maddie and Linh stayed around the apartment too, burning through a whole jug of oil for the communication altar. It's not like anyone could tell them off if they didn't turn up at the office. They also spent a lot of time cultivating. Too little, too late, but still never a bad thing.

He noticed that they performed a sort of dual cultivation. They sat on cushions back-to-back, letting their backs touch. They synchronized their breathing so that when one breathed in, the other breathed out. He could almost see the energy cycling through the room. He definitely could see the incense swirling around them.

It was quietly intimate—a spiritual closeness as well as a physical one. He decided to follow their example and cultivated under the heat of the sun. When he had taken in as much as he could stand, he switched to the Meditations. The cosmic rays were thinning. It was subtle, but he could just about feel it now. He better grab what he could while he could.

The scry got flipped on and off for most of the day. The news segments repeated a lot, sometimes with a tiny smidge of new analysis or a fresh picture. Then someone would get sick of the constant negativity and switch it off for forty minutes, then turn it on again "just to see if anything new had come up." There were raids, of course, people brought in for questioning, various parties claiming responsibility. Truth wondered how much of that was real. He certainly wouldn't take credit for someone else's atrocity. But then, he was new to this racket. Maybe that was normal.

Who exactly were they arresting? Was there some collection of usual suspects to round up? Nothing he could do about it. Instead, he turned his mind to the thought of using money to wash away sin. Based on what the priest had said, the *origin* of the money was immaterial. Truth smiled up into the afternoon sun. He was going to scrub away sin with stolen loot.

CHAPTER 45

THE OLD STRAIGHT TRACK

Truth hadn't eaten all day and resolved to fix that problem. Rather than raiding his hosts' weirdly sparse fridge, he decided to eat out. There was ample food available from street vendors, and in Jeon, the street food was *good*. The penthouse had a private elevator, of course. It had been depressingly trivial to defeat the security and, once he was in the apartment, to clone the control amulet.

It was quietly astounding to him. If you didn't know how the systems worked, they seemed utterly impenetrable. Once you were trained on them, once you understood what all those mysterious parts did and how they worked together? It was trivial to crack them. At most, it was a bit fiddly or time-consuming. The dirty secret of physical security—half bluff, a quarter reassurance, and a quarter sheer waste of time. And it was the waste of time that would actually hold off the attacker. It was their time you were wasting, after all.

Onto the street and into a rolling wave of heat and humidity. Summer was coming on in fits and starts, and it had decided to blast the late afternoon with a sneak peek of the coming weather. It was the kind of sun that promised sunburns and headaches. Smart beachside kiosks already had aloe salves set out for sale.

He had a late lunch of cold noodles with lots of vegetables and bean curd. A bit oily but satisfying. A lesser stomach might groan later, but Truth was literally made of sterner stuff. It was all good. From there, he walked up to the shopping district. The usual controls on who was permitted to enter that part of the city were in place; the floating identity scanners networked into security golems and the police to remove any undesirable elements. Like him.

Truth grinned up at the plank-shaped flying talismans. It was a crime for him to be there. It was a crime before he joined Starbrite, and it was a crime again once he had been terminated. The scanner wasn't very smart. It read Truth's identity by checking the theoretically unfalsifiable sigil on his forearm. It concluded that he was a High Citizen. There was no visible indication that he was permitted in. He just walked right past the scanners and went about his shopping. Truth Medici had returned to Jeon, and he would walk where he pleased.

Right now, it pleased him to walk around, looking at the high-end jewelry stores. He knew damn well none of these places had more than a token amount of cash on hand. Everything would be done by credits or by bank-relay amulets—invisibly shifting wealth from one account to another. Money reduced to bookkeeping. How did that square with the Pragerite notion of prosperity? Truth wondered. What happened when the money had never existed in a tangible form but had always been a fiction on paper?

He looked over the rings selection at Forquard's. His personal feeling was that bigger was better when it came to jewelry. It was all about showing off, right? So, big stones, surrounded by lots of smaller shinies, lodged into big chunks of gold or orichalcum, or something truly precious like mythril or frozen quicksilver. Could you make a ring from prismatic iridium? Presumably, but the important thing was that people should *know* it was very expensive from across the room. Brooches and necklaces seemed to fulfill his requirements even better in that regard. More surface area to work with.

Truth briefly imagined himself decked out in rings, necklaces, earrings, and pretty much every sort of decoration. He would have to do the piercing himself; normal needles couldn't handle it. Would Etenesh like the look? More to the point, did he like the look?

He thought about it. While he appreciated how much it showed off, it didn't really go with his low-key approach right now. Besides, people had to be able to see him before they could appreciate the conspicuous wealth. He wasn't prepared to let himself be seen in Jeon. Ah, well. Time for the old smash-and-grab.

There was a motherly looking woman talking to the clerk next to him.

"Yes, the earrings. Actually, do you sell cut stones without having them set in rings and things?"

"Loose? Madam, all of our pieces are crafted by the most famous brands and the very best jewelry designers in Jeon!"

"Yes, yes. I'm buying the earrings, aren't I? It's just, what with everything . . ."

The clerk's demeanor changed at once. "Ah, yes, sometimes a portable means of preserving value is needed. May I suggest our Romanov Line? Each piece of that exquisite collection uses one hundred percent pure rare metals, studded with quite striking, beautifully cut, and quite large gems. Available with and without enchantments, should you wish it."

"Do you have a brochure?"

"Better. I have the report from the bonded assayer."

Truth nodded slowly at that. He would have gone for steel knives and preserved food, but for a certain sort of person, a person with a limited amount of both information and imagination, hoarding non-cash wealth was pure prudence. And, of course, if they were shifting their money into gold, orichalcum, and gems, they weren't spending it on other things. For example, a new Starbrite-brand sofa or a new scryball. Or elixirs.

Not that Starbrite didn't own jewelry stores or control a big piece of the precious-metals market, too, but you had to figure this was taking a lot of money out of the economy.

Truth grinned. Time for the sinister mastermind to reappear. Not like the other spiders casting their webs around Buran. Here was a real villain. He stepped out of the jewelry store and looked around the shopping street. His grin deepened. He was a firm believer in prudential planning for the wealthy.

He started with a rather portly man blankly staring into space while his wife tried on extraordinarily large and massively enchanted hats. Little illusions of birds flew over and around the brim. She seemed to like it.

"She's *wasting your money* on hats. Hats. But what's a hat worth when *credits steal* all your money? Gold and gems. *Gold and gems hold their worth*. And you will need that wealth *when the Tiger rises and the Star falls*."

Over and over and over. He spent the rest of the day drifting around the commerce area, whispering his poison in as many ears as would listen. Planting the idea to buy as much gold and to hoard as much wealth as possible. And making very sure to plant the idea of a national uprising.

He made his way back to the jewelry store. The clerks looked exhausted but happy. They got paid on commission.

"A good day, but they know something. The rich know something. Something is coming. And they aren't telling you. You are going to get screwed again. The rich never give an honest person a fair chance. They are blood-sucking parasites. *The rich are going to eat you up!*" he said, drifting among them.

Truth watched the smiles fade to grim certainty. They were all Level One. The supervisor was a measly Level Two. Maybe the manager was Level Three, but they weren't on the floor. They didn't stand a chance.

"The wind moves the grass. *The Tiger stalks its prey*. It's time to take Jeon back. Back from the parasites and thieves. Time for the *Tiger to eat the parasites*."

The display cases were pretty empty at this point. He would bet heavily that they would be filled to bursting come tomorrow morning. He headed back to the food stalls and loaded up on some rice and stew. It was great. It was so damn good. He liked the food in Siphios, he really did, but damn, did he miss the flavors of home.

He spent the night in the guest room again. Linh and Maddie had an argument, mostly from the built-up stress. They talked it out eventually. Truth dipped into a novel for twenty minutes, then slept.

Awake and straight to work. Out for breakfast once again, and this time he got an egg sandwich. Except the Path of the Foodie would not accept a bland name like *egg sandwich* for this delight. Two pieces of soft, sweet bread, toasted in butter and slathered with ketchup. Then eggs with a touch of salt and sugar, scrambled and folded into neat sheets on top of the toast. The egg was topped with shredded cabbage and scallions and yet more ketchup.

It was impossible to eat without smiling. The contrast of sweet, salty, savory, crunchy, and soft was just so, so delightful. He took his time and really savored it. He treated himself to two cups of basically okay coffee and shopped around for the right mask. A tiger mask seemed . . . just right. It was a nice morning as spring made its pretty turn into summer.

Truth waited until just after opening before going to Forquard's again. It was upsettingly easy for Incisive to disguise him. There was an alarming amount of belief in this identity. Well. Whatever. He'd just take it as proof that he had been doing good work as a propagandist. He pulled down his mask and got to work.

He kicked in the door and lobbed in a couple of charms before quickly covering his ears and looking away. The *BANG BANG* nearly blew the glass out of the window. Even behind a wall, the light shone through his eyelids, making the dark world vivid red.

He kicked in the door again, yelling this time. "On the ground! ON THE GROUND! NOBODY LOOK AT ME!" He threw another charm at an activating golem. It froze up momentarily as the scrambler jammed its connections to the control net. Truth was moving faster than a Level One could even perceive, smashing open cases and dumping rings and necklaces into a sack.

Someone, probably more confused than rebellious, tried to stand. Truth rushed over, slapping him to the floor. "I SAID FUCKING STAY DOWN! I KILL THE NEXT ONE! I KILL THE NEXT ONE!"

He made a beeline for the Romanov collection, making sure to empty all the drawers behind the counter. At the speed he was moving, it probably looked like a series of explosions across the store—the display cases spraying glittering gems of glass as the jewelry vanished.

"WHERE IS THE MANAGER? WHERE IS THE MANAGER! I KILL SOMEONE EVERY BREATH UNTIL THE MANAGER COMES OUT!" Truth yelled, yanking a socialite up by her hair. She screamed, not even able to beg in her terror.

"FIRST ONE! SHE WILL BE THE FIRST ONE! THIS IS YOUR FAULT! YOUR FAULT!"

"NO! Please! I'm the manager. I—I am the manager!" An older lady stumbled out from behind the counter. Truth dropped the socialite and grabbed the manager instead.

"Open the safe right now or I kill everyone!"

"Yes, yes, right now. This way."

"EVERYONE STAY DOWN OR THE BOMBS GO OFF. YOU MOVE, YOU DIE!" Truth screamed. Surely, security should be on the way by now, right? The air-deployable golems should be seconds off at most.

"Here, here is the safe."

"Any tricks, you die first, then I take your wallet and find your family. You understand me?"

"No, no tricks. Please, no tricks! See, I'm opening it." Truth gave everything a quick check for tracers, dye packs, and any other little tricks that might be deployed against the careless. He dumped the jewelry in the sack, leaving the trays behind.

Just in case. Did he hear sirens? Prager's boiling balls, how bad has security gotten these days?

He gave the manager a quick slap, knocking her to the floor. "I SAID, DON'T FUCKING LOOK AT ME!" He dropped a couple more flashbangs as he ran out the door again, just to keep heads down.

Public security might have been a little slow off the mark, but the golems of the merchants association were coming in hard. Dozens of their smooth forms, leaping from roof to roof or scampering along the street. A blizzard of eye-spies were up too, locked on and desperately trying to make an ID.

Truth flipped them the middle finger and ran. He plunged into the sea of screaming, running shoppers, golems coming in hard behind him.

CHAPTER 46

ALL GOD'S CHILDREN

Truth dove into the panicking masses, letting them break his line of sight with the golems chasing him and the eye-spies above. It was far from perfect. They were still on him. But it helped. As he went, he shouted.

"The golems are killing people! They have gone crazy! The golems are killing people! Bombs, they set off bombs! Starbrite's gone crazy! They are killing people!"

He didn't even need to use Incisive. The words had all the effect he needed. Spells and charms started crackling out. Most people only had the Jeon National Universal Spell, of course, but these days, who didn't carry at least some sort of personal protection? It may be illegal, but again, these days, what did *illegal* even mean?

Not that homemade or black-market attack fetishes did much against commercial-grade security golems. Some poor bastard even had a knockoff needler. Truth watched the needles, pathetically free of any sort of attack spell, plink off the armored form of a golem. Maybe if he had a Sharp spell. Or one of dozens of anti-golem spells that were developed over the centuries. But he didn't, and the needles went *plink-plink-plink* until the golem caught up and smashed his head into the ground and crushed his hand and slapped a paralysis charm on him, leaving him on the ground and unable to scream as the rest of the mob charged over him.

"Don't let them get you! Don't let them get you! The golems are killing people. Starbrite is killing people!" He hadn't really thought about starting a panic beyond some vague notion, but his trainers in Siphios had been quite clear—provocation was the core of "freedom fighting," and overreaction by the provoked could always be turned against them.

He ran crouched between people, yelling as he went. Waste not, want not, all that. And it gave him a chance to subtly shape his identity, becoming harder to spot. Becoming one with the mob. He worked his way to the edge of a shopping galleria, the security shutters rumbling down fast. He dove under them—and vanished.

Truth idled around the locked-down mini-mall for an hour or so. Most of the store employees had been ordered to shelter in place, shuttering their stores and praying the mob didn't break in. Nobody knew what was going on. Nobody understood what was happening. This sort of thing just *didn't happen* in nice districts. Secure Citizen districts. This was the kind of thing that maybe, MAYBE happened in the slums. Not that they knew much about that, of course!

It was a point of snobbish pride for the stores there—the retail staff were all the children of Citizens, getting a little training in before their doubtlessly glorious future careers. The managers wanted to train their staff well—usually, the managers represented the bottom-most rung of salaried employees for a vast corporation. Their best hope to climb was a protegee succeeding and remembering their mentor.

Truth drifted along, looking through the shutters. That was how it was in Jeon. You were employed by Starbrite, or one of the second-tier great corporations, or your parents pretended you had died in the crib. He looked in at the clerks trapped behind the bars and mesh of the shutters or three-centimeter-thick enchanted-glass storefronts. They were pacing around in neatly pressed suits and skirts, with ties or neckerchiefs or hats all in the focus-group-tested, board-of-directors-approved color scheme. Attractive young "brand ambassadors" learning how to maximize shareholder value. Trapped in little boxes, waiting for the mob.

For once, the orders were correct. The mob had no interest in breaking in there. The safest place to be was out of the district. Truth walked over to a mostly empty food court and found a table. He had filled a good-sized sack with loot. A bit banged up by the rough handling but still very nice indeed. It was noticeably heavy. He grinned. Maybe he had underestimated the long-term earning potential of armed robbery.

Truth swung the bag back and forth a little bit. What could he buy with all that loot? Well . . . was there even anything he wanted to buy? Elixirs were always good, but elixirs for those Level Four and up were not exactly retail buys. Maybe at a major branch of the Green Lotus or some other top-notch subsidiary of an alchemist tower, but even then, he would bet that you had to put in an order and wait for something to become available. All those Starbrite Level Fours would be buying from the System Shop, too. That would take a big bite out of the market. Anyway, not something he could purchase with a stolen ring.

So, elixirs were out. What about weapons? Those could *certainly* be acquired with stolen jewelry. A needler might not be as delightful as it once was, but it was still immensely lethal in his hands, a heavy needler more so. And if he really wanted one, he could walk up to the nearest army base, present the "order" to the quartermaster, and be issued his very own, free of charge. No need to spend more than the time on the trip. So, that was out too.

A fancy firebird? His own flying cloud? Not practical under the circumstances or in the foreseeable future. Enchanted clothes? Overrated, mostly gaudy even by his standards, and Etenesh had made it clear she liked him in his skin, or as close to it as decency would allow. In retrospect, her saying, "*My pretty man has a god bod, and he should show it off*," probably wasn't just her flirting.

And just a tiny piece of his soul was so toxic to her, it drove her into paranoia and misanthropy. He was literally poison for her.

Truth gave himself two quick slaps and shook his head, trying to shake out the intrusive thoughts. She was recovering. His "gift" would help her survive what was to come. She still loved him. And he had to make sure they would have a future together. As well as get his revenge.

He stood, sweeping everything back into the sack. He wanted to grab a nap in the mattress store, but the grate was down. He'd make do with a bench or something. The district would be sealed for a while, but they wouldn't keep it closed all day. The losses for the stores that weren't robbed would be far too high. No, a few hours at most, and he would be off to hear the good word and to unburden himself of sin.

Truth walked along the road to St. Florian of the Loch. St. Florian's was on a major street, naturally, and on an enormous plot of land. Lush, immaculately tended ornamental gardens surrounded the church, itself a monument of stone and sculpture. Different sorts of sculpture from those found in Siphios. Not alive or moving, certainly. But massive and everywhere.

The walls were covered in niches for marble saints, or plinths raised so that Prager, in his many forms, might bless the masses. Granite lions guarded the wide, sweeping stairs up to the massive bronze doors of the church. The church made the stance of the faithful clear—God is great, and you are very, very small. God is eternal and you are temporary. Truth didn't have a problem with that—it was the literal truth, after all. But the subtext made the hairs on the back of his neck rise. *The Church is very big, and you are very, very small. Be obedient. Be grateful. Or else.*

Late afternoon. It should be pretty dead, he reckoned. Might be a bit tricky to track down Archpriest James, but he could ask around. He had a casual look around as he walked—a pretty normal Buran neighborhood. Citizens exclusively, of course, streets well lined with trees and shops. An awful lot of those shops had OUT OF BUSINESS signs on them. Truth kept his eyes roving, on the theory that you never knew what you might find if you were looking.

A Ghūl stood in an alley, half hidden by the shadows. Truth nearly tripped over nothing.

A Ghūl. Miles from the slums. Out at midafternoon. One hand covering its rotted eyes, standing deep in the shadows, barely ten meters from nattering ladies enjoying a blowout at the blow-dry bar. It turned to face him and softly beckoned him closer.

There was a strangeness to the moment. Like the world had suddenly gone soft and thin. Like pictures projected onto a fluttering curtain, only seeming to move because the wind blew the curtain about. Truth approached the Ghūl. Closer. The Ghūl beckoned him yet closer. The peeled flesh, the naked bone, the rotted away holes where ears should be. It called him over, and lost in the unreality of the moment, Truth went.

The Ghūl . . . embraced him. For a long moment, it simply embraced him, pressing a rotted hand between Truth's shoulder blades, the other wrapping around his ribs. For the space of a few heartbeats, it connected with him. A statement of fraternity, of acceptance. Then the breeze blew, and it was gone. Whatever he was was good enough for them. Without question or condition.

Truth stood in the alley, his arms wrapped around nothing. He couldn't put words to it. An illusion? But he should be almost impossible to glamor. Some Ghūl magic? But they didn't use magic. They were famous for not using magic. He felt like he was teetering on the edge of something. Some vast realization, and once he understood it, he would never be able to live in this world again. A truth so terrible, you would die if you knew it, and he was balanced on one leg, leaning over the precipice.

Truth had remarkable balance. The moment passed. He didn't know how much time passed before he returned to himself. The sidewalk was as solid as before, the church as grand. The ladies chattering away, getting their hair blow-dried and styled by hard-eyed professionals, hadn't missed a beat. The world was as real as could be.

He violently shook his head and walked into the church. He grinned nastily at some of the enchantments around the door. Specifically designed to drive away demons, ghosts, and malevolent magics. Well. Good luck exorcising him.

The interior of the church was quite spacious and almost entirely empty. The majority of the space was taken up by a single great room filled with hundreds of seats. They descended below street level and rose up to two stories high, simple white wooden seats on sealed concrete slabs. Easy to clean. The tiered chairs surrounded a pentagon in the middle of the room—nine stacked platforms, the last being painted metallic gold and ornamented with frozen quicksilver. He spotted projectors among the talisman lights, as well as a sound system that would do a concert hall proud. And that was it. It seemed like the ornamentation budget had been spent on the exterior.

Truth had an unaccountably irritable feeling, looking at it all. He remembered the dais from going to church as a kid. The priest stood up there and preached, turning to face the different parts of the congregation as he spoke. But he remembered music. The church in his memory was alive with lights and colors and the sounds of singing. This was dead. Sterile, even. Had there been some kind of problem? He walked around until he found a business office. Neatly dressed staff were bent over their ledgers and abacuses, fingers as busy as their eyes.

"Pardon me, I am looking for Archpriest Reik?"

The clean-cut young man jumped half a meter out of his chair in surprise.

"Glory! How quietly do you walk! Took a year off my life. You are looking for His Eminence?"

"Yes, he told me to call on him when I was in the neighborhood."

"You are a friend of His Eminence?"

"No, no, just an acquaintance, but he seemed very insistent that I come and see him."

"I am sorry, but you are both too early and too late."

"Pardon?"

"Too early because he will be here leading worship at seven this evening, and you could make an appointment to see him then. Too late, because he generally does his pastoral work between noon and five and has been out of the Church for hours now."

"Ah. Well. Perhaps I will attend the service and find him later."

"Wonderful. Our doors are always open. What name should I put on the appointment?"

"Johnny Bells."

"Could you spell that?"

"Probably."

There was a pause. "Sorry, force of habit. You wouldn't believe some of the names we get."

"No problem. I have to put down a deposit to hold the appointment, right?"

"Ah, no, not a deposit, no, of course not . . ." the young man started to explain hurriedly. Truth reached into his sack of loot and brought out a rather chunky ring. He casually rubbed off the ma'er's mark and serial number, then etched a crude picture of a rat on the inside of the band. The embarrassed acolyte thought he was fishing around for his wallet, and looked shocked when the ring clattered on the mythril-plated dish on the counter.

"Here, for James. I will see him after the service. I hope he's ready."

CHAPTER 47

WHAT YOU OWE AND WHAT YOU SOW

Truth sat about midway back in the pews. They were on tiers, like stadium seating. The church was trying to cram the most bodies possible into the hall and make sure everyone had an excellent view of the dais. No obstructed-view seats there. And the acoustics simply could not be beat.

He knew the last point because he had watched the sound check. Professional sound and light technicians, specialized mages in all but name, came out and flicked up the sound-catching talismans. They hovered where they ought to—either positioned next to an instrument or discreetly by the jaw of the technician.

"Test test. Test one two, one two." They ran through each talisman, testing the pickup, the noise isolation, and the range of captured sounds from bass to treble. They were clearly old hands—it took less than six minutes. The lighting check ran a bit longer. Truth was grimly unsurprised to see that the light talismans were, indeed, unreliable. They were highly modifiable—ranging from spot to flood to ambient, shifting through color gradients with deceptive ease. Until they exploded in tiny showers of sparks for "no reason." Only two or three of them, out of hundreds of talismans. He would bet cash none of them ever reached the end of their alleged service life.

Complexity meant more points of failure. Pack in a half dozen new points of failure in any kind of consumer talisman, run it hard every day, and sooner or later, they will start breaking down on you. Not that it was a big deal to replace the talismans. They had plastic bins full of light talismans. A tiny servitor golem flew up with the replacement talisman, made the change, the technician connected the talisman to the lighting array, tested it, and they were off to the next fault. No rush, no delay. Just another day on the job.

The band came out, a quartet of fit-looking people in their mid-twenties. Clean-cut, neatly dressed but just slightly too casual for church. Attractive but not startlingly so. The kind of people you would desperately want to chat up in a coffee shop or not-too-loud bar and think you just might, maybe, have a shot with them. A long way from the unearthly beauty of the idols or big national stars. They tested their guitars, drums, tambourines, and trumpets and ran their own sound check. Sounded good to Truth. They seemed to disagree, making minute adjustments to their instruments.

While they were working, the illusion array came to life. The projectors on the ceiling turned the bleach-white walls into forests, pristine beaches, laughing children, the spinning gold face of Prager, and the wrought silver of St. Florian. He could sense the illusory array trying to persuade him he was smelling things—cedar, the brine of the sea, or rich incense. Trying to make him feel calm or excited or loving. He didn't feel much.

The lights went out, then slowly came up again. Sharp white spots lit the dais, the top step blindingly golden in the harsh light. Softer, warmer lights lit the stairs for the seats. That old church music came up—the songs he remembered from his childhood. No words now, just instrumentals lifting him up. Making him feel something in a way the illusions couldn't. This was going to be something special. This was something big and real and he was part of it.

The congregation started filing in, families smiling and nudging each other as they found their usual seats. Everyone dressed nicely, some in suits or fancy dresses, most in what would pass as "business casual." Making an effort to be upbeat but respectful. It took a long few minutes to get everyone in. The house was packed. Everyone settled in. The house lights dimmed to almost nothing. There was quiet.

A sudden blast of music! The illusions burst into life, all brilliant colors and joy and hope and the face of Prager smiling down on everyone. Thudding bass and high-pitched horns got everyone up and cheering, thousands of them up and cheering, and from the rafters a robed preacher floated down on two wings, like a messenger angel bearing the word of God.

He waved, and the crowd roared back. He pointed to each section in turn, getting a roar, a cheer, feet stomping, hands clapping.

"Brothers and sisters. Those friends we know and those who we hope to know. Every living, breathing, loving soul in this building. ARE YOU READY?"

The congregation cheered and yelled.

"I SAID, ARE. YOU. READY?"

The congregation got even louder.

"I CAN'T HEAR YOU. ST. FLORIAN'S FAITHFUL, ARE. YOU. READY?"

They screamed and screamed like their throats would burst if they didn't get all the sounds out.

"IS THE HEAVENLY HOST HERE? I CAN'T HEAR YOU!"

One section seemed to lose its mind, hundreds of parishioners bursting into ululating shrieks, waving handkerchiefs and flailing their arms.

"ST. FLORIAN'S. ARE. YOU. READY . . . FOR BLESSINGS?!"

Oh, they lost it there. People stumbled out onto the stairs, shaking and crying and yelling. They were ready. They were so, so ready.

The band opened the service with a song. It seemed to be mostly about God raining blessings on them, Prager leading the way, and, occasionally, trees. The illusions of streams and soft rains on fertile fields and the smell of spring all lifted the song beyond the banal into something rare and special—showing how the holy and the material were really one and the same.

The preacher opened up with a few prayers, inviting blessings and warding away evils, reaffirming everyone's faith and devotion. Reminding everyone that this was no solo act—they were the glorious army of God in this sinful world, marching behind Prager's standard and flying the colors of the faithful.

Truth thought the preacher would give the sermon, but it turned out he was the warmup act. The actual archpriest delivering the sermon flew in on six wings, embraced the lead man, and sent him off the platform. Handsome but not too handsome. Perfect teeth, a good suit. You would buy a luxury boat from him, or try and get investment tips from him at the bar in the country club locker room.

The sermon ran for half an hour. It should have been agonizing, but Truth found it strangely compelling. It started with an odd little passage from the Writ—Child Zephram and the apple tree. The tree was old and withered, and wouldn't bear fruit anymore. Child Zephram prayed and prayed but no fruit. Then one day in the middle of winter, the tree suddenly burst into a beautiful crop of plump, delicious apples. A blessing out of season but perfectly timely for the starving boy.

The gist of it was that God would bless you, but on *his* schedule. He had a plan for the whole universe. All your blessings were ready, all prepared for you to receive them. But they wouldn't come when *you* wanted them. They would come when God decided the time was right. Even if you thought it was too late, the damage was done and all was lost. That was the precise moment God (through the intervention of Prager, the saints, and those who had received the blessings of priesthood through the apostolic succession from the hands of Prager himself) would display his glory and give you what you needed.

But, naturally, you could refuse his blessings. You could close yourself off from faith, live in pain and despair, make your life a little taste of the Hell to come. He wouldn't force you. The message was repeated again and again, in tiny homilies and anecdotes and one sentence quotations of the Writ, all reinforcing the same point— God is on his schedule, you will get all the blessings that are coming to you, but only if you made a way for them. Only if you were ready to accept them, by being faithful, patient, and humble.

One part in particular stood out to Truth—the resurrection of Oila.

"Now I'm sure you all know the story, but I ask you to, for today, consider that story another way. Pulim had called Prager. Pulim, who was full of faith, and Oila, full of faith, they called to Prager, asking for the blessing of good health. Prager was friends with them, good friends, but still, even as Oila got sicker and sicker, he didn't come. Now, the Writ doesn't tell us *why* Prager didn't come. He wasn't stuck in traffic. He wasn't getting his hair done and just lost track of time. The Writ says that Pulim called for Prager to pray for his wife, to pray for Prager's dear friend Oila, that she might be returned, healthy and happy to her family.

"And for one week, Prager did not come. On the fourth day of his absence, Oila died. Blessing God and Prager with her dying breath, she died. And the Writ doesn't tell us why Prager wasn't there. Prager and God don't need excuses. They don't need a note from their mom. We know why he wasn't there—it wasn't time for him to be there.

"On the seventh day, Prager came, and Pulim, full of grief, collapsed on his manly chest. He pulled on Prager's robes of celestial silk and divine gold. Weeping, weeping, he cried—'Why? We love you! We worship you! She died with your name on her lips. Why did you abandon us in our hour of need?' Prager said nothing. His own tears joined Pulim's. God knows the fall of the smallest hummingbird. How much more does he know the pain of men and women?

"So, Prager went out to the cemetery and walked up to Oila's urn and said, 'Come back, Oila!' Now, this is the bit I want you to think about. Go home and pray on it, wrestle with it, test yourself against it. Prager goes up to the urn holding the ashes of Oila and says, 'Come back, Oila!' and there is a pause. You can see it right in the Writ, right there at Miracles 23:2, there is a pause. He calls out, 'Come back, Oila!' and there is a line break. God *himself*, through the disciples and the testimony of the Writ, tells us there was a moment between the call and that lid jumping off the urn.

"Now, we all know what happens next—*The hand reached out of the urn. Then the arm reached out of the urn. Then the shoulder reached out of the urn.*"

The priest's voice was singsong, like a nursery rhyme. The congregation started singing with him, and the band's guitarist "spontaneously" decided to play the tune to accompany them. Truth realized with a jolt that he knew this song. It just listed all the different parts of the body as Oila slowly crawled out of the urn that held her ashes. He didn't know where he had heard it. It was just . . . around. Somehow, even not going to church, he couldn't escape it.

"Haw-haw! That's right. But think about what we talked about today. Think about Child Zephram and the apple tree. Prager could have been there on the *first* day. He could have been there and blessed Oila before she got sick. She was his friend. She never missed a tithe, and every little extra she could raise went to the Treasury of God. But that's not when he *needed* to be there. He needed to come after it was all too late and everything was lost.

"When he called out to Oila, when he resurrected Oila, there was no question that it was anything but a miracle. She didn't get better on her own. She was ashes and dust, her soul returned to heaven and God. This was a true, indisputable miracle, a blessing out of season, and it saved not only Oila's family, it also saved generations of believers. It saved every soul that heard of that miracle and opened their hearts to God.

"But remember—you get to choose! *Oila got to choose.* The Writ tells us there was a pause. The Writ tells us that the resurrection was not instant, that there was a moment where things could have gone either way. That was Oila's moment. That was *her* opportunity. Remember, Oila was devout and devoted. She died absolved of sin. Her faith never wavered. *She was in Heaven!* Brothers and sisters, Oila was in HEAVEN, kneeling before the Throne of God and as blissful a soul could be.

"Oila *chose* to return to the world. She *chose* to accept the resurrection, no blessing for her, so she could be a blessing for others. Her resurrection was an act of piety, devoting the balance of a mortal life to earthly suffering. A sacrifice for all those who would be saved in the future. She *chose* to be God's instrument in the world, safe in the knowledge of her place in Heaven and the eternal, perfect life to come. She chose to be a piece of Prager's shield, protecting humanity from all demons and evils of the world.

"I believe and declare: wagonloads of blessings are coming your way, favor, healing, the right people. Like with Child Zephram, 'who would have thought' blessings, dreams bigger than you've imagined, problems that look impossible suddenly turning around, the fullness of your destiny, in Prager's name.

"And if you received it, can you say *Amen* today?

"Now, I see the basket is going around, and I see you all are ready to contribute to the Treasury of God. Making sure those blessings and protections are here for not just yourself but all the faithful. But in these dark times, deadly times, times of wickedness and the oppression of the ungodly, the oppression of those who have not opened their hearts to Prager, it falls to the faithful to be a shield for the whole world.

"I am asking you, the faithful flock of St. Florian's, to be that shield. Today, we are doing something very special." The priest held up a little bit of colored paper, trimmed into the shape of a kite shield and bearing the symbol of Prager and St. Florian's.

"Each of these Holy Shields has been blessed and prayed over by myself, by Father James, Father Farsid. Each and every ordained priest here at St. Florian's has prayed over them and loaded them with blessings of protection against wickedness and demonic forces. And there is one prepared for each of you."

The crowd went nuts, screaming *Hallelujah* and *God is great*, some seeming to have seizures as the ecstasy of the moment took them.

"There are blessings prepared for each of you. That's the standard God sets, and we hold ourselves to that standard. Brothers and sisters, we have prepared the blessing for you, but have you prepared a blessing for others? We are asking that every member who can to donate what they can to the Emergency Treasury Drive. There is a shield for each of you, and if you can't spare even five wen, then you can't, and God bless you. But if you can, we ask that you donate at least five wen. To be that shield for your brothers and sisters and the whole world.

"Not part of the tithe—that's what you owe. This is what you sow."

After the celebrations ended, the congregation filed out, and the volunteers from the Heavenly Host came to sweep up, Truth made his way to the offices at the back of the church. The sun was setting later and later as the solstice approached—James's office was flooded with coppery light, painting the pale sin eater. Truth walked in, a bonfire of sin shrouding a hole in the air.

"Good evening, James. Find time to visit the slums?"

"My pastoral duties kept me occupied. Never thought a ghost would make an appointment. Or pay in blood gold."

"Blood gold? You could call it that. Someone certainly died for it. One way or another."

James flinched at that. Truth slowly poured the jewelry-store loot out on the table, raining treasures from the empty air in front of the priest.

"Here, sin eater. Ready to reap what you have sown?"

CHAPTER 48

TO UNBURDEN ONESELF OF SIN

The sin eater looked at the scores of rings, chains, and earrings scattered across his desk, spilling onto the floor. Each worn and rubbed, the maker's mark and serial numbers carefully removed by Truth's patient effort, waiting for the service to start. They all looked like they had been dug up, some possibly cut off the fingers of their late owners. The sin eater gingerly lifted a plain silvery band. It was heavier than it looked. Frozen quicksilver, banded with platinum. He had a similar ring.

"I am . . . moved by your piety," the priest said, looking a bit sick. "I took the precaution of releasing all the sin upon me and refusing any other appointments today once I learned of your . . . reservation."

"For the best."

"Just what manner of thing are you? I have read of some unquiet dead similar to you, and you don't quite feel like a demon, but—"

"I'm not quite one thing or the other?"

"Yes."

"Not really your problem, though."

"It is. It is exactly my problem. What am I for, if not to ease the burden of all God's children and lead them back to their father?"

"No idea. That is the question for everyone, isn't it?"

"The Church does offer some answers. The correct answers."

"That's nice."

There was a pause.

"You wouldn't happen to be interested in finding out what those answers are, by any chance?"

"No, not right now. Places to go, things to do. Also, based on the service I just saw, I don't think I would agree with your answers. 'Even if you die sick, in pain, believing yourself abandoned by friend and God alike, it's all part of God's plan, and the smart thing to do is obediently go along with it. Make sure you tithe generously as you go. God needs his vig.' Can't say I agree with the moral there."

"That wasn't the point at all!" James slapped his hand on the table, looking furiously at the hole in the air surrounded by sin. "The point was that prosperity *will* come to the faithful. That obedience to God will always result in blessings. Just not the blessings you might want right this minute. That the *timing* of the blessings is not a merely mortal question—they are all part of God's plan for the world. Are you going to help or harm that plan, Johnny? That's the point."

"But we know God's plan. He will leave us to die. He will let the world cleanse itself of humanity, and when the planet has been wiped clean, he will start again. After all, it's what we chose. We didn't have to make the world this way. We didn't have to be part of systems we didn't understand or fail to take alternatives we didn't know existed. We could have starved or frozen or chosen to die. Really, this is all our fault, not his."

"All arguments that the Church has failed, not God. And I will admit the Church has failed. We didn't save the planet in time."

"Saved from a fate as inevitable as a stone falling to the floor, without outside intervention."

"Our fault, not God's. And hope is never lost. Not now, not at the moment of death. Not in the time after death. The righteous will kneel before the Throne and enjoy eternal blessings. Those who fail to welcome God shall have what they wished for as well."

"Because the ignorant, those you have failed, have freely chosen Hell. We are talking in circles here, priest, and you have a job to do. It's what you are for, apparently."

The sin eater snorted. "Did you think I would run? I'm no hypocrite, ghost. I accept the burdens God places upon me. I am prepared to take them for the blessings they are." James stepped around his desk. "I would ask you to kneel, but I don't think you would."

"My knees are stiff. I seem to have the same problem in my neck and back. Just won't bend right."

"And yet, every relic and talisman I possess swears you aren't a demon. Well, kneeling or not." James gathered himself. Truth could feel cosmic energy gathering around the sin eater, moving in ways he had never really seen before. It was magic, just not the sort he knew.

"By the grace of the Father of Mercy, the Most High, by the intercession of Prager, the Saints and the Doctors of the Faith, and the offices of the Holy Mother Church, I accept your profession of faith. Be embraced by God, and be healed." The sin eater reached out and embraced the fire.

Truth could feel something slipping away. Something he couldn't quite put words around. It felt like he could suddenly breathe again. He hadn't realized he was choking. James screamed and collapsed.

Truth jumped back a step. The once fit-looking priest was covered in blood. Rotting holes had eaten through him in places. The holes were still appearing, getting wider. His ears fell off, his fingers slipped off his hands and onto the floor, one knuckle at a time.

It seemed that, whatever the jewelry was worth, Truth had given the priest too much sin. The priest truly was no hypocrite. Even now, he didn't call for help. He just thrashed on the ground of his soundproof office and screamed until his vocal cords rotted away.

Truth looked up and sighed. The purification must have worked. He didn't take any pleasure in what he was seeing. If anything, he was a bit nauseous. He was carrying all that? Bleugh. James had done him a real solid, if not for free.

"Well. I guess you can chalk this up as another miracle of God's grace," Truth murmured. "I don't really know how to use this spell right, and if you live through this, it will definitely be a miracle, so . . . you know. Have faith."

Truth looked over. Sin definitionally wasn't "right," right? Even if it was defined differently by lots and lots of people. And humans, as a rule, shouldn't have holes of burning corruption running and spreading through them. *So . . . let's fix this.*

The spell form for Cup and Knife spun out and surrounded the priest. It seemed to hate the sin as much as the sin eater did. Truth felt his cosmic energy drop hard. The corruption stopped, but he had the sense of holding back the tide with his hands. The corruption had to go somewhere. Truth grinned savagely, wrestling with the spell. He knew exactly where the sin should go.

A bare minute later, the sin eater was out of danger. Not healed, but ordinary magic could carry him the rest of the way. Presumably, given his job, he would have potions and things handy. Probably still a lot of sin to clear up, too. Regardless, Truth wasn't going to spend any more of his cosmic energy there—he was almost tapped out. Almost.

Truth leaned over and whispered in James's ear. "You want to know what I am? I'm one of Starbrite's bastards, finally come home. And I didn't come home alone." He let Incisive do its work. James was too out of it to notice the spell. "Why do I refuse to absolve God of blame? Because the God of this world is *Starbrite*, and if he is a *false God*, you have done NOTHING to tear him down. The Church is *complicit* in worshiping a false god. And if I am wrong? If your God truly is great and good, *prove it. Tear down that liar's throne!*"

He opened the door and walked out. He found one of the deacons hard at work, counting the day's take.

"Was that screaming you just heard? It seemed to come from Father James's office. But you shouldn't hear anything through the soundproofing. Is something wrong? *You had better check.*"

Truth smiled as he walked away. He could imagine the confusion on the deacon's face. He would find the injured sin eater on the floor, the penitent gone, and the fine wooden desk covered in reeking muck.

Truth walked out of St. Florian's in an odd, contemplative sort of mood. He had been embraced twice today—once by a Ghūl, or the illusion of a Ghūl, and once by a

Pragerite sin eater. He wasn't sure what to make of it. Both felt accepting. Liberating, in a way. He could vividly see the flesh rotting off James. Were the Ghūl beings so soaked in sin, they turned out like walking corpses? Truth doubted it. The Ghūl, horrible as they were, seemed to have no conception of "evil" that he could see. Intelligent, yes, but their lives were devoted exclusively to single-minded worship of their God.

He silently laughed. The Ghūl were incapable of sin because they were incapable of acting contrary to the will of God. Nobody anywhere agreed with the *details* of that life of faith, but almost everyone would agree that living life according to God's will was what a person should do. The Ghūl, nightmare creatures of torment, were innocent. Not a soul would believe him if he told them.

"Thrush, as a sin professional, how would you rate my current sin load?"

"I wouldn't, Master."

The little imp casually preened its feathers. Thrush had strongly requested being left outside the church wards, which struck Truth as fair enough.

"Self-preservation?"

"More that it doesn't work that way, from my perspective. I don't decide what souls are worthy of the care of Hell; I merely do my best to serve. So far as I know, it is not a question of either quantity or quality."

"Salvation through faith alone? The intercession of Prager and the Mother Church?"

"Your servant is lacking, Dread One. I can only say that you appear to be mentally less burdened by your choices. Do you remember my analogy of the coral growing over a gem?"

"Yes."

"You appear to have had some crude diver with a hammer knock off a chunk of that natural beauty."

"Still Hell-worthy?"

"All are worthy in Hell, Master. It is the nature of the place to make prince and pauper alike in dignity."

Truth grinned at that. Air demons. Thrush was okay for an imp, but goddamn if he didn't want to go murder the Hell out of some air demons just for fun. It sounded like James didn't get all the sin off. He would still be somewhat visible to those with James's strange blessing. It would have to be considered a tolerable risk. Or at least a risk he would have to tolerate.

"All this does lead to a fairly obvious question—what is sin? Why can some see it, but most cannot? What is it about 'sin' that sticks to souls even through death? Is virtue the opposite of sin? Is it also sticky?" Truth wondered.

"Above my pay grade, Master, to use an analogy you are familiar with." Thrush hopped around, digging for insects in the dirt.

"Which leads to the question of 'What is virtue?' and from there defining good and evil, and figuring out why they exist." Truth smirked, then mentally added, *I should ask Merkovah about that. He loves our little chats.*

He looked down the boring, ordinary street, past the ordinary shops and ordinary hairdressers, watching the ordinary street lights converting cosmic rays into sharp light. In a year or so, this scene would become mythical. Something leathery storytellers would describe to disbelieving children around campfires.

He had done everything he wanted or needed to do in Buran. He wasn't looking forward to the trip north, but it was time to go. He had a researcher to murder, fear to spread, and chaos to sow. He started jogging down the street, scarf around his neck, sword in his soul, and duffel of clothes and books on his back. Just another Jeon kid. The logical consequence of a billion bad decisions made for *it seemed like a good idea at the time* reasons. A rat on its hind legs, looking up and wondering just what was up there, outside the walls of what it knew.

CHAPTER 49

BACK AND TO THE LEFT

Truth started making his way toward the edge of Buran. He was wearily certain that there would be checkpoints on the roads, *again*, and doubly certain that the buses and trains would be filled primarily with plainclothes police officers and surveillance equipment. He morbidly wondered how there could be room for ordinary commuters under the circumstances. He'd take a damn boat at this point, but he was headed inland. As wondrous as his remarkable physique was, he was getting very tired of running everywhere and even more tired of playing suburban hopscotch.

Tired or not, he didn't have a solution. So, he sighed, looked beseechingly at the empty heavens, and got walking. The color, sex appeal, and wealth of Buran were concentrated in a dense pocket by the ocean's edge, then radiated outward. Like a lump of solid paint dissolving in clear water—it got progressively less colorful the farther from the source you were.

He was jogging at a normal Level One pace, not wanting to strain his cosmic energy so soon after draining it in the church. Just a nice, easy pace, letting his body carry the load. Watching the families collect their groceries, looking stressed and tense. The commuters on buses looked more miserable than even Jeon's buses should account for. The cram schools turning kids loose. Felt early for that. Maybe they were easing up. Can't imagine the SAT was all that important these days. Or not. The kids looked pissed and miserable. Not that he ever had a hope in Hell of attending a cram school. Not for his kind of rat.

Incisive gave a tiny twitch. Very slight danger, or perhaps opportunity? Truth slowed and looked back at the school. It was one of the students. A boy, maybe seventeen. Nobody talked to him. He had a stuffed backpack slung over his school uniform. A little bigger than his schoolmates. There was a flatness to his face, a rigidity of expression, and a deadness of eye that made the hairs on Truth's arms rise. He decided to follow the boy a little bit and see just what he was up to.

The boy stalked away from the cram school but didn't head toward the bus stop with everyone else. Instead, he walked up the road. Nobody noticed or cared when he went off on his own. He trudged up the street a solid six blocks, then went up an alley. He found a side door to an apartment building that had been left propped open, presumably so the people in the apartments could get to and from the cage full of trash cans easily. The boy then walked up the fifteen flights of stairs to the allegedly locked and alarmed roof-access door, opened the door without a hint of an alarm, and went out on the roof.

The boy walked to the ledge and looked out. And down. *A jumper? He probably wouldn't be the first in his class,* Truth guessed, but it didn't feel right. The boy was looking for something. Apparently, he found it. He reached into his backpack and pulled out a *very* familiar-looking case.

Where the HELL did this high school twerp get a goddam M-202A3 Heavy NEEDLER?! Is he even Level One? No, he isn't. Prager's filthy prick, he can't even lay a spell on the needles or guide them or . . . anything.

The boy quickly assembled the needler and stood rigid, eyes aligning with the targeting reticule. as the sun set behind him. Aiming at something or someone below. Truth couldn't stand it anymore.

"Wait! Stop! Don't do it!"

The boy spun around. "BACK OFF! I'll kill them, and I don't mind starting with you!"

"Not like that, you won't! You're doing it all wrong!"

There was a momentary pause.

"What?"

"You are holding the needler wrong, your setup is wrong, your angle of attack is wrong, best-case scenario you go to full auto and shoot into a crowd, but aimed shooting with this setup? Your odds of scoring hits on target are way too low, and your odds of getting captured and killed shortly after contact are way too high. I applaud your initiative; it's great to see the next generation stepping up like this. But just a little more care for the details will turn a botch job into a success story."

The boy looked like he was having a hard time processing, but Truth pressed on regardless.

"Look, I'm only a few years older than you, so I can really remember what life was like prepping for the SAT." Truth said, Incisive helped him settle into a "good" senior schoolmate identity. "I can also remember how incredibly homicidal I felt on a daily basis. Now, let your senior guide you. Who are you trying to murder here? Not your schoolmates or teachers, I see."

"What? No! I'm not shooting any teachers!"

"Whoa, hey, easy. Who are you shooting? There is an office building next door, right?"

"The PTO."

The what now?

"Help me out here."

"The fucking PTO! Parent-teacher organization, except it's all the parents and they use it to bully the teachers. They are backed up by the Ministry of Education, too; the teachers get no support, and they get blamed for every little thing."

Truth did not have particularly fond memories of his teachers, and the notion of a student taking up arms to defend them seemed . . . insane.

"All right?"

"I mean EVERYTHING. One student gets two sentences of praise and another gets three? It's emotional abuse, a complaint filed with the Ministry, and the family bangs on the teacher's door in the middle of the night to scream at them and demand an apology. Reminders to bring homework, pens, notebooks when they keep forgetting them? Emotional abuse, should be kinder, complaints to the Ministry. Trying to stop bullying? Stop a beating? That's physical abuse, discrimination, complaints filed, banging on doors, chasing them down on the street, making a huge scene, swearing at them and demanding they record an apology."

The boy was ranting.

"And the Ministry always supports the parents. ALWAYS. They never take the teacher's side. People get fired, lose promotions, kill themselves." He stumbled there, panting.

"Oh. Mom? Dad?"

"Sister. She was twenty-three and hung herself in her elementary school classroom. She had been teaching for less than a year."

"I'm sorry for your loss."

"Thanks."

Their words were empty and formulaic. You had to say something, but really, what could you even say? And what could you say to the empty comfort? Truth tried to get the conversation back on track.

"So, there is a PTO meeting in the office building over there?"

"Yes, one of the people in the PTO works there, and they borrow a conference room for their meetings. I'm not sure where the conference room is, so I thought I would pick them off as they come in and out."

"Makes sense, makes sense. Can you recognize them from the top, though? It's a damn steep angle across the street."

"Well enough." The boy sounded defensive.

"All right, looks like your senior needs to give some guidance here. First of all, you are Level Zero. You don't have spells, so you have to do everything by muscle, which actually means you need to brain first, muscle second. Let's clear the easy stuff out of the way." Truth pointed at the building.

"You can see through the windows of one whole side of the building. Most offices have conference rooms, especially a conference room big enough to hold an entire PTO meeting, in rooms with a lot of windows and, ideally, a view. This side of the building is the only side that doesn't have another building three meters from it, so the odds are decent the conference room is going to be visible from this rooftop."

The boy looked rocked but nodded along.

"So, you have at least a decent shot of picking them off when they are nicely grouped together in a comparatively small area, with a much flatter attack angle. This is going to really increase your hit probability and make spray-and-pray a much more viable option. You probably aren't going to get a second shot at this. You want to maximize the results, and this lets you do that."

"Yeah, that makes sense."

"Now, we can also call that the best-case scenario. Might be a shitty office with a windowless conference room, right? Well, what you *don't* do is fixate or get frustrated. You just wait. See, right now, you have the end-of-day crowd leaving the office while the night-shift guys are going in. But if you just *wait*, they go in mixed with everyone else, but by the time the meeting ends, they will be some of the only people left in the building. When you see a big clump of people exiting all at once—bam. There's your PTO."

"Damn. Do you do this professionally or something?"

"I got into private security work after my national service, then went independent," Truth agreed. Incisive was up and running, but really, this was taking no energy at all. It seemed the nation of Jeon had no problem with this identity whatsoever. The unsubtle nudges from the universe that he was born to be a gangster were getting depressing.

"And . . . you are okay with me shooting up a PTO meeting?"

"*Okay* is a *strong* word. I would prefer if you shot up a Starbrite building or something, but really, I spoke up because I couldn't stand to see you doing it wrong. I mean, you are standing upright, silhouetted against the sky, and supporting the weight of the needler with your arms when the building ledge is right there. It gives you cover, breaks up your silhouette, AND gives you a steady platform to fire from. These are the kinds of basics you need to master, you know?"

"Why Starbrite?"

"Because they are why the parents are doing this. They are why the Ministry is acting like a bunch of little bitches. Think about it—it's the SAT. Your whole life gets staked on one. Goddamn. Test. Your whole value as a person, as far as Jeon is concerned, is down to one COMPANY. Not the COUNTRY; a company. And those parents know it. They aré freaking out, trying to make sure their kids succeed. So, they act like assholes. They are a symptom. Starbrite is the disease."

"I . . . Uh. Huh." This was clearly a lot to grasp. Truth could understand that. It was an emotional day for this kid, and this was a lot to process at once.

"Look, what would you say to a warmup? Look down that street there." Truth pointed to a cross street on the other side of the building. "If you kind of squint, you should be able to see the bank?"

"Yeah?"

"Four Seas Bank. Starbrite owns a big chunk of it. Not an official Starbrite company, but come on. You really think any of the bosses there are going to argue with Starbrite?"

The boy shook his head.

"So, let's do a little proof of concept. It's a much longer shot, but because you are shooting farther away, the angle is flatter. Easier to hit, hopefully." And he would be cheating, but no need to mention that little detail. "Now, do you see the security guys out front? Gray-hat guys."

"Yeah?"

"You see the prick in the fancy suit next to them?"

"Yeah."

"Bank manager or higher. Might even be some bigwig from Harban come for an inspection." He definitely was. There was one of those almost-invisible-watcher things next to him. Watching. Plainclothes PMC hitters around him too.

"Probably off for a nice meal, hot and cold running whores, and a peaceful night's sleep. He would be so mad if you told him he was part of the problem. That he was *the person who killed your sister. They are all responsible for killing your sister.*"

The boy started fixating, hyperventilating.

"Now let's put it all together. Kneel behind the parapet. Just like that. Good. Rest the needler—you got it. Nice steady breath. I'll help you line up the shot. There. Hold it right like that. When I say 'Now,' shoot. Nice quiet needle from a long way off, plenty of time to get clear. Might even be able to come back and tidy up the PTO, if you still want to."

"Yeah."

"Here comes the carriage. Fancy limo! There goes security—" The watcher moved into line with the suit for a moment. "Now!"

The boy squeezed the trigger, the needle ripping through the air. Truth grinned. He had wanted to find out what happened when you killed one of those watcher-things for ages.

CHAPTER 50

A WHOLE PACK OF LONE WOLVES

The needle was quite long compared to a standard sidearm's round. Truth knew from experience it could smash through people without slowing down. That's what it was built for—smashing through problems and problematic people. Driven at brutal speeds by the enchantments on the talisman, it could turn even a Level Zero nobody into a legitimate threat . . . to someone completely not paying attention or with really shoddy personal protections. Assuming someone with a higher level nudged things along a bit.

Truth watched intently as the needle whipped down the road toward the Suit and the invisible watcher thing standing at his side. If he timed it just right, and if his subtle help aiming had worked, it should . . . Truth felt a tiny thrill of horror—in the bare second between the trigger being pulled and the needle reaching its target, the watcher had started to turn. Truth could see its head whipping toward the incoming needle. Not dodging, yet, just . . . seeing. If it had a second move, it didn't make it in time.

Incisive had caught the perfect moment. It let a Level Zero nobody kill one of Starbrite's secret weapons. The needle caught the watcher just above the eyebrows, a tiny hole going in, a shower of pink and gray gore spraying over the Suit a fraction of a second after the Suit caught the needle with his temple. It hadn't lost a whole lot of speed even by the time it came out the other side, spraying the F-Tier gray-hat security drone with "superior" gray matter. Not that the guard had much time to worry about his uniform—he caught the needle just below his neck before it finally smashed into a silvery disk on the pavement.

"Oh! Triple kill on your first shot! You may have a future in this, junior!" The boy was still trying to process what was going on, trying to comprehend what happened. His Level Zero body and mind simply couldn't keep up with what Level Four Truth was seeing. Once he had, he gagged, turned to the side, and threw up.

"Don't worry, kid; that's totally normal. Traditional, even. From what I hear, anyway; I never threw up." Truth's eyes narrowed. Incisive was starting to make a real racket in his head. He summoned the Tongue to his hand and *cut.*

The curse fizzled out, but Truth had a sneaking suspicion that was the . . . noob filter, for lack of a better term. The really nasty stuff wouldn't be so easy to shake. The boy was about to have a *really exciting* life.

"So, junior, do you have your scooter license?"

"Wha?"

"No time like the present. Let's learn by doing." Security was boiling out of the bank. He could practically hear one of those damn golden birds flapping their wings and getting airborne. He snatched up the needler, case, and backpack. Loaded the needler and case into his own duffel, stuck the backpack on the teenager, scooped up the teenager, and started running.

It was damn awkward, carrying everything and trying to run. The teen was still processing when he made the first jump between buildings, but by the time Truth made the jump to the *second* building, which had much more of an upward, vertical element, he had decided it was appropriate to start screaming. This, in Truth's opinion, proved that today's juniors were simply too soft and coddled. Well, he knew just the thing to toughen this kid up. Make a real man out of him. It was his duty as a senior, after all.

He got a good way down the street and, with a little care, was able to get to the sidewalk by bouncing between two buildings. It was good fun, only slightly ruined by the noise. Although he was pleased to note the lad didn't piss himself. Not a complete no-hoper. Truth beat it as fast as he could manage toward a parking garage, following the street signs. While he ran, he examined the schoolboy.

Truth wasn't an expert on divination. Only knew the basics, really. Still, he could make some reasonable guesses. It seemed that the whatever-it-was was built for detection and detection only. Quite fast reflexes, but apparently, it couldn't do anything with them. Because that wasn't its job. It was a component in a system. When its head got popped, its death triggered a curse on the person who killed it. Not much of one, but probably lethal if you were a scrub. Or, nastier still, maybe some kind of hard-to-shake marker, letting the PMC trace you back to all your friends and family.

Still, that was the superficial. And as he had painfully learned, Starbrite never left anything it really cared about unprotected. He couldn't detect any active spells on the kid. But passively? He'd bet cash the kid was marked and they were being tracked even now.

He looked around. There was a sweet little Koro-Bon 178 painted up in lime green and white. Supposed to run fast and corner sharp. A little bland, to his taste. A little lacking in color and character compared to his beloved iron horse. But it would do.

"All right, here's your ride."

"That's . . . not my two-wheeler."

"It is now. Look." Truth jammed a finger into the casing and severed a notoriously fragile control node. "It's not even locked or anything. See, it was meant for you. Better start running; they will be locking down the city any second now."

"But . . . what . . . why?"

"Kid, you just sniped a high-end banker on a junket from Harban AND picked off two Starbrite security guards. One of which you didn't see because they were that high-end. You have been most assuredly marked for arrest, followed by torture and a particularly degrading death."

It was hard for the student to turn whiter, but the kid wasn't a quitter. He found a way.

"Now, I'm not heartless. I will dispose of the needler for you—that's way too hot for you to handle. You have a fast two-wheeler, and here—some walking-around money. Welcome to the world of the revolution, junior. You are going to fit in just fine."

"Revolution? I'm not a revolutionary! I just wanted—"

"To be a lone-wolf terrorist. I know. Believe me, I know. But the revolution finds its way to all of us. Don't worry; you can still be a lone-wolf terrorist. But if you want to live to be an *old* lone-wolf terrorist, *RUN NOW!*"

He pushed on Incisive and let a wisp of his killing intent seep through. The schoolboy bolted, nearly plowing into the wall at the first corner. He managed to brake in time, then muscled the two-wheeler around the corner. Truth kept an ear out. Sounded like he had made it out of the garage. Good for him. And they were right next to the freeway onramp, too—headed west.

Truth watched him go, slowly letting the persona fade away. It was a curious moral position, he supposed. Better that this kid (and when did a seventeen-year-old become a kid to him?) become an anti-Starbrite rebel than shoot up his local PTO. In either case, the police would have hunted him down in short order. He would already have been recorded by innumerable surveillance talismans—the dots would be pathetically easy to connect. This wasn't some crummy little town. The cops were active and interested in Buran.

Well, interested if someone shot up a room full of Citizen parents. This was the kind of blood-soaked atrocity that could actually move the people who liked to complain to the police. The news programs would love it too. Assuming they weren't "advised" to the contrary.

But there would be no news reports about a Starbrite suit getting sniped by a seventeen-year-old lone-wolf rebel. A rebel who, when caught, would reveal that he only committed that crime because a senior strong-armed him into it. A senior rebel. A real rebel, not one of the shadows they had been chasing about.

He reckoned he had, at best, half an hour before the kid got picked up. Call it . . . fifteen minutes conservatively. Maybe an hour, absolute maximum, to get him in an interrogation cell and crack him. Realistically, he might crack while he was still pinned down on the pavement before they even dragged him into the wagon.

Ah, no, wait. If they took him alive, they'd slap coma cuffs on him, make sure he couldn't suicide before interrogation. Yeah, absolute maximum, one hour from now, this part of the city would be 50% Internal Security by volume, if not weight. Time to run like Hell. He looked around the garage. There were more iron horses, but his weird loyalty stopped him from grabbing one.

Truth opted for a sweet Rixowip Cevis only slightly younger than he was. Sure, it smelled, but at least the cooling charms didn't work. The brakes sort of worked, but only if you got the pedal in the exact right spot. Push too far, and they didn't engage at all.

Why not use the bound demon to drive the wagon? Because, despite everything, despite the profound cruelty and mad sadism of the world, Truth chose life. That demon couldn't be trusted to tell which way was up, let alone north.

The highway traffic was slowing down. Truth made certain he was heading north, not west. All practicable speed and all that. He very quickly concluded that "all practicable speed" in a frigging twenty-plus-year-old Cevis with shot brakes and a beyond-dodgy demon was slower than he could run, by a fair bit. He grimly pressed on. It wasn't about speed. It was about not burning through his limited supply of cosmic energy. It was a long way from being fully refilled after a busy day.

He would drive this smelly, greasy, revoltingly stained Cevis. He would drive it to the nearest small town, then set it on fire. He would stick a big metal drum on top first, fill it with good, clean water and loads of soap. He would boil up the water on the burning Cevis, so he could scrub the sense of filth off himself. It was like a fungal growth, the unclean writhing and spreading from the horrible seat over his skin, reaching for his face. Trying to sink its vile pseudopods into his tear ducts and throat and nose.

He had felt cleaner in the Ghūl nest. What the Hell had possessed him to take this carriage? Truth watched a police cruiser whip past on the highway. Right. Stealth. Just another little imp in the system, trudging back to his little box for drug-induced sleep. Definitely not off to murder one of the leading minds of the era with a heavy needler he had stolen off a high-schooler.

Truth missed his iron horse. He missed Etenesh madly, and Jember a great deal, and he even missed Merkovah, grumpy old bastard that he was. But he really missed his iron horse. You had the sense that you could run off anywhere and be okay. No matter what happened, it would carry you there and take you away again. Not this thing. In the Cevis, you lived your moral depravity. If depression was a heavily used entry-price sedan, it would be the Cevis. There was a bit of fermented cabbage, desiccated now, stuck to the side of the passenger door. Horrible.

He tried to get his head in the game. There was a service station up ahead. They were just outside the Buran ring road. There would be a wagon headed up north. It wouldn't be comfortable, but he could sneak in the back and sleep for a bit. Maybe do a bit of on-the-road cultivation. And in a few hours, he would hop out and do it again. Yeah. That worked. Keep security guessing. After all, if he didn't have a plan, how could Internal Security guess his plan?

There was probably a flaw in that logic. If only the piercing, layered smells of the Cevis would let him concentrate on it. No, he wouldn't dwell on minor issues. He was off to assassinate a scholar. A mage and a gentleman. Someone who would be heavily guarded and capable of immense personal violence in their own right.

Easy.

CHAPTER 51

CERTAIN UNPLEASANT PRACTICALITIES

The Cevis bubbled pleasingly as it drowned. The grass-green pond scum frothed a bit around the smashed-open windows, pouring in to give the interior the closest thing to a cleaning it had ever known. The fungal life within the carriage would finally have a real fight on its hands. This pond had never had anything good living in it. *Welcome to the jungle, trash. It's got what you need.*

That rang a bell somewhere. No idea why. He wouldn't worry about it. He would just enjoy watching the source of the last hour's oppression slowly sinking to the bottom of a pond just two kilometers from the rest stop he was targeting. The sheer satisfaction of watching the carriage drown was worth savoring and, like all truly good things, seemed to end too soon. The algae drew its toxic curtain closed on the play. Truth sighed, checked that he had everything, and set off for the rest stop. Next stop—north.

Truth hiked through the exurban scrubland, trying to leave as little trace of himself behind as he could manage. Between his Blessings and Thrush, he might as well have been a breeze through the tall grass. The rest stop was pretty typical of its sort—pay showers, enormous ranks of bathrooms, a food court with a whopping three chain restaurants, and a convenience store larger than most homes. Level Ones and Level Zeros drifting to and fro. For once, Truth could imagine they shared his assessment of their existence—ghosts haunting the freeway.

He hung out near the line for coffee. Regrettably, none of the drivers were bored enough to discuss their destination. They had other complaints.

"It's going to be the end of us."

"It's not that bad."

"It's exactly that bad. Remember when the drive-assist demons came in, and all our wages got cut by two-thirds?"

"No, because it happened before either of us was born, Joarle."

"Oh, fuck you, Pasie; you know what I mean. Every time there is a 'huge improvement,' who gets screwed? Me. You and me."

The other driver shrugged. "Yeah. So, what are you going to do about it? Changeover is in, what, three weeks?"

The wiry man, Joarle, seemed to deflate. "Two. I don't know. I really don't know. Don't suppose you have any good ideas?"

"Well"—her voice dropped—"wouldn't be the craziest idea for some goods to be 'damaged in transit,' you know? But not sold. Stockpiled. Just in case."

Joarle hissed and recoiled. "Pasie—"

"Just saying."

"The risks—"

"Are what, exactly? If things are as bad as you think?"

Joarle mulled it over. "I've been with Totte for nineteen years."

"Yeah, you have."

The conversation lapsed. Joarle put in an order for two large coffees, then looked over at Pasie and got her two, too. They moved to a table. They sat for a moment, just sipping their terrible coffee and thinking their own thoughts.

"It's just—"

"Oh, I know." Pasie nodded. They lapsed back into silence for a minute longer.

"You really think it's worth it?"

"I think you have to make that call. One way or the other, you have to be ready for . . . whatever is coming next. Because one thing we agree on—it can't be a good thing. I've got two more stops today. You?"

"Just one, but it's a long haul."

"Damn. Well, here's hoping no checkpoints." She chuckled.

"I can't say I'm surprised management refused to change the late penalty when those started rolling out," Joarle grunted. He picked up his coffee and walked out. Truth followed behind him. They were on the southern tip of the peninsula. A long haul could only be headed in one direction. North.

Truth followed the driver out to his wagon and looked it over. Pretty standard—a cab hauling a shipping container on a trailer, basically. The cab's eyes of gold and flame glared around the parking lot, ready to set off as soon as it got the order. Truth was stuck—you couldn't close the doors of the container from the inside. On the other hand, he wanted to nap and cultivate if he could. Fortunately, there was a tiny sleeping compartment behind where the driver sat. It wasn't much more than a cot, a drawer, and a reading light, but he would happily take it. It had been a long, eventful day. He got settled in as the driver set out.

The cultivation before bed went . . . not well. It was fine in that he was pulling in more cosmic rays and filling his apertures and generally doing what a mage should. It was not-fine in that he could definitely feel a hint of thinness in the energy now. Like that touch of breeze in summer that lets you know winter is coming. And there is nothing at all you can do to stop it. Just a hint of cold now . . .

He shook off the feeling. It took a while, but he got his head straight. He knew this was coming. He, of all people, had no excuse for being shook up by it. Can't fix it? Deal with it, then. *Any progress on how to replicate that energy-sealing spell we stole from Gullvar using the Meditations?*

<<Yes, but you aren't going to like it. Visualization.>>

Elaborate.

<<It's what I said. You have been hijacking the Nine Worms to supercharge your med-itation practice, but it always comes back to visualization. That's its deal. You visualize, meditate, and the Meditations of Valentinian slowly brings that vision into reality. So, your undead ass needs to incorporate a little extra something into your visualization. The good news is that you will be an even more monstrous pain in the ass to scry on once you have some mastery.>>

Truth groaned. He didn't like it one little bit. He was used to doing jobs he didn't like. Pissy and resentful, he began to meditate. *What's the old joke? That's why they call it practicing meditation? Something like that.* Truth grumped to himself, not realizing he had never in his life heard a person ever make that joke.

Wait, there were two spells. Have you cracked the second one yet?

<<No.>>

What do you mean, "No"? You were able to take a stab at Knife and Cup in way less time than you have had with that . . . whatever it is.

<<No, Truth, means no. Which you know perfectly well, no matter how much it pains me not to roast you. After careful study and comparison with other spells, I don't know what that spell does, what it's for, or how it is supposed to work.>>

Say more.

<<Most spells share something in common. Parts of the spell form, the incantations, something. Some parts of their essential geometries are recognizable and can be used to analyze other spells. A spell that enlarges things isn't going to have a lot of crossover with a spell that ensures even dispersion of carbon through iron in the steelmaking process, but there is something. I can't find that something here. The only reason I know it's magic is because it says, "The mage then projects the spell form and channels their cosmic energy into it" and things like that.>>

Could this be a spell from whatever branch of humanity Anakson is from?

<<I don't have a better idea.>>

Not safe to cast, then.

<<No.>>

Truth mulled it over, then shrugged. Another item for the *I can't do anything about this* heap. What he could do was get to work visualizing. So he did. It was a slow grind, but then, he knew he was in for a long haul.

Six hours into their journey, the wagon came to a full stop. Something about it jolted Truth from his nap. He instinctively cast Incisive and was immediately alarmed—danger all around. A quick peek out the window was explanation enough. They were just outside of Harban. They had hit a checkpoint. The good news was that the traffic was moving reasonably quickly through it. The bad news was all the watcher things. Which practically coated the streetlights hanging from dozens of posts.

Nowhere to run. Absolutely nowhere to hide. Welcome to the highways in the middle of the night. Truth thought fast and tried to figure out the best way through. Fight? He probably could—briefly. Then, a whole mess of high-levels would be on him, and that would be that. Run? Faint hope. Not no-hope, but faint. Truth gritted his teeth. There was only one thing for it, then—stack as much protection on himself as he could and try to hide.

He risked another quick glance. They were checking everyone's identity sigils, not just the driver. Running spellhounds around, too. Taking no chances. That ruled out pretending to be a hitchhiker. Or even a dog. His thoughts raced. *Ah.* There was one identity that didn't need proving. He could be dead meat.

He did his best to seal himself up. Like the System urged him to when he was fighting the anti-theists. Like a snake trapping the water inside of his scales during a dry spell. All the active processes of a living body, the absorption and emission of cosmic energy. His heat. His smell. At Level Four, he could stop his heart, stop his breath, for a time. He let his body fall away.

He was dead meat, floating in a well. Meat being taken for butchering. Not human meat, nothing worthy of even that much attention. Just meat. He kept only enough of his mind active to keep Incisive running. Maintaining the identity. Maintaining the Blessing of the Silent Forest. He could vaguely sense that his alarm should be increasing, that he should be very afraid. Meat didn't fear. Meat was meat. Already dead. He let his consciousness drift off, too, afraid that even that could be detected somehow. He was just meat. Just meat. Just meat.

He hung in the dark well. Timeless, at first, but pressure slowly grew. The pressure of a heart to beat. Of lungs to breathe. Of a mind to think. The pressure to be born out of this darkness. Something was pulling, too—something pouring out of him, like a slit vein in his leg and throat, not even air pressure slowing the flow of blood. Something important, vital, racing out of him. He couldn't hold it together long. The pressure grew. More and more. It became harder to just be meat. To hang in the well. But he was meat. Just meat. Meat wasn't afraid. Meat didn't worry about pressure.

Pressure didn't worry about the opinions of meat. It just grew. And grew. The drain got worse and worse. Eventually, the drain tapered off, but by then, there was nothing left to keep the meat in the well.

Truth opened his eyes and gasped. He was almost drained dry. Covered in sweat. Everything hurt. But he was still in the back of the truck, and they were moving. When he was strong enough, he peeked through the window. They were through the checkpoint. He sucked in rasping lungfuls of air. His body was suddenly drenched in sweat. He was nauseous, light-headed. He wanted to throw up and piss himself at the same time. He didn't. He just cultivated as hard and as fast as he could.

He could make it past the watchers. Just barely, and it took everything he had. But he could do it. A rictus grin spread across his face as he desperately tried to bring his body back to order. He could get past them.

Starbrite was *fucked.*

CHAPTER 52

FRAGILE BUBBLES

Truth alternated between sitting cultivation, his least favorite sort, and trying to remember how his body worked. Everything hurt or felt wrong, or hurt while feeling wrong. In a brief moment of lucidity, he decided that *wrong* was unacceptably imprecise. If an elbow could feel nauseous, it would feel like this. And he had to remember that blood needed to pump and the lungs needed to inflate and deflate, and it all needed to happen without his conscious involvement, thank you very much! Because right now, his body was operating on manual controls, and that just wasn't going to work.

He also needed every scrap, every tiny particle of cosmic energy he could grasp, because he was a hair, a wispy, thin hair, from being totally empty. And that meant he was seconds from having his apertures start to collapse. It wasn't normal to test your reserves this way. The one time he had overdrawn himself in the PMC, he got serious medical attention and an even more serious chewing-out by Sergeant Murthey. "Dumbfuck Medici" was his formal name and rank for the purposes of that discussion.

It was the universe's way of hinting that he was doing it wrong. That he was brute-forcing it instead of using his brain. Truth could see that plainly. He just didn't know how he could do it better. Every time he pushed himself to the limit and lived, he lived. If he hadn't pushed as hard, he wouldn't have lived. He would, therefore, have to deal with the pain.

His gamble worked, but he couldn't do it a second time. Not today, at any rate, and probably not tomorrow. On the other hand, he didn't want to ditch the wagon and go to ground. He was finally making good time going north, certainly faster and more directly than he could run over such a long distance. So, he cultivated like mad, hauling in every bit of energy he could, trying to keep his lungs going without his reminding them, and squinting out the windows for any hint of roadblocks.

He did not enjoy his ride in the wagon. He had lost track of time somewhere—it was the middle of the night or creeping toward dawn. The horizon hadn't lightened yet, and spring was rolling into summer . . . he would go with *so late, he really wished he was asleep.* His driver, Joarle, agreed. They didn't run into a checkpoint, but they did pull into a rest stop. A brilliant bubble of bleach-white lights shone down on gray-and-gold-trimmed corporate livery. A sprawling complex engineered to quickly empty what was full and fill what was empty.

They both got out of the wagon at speed. Both went for a shower. Both went for coffee, which Truth had one sip of and flung violently into the trash. Joarle's palate wasn't so refined. He chased his tall coffee with a couple of pills from over the counter at the convenience store and settled on an outdoor bench to smoke a quick bowl of something energizing.

Truth opted for a big bag of chips, two liters of fruit juice ("Guaranteed 5% real fruit flavor!"), and a big sack of crispy, sesame-flavored seaweed. He would have gone for the jerky, but it was now being kept behind the counter and under glass. Meat was getting very expensive very fast. The little bench, fake-cherry-flavor red and made of metal, was at the edge of the bubble of light surrounding the rest stop. More bubbles of light shone down from the towering lights over the parking lot, giving the wagons their star turn for the spotlight as they pulled up.

They recharged in companionable silence, for all that only one of them knew he had a companion in the dark. But the life of a trucker *was* a lonely one, and companionship, like the showers, was rentable at the rest stop. She had put on heels and a skirt as short as the money that bought it. A top that stretched nicely over nothing much. She didn't saunter; she just walked over on aching feet. "Hey, Joarle. Got a hit of that for me?"

"Sure, Marcy. Here, finish the bowl." He offered it over with easy familiarity. Truth stepped away from the bench so they could sit together, and wound up leaning against the lamppost. She took the glass pipe casually and dragged deep, taking the edge off, but only just. The tired was ground in deep.

"Doing all right?" Joarle asked.

"Been better. Tommy's got a bad cough."

"Must be really bad if you're mentioning it."

"Some kind of fungal thing. I always think it sounds like mushrooms growing inside of him, but it's not. His body just can't fight it off like with a cold. You can get a charm for it, but it costs. Well. You know how it is."

"Yeah. Suppose I do. Different when it's your kid, though."

She sighed. "Not as much as you would think. Always been me and him since he was born. Not saying none of it's been for me—I gotta eat and pay rent too. But it's been for him, mostly. 'Cause without him, what even am I?"

"I have Bresla and Nadi's pictures up in my cab. Every long haul I make, I look at them."

They fell back into silence. Marcy took a hopeful drag on the pipe, but it was cashed. She sighed and put it down between them, letting the glass cool. Joarle offered some chips. She took a couple.

"Sleeping here?"

"Can't. Got stopped by a checkpoint over near Harban. The goddamn penalty clauses kick in if I'm late, and with everything—"

"You can't be late." Marcy leaned back, trying to relax her shoulders and rest her tired feet.

"Can't be late. Sorry." They lapsed into silence. Each just existing, trying to float in their fragile bubble of light, seeing the cold dark around them. Trying to be brave.

Joarle took a look at his watch and did some math. "I'm here another ten minutes. I can spend them on this bench or in my bunk."

"You're a good guy. Sorry about laying the sob story on you."

"Only story anybody's got these days."

"Somebody ought to write a comedy." Marcy stood. It seemed to take some effort. Joarle got up almost as slowly. "Everybody knows everything is rotten and terrible. Who needs to be told that? But something that makes you laugh, that takes you away from it all for a while? I'd like to see that."

They walked over to the cab of the wagon. Truth stayed on the bench. Plenty of time to catch up when they were done. He felt very cold without his companions in the light. But he wouldn't grudge others their little warmth.

The geography of Jeon got more claustrophobic the farther north you went. The number and size of human settlements dropped hard forty kilometers north of Harban. The number and size of mountains rose proportionally. They might be stumpy little things in the south, but up north? Some green, some gray, all forbidding. All grudgingly permitting human settlement in the narrow valleys or on the scraped-away tops of foothills. There were mines there and some heavy-pollution industries. Some of the higher-volume and toxic production lines from the alchemists were set up along railroads through the north. Truth remembered there were PMC offices up there, too, and a small training camp.

Joarle drove his wagon through the night and into the dawn. It was because of the law, apparently. The demon bound to the cab did all the actual steering, navigation, braking, signaling, and all that. But, to reassure the public that a multi-ton cargo wagon wasn't going to freak out and plow through a crowd, each was required to have a driver. The spells would not engage until the driver was in their seat and had one hand on the steering wheel. The wheel wasn't connected to anything, of course. The steering spells only kicked in if the driver pulled the big red lever on the dash, and they'd better have a DAMN good reason for pulling that, because the truck was company property and you would be liable for damaging it.

The truck driver's job was sitting in the cab, one hand always on the wheel, staring out of the cab. Not moving except during their approved rests. Barely able to nudge the demon into stopping at a rest stop. Trapped in a glass box, watching the most boring parts of the country slip past. Ghosts watching ghosts. They mostly helped with the loading and unloading at their destination. Another tiny component in the great national working: summoning money for Starbrite.

They didn't run into any more checkpoints. What was there to inspect? Truth focused on cultivation and recovery. He didn't even want to think about the hit. Well, that and he didn't actually know where Joarle was taking him, beyond "north" and probably to a Totte distribution center. Where, thanks to him, they would definitely have security. He waited until they were in a good-sized town, then he hopped out of the wagon. There were a few Level Zeros on the street, which made it close enough to empty for his needs. He was still feeling tender. Best to take it easy while keeping in motion. He stretched, looked around, and decided to find coffee before plotting his next steps.

It was at this point that Truth realized he had screwed up. Again. This was not a "good-sized town." This was a very dense cluster of houses next to a train station, giving one the *illusion* of a good-sized town. What it actually was was a crummy little mountain village that seemed to exist mostly to house factory workers, miners, and their dependents. There were one convenience store, the train station, and a combination police station/doctor's office/stationmaster's office. Truth had a sneaking suspicion that they were all the same person.

The sign on the train station read YAGDOK, and while the schedule grudgingly admitted that trains *did* stop here, it took vindictive pleasure in informing him they did so only twice a day. Freight trains came through all the time but never stopped. Kilometers long, traveling barely faster than a Level One could walk. The worm demon pulling them was a huge, brutal thing. Monstrous even for an earth demon, coated in sigils and spell formations, the lines etched into its form, rods of punishment and control piercing through its head. Rippling along the track, it hauled the carriages behind it.

"I wonder if it even knows it's out of Hell," Truth muttered. Thrush watched the earth demon go past, managing to sneer with a beak.

"It knows. The dumb thing may be suffering, but it's used to that. If anything, it's happy," Thrush said.

"That looks happy to you?"

"Our emotions are different to yours, Dread Mage. I'm trying to make the best comparison I can. Perhaps *satisfied to be fulfilling its purpose* would be closer in meaning."

"Increasing human misery?"

"Master, please! Such is never a *demon's* purpose. A necessary byproduct of it, on occasion, but never the purpose itself."

"Go on, then. Why is the bound and tormented worm demon 'happy'?"

"Because it is useful to a more-powerful being. It views suffering as proof of service. And they are so stupid, they make no distinction between masters. Time is a meaningless concept to them, so only pain and labor define their existence. To the extent that it is aware of humans at all, it looks at them with as close to approval as it can manage."

Truth laughed quietly. He dug out his now badly battered road atlas and gingerly hunted through the index. It took an alarmingly long time to find Yagdok, even with the coordinates. A tiny speck of nothing, not interesting enough to be in the middle of nowhere. He was still well southwest of where he needed to be. He traced the rail line running through town. It ran, slowly, from northeast to southwest. He could hop on a northbound train for a while. It would give him time to plot the hit. And rest.

He ran to the convenience store, loaded up on as much junk food and water as he could grab, snagged a tarp, hit the No Public Toilet toilet, and zipped back to the station. The same train was still rolling through. He needn't have rushed. Truth briefly debated about which open-topped bin would be the most comfortable and hopped in. Pea gravel. It could be worse. He could explore the train later, if he felt like it. He buried himself in it, wrapped in his tarp. The weight of it was strangely comforting.

"Thrush, wake me if we approach a town of at least five thousand people, if you see any sort of checkpoint or security inspection, or if the train reaches its destination."

"Yes, Master."

And with that, Truth finally slept. Getting closer to murdering a generation's genius.

CHAPTER 53

CONSIDERING OLD EMPLOYERS AND COWORKERS

Truth awoke in a minor panic, feeling smothered by the plastic and the gravel. For a horrible second, he thought he had died in his sleep. For a horrible second, he thought he was back in that well of nothing, feeling the pressure growing. He kicked his way up and out in a hurry.

"How long did I sleep?"

"Five hours, Great One. This stupid worm is quite slow, and we passed nothing and no one of any note." Truth looked around at the crummy one-lane road jammed between the railroad track and the looming mountains. It was empty. Looking the other way, there were more mountains with a few patches of trees on them. Presumably, some manner of animals, insects, and demons lived in those woods, but he had a hard time believing it. He believed the demon instead—this part of the country was empty because it sucked.

Truth kicked the pea gravel into the rough shape of a seat and sat in it, watching the nothing go past as he got to work on his assassination plot. The information crystal provided by Siphios had been destroyed as a security precaution, but he remembered it well enough. Merkovah knew his man—no plan had been provided, just a target.

The researcher was Constan Borges, MThaum, PhD, DThaum, DTheo, and with a string of honorary degrees so long that they must be quite tiring to write out in one sitting. Truth was a little vague on what he had actually done that made him so blasted important to Starbrite and, apparently, the world. The dossier used words like *revolutionized* and *pioneered* but connected them to terms of art he had never come across before. He had a sneaking suspicion that this was his terrible education coming back to bite him in the ass again, but it could be that the researcher's work was just that advanced.

The dossier was blessedly specific on where the good doctor lived and worked. He lived in a surprisingly reasonable home in the tiny flyspeck village of Happori, way the hell up in the mountains. He also worked in the tiny flyspeck village of Happori because Starbrite had built him his own research base there. A three-hundred-meter-tall twisting vine, thin as a lady's finger, holding up a flower a kilometer in diameter. The research station was built on top of it.

Access was strictly controlled. One had to be vetted at a base station and then ride up on the butterflies that fed upon the flower. Thousands upon thousands of butterflies, whose combined bodies and wings formed a platform strong enough to lift both researchers and equipment. Apparently, it all worked thanks to some of the discoveries made by Dr. Borges.

Why build the research station that way? Because when one of the greatest minds of his generation, and one of your most successful drones, wants a fancy toy, you give it to him. Especially if the toy is intended for your benefit. It will inspire others to work harder. And it *was* quite pretty. Most of the staff lived up there, and Dr. Borges seemed to spend virtually all his time there as well.

Reading between the lines, the home in the village was more a place to keep his wife, his dogs, and, should he ever decide he wanted them, his children. The dossier had specifically instructed to avoid attempts to use the wife, as she was a product of the Lovers tab in the System Store. She could no more harm Borges than she could fail to laugh at his jokes. She was a modified human, though just how much she was modified beyond the merely cosmetic was uncertain.

Considerably more concerning was the security. There was an awful, awful lot of security. Those observer-creatures were there in bulk, naturally. The PMC kept a full platoon of Level Three veterans on site 24/7, with rotating squads of Level Twos to man the base station. The list of surveillance golems, security golems, trap demons, and floating curses ran on to a second page, and it was repeatedly emphasized that this was only what could be observed. There were *unquestionably* hidden experts on site, too. Level Five, at a bare minimum; Level Six or Seven would be more likely, given their protectee was Level Six.

So. A frontal assault was probably out, and infiltration would be a . . . real challenge. Supplies came in and out via the base station, brought in by spell birds or extraordinary spirit beasts. There was a regular supply shipment, but if Truth were in charge of the base station, the guards there would know that "delivery day" was also "Surprise Inspection Day" by the senior officers, making sure that nobody got bored with the routine work. An idea he had gotten directly from Sergeant Murthey, now that he thought about it.

Truth lay back on the gravel and lightly closed his eyes. He was stronger now than he had been when he went into the well. But was he more dangerous? He played out the fights in his mind. As a Level Four, with intensive body cultivation, he was far faster, more durable, and almost immune to low-level spells. He had extraordinary Blessings and a holy sword, and his spells synergized fairly well together. He was still trying to figure out how Knife and Cup worked, but the System gave him at least a bit of flexibility in how he approached problems. Mobility, range, stopping power, healing, he was incredibly capable by any standards . . . except those of the Starbrite Private Military Company.

He ran the fight in his mind—Level Four PMC officer versus him. Assume they had armor, defensive charms, and the standard-issue needler.

Assume there was no ambush and he was running right at them. The officer would be much slower due to the, at best, limited body cultivation available. If Truth could close to sword range, the fight would be over very quickly. The physical advantages and the power of Incisive to guide him through a fight were nearly insurmountable at the same level. If Truth could close. But what if he couldn't?

He ran the fight again, charging forward. The op saw him coming and dropped a shield directly in Truth's path. Truth cut it away, but as he did so, the op caused the earth below him to slam upward mightily, launching him into the air. The PMC soldier switched to their needler and started firing rapidly. Auto fire, using Graeme's Arrow, Enlarge, Sharp, and Plutonian Chains so that in the event that this somehow didn't kill Truth, he wouldn't be running anywhere afterward. This fight, too, ended quite quickly. He might be spell-resistant, but he wasn't *big chunk of pointy metal hitting you repeatedly in the face and chest at very high speeds* resistant.

He ran it again and again in a variety of scenarios. He could shrug off lower-level spells. He could endure standard needler rounds without too much trouble. But that was the thing about the System. Sooner or later, the PMC soldier would find the right combination of spells to take you down. It might not be as fast as they wished it was. Truth had certainly seen plenty of his former comrades die. But it was never one-on-one. They always fell to a volume of fire.

Take the sword out of the equation and switch to the heavy needler. Truth played it out, and things were . . . odd. The Level Four's ability to combine four spells on the fly let them do some downright alarming things at long range. He hadn't had the energy for it at Level Two, but it occurred to him that it would be possible to replicate mortar fire with a needler and spells, making cover irrelevant. And if the range was long enough, spotting, tracking, and targeting spells could be layered on to the needles. Again, things Truth had never bothered with, given the limitations of Level and mission requirements, but you absolutely *could* do it.

Balanced against that was the simplified nature of the spells. No single spell had the utility of Incisive or Cup and Knife. Or, for that matter, the Meditations of Valentinian. If anyone kept an active effect like Incisive's foreknowledge going at all times, he had never heard about it. So, if he was sniping, he could clear the field *very* fast. Until the real experts came out.

With intense reluctance, he added Obliteration to the mix. It wasn't quite as decisive a weapon as he might have wished—it did nothing to blunt the enemies' offense. But the damage it did was horrifying. Even a glancing blow was crippling, as the cosmic energy within a person just evaporated or boiled away. He couldn't really imagine the damage it did to the magical System inside a person, but it had to be awful. It also negated any magical armor or charms, of course.

Would it negate foresight? He didn't know. He had never heard of the anti-theists before fighting them, but they had apparently been around forever and existed off-world. It would be insane to think that Starbrite didn't know about them and hadn't taken *some* precautions.

He briefly imagined cutting down the vine and causing the whole research station to fall out of the sky, but that was just silly. It wasn't the stalk holding up the station. And a single casting of Obliteration would most assuredly not drop it from the sky. Any ritual that could empty the cosmic energy around it would be so slow to take effect that everyone could evacuate before it finished.

Truth puzzled at it for another hour, then set it aside. It didn't occur to him that he had spent the whole time visualizing, something he had used to struggle mightily with. Missing that growth spurt.

They were slowly, painfully slowly, approaching the town of Rhemv, which his atlas swore was a decent size and likely to have at least one restaurant. Time to get off the train and pick up the pace. Dr. Borges wasn't going to kill himself, after all.

A walk, stretch, and trip to the bathroom later, Truth acquired a box of fried chicken and the bus schedule. Both were disappointing. The bus ran rarely and didn't head anywhere near Happori. Which was fair enough, in a way, because Happori was deep into the mountains, and there was no reason for a stranger to go there. The fried chicken had no excuse. Lousy batter, under-seasoned, and the cost was outrageous. If someone had told him six months before that he would ever, under any circumstances, pay thirty wen for a four-piece box, he would have had them exorcised.

He looked around Rhemv. Another tiny, gray mountain town, equal parts misery and meth. He couldn't get out of there fast enough. Literally could not; trying to find a stealable vehicle was frustrating. They were all in use. Nobody walked more than a few hundred meters. Farther than that—carriage. Ancient wreckers, all of them. It felt unsafe just standing near them. But this would be a very long trip indeed if he had to run all the way to Happori.

He briefly imagined hiring a local to drive him around but quickly gave it up. The idea was to leave fewer traces, not more. He hunted about the town, breaking into garages and exploring backyards. At this point, he would take anything with four wheels, effective brakes, and a functioning demon. He was lucky to get even one out of three. He didn't know what sort of terrible crime the people of Rhemv had committed to be punished with such a comprehensive curse. It must have been spectacular.

"I give up. Thrush, find me a treasure—a functional or near-functional vehicle in this pisshole town that is not in use. It cannot require more than minor repairs to be fully functional. That includes a complete absence of rodents fucking and shitting in it."

Thrush ducked its head briefly but hesitated before flying off. "What about other animals? There is a carriage with a foxes' den dug into the back seat that otherwise meets your needs."

"No."

"As you command." Thrush managed to sound like a vizier indulging a particularly cruel young prince. A few minutes later, he came back.

"I found a vehicle that I believe meets all your requirements."

"Lead on."

"I caution you that it is . . . unconventional."

"Sounds like my life. Let's do it."

"Very unconventional."

"Just show me already."

"Here, behind the hovel."

Hovel was a fair description of the house, as it was for all the houses in Rhemv. The backyard was a heap of scrap, hauled over and dumped for reasons known only to the dumper. Buried under bits of houses, boats, and household trash was . . . something.

"Thrush, what am I looking at?"

"I believe, Dread Master, that it is a moderately broken, single-person, demon-assisted spell bird. With some effort, you may yet rise above this rabble."

CHAPTER 54

ABOVE IT ALL

Truth had to fish around in the garbage heap to collect what was probably all the surviving pieces of a miniature spell bird. As best he could tell, it was some kind of kit project. The parts came together with simple fasteners, all the talismans were neatly marked where an unskilled assembler could line them up, and nothing in it was particularly unintuitive. And you certainly would be making this as a hobbyist. Truth couldn't imagine a single commercial purpose.

Every spell bird Truth had ever seen, from the smallest puddle-jumper to the huge, transcontinental geese, had one crucial thing in common—seats. You sat in the bird and directed it where to fly. Most of the actual flying was done by the bound demons, but there was still a human operator to set the bird's course. This hobbyist construction subverted that.

It was shaped like some sort of swallow. From what Truth could tell, it opened along the spine. You stepped into its legs, stuck your hands in its wings, and your head into its skull. Then the whole contraption sealed up around you. You would be within it—a swallow ready to leap into the air, flying swiftly along the mountain valleys, green mountains hiding gray lives beneath. Diving up into the pale blue sea of the sky.

Truth looked it over carefully. Some of the bolts had sheared off, screws were missing, and metal struts had bent. More damningly, some of those broad, simple talisman lines had been cut. Some clearly on purpose, others by accident. It wouldn't be a quick fix, but the construction had been designed for easy assembly by amateurs, and the all-important bound demon was still in place. It would provide most of the energy used for flying, as well as providing the bird "instincts" on how to move.

Truth got stuck in. He didn't have any better options at the moment, and there was something quietly satisfying about it. Here was a broken, complex talisman device. It didn't take a ton of skill to repair, but it took training, care, and attention. He cleaned away rust, smoothed out bent metal, and fished out new fasteners from the junk heap. Broken talisman lines were buffed out and redrawn. Bit by bit, he put the broken bird back together. It only took a few hours, and in the end? He had fixed it.

The swallow looked a bit raggedy. Some of the paper exterior had been torn, and there was no good way for him to make it whole. The paint was scuffed, but then, with black feathers, a white belly, and a ruddy face, swallows were never the most glamorous birds. Their beauty was in flight.

Truth climbed inside. The fit was snug, but then, he supposed it was meant to be. The bird gently tightened up around him, his fingers stretching flat, his stomach getting support. The bird suit closed around him. It was a little awkward but not terrible.

"If you will permit me, Master—you should leap strongly, then start flapping your wings. Let the demon guide you. This is its purpose, after all. It should feel like only a minor effort if you are working together properly."

Truth nodded at that, pushed off harder than ever a swallow managed, and leaped into the sky.

It was awkward at first. Truth was not comfortable shifting control of his movement to anything, but once he stopped trying to overrule the bound demon, it all just . . . worked. He moved his arms and flew upward. Over the houses and trees. He circled the town once, learning how a swallow moved. Its speedy dives and sharp curves. It didn't glide well, but it could corner hard. Above all, though, was the sense of freedom it offered. The ability to move with slight effort in any direction, all three dimensions available for him to play in.

The locals never seemed to look up. There was hardly any pull on his energy. Truth smiled broadly and started flying up the valley. He thought he could get addicted to this feeling.

"Thrush, you are responsible for navigation. Guide me to within forty kilometers of Happori Village. Bring us in on the mountainside, above the village. Keep us away from human settlements and habitations as best you can."

"I obey, Great One."

It was delightful. The duffel bag, now full to bursting with the addition of the heavy needler, was uncomfortably stuck between the skin of the bird and his own flesh, but it was an acceptable price for being able to fly. To be able to look down on the world like an angel or demon. Or God. It was different from flying in a commercial spell bird. When you went up in one of those, you were a passenger, traveling in a little bubble of isolation. This was *flying*. Feeling the air lift you and drop you and the wind try to push you around. Feeling it. Smelling it. Seeing it in marvelous detail as the bird's eyes could enlarge and focus on what you looked at.

Even in the remote north, you couldn't completely escape humanity. There were shacks out in the woods. Mines. Carriages and wagons dotted long macadam roads along winding mountain ridges. The steaming, smoking towers of alchemists and steel foundries rose like infernal mushrooms, spreading an ash spoor over the houses around them.

You couldn't see people, though. Not without getting low and really looking. They were too small and too wedded to their structures. Their little bubbles of shelter where they lived, worked, traveled. Loved, perhaps. Worshiped, certainly, for there was no trouble finding steeples. Pragerite churches studded the countryside. Attendance was booming, it seemed. He could hear the bells ring as the sun set. Calling the suddenly faithful to give that they might receive.

The mountains were littered with the artifacts of human artifice, without human affection. Carelessly scattered *whats*, waiting hopelessly for some cosmic eye to look for the *why*s. As for the *who*s? That would be too much to ask. You could infer that people did live there. You could infer something about how they lived, what they valued. But who they were? Never.

The ghosts of Jeon, of this world. Becoming less and less visible and tangible with every remove. No longer qualified to be ants. No longer a rat that could look up and climb. Just the time served, demonstrated in concrete and steel. Before the rains and the rust washed away even that.

It was very free, up in the sky, but very lonely, too. He could understand why birds flocked. You wouldn't want to face that big empty alone. Was that the secret? You only really saw what was on your level. Above and below might not even exist to you. So, you didn't worry about them or care about them. They only intruded into your consciousness when they became a problem.

He made it most of the way to Happori. It would only be about an hour farther in the morning, traveling on foot. He made a cold camp, ate some junk food, drank store-brand water, wrapped up in his tarp, snugged his scarf just right, and went to sleep.

To the System's immense shock, Truth dreamed. No horrible torment involved.

Truth found himself in a vast, rectangular room. A hall, really, or a temple with a single room. One end of the room was considerably higher than the other, as the floor was made up of shallow steps, each several paces wide, leading up to the top. Tall, heavy stone columns rose to a ceiling so high, he had to squint to see it. *This is a place of grandeur*, it seemed to say, *and you are very, very small*. Which was a pretty cocky take, Truth felt, given that it was still under construction.

Here and there, angels darted about, etching holy names into the walls, laying blessings, impressing the authority of God upon this place. Demons scurried about too, fish heads on bodies like a thousand centipedes carefully painting the walls with immense care. Each section of the wall was its own tiny masterpiece, but still part of the great work. There were bigger projects underway, too—headless cherubim with six wings covered in eyes and legs ending in calves' hooves lifted enormous braziers into place, set down vessels for baptism and purification, and hung chandeliers of stars. And overseeing it all was Etenesh.

She floated in the middle of the hall, strong with her God as Truth had never seen her before. Even more so than the duel. Her wings of black and gold beat slowly; her raptor-clawed hands and feet seemed ready to tear open the bellies of the slow or careless. Her eyes blazed ocher, in a face so beautiful, you wanted to break down and gratefully worship her. She was God's Consort, She who came to be, that all necessary things might come to be.

Truth looked at her in awe. Then snorted. "Figures my first dream is Etenesh setting up our house."

Her head snapped around, looking down and seeing him there. She sucked her teeth at him and rolled her eyes.

"Oh, my pretty man is here, is he? No, little figment, this is my dream. My man has plenty of his own."

"Haven't."

"Have so."

"Nah."

"Look, I'm working here. Everyone dreams. Everyone. Away with your nonsense."

"I don't. Never have."

"Nonsense."

"Bet you a birr?"

"You are a figment; you don't have a birr."

"Bet you a cheese-flavored plantain crisp?"

"Now, that's raising the stakes too high," Etenesh grumped. Which was adorable on her, but he could see the embodiment struggling. God's Consort *did not grump*. "Why are you here distracting me, little figment? Can't you see I'm working?"

"Yeah, but you are doing it wrong. I'd be a bad boyfriend"—she fixed him with a look and he looked right back—"if I didn't at least try to help."

"My HUSBAND, a man famously indifferent to interior decoration of the theological type, has opinions on sacred architecture, does he?"

"Yeah. All the proportions are off."

"They are not." She glared down at him. "They are becoming more and more perfect by the hour."

"Maybe if you are a God looking down, but as a rat looking up—"

YOU WILL STOP THAT AT ONCE! Etenesh didn't speak. The whole temple shuddered with her will. "Again and again and again, you call yourself a rat. A slum-rat. I hate it! I will not abide it! You are no rat!"

"Looks like the anger is touching you now. You might have laughed that off before. Now it hurts you, so you lash out."

Her ocher eyes narrowed. She murmured as though to herself. "A week ago, someone reached over my shoulder at lunch. They picked an apple off my tray. Marsa, one of the other guests at the hospital. I spun and rose before she could even bring the apple up to her mouth. I let the momentum carry the tray in my hands, the strength in my legs pushing up and forward. I smashed my lunch tray into her throat and would have killed her on the ground if they hadn't grabbed me. When I was calm again, they asked me, 'Why did you try to kill your friend?'"

Truth nodded. "And you told them, 'Now it's an apple; next time might be my ass. And she ain't my friend.'"

"Yes. Exactly that."

"So, here you are, making a very inefficiently heated, excessively public home for the two of us. With no hot tub, I note, or a big comfy bed."

She sighed, wings drooping slightly. "I just want our house to look good. It looks right from on high. And we will be seeing it from on high."

"But what about the rats? Will we be gods over a world of blind rats, so small we cannot even see them? Or will we make a world for people? People who can look up and see the wonders of your creation?"

"I said not to call yourself that! Why won't you see yourself as a human?"

"Because I don't think I have ever lived like a human. Whatever that is. I think I would like to be one before I become a God. It would be a shame to be stuck at King Rat."

"Well. That's fair enough. I'll think about it." She looked troubled.

"If it makes you feel any better, I've troubles too."

"Oh?"

"I realized I'm never going to have a threesome." Etenesh nearly fell out of the air.

"You what?!"

"Never going to have a threesome. Can't imagine you tolerating it for even one second, and I'm not going to run around on you. No threesomes, ever. Shame. A monogamous God. Ah, well. The one time I had sex was pretty great, so, you know, hope for the future and all that."

"This is your *big troubles*?" She was having a hard time holding on to the embodiment now. Truth's eyes gleamed with mischief.

"Well, that and I thought it was pretty fun to be a bird. A swallow. Pretty birds."

"Yes, quite lovely, especially when they are flocking. So, not the, you know, guerilla campaign against the most powerful man in the world—"

"No, that's going fine."

"You have bird troubles."

"More like bird solutions, but yes. Merkovah tell you I asked after you?"

"I haven't spoken with him in a week."

"Well. I did. Ask him. I think I'm waking up now."

"A figment of my dreams is waking up. Sure."

"Love you, my Etenesh."

"And I . . ." She paused, then smiled joyfully. "I can say it here! No one can hear us or hurt us here! I love you! I love you, Truth Medici! I count the days until the world ends and we can be together forever!"

Truth laughed himself awake.

And across the world, Etenesh woke from a late-afternoon nap. Crying and smiling.

CHAPTER 55

NOSE PRESSED AGAINST THE WINDOW

Truth knew that it was dangerous to make assumptions without enough information. Paranoid speculation, however, was different. He would explain why, but some bastard would take advantage. Right now, he had the horrible suspicion that the "good doctor" and his team at Happori were trying to minutely alter the rules of reality, creating a zone of complete control. Not straying too far from the established order. Just pushing. Slightly.

Two immediate possible interpretations leapt to mind—one, they wanted to alter local reality far enough that they could continue to benefit from stellar rays and keep their technology and apertures up and running after the collapse. If the world becomes too unreal, make a spot that is real enough to work. A new holy land for the Starbrite faithful, that they might work their miracles in the world to come. As backup plans went, it was top-notch. Really leveraging the current power and resources of the corp. Truth didn't quite buy it, though.

Starbrite was king of the world. It wouldn't benefit him more to become the God of it. He didn't want worship. He never appeared in public, never gave philanthropy, never pretended to care about people or nations. The *company* cared. They had endless programs to show just what good corporate citizens they were.

Your manager cared about you. Cared *so very much*. You think just anyone gets pizza in the break room once a month (access to the break room must be scheduled in advance, unpaid but mandatory pizza-party attendance for qualified associates, enthusiastic participation encouraged for those seeking promotion)?

But the man himself was practically mythical. What was the upside to staying on this planet after the collapse? Truth couldn't see any. There would be no more natural treasures or resources worth collecting. His path to power would be severed. He would have stripped all useful assets from the planet. Time to offload the cleanup to some sucker.

What if this village was a test bed for cracking the magical technology of the Black Ships? That researcher he murdered, the theosophist, thought the ships worked by knowing their reality so perfectly, they could manipulate it. What if that was just the first step? Perfectly know yourself and your environment, then make changes?

Alter the local rules to let them cross the shattering void between the protective embrace of the stellar eminences?

Truth looked through the green woods. A lot of spiky-looking trees. He would guess . . . pine? Or some kind of evergreen? They didn't grow in Harban; that much he knew. And above them, the sun. Was that grandee's face clouded by more than atmosphere? He couldn't tell. He got back in motion, slower now, no longer worried about speed and purely focused on concealment and minimizing his energy expenditure. It was going to be a long day.

The woods slowly revealed its hidden dangers. The outermost ring consisted of surveillance in the form of spell birds and beasts. Some talisman creations, others were witch-crafted or corpse puppets moving with an uncanny semblance of true life. Deeper in, he found arrays for detection. More arrays to deploy barriers or attack spells. Golems hidden in trees. Summoning rings. Banishments. Spell bowls tailored for a variety of needs. Leaves sprayed with subtle poisons that gave unsubtle results.

Truth came across a deer trail winding through a small stand of thorn bushes. The bushes had been alchemically toughened. The trail had no less than three explosive mines hidden on it. People with time, who genuinely cared about their work and had the budget to make things happen, had put years of effort into making the forest a nightmare for infiltrators.

Truth was genuinely impressed. Pissed off, frustrated, but impressed. It took him the whole morning to get to the edge of the village. Six hours to go twenty kilometers, and it tired him out more than sprinting down the highway. He almost laughed with relief when he finally found a physical patrol. Then he stopped laughing when he realized the path the patrol was following had a "unique" feature. The parts of the trail just ahead and to the sides of the patrol would be subjected to a barrage of active-detection magic and sweeps by mini-golems. The area directly behind them would see small explosive arrays arming for a few minutes before sinking back into inactivity.

The patrol wasn't there to find people. They were there to invite an ambush, then counter-ambush. Say what you like about the PMC, they weren't soft. Truth gave the patrol plenty of room. He had thought about inserting into the back of the squad, letting Incisive and the Blessings of the Silent Forest help him blend in, but no. That was just silly. They would have taken steps to prevent that.

When he finally breached the external defenses and got within eyesight of the village, he took a moment to look it over. The point of coming from higher up the mountain was to give an elevated view, after all. The village was patently phony, in the way that planned developments always are. Too clean, too samey. All one-floor ranch-style homes with big sloping roofs to shed the snow. Mass-produced houses in one of four approved colors, built around backyards and "informal living spaces" in one of four approved styles.

No streets, he noticed. Wide sidewalks everywhere but no streets. It was quite densely built. You could walk everywhere, and if something heavy needed to come in? It would get flown in and then carried to your house on a floating platform.

Nobody living in this village was a nobody, after all. They had the credits to cover whatever they wanted. Especially since the System helped temper those wants to a more reasonable, productive level.

Lots of very pretty people having bland conversations over garden fences, keeping house, keeping fit. Waiting for their most important person to come home. However long that might take. They would run up, wagging their tails and making a happy noise, letting their people know just how happy they were to see them.

Truth despised himself for seeing the appeal. The utter safety of it. Everything was comfortable. Everything was just the way you liked it, within the established, written-down and published rules of good taste. And if you wanted something a little spicier, a shot of espresso after all the milk tea, you could have that too. Behind closed and soundproofed doors. And the human cost? The lives burned to make this artificial world possible? Don't worry about it. Really. Don't.

The staff had more important things to worry about, like work, or cocktails with the Cavendishes. Yivonne is always such a hoot. Someone did a great job turning her into the perfect hostess. You could upgrade your lover to be just as good, of course. Wouldn't even have to press a button. A thought would be enough, and the System would "adjust" as needed. Credits permitting.

It was more than just the company-issued lovers, of course. It was the houses and yards and picket fences and the airlifted food, booze, medicine, entertainment. It was the thousands of laborers grinding away invisibly to keep this village of a few hundred aloft. The gray-clothed, gray-souled factory laborers. Factory farmers. People who are not allowed to have things like clean air or clean food. People living in seventy-story apartment blocks, in rooms more like an insect nest, trying to eke out an invisible existence between Heaven and Hell before they died. Living to make sure Hwang had a new novelty tie every time he hosted one of his famous patio parties.

Truth closed his eyes and willed his thoughts away from the village. The cruelty was the point. He had known that since he lived in the slums. Nothing new there, and he was unlikely to catch his target at home. He forced his attention over to the research institute, then closed his eyes again.

He had a better imagination now. The books, the travel, the people, they really had broadened his mind. He understood what he was seeing now. The true arrogance and cruelty weren't in the village. They were in the flower facing the sky.

It was something like a lotus or pond lily. Beautiful colored petals unfolding in long, raised spikes. The buildings were scattered across the petals. From this height and angle, he could just about see them. No bridges—you moved from place to place on little flying clouds, or swarms of butterflies, or other dreams and whimsies. If the village was a mortal dream, this was the playground of gods. An immortal garden, floating above the world.

The umbilical vine connecting the flower to the mountain was purely decorative. You could see it was fragile, ready to fall away at any moment. Not that the flower could fall—never that. It was just a constant reminder to those in the village. A human's path to immortality is fragile. The heavens and the earth are eternally separate, and the existence of the path is a gift from those above, not the birthright of those below.

You could live in the village, already a hallucination of maddened urban desire, and live as well as a human could hope to. Or you could be one of the elect, joyful in their work in the land of the gods. No wonder most of the researchers and staff spent all their time on the campus. Truth wouldn't want to descend to the village either. Living below, looking up at a tangible Heaven, knowing you weren't good enough to even visit. A life in the mud, existing to satisfy an artificial nostalgia for mortal existence. Not even something valuable for itself. Lives reduced to props, stand-ins for things that never existed.

He assembled the heavy needler, activating the telescopic-vision talisman carved along its back. Sighting down onto the flower platform. With Graeme's Arrow, it was technically in range. He didn't for a moment imagine it was unprotected from sniper fire. He watched a pair of researchers board a hummingbird the size of a chariot and flutter to a different petal. They looked like they were really into their discussion. He put his reticule right over the head of the one on the left. Boring-looking guy. Skinny, black hair, animated face, and he made sharp gestures with his hands.

You wouldn't look twice at him if you ran into him at the convenience store. Not really the stuff of immortal dreams. Unless you were the "lover" at home, waiting by the door.

Truth spent the afternoon shifting around on the mountainside, learning the rhythms of the place. Trying to nail down patrol routes. Checking the contents of the information he had received against what he was actually seeing. It was holding up pretty well. He hadn't been expecting much, so *Only a bit wrong so far* was quite acceptable. No sign of the target or hidden powerhouses so far, but that was also expected. Wouldn't be very hidden if they were out in the open.

The afternoon shifted to evening. A few people descended, returning home for . . . pot roast? Curry? A kiss, a promise, and a healthy green salad? The petals slowly began glowing. No longer reflecting the sun, they made their own brilliance. Lights switched on in the laboratories, and the hard work of discovery continued. The lower petals blocked the light for those living below, he noticed. How thoughtful.

It got cold in the mountains in the spring. Truth just sat, watching. Moving now and then to get a different view. Dew condensed on him, dripping down, soaking his cotton clothes. Birds went quiet, but the insects were noisy enough on their own. The PMC patrols didn't let up either. There were an implausible number of owls and bats flying around. Subtlety had a place there but a limited one. If his target had ever come out in the open, he hadn't spotted him.

Just before dawn, Truth exited the secured perimeter. It was much faster now, having plotted his routes and figured out how to evade the thousands of watchful eyes. He would spend a few hours sleeping, hidden under pine boughs. Then, refreshed, he would break in. One way or another, he would topple the heavens. Just a matter of finding where to stick the lever.

CHAPTER 56

HAPPY WIFE, HAPPY LIFE

Truth got up a little before dawn and made his way back toward the village. The information he got from Merkovah had listed Dr. Borges' address and included pictures of the house. Truth thought he would start his hunt there. Not because he expected to catch Borges at home. He was never going to be that lucky. His hope was more pedestrian—that Borges would fail to practice impeccable security hygiene and would take some of his work home. Something that would give him a lead on where on the research campus was actually located.

Besides, he had come up with a backup plan during the night. If he could make it work. If it was even possible in the first place.

Less of a plan and more of a strategy.

A pretty sophisticated idea.

It was *an* idea.

A borderline-insane idea, lacking the qualifications even to be a stupid idea.

It was also the best idea he had, so . . .

He picked his way through the surveillance net around the village. His preparation the day before had sped things up considerably, but that was only in comparison to the day before that. It was slow, painful going. The PMC was depressingly competent. They had changed the patrol routes of humans, golems, witchcraft creations, animal puppets, spell birds, eye-spies, and floating curses. The only mercy was that the overwhelming majority of them were Level One and Two.

It was a cost-effectiveness thing, Truth knew. No concealment system was perfect. Everything showed a hole at some point. It might be tiny and only there for a minute. Perhaps it was allowing a trace of smell to escape or a shimmer as you moved across a bush. The soft sound of grass brushing against legs. All you needed was *something* to catch a hint of a trace. It was much, much cheaper to flood an area with small, low-level things than a few high-level things. They could be kept moving around in the field at negligible cost.

Sooner or later, they would catch something. Then the net closed in. More specialized, powerful hunters began their sweeps. Ninety-nine times out of a hundred, they would find it. Even if it were just a tiny field mouse, they would find it.

Truth had always told himself he was nothing special. Just another slumrat trying to make good. Well, for today at least, he was a one-in-a-billion slumrat. A big fat chance like one percent was too juicy to pass up.

It took time to pierce the surveillance cordon, but it was manageable. Soon he was on the edge of a backyard on the village fringe, and he had to make a choice. He could try to go in full unnoticeability mode, but the village was coated in recording talismans and those unnatural "birds." He reckoned it was manageable—the population density was low and most of the spells were passive, low-level, and not targeted at him. The draw on Incisive and the Blessing would not be *too* excessive. However, they would burn through his energy significantly faster than he could replenish it.

Going around with an assumed identity would be much, much easier on his energy, so long as it was a plausible one. His concern was that the surveillance system would be based on a whitelist. Not like there were any strangers that came to the village. It wouldn't be too crazy to command your spells to report anyone without a Starbrite sigil directly to security. And there wasn't really any good way to test his theory.

He hesitated a long minute and decided he would have to split the difference. Go in as unnoticeable as he could manage, try to stay out of sight to reduce draw, and if he saw someone whose identity he could assume, he would do so. He was about to hop over the fence when he spotted the recording talisman aimed at the backyard. Cheap little thing, mass-produced on an assembly line. It would barely put out the energy of a Level One spell. A Starbrite product, naturally, through a subsidiary that owned 35% of another company and had 100% functional control of it.

Truth slid his eyes over to the next yard. Same exact talisman, same exact placement. Must be a standard part of the security system for each house. Well. At least the fence and yard weren't warded?

He vaulted the fence and started making his way toward Borges' place. He would stick to the backyards. Fooling one Level One talisman at a time was better than trying to evade everything facing the street. He had had a depressing amount of practice doing this since he returned to Jeon.

There were occasional people in the backyards, watering flowers, mowing micrometers off grass already mowed to unnatural evenness. Everyone was smiling or at least looking content. "Lovers" going through their programmed routines while their leaseholders were at work. Not owners, of course. Starbrite wasn't in the slave trade. This was nothing more than the exchange of labor for money. And what could be wrong with that?

It occurred to Truth, watching a blandly pretty woman tanning in her backyard, that these days, there would probably be a queue down the street to replace her. She was fed, protected, sheltered, far away from terrorism or anarchy. She was compelled to be happy and content with her lot. Probably.

He had never gotten the chance to find out firsthand. He had spent all his pay on elixirs and those blasted, thrice-cursed "Friends and Family points." And didn't he just PRAY he got his hands on the bastard who had thought them up.

Not that he didn't love Etenesh. He absolutely did. But looking over the engineered "perfection" of the lady on the lounge chair, he couldn't help feeling like he had missed out. At the very least, he missed out on the opportunity to experiment. To test without risking hurting someone he cared about.

<<*Told you the sadism was always there. The need to prove your superiority, the need for control. Not something terrible. Lots worse traits to have. God knows so many of these animals deserve it. But you need to be aware of it. Take control of it, not let it control you. Letting Etenesh take the lead at times was like getting stabbed for you. Not a healthy mindset.*>>

Yeah. Not the time, but yeah.

He kept moving. The same bland houses with bland decoration. He did occasionally break in, just to learn the security system. Nothing special on its own—a high degree of security compared to most homes, but nothing that wasn't available off the shelf. Well. Available off the shelf a few years before. Now? Maybe not so much.

The only thing that gave him pause was the whitelist. The concept was alarmingly simple—if you were in the house and not on the whitelist, an alert sounded. If the alert wasn't muted, an alarm went off. Only someone on the whitelist could mute the alert and provide temporary access to the house. Truth wasn't particularly concerned; the spells were still roughly Level One in power output, but it suggested a mindset. Truth was certain Borges had more security at his place.

He took a quick look around the home he had broken into. Truth was back out the door before it had finished closing from his entry. There was just nothing there. A whole suburban home full of nothing anyone could care about. Expensive nothing. A big scryball setup. Big sofas, big bed, big glass windows looking out over the yard. Nothing that you couldn't buy in bulk from a catalog. Not even a diploma on a wall. Just a couple of pictures of a man and a woman pressing their heads together and smiling happily for the camera. It looked like the stock pictures in frames you could buy at the store, but worse.

It would be easy to assume this identity. He would just smile and pretend he wasn't there at all. No one would ever spot the difference. Assuming that it was the man who was the Starbrite employee, of course. He really couldn't tell.

Press on, press on. He made his way steadily to Borges' place. When he had to cross a wide sidewalk, he did so in the air. It was an easy jump up to the roof, then a quick sprint to the ridge line, Abner's Amble, push hard, and across he went. Harder to blend but less time visible. He figured he came out roughly ahead on the trade.

Borges' place was depressingly identical to everyone else's. The largest layout of the four approved house models, sitting at the very back of a dead-end street. Looked normal. Truth was certain that the neighboring homes were packed with PMC hitters and every sort of unpleasantness. The quality of talismans got much higher, too— those backyard recording talismans were now pumping out Level Three energy. Very expensive. Not something mass-market at all. The lonely lovers on the street all had a certain similarity to them. A glassiness of eye that suggested heavy glamors and intensive mental conditioning. A special street, then, for special people. When they could be bothered to come home.

Truth got to work on the back door. He could hear someone moving around inside the house. A peek through the window confirmed that it was Borges' lover. Truth had never bothered to learn her name. She was Level Two and utterly, utterly incapable of harming Borges in any intentional way. It would be slightly more draining moving around her, but nothing terrible. Less than the surveillance system demanded of him.

It was intensely awkward, therefore, when she came out onto the back porch with two glasses of lemonade.

She stood there, looking around like she was expecting to find someone. Truth froze, wondering how he had been spotted, only relaxing when she marched up to the fence and said, "Hi, Tom!"

Tom, the next-door neighbor, had been crouched behind a flowering bush, doing some kind of gardening work. Partially hidden, though there was nowhere to really hide in these yards.

"Oh, hi, Maysi." His voice was full of forced jocularity, but Truth could see the eyes of a man wanting to run.

"I saw you working out here, and thought I would bring you some of my famous lemonade. Here, drink up."

"Oh, now, you didn't have to do that. Really," Tom said, backing away a little, waving away the glass.

"I know. It just seemed like the least I could do. Or something I could do. It really is good lemonade, you know." Her voice went quiet.

"Please . . ."

"I have always loved you, Tom. I want to have sex with you. Right now. Let's cheat on your wife together. I know you want to cheat on your wife with me, Tom."

"No." He barely breathed the word out before he collapsed. His body started going into seizures. He was crying, soundlessly, as he tore at the immaculate grass. The tendons rose under his skin as convulsions of pain ripped through him. Maysi started crying too.

"I'm sorry. I'm so sorry. I can only remember them when I hurt someone. There is another way, but I can't remember what it is. Only that trying to think about it makes me want to kill myself. So, I have to hurt you. I'm sorry. But I can't forget Sarah. Or our son." Maysi's tears dripped over a smile now. "She is so beautiful, Tom. You can't imagine how beautiful she looked holding our newborn son. Our beautiful boy. Or how she looked at sunsets, or walking between the stalls in the market. She is so sweet. So, so sweet. And he only lets me remember her when I hurt someone."

Tom was trying to say something, mouth something. Begging.

"Just . . . a little longer. I'm sorry. But just a little longer. I'm starting to forget things. I couldn't remember Al's fifth birthday last time. I don't want to forget anything else. So, please, just a little longer. I promise it will be the best sex you ever had."

She sobbed a little as Tom's convulsions got worse. "Just a little longer, then you will get better and forget this happened. Mostly forget. You are remembering the pain, just like me. I'm sorry. I just can't forget anything more. I'm sorry. I promise I will hurt Sonya tomorrow or Paul. You can rest then, okay? You can rest then. We'll both forget for a while. I promise. I promise."

She kept him in agony for an hour, deliberately tripping his enchantments, turning them against him over and over and over, until her own enchantments kicked in. Truth could see the light drain out of her eyes as she picked up the two untouched glasses of lemonade and turned back toward the house.

"Whoops! I had so much fun chatting, I lost track of time. I have yoga with the girls, then it's straight into my spin class. You have a great afternoon, now, Tom." Truth followed her into the house. He'd had plenty of time to get on the list.

CHAPTER 57

HOMEMAKER

Truth felt the security systems brush past him, like walking through cobwebs. Knowing that somewhere in them, spiders still hunted. His work cracking the system, his own spells, and the seeming "invitation in" by the lady of the house was enough to get them to look the other way. For now.

Borges' house was curiously decorated. Superficially, it was the same suburban blandeur—imposing sofas in grays and browns, a big scryball, what was clearly intended to be *his* recliner, with a sparkling-clean ashtray next to a table lighter and fully stocked humidor. There were fleece-lined leather slippers under the coat hooks by the door. The walls were painted a light olive. One lamp had pressed leaves in wax paper for a shade. So far, so dull.

Maysi went upstairs to get changed. Truth stayed on the ground floor, trying to figure out what was bothering him about what he was seeing. The sofas and recliners and slippers were all quite ordinary. Nothing special about the cigars or lighters or any of the dull brags of suburban success.

His eyes drifted to the bookshelves. All perfectly dust-free, naturally, and with perfectly undamaged covers. He would be shocked if anyone had read them. The titles all sounded like things that got put in the front window of bookstores, then returned to the publisher a month later.

There were little knickknacks scattered around the shelves. A glass paperweight, geometric shapes cast in bronze, things like that. Maybe they had some meaning or emotional importance to Borges. He couldn't imagine why. There was a coin in a clear plastic case. Truth picked it up and examined it. The case was carved and polished to make the coin look bigger when you held the box up to your eye. You could get a quite-close look at all the sides of the coin.

On one side of the coin was a regal face wearing a crown. Words in some language Truth didn't recognize, in an alphabet he had never seen, circled the face. The edges weren't quite even, the coin a little too lumpy to be perfectly circular. The back was a tiered platform, clearly huge, with tiny people around it. There were three stars hanging in the sky above the platform. Symbolizing what, he didn't know. A funny trinket, but Truth couldn't imagine what its relevance to anything was. Though he couldn't quite bring himself to put it down.

The king's face was handsome. Strong. He was a good king. The writing was neat and formal, but it flowed elegantly. Someone had done really good work there.

The edges of the coin must have deformed with time. The platform on the back only grew more impressive the longer he looked at it. The tiny people gathered around it in worship.

At the top, they would be making an offering. Worshiping the stars above. The king was no doubt up there, leading the sacrifices. Just what, or who, would be going under the knife? Feeling the terror rise to such a peak that it was no different than ecstasy. Losing themselves in the void between life and death, orgasm and extinction, until they tipped over and the gods took their due.

It wasn't right for this coin to be left around like this. It was . . . blasphemous. It was too precious and special. Truth felt a pressure building in his head. There was an increasing dissonance. The coin seemed to get blurry in his hand, or maybe it was his eyes that were going. The coin seemed to eclipse the room in his perception as he fought to wrestle it down.

His hands smoked furiously, his whole body steaming. He wasn't worshiping at the foot of the ziggurat, a word he had never known before today. He wasn't the priest or the sacrifice. He snarled silently, forcing the coin to be a coin.

He was Truth Medici, and whatever he was, he was no king's slave. He wrestled to put the box down, still unable to fling it away from him. In a moment of desperation, he tried casting Cup and Knife. He could feel the spell raging at the *wrongness* of the coin, but he couldn't figure out how to use it. How do you "correct" something like that? Peeling back one finger at a time, he managed to drop the thing on the floor.

Truth collapsed on the sofa, sweating. Gasping for air. He could smell that place, whatever it was. He could hear the chanting, the screams of the sacrifice as they balanced on the limit of experience. The holy born from the profane, finding the ecstatic spirit in the split chest of the sacrifice.

He could feel the awesome majesty of the king. His rule was blessed by the gods above and venerated by the people below. A living god, bestowed with the right to determine life and death, to divide the earth and the waters, to make all laws that bound those who dwelt between Heaven and Hell.

The king's harem was filled with women from every corner of his dominion and from every nation begging his benevolence. His storehouses groaned with gold, silk, and amber. Precious perfumes and oils were his, as were the rarest fruits and nuts. All earthly glory was his due, confirmed by the heavens above.

Truth shuddered, feeling the coin tugging at him. He heard Maysi walking down the stairs. She looked nice in her yoga gear. Hair up in a ponytail, everything form-fitting. She looked pleased to go get a workout in her cute little white sneakers. She didn't look like someone who tortured her neighbors. Right now, he supposed, she wasn't.

Truth could easily understand why Borges kept such a cursed coin in the living room. The message wasn't subtle. But it didn't explain by itself the wrongness and the power of the thing.

Maysi went out, leaving Truth in the house alone. He didn't know how long he had before the spells marked him as an intruder. Probably not very long. He could keep hidden from them, but it would be tiring. He had to get up off the sofa and get to work. It seemed mildly impossible. Deep breath. Impossible or not, he had to do it. He heaved himself to his feet and got searching.

The basement was cleaner than he expected. The floor was sealed concrete. The walls were smooth and painted white. There were storage boxes of old clothes, hiking gear, and skis. A punching bag was hung from the ceiling next to a dusty bench and rack of dumbbells. It all looked in mint condition, if in need of a wash.

The wine rack saw heavier use. It was almost fully loaded. There was a high table next to the rack with a decanter and a pair of glasses set on it. Perhaps Borges had tastings down there. Truth didn't know much about wine, hardly anything, actually, but at a guess, these were expensive. A couple of trophies had been stood on their bottoms, proudly displaying their labels to the room. He gave them a second look, then turned away, shuddering. The labels were in the same language as the writing on the coin.

He tried not to speculate. Too soon to speculate—he needed more information. Still, he was steaming so much, it looked like he was being prepared for a light supper. It seemed that whatever this was, it was not in conformity with "orthodoxy." Truth smiled a little at that. His mad idea of a backup plan was looking a little more plausible.

The rest of the house was more of the same. Bland, safe, suburban, sprinkled with little artifacts from that strange world. There was a home office, but a careful search revealed that it was used exclusively by Maysi to organize parties and the very import- ant activities of the village—the Gardening Committee, the Festival Committee, and the Running Club. The den saw a little more use—more cigars, decanters of whisky, comfortable club chairs, and books that looked like they actually had been read. Most nonfiction, historical stuff. Some books on spell theory. Those were unread. He couldn't understand why until he saw Borges listed as the author.

Next to one of the club chairs was a volume of an encyclopedia. Truth opened it, letting the book fall open wherever it wished. It opened to an entry about some ancient country called Uqbar, long lost, or perhaps still existing on another planet. Or possibly existing on this planet before the most recent human settlement. Its location was precisely set between mountains, rivers, and the ocean, for all that its existence was ambiguous. The entry was quite long, giving a detailed description of its history (bloody), its politics (distressingly simple), and its philosophy (endlessly complex). It felt . . . true.

Truth dropped the encyclopedia back on the side table and glared at it. He had noticed the way his hand was steaming when he picked it up. Was this house a testbed for the reality alteration going on around the whole village? Something more dramatic than the invisible alterations made before? Truth wondered if whatever Borges had done to Maysi was part of it. His first thought was that it was a deliberately repressed memory or perhaps an implanted one. There were no wife and children waiting for Maysi, but when she hurt someone deliberately, she believed that she had once been happy and loved.

It didn't quite feel right. Not after searching the house. The house was boring. It lacked any of the paraphernalia he associated with the recreationally cruel. Other than the "artifacts," it seemed to lack anything at all that smacked of creativity or imagination. Which couldn't possibly be right. Borges was one of the leading researchers of the age. He had to be some kind of creative.

Truth could vividly remember being beneath the ziggurat. He could remember the fear and worship the king tried to press into him. He could remember the cries of the sacrifice and the smell of that strange earth. The memories were slipping away, their vividness fading, but he could still remember Uqbar.

What if the doctor wasn't trying to torture Maysi?

He spun the idea around in horrified fascination. What if the doctor was trying to show Maysi a better life, a life of freedom and joy in another world? Such memories would come at a cost, of course. Pain. Sacrifice. Proving your strength by making another pay the price for your happiness.

The king didn't look much like Borges, but that didn't mean anything. Maybe it was what Borges thought he should look like. Or maybe it wasn't Borges at all, and the king was Starbrite or the current CEO, or some designated puppet. It would seem to line up with how the System Astrologica liked to work. Create your own chains, and be grateful to serve.

He searched through the house again, cataloging the artifacts and hunting for anything that might undercut his theory. He didn't find so much as a skin mag shoved under the mattress or a little vial of Mother's Helper in the vanity.

If Borges had more colorful sins, he kept them at the research center. If Maysi did—but she couldn't, of course. Starbrite did fine work when it made custom goods for its top employees. And Borges was a proud B-Tier elite. Maysi would have been delivered with a certificate of authenticity and a comprehensive warranty.

Truth laughed at the audacity of it. The researcher he had murdered thought the Black Ships could move through the void because they perfectly understood their environment, which gave them power over it. That junior was stuck in an anonymous suburban office park, licking copper cubes. He didn't get his own research center on a giant flower with a complete village attached. He thought too small. Borges? He thought big. Big enough to move Starbrite.

It wasn't just about building an escape ship for Starbrite. It was about everyone. Borges would do his part to get the boss off-planet safely, then afterward? This planet would have the God-King it always deserved. Worshiping the God it always deserved. The planet would wait for the millennia to pass, worshiping its king, consecrated by Starbrite. And if they weren't able to capture the cosmic rays anymore? No problem. There was another source of power available. Sacrifice. And he would have billions of people to choose from.

CHAPTER 58

WHATEVER THE BOSS SAYS IT IS

Truth sat in Borges' living room. The deadly coin was safely trapped under one of the doctor's slippers, waiting to be scooped up and returned to the shelf. He needed a moment. It was all kind of a lot. He was gently steaming just sitting there. Sooner or later, the alarm spells would start getting cranky. Probably sooner, but he still needed a minute. Just to pull himself together.

He had experienced flashes of unreality before. That sense that reality was a soap bubble, a thin film of being, and humans, Truth in particular, just a smear of color on its side. Soon, the bubble would pop, for one reason or another.

Once in a great while, you could see through the bubble. See some little piece of the world beyond, maybe. His understanding of what he saw was essentially nonexistent. The notion that you could paint your own soap bubble, paint it so convincingly that it became the "real" soap bubble when the old one collapsed . . . he could hardly conceive of it.

Of course, this meant that his *barely an incoherent idea, in no way a viable primary plan* plan just got moved into the *urgent action* pile. He would have to do some experimentation later tonight. He stood. There was a brief moment of vertigo. Then he scooped up the slipper and got to tidying up.

Time to go and see what else could be done. Borges wasn't going to kill himself, and it was quite clear just how valuable he was to Starbrite. Which meant that Truth would have to spend serious time considering his exit strategy, too.

Nobody mentioned how tiring international terrorism was. It just wore him out.

Truth started making his way over toward the giant flower that held the research center, drifting from hedge to tree, hiding behind the corner of houses, and, when absolutely necessary, walking right down the middle of the sidewalk. Just a maintenance tech on his way to the next job. He could feel the draw on the Scales like a soft but constant tugging. A constant drag on his energy and attention. Making him sacrifice the energy within him.

The image of the ziggurat stuck with Truth. The sacrifice of people to fuel magic. It wasn't a novel concept. It was how magic worked at its core. You made a "sacrifice" of some accumulated magic within you, magic you could have focused on propelling your cultivation or some other purpose, and you burned it up. You forced it into a form the cosmic rays that flooded the universe could interact with. The rays then created the outsized result you were looking for. The main power came from that stellar energy—the indiscriminate blessings of the heavenly demons and, ultimately, God. Remove God's blessing from a world; if he simply dropped you from his eyes, the stellar rays would ignore you too.

The magic in you was a sacrifice, and it was leverage. Like a small man throwing a bigger one over his shoulder—you needed *some* muscle, but the real secret was leverage. And the energy didn't have to be your energy to work. The universe was indifferent to where the power came from. The demon-summoning terrorist attack Truth had stopped in Siphios was an example. All those murdered people fueling the portal.

Truth watched a group of joggers go past, keeping fit. One-two-one-two, chatting about nothing as they ran through suburban streets in workout clothes worth more than Truth had earned in six months when he was a kid.

What do you do with all that internal magic if there is no external magic to interact with? What do you do when there is no way to refill, naturally, the internal magic? Use external magic for both.

The death of humans triggered a release of energy that magic could interact with. Sacrifice on a grand scale to bring the rains and drive away floods. Humans breed rapidly under the right circumstances. Keep agriculture going, and you will soon have a surplus of lives. Kings and priests could spend the extra on useful projects like wars or domestic stability. Sacrificing a few to keep the masses content and the elite in comfort and power.

He skulked his way closer and closer to the base station for the research center. Not a very big building—it was there for cargo handling and people coming to and from the village. There was a security office attached to it for the PMC, and a workshop for the golems and other security devices that flooded the area around the village.

He could probably break into the workshop. It wouldn't be too hard to assume a functional identity in there. Hell, if he had stayed in the PMC, he could imagine himself transferred there, protecting one of the researchers. And he would need some kind of assumed identity. The research station made the village look unprotected by comparison.

Birds perched all over the long, winding vine, flocking in vast swarms or swooping "randomly" about. All hunting for the very smallest bugs that tried to sneak their way in. Wards, complex, multilayered, and powerful, carefully coated the entirety of the flower. Beyond the wards were the endless enchantments that stabilized and maintained the whole structure. A dizzying multitude of systems, all working together.

He couldn't grasp the entirety of it. He wasn't even willing to guess what it all was for. The stem wasn't holding up the flower; that much he could see. He had the vague image of the flower absorbing energy and transmitting it down the stem to be stored in underground roots until it was needed. But he had no real basis for thinking that.

As for more-active, less-discreet defenses than golems and the PMC? Oh, yes, there were plenty of those. Banks of heavy needlers, explosive launchers, nozzles whose purposes he didn't care to test, traceries of enchantments forming subtle, hair-raising networks, all combining to promise death to entire armies if they dared make an assault. A promise Truth absolutely believed would be fulfilled.

He would not be attempting a frontal assault. Or any kind of assault. Not if he could help it. He found a house with a view of the maintenance depot. His plan to break in and do a light stakeout was immediately derailed by the surveillance system on the house. Though it was visually the same as other basic-tier recording talismans, Truth felt a sudden hard drain on his energy as he approached the back door.

After retreating and a more-careful examination, he discovered that the recording talisman was actually bait. The whole back of the house was coated in counter-infiltration and high-power surveillance tools. Truth thought he could be considered both experienced and careful, but he had to admit he never would have spotted them without Incisive and his Blessings.

It was a dilemma. He needed more information. Surveillance was the lowest-risk solution. But the paranoid bastard that designed this house would have made a point of plugging any and all gaps. Truth was privately certain that anyone setting foot into this house, on a whitelist or not, would soon regret their life. He had to assume that other houses with views of the station were likewise rigged. A tiny cost compared to the rest of the installation.

Truth felt incredibly stifled. He choked down the urge to do something rash. That was what the designer wanted, and he would be damned before he gave them the satisfaction.

Truth dithered for a few minutes but eventually concluded that the defenders had won this round. He retreated. He had some very poor ideas to experiment with, some junk food to eat, and then an early bedtime. Tomorrow was going to be another busy day.

He had barely reached the edge of the village before he remembered he also had to check out his escape routes, not just from the village but the whole damn stretch of mountains it was in. Swearing silently, he got to work.

Truth awoke, feeling uncharacteristically sorry for himself. His snacks had run out, the opposition was alarmingly competent, he missed Etenesh and Jember, the ground was uncomfortable to sleep on, and he was pretty sure he smelled. Also, nobody likes digging a hole and taking a crap in it. It's just not a good time. He did feel damn smart to have bought toilet paper.

Had he stolen it? He couldn't remember. Not really important. Having hosted his pity party for as long as he would tolerate, Truth started the business of the day. He spent a few hours working on his insane idea, scouted around some more, and then spent a few more hours on the borderline suicidal scheme.

After a hearty lunch of water from a mountain stream, he set off. He ran fast, well outside the village security perimeter. It felt wonderful to finally stretch and move like he knew he could, even with the heavy needler strapped to his back.

Truth made his way to the opposite side of the village from where he had his cache and started his infiltration. He hadn't scouted this area as much, so it was slow going. He chose to think of it as a dual-purpose activity. Patience was a key virtue, one supported by a positive mindset. He kept at it, just to the point where he could make out the flower holding the research institute. Carefully, he climbed a tree and got a better view.

Using the tree as a brace, he popped up the magnifying sight on the talisman and found a comparatively empty patch of the underside of a petal. *Comparative* being the key word, as it was still crawling with wards and more-esoteric enchantments whose purpose he didn't care to guess.

He put the distance at about five kilometers. Given the size of the target, precision was more or less irrelevant. He laid a careful series of spells on the needle. First Graeme's Arrow, then Incisive, then Tool to make sure everything went as perfectly as it could.

Graeme's Arrow was still a struggle to cast; it seemed to buck around in his mind, not willing to put up with being a temporary addition to his arsenal. Silly to say a spell "wanted" something, but these days, he was less and less confident in "common sense."

He gently activated the talisman, loosing the needle between the beats of his heart. Even for him, five kilometers was a long, long way to send a needle. Big target, though. That always helped. The needle whipped between the trees almost silently, a faint ripping noise marking its passage. Truth couldn't silence it, but he could make it part the air smoothly. It raced across the air in an almost-flat line, the whole point of shooting from the side of the mountain, and plinked off the wards. Truth was watching very closely, and as best he could tell, the needle just smooshed into the wards and dropped straight down.

Disappointing, if expected. Now was the important part—the reaction. *One, two, three* . . . As quickly and silently as he could, Truth shifted a kilometer away from his firing position. He dove into the prepared blind, keeping his eyes focused on the patch of wood he had just left. He was somewhere between *twenty-nine* and *thirty* when the birds came swarming in. Subtlety be damned, apparently. They converged from all directions, some flying hard toward the point of origin, others hunting as they went.

Truth didn't stir out of his blind for the rest of the day. The woods were being aggressively swept, and indeed, his blind was "confirmed empty" six times. Annoying but, again, expected. Of course they would log the impact, trace the direction of impact, measure the damage the impact caused, determine it was not natural, and order a search. It would have been the work of a fraction of a second for a genuine spirit of intellect. It was boring to wait so long, but it was necessary, so he did it.

Once the search died down, driven by a profound sense of malice over the exhaustion the oppressively robust defenses of the research station had caused him to suffer the last few days, he returned to precisely the same spot on precisely the same tree and lined up the heavy needler at precisely the same spot he had shot at before. This time, however, he loaded in one of his test needles. It had taken ages to make, but it was the point of all this. It would be nice to get it right on the first try. Breathe in, out, in, out, hold, wait for that double thump—loose.

CHAPTER 59

CATHARSIS

The dim twilight was no hindrance to Truth—he watched the needle fly toward the wards through the magnifier. It hit the ward . . . and went straight through. He lost track of it there, but he didn't see anything bouncing off the flesh of the flower. He bounced out of his spot as soon as the needle vanished, this time running three kilometers away before going to ground. He waited, watching, holding his breath. Every nerve strained.

The trees rustled. Were the birds coming? Or was it the wind? The cries of animals, the chirping insects—was the net closing in? He forced himself to be still and watch. He forced himself to breathe, long and slow. Forcing himself to relax and wait. An hour later, there was still no reaction. Nor an hour after that. He crept closer. The woods were lousy with the surveillance critters, but not many more than there had been this morning. It seemed that the second needle had slipped through unnoticed.

He didn't collapse on his back and start laughing. He really, really wanted to, but he didn't. He chose life instead and evacuated. He had his proof of concept. He would fall back up the mountain, settle in for the night, and prepare. Then, tomorrow, he would set about cutting a flower.

Truth stretched as he made his way back into the woods around Happori. He knew the stiffness was in his head. His muscles, tendons, and fasciae were all supple enough to make a contortionist weep with envy. Didn't matter. After spending the night on the dirt with no blanket, he felt stiff.

He was probably sleeping more than he needed to, physically. That didn't matter either. He needed the mental rest. He looked up at the cheery sun through the light-dappled, tender leaves of spring. Today would be a good day. He would make sure it was.

He smelled the soft loam, the trees, and the wind as it wound around the mountains. Tasted the spring air, clean and sharp and herbal. Yes. Today would be a good day. He climbed up a tree and picked a spot on that towering flower that *didn't* have a lot of surveillance birds around it. He took his time, putting three needles into it.

At five kilometers, the degree of spread was significant, but that was fine too. Precision wasn't important there. He climbed down again, taking the time to savor the feeling of the bark under his hands and how the strength in his body made moving effortless. Then it was off to the next location.

It was a thirty-kilometer hike through pathless mountain woods, hiding from surveillance, avoiding traps and patrols, and doing his best to leave no trace. He had to get uncomfortably close to the village to find a decent shooting angle from the downslope side. It still managed to be quietly pleasant. He really had no way to test that this would all work out how he hoped it would but . . . screw it. He had enjoyed a revelation last night.

It was important to kill Borges. It was. He was clearly a crucial piece of whatever puzzle Starbrite was assembling. Killing him was *The Job*. On the other hand, the stated reason he was killing Borges was to pull attention and resources away from Harban and the System Astrologica. A goal he could achieve by other means.

That's all the assassination was—a means. The end was something else entirely. It wasn't worth killing himself over. It wouldn't save his siblings. It wouldn't save Etenesh or Jember. It wouldn't get Merkovah his dreamed-of revenge. Dying there would be a terrible waste.

The thought was incredibly liberating. He could do his best . . . within the bounds of whatever he considered reasonably safe. The Job couldn't demand more of him than that if he didn't let it. Once he realized that, things snapped into place.

One person, no matter how blessed, skilled, or sneaky, was going to crack in days the fortress Starbrite had spent years building. They were waiting for someone exactly like him. So, he would change the rules. He would hit them with something, some *things* they couldn't prepare for. And if he got very lucky, he could pick off Borges afterward.

He listened to the twitter of undead birds in the trees, feeling the wind on his skin. Yeah. It was a good day. He made a full loop around the village and the research station. The station hung in the sky, the vine or root hanging down to the earth below. It was like you were on the bottom of a pond, looking up at the lily floating on the surface. It was beautiful. It was simply beautiful.

Once he finished the loop, he made his way back toward the village. He popped by Dr. Borges' house just to see if he was home. He was not. Truth didn't take it to heart. He knew he wasn't that lucky. Still, he'd more than kick himself if he didn't at least check.

He found a children's playhouse in a backyard and managed to shove most of himself into it. It wasn't very comfortable, but it did provide almost-total cover from the endless surveillance. He meditated for forty minutes or so, just to top up a bit.

Figuring there was no time like the present, he went out and got himself a seat on a roof. You could see the research station from anywhere in town, so any house was as good as another.

It came down to jank, Truth had concluded. You take two things that don't exactly work how you need them to and combine them into something that does what you need it to in a shoddy, inefficient way. Jank was a sign of poor quality, sure, but it was also a way of life. It might be "poor quality," but it *did* work, and now you had a tool or functionality you didn't before. He pulled out his homemade . . . well, under-a-tree-in-the-woods-made talisman-control amulet. If he got this right, the result should be pretty spectacular. He pressed the glass "gem" and waited.

And waited.

And waited.

After five minutes, he had the thing flat on the roof while he looked through the etchings, making sure everything was connected properly. Amazing how often it was something simple like that. It wasn't that simple. Talisman looked fine.

He fished out one of the customized needles he had been shooting into the flower, looking over the incredibly detailed spell tracery on them. They *looked* right, but clearly, there was something stopping the trigger from reaching the needles. Could it be interference from some built-in defense on the research station? But there shouldn't be any with what he was trying to do.

His fond feelings about the power of jank flew away as he desperately wished he had a proper workbench and a stack of technical manuals to work with. He was a mainte-nance tech, not a damn talisman designer. This wasn't covered in his vocational classes.

After bashing away at it, he tentatively concluded that it wasn't working because the needles were too far apart to start the cascade, and he needed a big cluster to get them going. Except he had used most of his customized needles already, going around the *damn huge* flower. The good news was that heavy needlers held in excess of a thousand rounds per big box magazine, and he had plenty of ammo left. The bad news is that it was still a complete pain in the ass to etch the damn needles. Silently swearing, Truth got to work.

Once he had made a few dozen, he ran a quick test and found no less than ten that were broken. Truth swore even more and fixed them. Two were still broken. He destroyed them carefully. They might not be cursed in the technical sense, but a certified talisman-maintenance tech knew the practical side of such things. These were cursed and must be destroyed.

Evening was settling in, and as expected, only a handful of people came down from the research station and made their way back to the village. Truth made a last, quick trip to check, and no, Borges hadn't popped home for a bite of dinner. He took a final moment and forced himself to appreciate the sunset. It had been a lovely day, and he should try to hang on to that feeling.

He managed almost three whole seconds of looking at the light show before spin-ning around and shooting the thirty-seven modified needles into the flower holding up the research station. This close, grouping wasn't a problem. Just to make sure none of them hit each other, he put them all in a roughly one-square-meter area. Should be plenty. And if it wasn't? Well, back to the damn, thrice-cursed drawing board.

Some part of this must be working; the needles were getting through the wards and not triggering the alarms. Briefly praying to the god Etenesh thought he was, he squeezed the activation talisman again.

There was a conspicuous lack of anything happening again. He waited for it. Reminded himself that these things took time. It would be weird if anything happened immediately.

A blizzard of birds took off from their roosts on the vine and started swirling around the flower. Truth smiled, then jumped to the edge of the roof, reached under, and ripped out the recording talisman. He needed proof. A quick factory reset later, he set the talisman up on the ridgeline, aimed at the sky-lily. Just in time, too.

A heartbeat later, swarms of heavy needles smashed down into the village west of the base. Some unspelled, most coated in acid or electricity, or heated to a thousand degrees. Sprays of acid started washing down the torn-open homes and shops as garbled alarms sounded and bright lights stabbed down. Then the needles opened up on the south side, wards snapping up and out, then up again. The air crackled and seethed as the defenses were created and demolished within seconds.

Golems fell out of hidden hatches in the base of the flower. Truth hadn't spotted them at all. Dozens of them, hundreds of them, pouring down like pollen. Security teams on flying platforms came rushing out too—must be the rapid response squad.

There was a heavy *thump*. Truth couldn't see what it was from there, but it must have been important. There were so many wards popping up and vanishing, it looked like a rainbow caught in a hurricane. The random magic discharges were playing hell with all the bound spirits, Truth knew. To say nothing about what he had actually done.

One of the petals was strobing magenta. He had no idea what that was about.

It was the power of jank. Truth nodded sagely to himself as billions of wen in precision-engineered, professionally manufactured and installed magical technology tore itself apart. You took things that kind of worked, mashed 'em together, and blew shit up. It wasn't just him that did it, either. People spent entire careers making the best jank they could.

Take, for example, the Siphios Office of Temple Security. Using magic, using cosmic rays to recreate the anti-magic of the anti-theists? That was the dumbest thing he had ever heard, and the fact that it basically worked was a continuous wonder to him.

Or the fact that needler rounds were designed to be used with spells cast on them. They held on to magic like nobody's business and were childishly easy to enchant if you had good eyes and a steady hand for the carving. And a ton of patience.

Or that Incisive had absolutely no problem imprinting needles with the effect of being sharp and stealthy. The invisible bite whose poison isn't felt until far too late. Sure, the spell wasn't *intended* to work like that . . . probably . . . but it could be made to work like that.

As petals started dripping streams of fire onto the base below, Truth could only regret that he didn't understand Cup and Knife well enough to add it into the mix. It sounded like an evacuation alarm had gone off. Sensible. Truth lay flat on the roof and settled in with the heavy needler. He was only a bit more than a kilometer away.

Shooting up was always harder than shooting down, but he reckoned he could manage. Didn't have to make the head go *pop* if the magic cloud the target was standing on suddenly disappeared for "no reason."

Oh, was the flower starting to tilt over? Not long until it fell, then. Truth felt the grin stretching across his face.

"Squeak, squeak, motherfuckers. Run for me."

CHAPTER 60

CUT FLOWERS

The floating sky-lily was tilting over. Systems were exploding now or activating without reason. Mindlessly running. The defenses raked the village, shattering homes, shattering the streets. Shattering lives. Truth looked carefully, but it seemed the heavy needles weren't coming anywhere near him. Small mercies.

Some people on the flower were trying to evacuate, but for some reason, the clouds of butterflies weren't coming together like they should. They were just . . . swarms of insects with no notable load-bearing capability. The flying clouds were doing much better, but then, they weren't a product of the research center's magic. They were straight off a factory production line. Truth picked one that was out ahead of the others and lined up his shot.

Infiltration? Starbrite had prepared for that. Assault? The defenders wished you would try. Even dispelling magics or the anti-magic of the anti-theists was prepared for. Backups, redundancies, shunts, emergency preparedness drills, every reasonable precaution taken. At least, that was Truth's assumption. So, he was deliberately unreasonable.

The enchanted needles were never going to drop the base. Not nearly enough power. Not remotely enough. But the base had plenty of power. He just needed to turn that power against itself. Use the base's own power to fuel the enchantments on the needles until the needles burnt out. Overwhelm all the backups and redundancies and shunts by creating faults everywhere, all at once. Force the different systems to compete for resources internally while things break at an accelerating rate.

Truth cast Obliteration on a needle and drilled it into the flying cloud. The driver sensibly wanted as much distance as they could manage from the randomly firing defenses of the base, so they were flying straight over the valley, a few hundred meters up. Whatever they tried to cast before they hit the ground didn't appear to have worked. Or maybe it did, and he just lost sight of them. Didn't really matter much. As long as they weren't flying away.

He quickly picked off all the clouds he could see on the ground or in the air. It must have looked like steam blowing away to the frantically evacuating researchers. Six figures' worth of smoke up in the air per cloud. As the flower tilted farther and farther to the side, it got harder and harder to cling on. Watching the clouds blow away into the night sky.

One bright spark figured they would try to fly. You didn't see those spells too often. The spells rarely worked well. Bright Spark got up off the platform a ways. Truth got ready to pick them off so as to discourage other quick thinkers, but there was no need. It seemed the system targeting airborne threats was having a bad time. The swirling undead birds tore apart the "invader" before he could cause any harm.

The flower started to slowly spin counterclockwise. Still tilting farther and farther up, but starting to roll now. This was not, in Truth's opinion, a good thing, as it meant finger-long heavy needles and sprays of acid were now being distributed even more randomly. He was a ways off from the station but, as his own, comparatively small, heavy needler proved, well within the effective range of the emplaced weapons. It was sliding downward now too, the motion getting wilder as the spells holding it up came apart.

It was only at this moment that Truth considered what might happen when a giant flower packed so full of magical energy and enchantment that it could keep an entire research campus floating in the air crashed into the ground. Violence, explosions, and death, yes; he had his fingers crossed for that. It was just that he had maybe, just possibly, failed to fully appreciate the scope. For example, just how much energy it would take to keep something that size up in the air.

He grabbed the recording talisman and dove off the roof. The village was built on the side of a mountain, with bedrock a bare thirty centimeters under the surface. But his trainers in the army had been adamant—if something was going boom, any amount of being underground is better than being on the surface. He called the Tongue to his hand and started madly hacking away at the dirt. Between the sword and Incisive, he had a trench two meters long by two meters deep dug in seconds.

He got in just ahead of the boom.

There was a sudden pressure forcing him into the bedrock. A sort of high-pitched squeal that shifted almost instantly down into an infrasonic bass that vibrated his viscera. The bedrock shook for a second. Bits of the house he had been up on rained down on him, the jagged splinters bouncing off his hardened body. The inane thought of *I hope the recording talisman is okay* popped into his head. He checked it briefly. Looked okay. Still recording. He felt lightheaded as he started to stand. Incisive SCREAMED, and Truth dropped flat on his belly.

Something he couldn't describe changed in the air. Something primal, like bitter aconite on the tongue or the smell of rotting milk. Something in the snake brain, stretching down through your spine and telling you that there was nothing good there. *Be a smart snake. Stay low.* Steam started boiling up around him, the Blessing of the Sea of Brass furiously resisting the changes polluting the world around him.

Truth tried to lie as flat as he could, but he could feel his energy pouring away, the Blessing drawing down his reserves fast as it struggled against the changes. He could feel himself fraying away, boiling away in that same steam. Something was wrong, something was wrong with him. Something was wrong with the world, and he couldn't stop it couldn't stop it couldn't stop it, and it was happening, and there was nothing he could do—

In a fit of desperation, he tried casting Cup and Knife but couldn't find a target. This wasn't "sin" or "wounds" or demons or spirits; it was someone's mistake changing the fabric of the world in ways he didn't have words for. He flailed with it for a moment, imagining "cutting" away a little coffin-shaped box with him in it, isolated from all the madness around him. He felt something shifting around, like a nail pressing almost but not quite through a balloon.

There was quiet. The Blessing lightly steamed for a few seconds longer, and then that stopped too. Truth hyperventilated, trying to bring his emotions back under control. What . . . was all that? What the hell just happened? How did that happen? What did he just cast? He could see the air twisting and blurring above him, the night air turning into oil sheens and soap-bubble smears of color. Painting the surface of his little coffin. There was still a small drain on his energy, but it was manageable. Not like before.

What the hell was all that? He had expected the . . . reality warping or overwriting or whatever, devices . . . or whatever they were, to break. That made sense. But this? How does something explode into whatever this was? How long could it last? It couldn't be permanent, could it?

Could it?

Even at Level Four, he could only last so long, trapped in his little coffin in the grave he dug. He might have stopped most of the bleeding, but he wasn't replacing his energy, either. Sooner or later, he would have to rise again.

Truth tried to get a sense of what he had managed in his desperation. It was a little bubble of isolation. He had defined a little area and cut it off from . . . what, exactly? He couldn't tell. Not light, because he could see what was directly above his grave. Air? With how small the box was and how much he had been hyperventilating, he would have used up all the air by now, right? He didn't know. He could feel the rock under him, feel the weight of his body, so he was not cut off from the earth or gravity. So, he could not be said to be cut away from "reality" or the world. Which meant that his original assumption, that this was some kind of reality-warping effect, was either wrong or incomplete.

He forced himself to breathe slowly, to calm his heart and work it through. Funny to think—that was the first time he had freaked out like that in a long time. He really couldn't think back to when. It was the loss of control. The world was spinning out of order, and he spun right along with it, no longer in control of body or mind.

He smiled bitterly up into the night sky. He might say "okay" to a lot of things, but that was because he decided that it was, in fact, okay. Nobody got to decide for him. Not anymore.

He didn't understand what Cup and Knife actually did. It had taken him weeks of practice, a vision of Botis, and daily tuition from an expert to achieve an initial mastery of Incisive. Screwing around with Cup and Knife a couple of times really wouldn't do it.

Shame he had blown the base up rather than infiltrating. He would bet they had a great library and there were nothing but experts up there. A few *minor* problems with that plan, but hey, as long as he was dreaming.

It looked like the pollution outside the grave was clearing up. Whatever had happened, it wasn't permanent. Reality was reasserting itself. A bit of blown-up whatever wasn't going to overwrite the belief of even a disinterested God permanently. What would happen when he got out of his little coffin? He wasn't in a rush to find out.

He let the spiritual pollution clear up a bit, then tentatively stuck a corner of his shirt up through the invisible lid of his coffin. It went through without resistance, though it very faintly steamed when he drew it back. Not yet, it seemed. He waited a few minutes longer and tried again. Nothing visibly steaming. No damage to the fabric.

He tested with the tip of his pinky, then his whole pinky. No problems. Nothing at all, actually. No resistance or tingle or warm feeling or any other indication that he had passed through some kind of barrier. Pinky was fine. Wasn't even steaming. It seemed that whatever reality-bending things had been going on around the village had come to a firm stop.

He burst upward, smashing aside the few boards that had covered parts of his trench. He could smell fires—burning homes and metal and plastics. The house behind him wasn't on fire. It was just gone. Shattered rubble. He didn't see anyone moving on the street. He dropped back into the grave, grabbed the recording talisman, and tied it to his chest. The cosmic rays were hitting him now, getting passively absorbed by his body. Not enough to offset the drain from his Blessings, but nearly. It seemed there weren't many people left nor active surveillance. Just in case, he assumed an identity. Starbrite Security PMC, rushing to search through the wreckage for high-value survivors.

He moved swiftly through the ruined, rubble-lined streets. There weren't as many fires as he expected. The blast seemed to have blown things too far apart for a big blaze to spread. He could see things and people thrashing in the wreckage. Not his problem. He kept moving, eyes on the broken flower. There were survivors, he could see. People smashing at the wreckage, trying to pull out those trapped underneath. High-leveled, he assumed, and well warded. Or something.

He came up behind one—a fellow Level Four. Almost anywhere else, he would be an elite. A powerhouse, even if he had never trained in combat. Truth called the Tongue to hand and, with a swing, extinguished one of the finest minds in Jeon. He looked around the rest of the survivors, making sure the recording talisman was snugly in place. He might not cut off Starbrite's path of retreat with this. But after tonight, it would be a lot narrower. He raised the blade again and got to work.

CHAPTER 61

THE RUBBLE OF A DREAM

The few survivors were shattered, exhausted. Confused. Hurting. Their energy had been spent to the last drop, keeping themselves alive any way they could. They were very smart, possessed of abundant magical power, and surrounded by the best talismans and personal protections money could buy on this planet. Empowered by a System that gave them access to a bewildering number of spells in an instant. For most of the people on the sky-lily, it hadn't been nearly enough to survive the explosive collapse. For those lucky, smart, strong few who did survive, there was nothing left that would save them from Truth.

Truth moved through the smoke and darkness, letting the light of their burning homes blind his prey. They would see what lived in the darkness and the shadow soon enough. The Tongue struck, snuffing a life, then returned to his soul until it was needed again. Without noise, without light, it destroyed mortal lives. The sword had no qualms about this. Angels had always despised humans, especially those who had strayed from the appointed path. Truth was just glad the Tongue tolerated him.

He kept Incisive active. Who knew what modifications these researchers had made to themselves? What spells they still had available to them? He moved quickly, letting himself fade into the background, and if someone managed to see him? They would see a Starbrite Man, a strong brother in the PMC, rushing to do his duty.

He didn't keep count. If it mattered, the recording talisman would keep track. He just tried to capture the faces for identification later. It was just the job. He had been paid in advance and paid richly. Besides, he just plain didn't like what they were doing there. So, he did the job and killed everyone he found. Not that they all went quietly. The PMC had a large presence on the sky-lily, and they kept their heads in a fight.

He found a squad of Level Two mercenaries led by a Level Three lieutenant. They were wearing the BDUs and combat boots Truth remembered, but in addition to the usual needlers, they carried bronze spears and had on face-covering bronze helmets. He could see the sparking remnants of spells and talismans still lighting up around them. No idea where the second squad or the sergeant was.

The lieutenant seemed to be trusting his instincts, looking hard at the shadows, jabbing at them with his spear. Truth just casually stepped to the side and avoided it. As soon as the lieutenant looked away, Truth stepped sharply forward, calling the Tongue to his hand and beheading the officer in an effortless blow. He *should* have been able to exterminate the Level Two soldiers before they understood what had happened.

"Uqbar! Uqbar!" Truth was suddenly faced with four squaddies jabbing spears . . . roughly where he was. They were far, far too slow to hit him, and they clearly weren't seeing him, but somehow, they had reacted more quickly than they should. The end was the same—their heads rolling next to their lieutenants, but the experience shook Truth.

He was on the clock, but . . . he poked at one of the heads, helmet still attached, with a bit of wood. The helmet looked like normal bronze. It didn't even look particularly enchanted.

<<*Look closer—no straps holding it on. Poke the skin at the base of the helmet.*>>

Truth did, then stood. The helmets were fused to the faces of the soldiers. Whatever had been done to them, it was intended to be permanent. A lot to pick apart there, just not now. He grabbed one of the spears and looked it over. No obvious enchantments, but the edge was wickedly sharp. He smashed it into a bit of fallen concrete, then examined the spearhead again. Damage, but less than he would have expected. Hmm. He tossed it away, then had his attention yanked back to it.

His handprints were etched into the wood. He picked it up again. The steam boiled up, seemingly melting or eroding away the wood. It seems that whatever they were, they were *really* unorthodox. He took a few seconds to obliterate them with Incisive and the Tongue. Investigators would know this was not an accident immediately, but there was no reason to give them any easy clues.

The hunt continued. He didn't know how much longer he had—not long, he was sure of that. Orbital drop wasn't possible, thanks to the Shattervoid, but you could move something through the air in a *big damn hurry* if you had the magic and the money. Starbrite had both, and Jeon wasn't all that big. Someone alarmingly high-level was in the air and on their way, right this second.

He moved as quickly as he could, trying to listen for anyone moving through the rubble, voices crying out for help or to help. Silencing them. At this point, it wasn't important who he was killing. Each one would hurt Starbrite badly. He didn't see any loot worth grabbing, but then, would he even recognize it if he saw it?

Truth knew perfectly well that he understood hardly nothing he had seen there. How was he going to find the Top-Secret-Explain-Everything-Simply File in the rubble? Besides, anything really good would be stored by the System. That much he was sure of.

There was a sizable noise deep in the ruin. Huge chunks of flower and rubble were flying around. Some kind of Higher Level mage or powerful golem was at the center of it. Truth moved quickly. If it were the former, he would see if he could manage a kill. If the latter, he'd see if he could turn the busted thing on everyone else.

"Have you found the library yet?"

"No, and frankly, it doesn't matter right now. This was an attack. We need to get you out of here, Director."

"The hell with that! The library is the key to everything. Without it—"

"Director? I have a mission now, and I'm pretty sure you do too. Without the library, we have you. We can make more books with you, but no amount of books can make you. Please."

There was a pause. Truth got a lot quieter. He was lucky, in one sense. He had found his prey. Unlucky in another sense—his prey was still alive and had two Levels on him, the System, and a Starbrite-issue bodyguard. His senior. He didn't know quite how he felt about that.

Borges and his bodyguard were at the bottom of a small pit, digging for something. A "library," presumably. Borges was thin, older-looking, and not particularly handsome. An impressive degree of asceticism, given his wealth and class in Jeon. Or perhaps he relied on illusions and the charms had broken. His left arm was torn off at the shoulder, but he didn't seem to mind—a green field covered the wound, stopping the flow of blood. He was a mage. He didn't need his arms to be strong. He could fling one-ton rocks with a word and a thought.

His bodyguard was in considerably worse shape. His limbs were attached, but he had several bowl-sized holes clean through his chest and belly, eating away at him with some corrosive force. He was trying to keep them neutralized with his own healing spells, but it was not going well. It seemed that Borges had finally noticed that fact too.

"How are you holding up, Tae?"

"Not great, Director. I will hold together for long enough. If we go. Now."

The director looked bitterly around the ruins. "This was to be the first flower, you know. I was going to build an entire pond full of lilies, then sever their earthly roots and let them drift through the sea of clouds. Shedding the light of Uqbar on the world. Blessing its people with prosperity and hope, in the era of dead magic."

"You still can, Director. You still can."

"Oh, I know. It's just the stupidity of it all, the cruel barbarity. Whoever did this had no conception of what we were making here. They just destroyed it for the sake of destroying it. It's important to Starbrite, and that's reason enough. The logic of babies. Animals."

Tae nodded gently. "Plenty of time to prove them wrong. Possibly when they are strapped to the altar."

"I look forward to it. Hah. Well, I can't do much, but I think I can stop the corrosion, at least." Borges closed his eyes. Truth could feel the world starting to twist, ever so gently. The steam started rising off him faster and faster. No more time to watch. He was starting to charge in when he had a nasty idea. Since it had worked once . . .

Truth timed it carefully. Just when Borges started raising his hand to do . . . whatever he was going to do, Truth cast Cup and Knife, cutting around the two. The results were anticlimactic, from his perspective. Nothing happened. The two in the pit, however, saw it differently.

"Tae, I can't reach Uqbar. I can see it, feel it, but I can't reach it."

Tae went white and dropped to one knee. "It's leaving us. Me. Director, run! I can't hold out. RUN!"

"Damnit, I've lost too many people today! Come on, Tae. This time, it's me carrying you." Borges rushed over and threw his good arm around his bodyguard, lifting him to his feet. "We have this. I've enough strength left to clear us a path. Someone will have a sprit beast they can summon. We'll get out of here and get you to a hospital."

Truth moved silently behind them. Some instinct must have alerted Tae, some bone-deep pride as a bodyguard, because he tried to look over his shoulder. Tried to put his body between Truth and Borges. Truth didn't give him time to react. It all worked in concert—the Meditations, Tool, Incisive, and even Cup and Knife. They all stacked on top of the Blessings of the Silent Forest and of the Sea of Brass. And those, in turn, built on the instinct for violence he had been born with. The Tongue of One Who Speaks for God spoke powerfully and established Truth's orthodoxy. These two were not allowed to live.

There was barely any resistance. A brief spike of energy as the bane in the sword made sure there was no hope of recovery. And then two heads landed in the dirt.

Truth immediately cast Cup and Knife again. The souls of these people were mutilated and wrong. Evil. They should be shredded to their most basic essence and returned to eternity. The spell struggled with that one, but he could feel it drawing on his dwindling power. Eventually, it stopped. Hopefully, that did enough. Two fewer souls for the System Astrologica, and less information for it to work with. He cast Obliterate on the bodies, just to be sure, and stabbed them in the brain and heart, just to be *very* sure. He double-checked that the recording talisman caught both faces. Then he turned and ran from the ruins. The heavy needler was a pile of scrap somewhere; he wouldn't worry about it. It was stuck under the rubble of the house he had sniped from anyhow. He just needed to run. Fast.

He had made it to the tree line when the sky in the south started to glow. It looked like a swarm of shooting stars approaching, getting larger, turning into comets with long fiery tails, rushing toward him. As they came closer still, he saw they were firebirds, being driven to their limits, then faster still with heavy enchantments. Riding on their backs were mages. PMC hitters and off-the-books specialists in upsetting fields. If there was a soul up there below Level Four, they were hiding damn well. But of course there wasn't any. He'd bet the peak of Level Four was the minimum required cultivation to stand with these powerhouses.

Starbrite had arrived in force, and they were bound and determined to make sure *somebody* paid for all this. Truth suddenly wished he had been born with four legs. No matter how much he cultivated, he couldn't seem to run fast enough.

CHAPTER 62

A RIGHTEOUS CAUSE

Truth didn't look back a second longer. He knew what was behind him. All that mattered was forward. Or, more to the point, *away*. There was enough magical force coming his way to level a small country. Give them a few minutes for the equipment to catch up, and it would be a large country. If they caught him, he wouldn't have the luxury of death.

He was already running flat out. He tried to go faster. He didn't dare use Abner's Amble, not a single extra scrap of energy beyond what was needed to hide. His body could move fast enough. It would have to be fast enough.

Truth raced along his escape route. Most of the obstacles had been demolished by the explosion or the strange aftermath. Dead animals, long dead, littered the ground. No true animal would eat them. Not with everything done to the corpses. It was an open question if anything would grow where they fell. Truth couldn't pay attention to it. He was just grateful there was less of a draw on the Blessing of the Silent Forest.

The woods were awake after the blast. How could the animals and insects not be awake? They were screaming, shouting, demanding answers, and making threats. The smarter animals had long since run. Nothing good was coming after all that. Truth was right there with them. The wave of powerhouses coming up the valley was like the sun rising at midnight. The unnatural heat of them burning away the comforting dark.

They were close now. Close enough that he had to slow down and focus on stealth over speed. They would seal the area, he knew. Lock down everything around the village and work outward until they find *something*. Search-and-rescue wouldn't take more than a few minutes. Sifting through the rubble would take considerably longer, but that was work for juniors. These were seniors—officers, department heads, regional managers of this or that, and they were there to investigate and avenge an atrocity. A village was massacred, and a genuine wonder was destroyed. Their cause was just, and no half-measures would be accepted.

Truth had an almost-hallucinatory memory—the Silent Night before the SAT. All the parents roaming the streets, ropes in hand, to strangle the noisy. His own parents, abusive and monstrous as they were, participated. They loved every minute of it. They might be monsters, but that night, they got to be monster heroes. Or so they told themselves. He shook the thought from his head and kept moving. Up the mountain ridge, toward a notch he had scouted. Silent as could be.

In a few days or weeks, he would circle back and pick up Thrush and the micro-spell bird. He left his scarf, the Freedom of the Terraces, there, too. It wouldn't have survived the assault. Bird wouldn't survive, either. Not a good day to be in the air anywhere near there.

The rescue party had reached the village now. He could hear the crying birds circling. Some would be racing outward to create a perimeter. Truth threw himself into the shadow of a tree and tried very hard not to exist. Letting the forest wrap itself around him.

A fiery bird roared overhead, sharp eyes piercing the canopy as the hard sur-veillance of the powerhouses above scraped the earth. There was intense pressure, a strong draw on his rapidly dwindling energy, then they were past. This was just the first sweep. The real hunt hadn't yet begun. Truth forced himself back into motion. Every step forward was a victory. A meter farther was a meter safer. That had to be his mentality now. The bigger the area they had to search, the harder he would be to find.

More cries went up; light talismans were launched into the air in their dozens. The village was exposed, raw and bleeding, under the harsh illumination. He could feel spells going off, big, wide-area magics. He had no idea what they were doing down there and didn't intend to find out.

People run downhill when they are fleeing. It's easier. Faster. The instinct is to work with gravity and run, run, run, down and away from the hunters. It's why Truth made sure his route went up. They would search upslope, of course, but they would look for streams. They would look for routes to nearby towns or a road. Maybe they would use ground-sensing spells to hunt for caves.

He had considered, strongly considered, hiding in a cave. But no. Like running downhill, following a stream, or stashing a vehicle on the road, hiding in a cave was too obvious. Too static. He had to make them waste their energy checking the obvious first. While they did, he would run.

Another bird flew overhead, a spell bird this time, dropping . . . something. Dark shapes falling from two hundred meters up, arresting their fall in a thin bubble of light just before touching down. Cats. Big, eyeless cats, coated in the same rubbery material as the watcher things that had plagued Truth on his every road journey since coming back to Jeon. They moved through the forest like a black wind. Did they have the same sensory capabilities as their humanoid counterparts? Truth hoped not. There were a lot of cats, but the volume of space to search got bigger and bigger by the second. And there were ever so many things to find in the woods.

Truth didn't look at the ruins of the surveillance and counter-infiltration network in the woods for a single millisecond longer than necessary. But he did look at them as he raced past. How could he not, when spells were going off at random? Alarm spells, the ones far enough out to survive the double explosion, were going off. Firing red flares, screaming madly, triggering defensive spells. Explosive blasts shot out regularly from the recharging spell traps. Other traps mindlessly pissed streams of acid into the breeze. Truth had had no idea that was going to happen. Lucky accident. He smiled slightly.

He really should have known better than to entertain optimism.

It was the birds that warned him things were not as they seemed. Just like when he went into the village for the first time. One of the dead, twisted things was bulging. Truth might have thought it was a simple alchemical reaction to everything that had happened, but the bird used one of the tumors rolling along its back to get to its feet. It moved around like it was trying to figure out how wings worked. How moving while trapped in matter worked.

Borges and his team had been playing games with reality itself. Alchemy left alchemical waste, which could poison or rot those near it. Kill those who touched it. Talisman production was no better. So, he had to wonder, what was the waste product of reality modification? What rats would come to eat those scraps?

The very best spirit of intellect couldn't have answered the question faster than Truth. The answer was "Not his problem." He kept up the pace, happy to leave the cleanup to Starbrite. Happy thought, maybe the cats and whatever was wearing the birds could play together. Maybe they would be friends.

Downslope and east, there was a piercing, mechanical whine, and a burst of blue-green light. Then a second. Flying platforms swarmed over, followed swiftly by one of the firebirds. Above the village, a vast spell formed in the sky. Kilometers wide, made of ice-white runes and geometric filigree, supported by locust swarms of talismans.

Truth didn't recognize it at all. Above his pay grade and Tier. And Level. Far above. Something out there didn't like it, though, because the undead . . . Re-undead? Possessed corpses? . . . started flying up and attacking the talismans. Trying to break the formation of the spell. Mages were blasting them out of the sky. What was more alarming to Truth was that some needed a few hits to go down. Some of the ones that did go down were getting up again.

Every one of those mages was an elite. If something could survive a couple of hits from them . . . well, it was good that he was already running away. He had a feeling that, just possibly, maybe, he might have overachieved. He did remember being warned by Sergeant Murthey not to do that. "*Do the job you are told to do and nothing else, unless they pay extra.*" That was good advice. Could he run a little faster without breaking concealment? Probably not, but maybe he could be more efficient in his route planning. Really link together that cover for a smooth transit.

He could hear a rattling in the woods now. A sort of hissing, then a metallic clatter, like bones down a playground slide. He could see flashes of movement around him. Things hunting one another, or hunting for him. Looking for traces amid the chaos. A wrist-thick stream of blinding white plasma sliced through the mountain for a hundred meters ahead of him.

Truth looked up over his shoulder. A powerhouse on a firebird. The senior had seen *something* there and was willing to break out a particularly brutal fetish to burn it down. No crude acid bolter. This was a custom job. All sleek ebony wood and refined orichalcum. Delicate spellwork in mythril covering its working components, no doubt.

Truth was absolutely certain that if he caught even a glancing hit from that, there wouldn't be enough left of him to cremate. He wouldn't even have ashes—just rapidly spreading gas. He lay very flat on the ground, not even daring to look at the senior, lest they detect his gaze.

While he was clinging to the ground, wishing he could burrow through rock and vanish, it occurred to him that he was a disgruntled former employee. Those guys got blamed for everything. Any time something went wrong, companies blamed "disgruntled former employees." And look—for once, it really was.

A wave of black, twirling, sickly, viscous, the black of rotten meat, visible thanks to the fire and explosions across the mountain, flew toward the senior on the firebird. The bird flew up, vomiting liquid fire on the black mass as it went. The flames were sticky, somehow, clinging to the putrescence but failing to destroy it.

The senior snorted loud enough to hurt Truth's ears sixty meters below and struck again with his fetish. The blinding-white beam burned through the wave and struck something. Whatever it was lived long enough to scream, first with outrage, then pain, then fear. Then went silent. The beam lasted a second longer and then stopped. Truth could hear the heavy panting of the senior and could feel the rush of energy as he drew the cosmic rays toward him, needing to recharge. Then he was on to the next monster to kill.

Truth kept his head down for exactly sixty seconds longer and got back to moving. He wasn't clear yet. But he was getting closer to the edge of the surveillance zone the village had set up. Soon, he would be in the real woods. Fewer distractions for his hunters, but it didn't seem like that was a problem. They looked plenty distracted. He could pick up the pace.

The giant spell shuddered into life. Something vast and terrible formed—a summoning. Something angelic? But that would be insane, wouldn't it? Even if you had to put down a load of demons, you wouldn't . . .

Oh. Wait. You didn't necessarily have to summon the whole angel. He'd done this trick once before. Truth broke out of cover, running flat out as hard as he could away from the summoning circle. Everyone else was doing the same thing, except they had firebirds and wards.

An obliterating light fell on the village. Not even white—it was beyond white, as it was beyond the very concept of color. It was *LIGHT*, the essence, the primordial meaning before the word. The concept of illumination falling raw and angry on the world. A world that couldn't endure its weight.

Whatever came below the light was simply . . . evaporated. All that was God was returned to God. All that was not was cleaned away. Truth knew they would be switching off the spell any second. Job done, demons banished. Whatever they were worried about, removed. But these were seniors. Powerful old monsters. Most were over a century old. Not quite caught up with the times.

IMPUDENT

Truth lost track of things after that.

CHAPTER 63

ON THE SIDE OF THE ANGELS

Truth hung in a void of fuzzy gray. Bursts of color and noise broke in and faded away without cause or sense. It was a void so total, his mind was inventing stimuli. He didn't know how long he was there. *Forever* and *For the smallest unit of time possible* seemed equally likely. And then there was an angel.

The angel's size was impossible to define—nothing to compare it to. Truth had no idea if it was close by or far away. It felt big. Like a sun with an eye in it surrounded by wheels made of dozens or hundreds of eyes. Some of the eyes looked sort of human. Most did not. All of them looked at Truth with crushing contempt. And maybe he was just projecting there, but he thought that there was a trace of confusion in them, too.

AT LEAST YOU BATHED

Truth was on the mountainside, running hard for the gap between peaks at the top of the ridge. He could hear birds flying away, people running like hell through the sky, getting away from whatever happened. Then he couldn't hear anything. The noise of whatever the angel was doing was so loud, it overpressured his ears. He could feel his body cultivation barely hanging on, keeping ruptured eardrums at bay.

Which is not to say that it wasn't agonizing. Like knitting needles pulled from a furnace and pressed slowly inward.

The trees lit up in flashes of color. First electric blues, then searing pinks and smoky reds. Occasional flashes of impossibly harsh white light. He didn't look back. He could smell the sea. Smell salt. There was nothing good for him here.

He knew that there would be survivors. None of those seniors would die easily, angel or not. These were paranoid old bastards. They would have an ace or three hidden. Wouldn't surprise him if the System started handing out free spells, too. Best he could hope for, for the very top tier, was injuries and confusion. Best he could hope for . . . was time.

He got his head down and pushed hard up the slope. No more thoughts. Just running.

The woods had gone silent. All the little insects in their mindless fury, all the birds, all the scurrying animals, all had gone silent. It was only the humans who dared still make noise. Truth's footfalls made no sound. He left no trace on the earth or scent in the air. Nothing marked his passing. He ran through the gap and down the other side of the mountain ridge. "Safety," or close enough to it.

Truth collapsed into a mountain stream miles downslope. The water was bitterly cold, but he scarcely felt it. He tore off his clothes, scrubbing the water against his skin, scooping up sand from the streambed and scrubbing, scrubbing, scrubbing until the sand turned to powder. Bathing was important. Very important.

He found a rocky overhang and burrowed under it, carving himself a cold, dry cave. He covered the entrance with as many bushes and saplings as he could quickly grab, curled up into a ball, and hung on to himself. Wrapped his arms around his knees and squeezed. Trying to feel something but not too much.

He didn't crawl out of the cave until after noon. He wouldn't describe himself as "well." His clothes were still wet on the side of the riverbank. He tried to remind himself that what he was feeling was normal, a very normal reaction to being summoned before a higher-tier angel.

They were existences, very literally, on another level from humanity. Something that had never been born, that had never been made of flesh, that had never had a reason to learn empathy or compassion or mercy. Such qualities belonged to God. His servants just needed to glorify Him and do as they were told in the lower realms. Most especially, they had to keep the rats from pissing in the flour.

It seemed Truth was considered a reasonably hygienic rat. Arguably the highest compliment of his life. No offense to Etenesh. A completely alien being considered him "not smelly." Which, apparently, was enough to spare his life.

He had encountered other angels before. Little ones, summoned, bound by Names and pacts, restrained in their presence and methods. Even the seraphim overseeing Etenesh's duel was a faint projection, doubtless summoned at immense expense. This? This was not that. This was a true Power or Dominion, a being of the Second Hierarchy, and who knows what Step before the Throne of God. He had been summoned before some true fragment of that incomprehensible being and had survived.

There was a reason *angelic* wasn't a compliment any more than *demonic* was. It just described a thing's nature. Whose side it was on. Truth laughed, an odd-sounding noise even to him. *Well, I don't think it's a compliment. Others probably disagree.*

He wasn't discounting the use of having the Tongue in his soul, but he was a realist. The Tongue was forged out of scrap, a bit of trash from a broken weapon. How "moved" would you be if some random person turned up with some of your trash buried in their guts?

He didn't understand what had just happened. He didn't have to understand. He had, he suspected, overachieved. Starbrite had most assuredly started moving forces out of Harban. They were now short an awful lot of very skilled people.

Good job, well done. On to the next thing. Keep spreading chaos until he was ready to make the move back into Harban. Not too long now.

He took a look around. He was naked, carrying a bundle of damp clothes, through the late-spring woods in the mountainous wilds of northern Jeon. The recording talisman was unsurprisingly dead. The trees were pretty, small flowers bloomed, and watching mosquitos try and fail to bite you never ceases to bring pleasure. The soft wind rustled the tender leaves, bringing a cool green scent with them. It was idyllic. A place untouched by the horrors of the human world. The collapse would touch this place lightly, if at all. A good place.

"I'm completely lost, aren't I?"

Truth quickly got good at using Abner's Amble. It was a modern magic spell, prioritizing simplicity and ease of use over power or complex effect. Every step took you farther than it otherwise should. Nice and simple. Modest energy cost, too. At Level Four, keeping a moderate pace, Truth could run it for hours without strain. It was crucially important that this was the case, as Truth was using his patented *Overcome complexity with radical simplicity* method to solve his *being lost* problem.

He could figure out which way was east from the sun. The nearest coastline was to the east. Most of the towns and cities in the north of Jeon were on the coast. So, if he ran east, he would eventually encounter roads. These would have road signs, which would lead him to human habitation and clothes that weren't dirty, wet, and full of holes. There might even be food.

The fact that achieving this would require running across literal mountain ranges for an indeterminate length of time was unfortunate, but lots of things were *unfortunate*. Being the focus of an enormous manhunt, with roadblocks, search parties, eyeless homunculi, and other unpleasantness, could certainly be classified as *unfortunate*. So, looked at in that light, running cross-country wasn't that bad. The opportunity to escape could even be considered *fortunate*.

As for being cold, hungry, and uncomfortable? He had lived through that before. He could do it again. He was Level Four. He could deal. Things wouldn't get better unless he made them better. So, he kept the sun at his back and ran on.

As for doubling back to the village and working his way south from there? He chose life. Nothing good was waiting on that side of the mountains. Not a single thing.

The woods were considerably less interesting than he had hoped. He didn't understand what he was looking at, so there was no particular joy in spotting a mushroom or seeing a bird. It was just a 'shroom or a bird. Not a yellow-beaked something or other. Green leaves, brown trees, brown forest floor.

You run up the mountain, then you run down the mountain. Down was more fun than up. Down let you jump, giving you ages of free fall until you landed on a branch far below. Then it was on to the next tree.

At night, he hung his now-mildewy clothes out next to a small fire. He didn't know much about setting fires, but he figured it out eventually. Then figured out that there would be a damn forest fire if he didn't scrape back all the dead leaves and things, then got paranoid and shifted the whole fire onto a big rock. He could pick up the burning sticks with his hands. Ordinary fire could no longer touch him. Still, its light and warmth were comforting.

He woke before dawn. Cold, naked, clothes still damp, hungrier, dirtier—the night had not much improved his condition. He had, however, slept, so that would do. Truth greeted the dawn with a round of morning cultivation. In the dark, he was cold, naked, filthy, hungry. But as he moved his body to the rhythms of his cultivation, as the cosmic rays were refined along the Nine Worm path, he was cleansed and warmed. His apertures were full, so his empty belly troubled him less. As the sun rose above the horizon, that great Lord clad Truth in golden light. Tall, mighty, beautiful. Anointed by heavenly fire.

He buried the clothes before he left his camp, shoes included. He would dress himself entirely in clean clothes when he reached civilization. Not like anyone could see him, anyway. Truth laughed at himself. The poor and weak weren't allowed to look at him even when he dressed in their clothes. He wouldn't worry about it. For now, he was free, strong, and clad in glory. It was enough.

I had accepted that the world is an evil, cruel place that wants to hurt me. But this feels spiteful. Personally spiteful.

<<Oh, don't say that. Sure, you slept naked on the dirt in an insect-infested forest, starving, alone. And sure, there was no need for you to have done any of that.>>

There was a pause.

But?

<<But what?>>

I didn't have to do any of that but?

<<Oh, no buts; I just didn't want to hear you whining. Yeah, missing a luxury hotel on the other side of the mountain is pretty embarrassing. Look at all this hand-polished wood on the floors. It's practically glowing. I bet the beds are super comfortable, too. Really leaning in to the whole rustic but actually obscenely expensive *thing. Oh, see the sign? There is a natural hot spring attached. Good for the kidneys, apparently, and the skin. I know you wish you had a hot soak yesterday.>>*

Truth nodded decisively. He didn't see a receptionist, or anyone else, for that matter. That made things easy. Stark bollock naked, he followed the signs to the hot spring, snagging a towel and bathrobe along the way.

The shower room was quietly luxurious, with light stone tiles contrasting with the warm, well-polished wood. The soaps and shampoos all had a delicate, intriguing herbal scent, seemingly activated and lifted by the not-too-hot water from the showers. It felt indecently good to scrub away the grime. Truth remembered a snooty lord in a romance novel defining civilization as hot baths. That lord had a point.

Also, that lord had just barged in on the heroine in the tub. The characters in those books had real problems with boundaries, he noticed. And, okay, she was planning on turning into a giant snake and eating various members of the lord's family to fuel her rise as the terrible Witch of the Blighted Heaths, but still. Privacy.

Cleaned and refreshed, he stepped out of the shower and into the hot-tub area. There were two seniors there, relaxing with little folded cloths on their foreheads.

There was a little floating tray between them with snacks and a bottle of wine. He couldn't feel their cultivation, so nothing to worry about there. Out of a puckish sense of politeness, he silently bowed to the two of them, then eased himself into the spring.

It was hot, piping hot, hot enough to poach an egg. Just right for him. He sighed long and deep, letting himself almost dissolve into the water. The aches of the last few days seemed to float out of him, pulled away by the minerals of the bath. Was it good for the kidneys? He had no idea. It was certainly good for him.

"So, junior, what brings you out to the mountains?"

"Oh, it's embarrassing, but I got lost."

"Lost? All the way up here?"

"Yeah. I had a little flying bird suit, lost my bearings, and it crashed. I got lost. Just hiked out of the forest."

"Damn! Is your family worried?"

"Probably."

"That's no good, that's no good. You have to let them know you are okay!"

"Soon enough. For now, I'm going to soak."

"Haha, how mean. Your poor parents."

"I'm an orphan, actually."

"Eh?"

"My wife is the one who would worry."

"That's almost worse!"

The two old-timers took turns scolding him. Everyone had their eyes closed, just relaxing in the tub. Truth opened his eyes slowly, staring up at the blue sky.

He hadn't released the Blessing of the Silent Forest. They shouldn't be able to perceive him. He couldn't detect their cultivation. The only way those facts lined up would be . . .

"Ah, it does you good to relax after a trying few days, doesn't it?"

If they were above Level Seven.

CHAPTER 64

LIVING NATIONAL TREASURES

Truth kept his breathing steady. Incisive hadn't warned him, so these two were not a threat. Probably. At least for the next few fractions of a second. They looked melted in the hot water of the springs.

The outdoor bath was enormous, larger than the hotel it was attached to. Crystal-clear blue water covered wide, flat stones. Here and there, boulders rose from the steaming water, adding even more charm to the scene. The pool narrowed at the back, where the spring rose from the mountain, and widened out as it reached the waterfall that would cool it and lead it to a mountain stream. The icy stream water and the hot spring water made the area perpetually misty. In the spring, with the forest dappled with green and the blues, purples, and whites of little wildflowers . . . it was lovely. Serene.

The two seniors in the bath, really the only two people he noticed in the whole hotel, were happily sprawled against the side of the spring, looking out over the waterfall and across the valley below. With their wine and snacks, they could hardly have been more comfortable. Truth was doing his best to replicate their relaxation, with middling results. The two made an interesting pair.

"So, kiddo, what's your trade?"

"Ah, would you believe I'm a professional bodyguard?"

The two old-timers chuckled. "A Level Four bodyguard? Must be some tycoon's family."

"I'm sorry; I can't say more."

"No, we understand, we understand. Privacy is important."

"Yes, thank you."

The two old men were a study in contrasts. One was deeply tanned, with a round torso and thick, brutal features. Fat lips, small eyes, embarrassingly thin strands of hair combed over a bald head, and a thick scar running from forehead to cheek over his left eye. Truth could see the muscles moving under the fat—the old man was built like a powerlifter. One who had gotten huge in prison, where he did a dime for those terrible, terrible things and would have been executed if anyone was brave enough to testify against him.

The other was pale to the point of anemia, the hot spring bringing only the faintest flush to his cheeks. His full head of hair was neatly parted even now, the silver locks losing none of their vivacity and luster. Thin, delicate fingers lifted the wine cup from the floating tray, and quietly smiling lips took a gentle sip. His eyes were soft brown, thoughtful, and kind. Wise. Even his breathing, quiet, long, steady breaths, had a feeling of elegance and compassion. He looked like a grandmaster calligrapher who donated his time and earnings to a local orphanage.

"If I'm not being too nosy, may I ask what brings the two seniors to the mountains?"

"We came for the hot springs, kid, the hot springs," the brutal-looking man said with a chuckle. "My kidneys can't keep up. Ah, one day, you will learn how it is." His laughter was upsettingly vulgar. Meaty. Wet.

"Oh, don't tease the child. Well, it's true we did come for the spring. We try to get up here once a year or so. Lots of happy memories in these mountains. We were up here for work anyway, so we thought, *Why not?*" The elegant man nudged his companion. There was a musicality to his voice, a stately rhythm. Truth would have happily listened to him read a train timetable.

Truth desperately wanted to ask what possible occupation could employ a musical saint and the person known on wanted posters as "The Meat Man," but knew it would be rude to ask. He didn't have to. They were used to people wondering.

"Don't strain yourself too much. I'm an artist, and he's a philosopher. The cruel bastard." The coarse man laughed.

"Don't listen to him. I'm the artist; he's the philosopher." The elegant man chuckled.

"Seniors?"

"Ah, it's like this. Silver-hair here is a poet and calligrapher." Truth nodded. That sounded exactly right. "And his poems make people want to stab him constantly, so he has turned into an absolute homicidal maniac." Truth did a double take while the refined gentleman sighed and resolutely looked away.

"Forgive me, but I have a hard time imagining it."

"Oh, I can prove it." Fat lips pulled back over alarmingly strong teeth. "Do you read much poetry?"

"None. My education was famously lacking."

"I won't recite any of it, then. Here is the gist of one of his famous ones—*If it is in our power to prevent something bad from happening, without thereby sacrificing anything of comparable moral importance, we ought, morally, to do it.*"

There was quiet in the hot springs for a moment. Somewhere, a cricket called out for love. The steady rush of the waterfall was just loud enough to make one sleepy but not so loud as to disturb the mood. Truth had to admit he didn't see a whole lot of application of the idea to his life, but it didn't strike him as stab-worthy.

"All right?"

"Think it through. Would you watch a child drown in a fountain?"

"Probably not, no."

"You might get your pants wet if you go in and save him."

"So?"

"Ah, the sacrifice is far outweighed by the virtuous act. No morally equivalent sacrifice. Well, what about famine in Ben Zhu?"

"No danger to my pants, thankfully." Truth nodded. The big man slapped his forehead with an enormous hand.

"There are charities, good ones, that do famine relief. If you donate your income, everything beyond what you need to survive, to those charities, they would save hundreds, perhaps thousands, of lives. A far more morally useful use of your money than, say, a hot-springs retreat."

"Ah. All right."

There was another long pause. The steam drifted between the standing stones, blurring the world beyond the spring. It must be getting colder—the steam was slowly getting denser. The silver-haired man started laughing a little painfully.

"Kiddo, the argument is that by failing to donate the money, you are committing an immoral act. You are choosing to let people suffer and die even though you would be giving up nothing of morally equal significance." The flabby hulk started laughing too, jiggling the hot spring's water.

"He told everyone, with irrefutable logic, that they were evil, immoral people. And then the old monster had the nerve to turn it into a touching, beautiful poem. I cried." Truth had the image of the ugly bastard crushing someone, letting their tears drip onto his cheeks, and claiming them as his own.

Truth thought about it. "I can see how that would make people mad, yes." And yet, the old timer was at least Level Seven, and Truth would be buggered by badgers before he believed a good person could cultivate that high. Those elixirs cost more than just money, and the time cost of the cultivation was huge too. He wondered if the term *homicidal maniac* might have been literal.

"Might I ask what art is created by senior?" Truth asked. Presumably, it was something made out of screaming children and dogs.

"I'm a sculptor." The bald man leered. Still on track for the screaming children and dogs, Truth noted.

"He's a philosopher. He just uses clay and found objects as his medium." The elegant man decided to butt in.

"The senior expresses his philosophy in art?"

"Eloquently."

"Bullshit. I make what sells."

"Which is also a form of philosophy, though not the one you demonstrate. Tell me, boy, have you wondered what it means to be a human?" the poet asked.

Truth jolted. "A lot. I have come to imagine the world as a slum, and most of the people in it as slumrats. I am wondering what an actual human looks like. Can the seniors please advise?"

That got him two matching sets of sharp looks. "Oh, we have a third philosopher in the bath. I don't suppose you make art, do you?" the big man asked.

"I must disappoint you."

"One day, you should give it a try." The poet smiled kindly. The mist had thickened. Truth felt a cold breeze come down the mountain and across the hot spring. It blew away the steam momentarily, then the steam came back with a vengeance. The mountains, the valley, they all took on a dreamy, unreal texture. Truth let his body float a little more in the water. It was surprisingly easy to relax away the strain of the last few days.

"I cannot answer the 'human' question any better than you can, it seems, but consider this—what if a human is not a fixed thing but a thing constantly inventing and improving itself?" the pallid senior asked.

"Even if it's changeable, there must be a core to improve on, right?"

"Yes, but if we can't define it directly, can we observe things about it indirectly? Did you know you were a transhumanist, young man?"

"No?"

"You certainly are. You cultivate. Cultivation is a learned skill. It is something done for self-improvement. There is something in you that you dislike, and you change it by artificial means. Cosmetic glamors—transhuman. Fertility-controlling drugs, mood-stabilizing medication? Transhuman. Prosthetics? Transhuman. Transplanting a ghost into a golem? Ah, tricky, but I would argue it's transhuman too." The elegant man nodded. "Which is what this lunk does. He makes beautiful homes for ghosts."

The big fellow snorted and looked away.

"Incredible. Just incredible."

"The ghost homes go to the heart of his transhumanist philosophy, you see. It is the distinction between us. I see only"—he waved an elegant, if bony, hand—"what is. I want to stop the pain *now*. Not later. Now. I cannot control the future nor change the past. I concern myself only with the safety and well-being of the present."

The big man's face seemed to be drooping in the heat, his teeth getting bigger and blockier as his lips retracted from his gums. "I, on the other hand, think the world has always been fucked, is currently fucked, BUT does not have to be fucked in the future!" He chuckled as he made chopping, thrusting motions with his hands.

"I make homes for ghosts, new bodies, new forms, because ghosts are creatures without a present or future. Their minds, such as they have, can only comprehend their past existence and lash out in anger or pain when the world doesn't correspond to their memories. It isn't 'wrong,' it's just their nature. Human nature, since ghosts are humans once the meat is off the bones. So, can you give a 'human' a prosthetic future? Even if that future is one that isn't human-shaped?"

"You say yes."

"I say yes." The mists had totally enclosed them now. The sun should have been bright, coming up on midday. Instead, the sky seemed to be locked in an endless gray, blending with the drifting steam. "Some leave as umbrellas, others as trees, some I form in to exquisite bodies of mud or clay or stone. Others are formed from scraps picked from the homes of happy families. Others unhappy families. Each unique. Each piece asks the same question—do the materials define our future existence? Or do we build the future from that 'core' humanity you speculated?" The fleshy brutality of the man was shifting some. Something of a pig was in there, and something of a bull.

"I calm the ghosts with my calligraphy and poetry. Sometimes, they are angry. I quell their temper, release them from their confusion and pain." The pale, elegant man smiled softly. Something was emerging within him, too, somewhere between bird and snake. "And obviously, setting up our workshop near a ready supply of materials is just good sense."

"I can see that, senior." Truth "casually" looked around at the exits. When you got right down to it, he could just jump down the waterfall.

"You have saved us a lot of work, kiddo! I thought we would be pissing around these mountains for days. But look at the harvest now!"

"The harvest?"

"Why, all those people you killed," the pale man murmured. "How do you think you found this inn?"

The piggish man grinned his tombstone smile. "Lots and lots and lots of angry ghosts to work with. Now. What can we make out of their killer?"

ABOUT THE AUTHOR

Warby Picus is a lifelong fan of science fiction and fantasy. One day, he figured he would see if writing books was as much fun as it appeared to be. He hasn't looked back since.

www.ingramcontent.com/pod-product-compliance
Lightning Source LLC
Chambersburg PA
CBHW020647120726
47906CB00001B/165